The spray hitting the Revo's hull was quickly becoming a silver shroud that threatened to send the crew to their deaths. The weight of the ice dragged the battered tank closer and closer to the sea's surface, and sooner or later, a towering wave would rise to snatch the vehicle to a frozen death. The crew took turns chipping ice from the hull.

Kneeling on the aft hull, one of the crew would pound away at the spreading ice with a heavy hammer until he broke through to the vehicle's armor. Then the wind would rip the ice from the surface of the tank in huge sheets. The first time they had tried this, the peeling ice had nearly taken Coazctal off with it. They were more careful after that. Zomna experimented with rotating the turret to shed the ice clinging to the tank, but that system only worked after a dangerous amount of ice had built up. The battered vehicle continued to move south.

FROST
DEATH™

Other FASA Novels

Renegade Legion:
by Peter L. Rice
Damned If We Do...

by William H. Keith, Jr.
Renegade's Honor

BattleTech:
by William H. Keith, Jr.
Decision at Thunder Rift
Mercenary's Star
The Price of Glory

by Michael A. Stackpole
Warrior: En Garde
Warrior: Riposte
Warrior: Coupe
Lethal Heritage
Blood Legacy
Lost Destiny

by Robert Charrette
Wolves on the Border
Heir to the Dragon

by Robert Thurston
Way of the Clan
Bloodname
Falcon Guard

FROST DEATH

BY
PETER L. RICE

FASA CORPORATION

1991

Copyright © 1991 FASA Corporation.
ALL RIGHTS RESERVED.
This book may not be reproduced in whole or in part, by any means, without permission in writing from the publisher.
Printed in the United States of America.

INTERCEPTOR and RENEGADE LEGION are Registered Trademarks of FASA Corporation. CENTURION, LEVIATHAN, TOG and FROST DEATH are trademarks of FASA Corporation. Copyright © 1992 FASA Corporation. All Rights Reserved. Printed in the United States of America

FASA Corporation
P.O. Box 6930
Chicago, IL 60680

Cover Art: Steve Venters
Cover Design: Jim Nelson

Prologue

In the nearly five thousand years since Humans first left Terra and took to the stars in 2056, the history of the race has risen to peaks of glory and descended almost to the point of extinction.

Now, in the year 6831, it is Humans who dominate the galaxy under the sway of the Terran Overlord Government, or TOG. Ruled by Caesars out of New Rome, this government holds that the Humans of Terra are superior to all other races, and enforces its absolute power through any means necessary—be it propaganda, terror, brute force, or enslavement. Faced with TOG's eight million Legions and its iron-fisted Caesars, who dares oppose the mightiest army the galaxy has ever known?

The answer lies across the galaxy, some 70,000 light years from Terra at the far end of the Orion Arm. These thousands of stars encompass the government known as the Human-Baufrin Commonwealth, the seat of armed resistance to TOG since the Terran Overlord Government first came to power in 6681.

In that year, a number of Imperial Legions fled the tyranny of the new TOG government, finding refuge among the people of the distant Commonwealth. They and their descendants are now known as the Renegade Legions, fighting side by side with their Commonwealth allies against TOG.

1

1145, 1 Martius 6831—Showing both Commonwealth and Naram insignia, the Bata Revo grav tank drifted silver against the frozen blackness of the night and sea. Shattered crystalline-titanium armor hung down from the light tank as though reaching for the roiling sea fifty meters below. The waves resembled spouts, boiling up from the surface to be shattered into swirling spume by the force of the tempest howling across Uxmallt, the inland sea dominating Alsatia, the largest continent on Caralis.

The Naram tank crew, as was their nature, were making the best of a bad situation. Their race was older than the Human race; having survived several bouts with near-extinction, they learned along the way the importance of taking life day by day, and valuing above all loyalty and commitment to family. The three men in the tank were not much different to look at than Humans. Biologically, the two races are almost identical. The Naram race's one distinguishing physical feature is luxuriant hair, worn long and usually kept braided. In Naram culture, for reasons unclear even to themselves, long hair represents long life. Narams who join the military usually cut their hair to signify that they expect their lives to be short, but this crew had optimistically chosen to keep their hair long.

The most distinguishing psychological feature the Naram possess is their strong sense of family. Within their own communities, extended families live together in single dwellings, often adopting Naram who are permanently or temporarily separated from their own families. The tank crew of the Bata Revo had adopted each other as family.

The Naram had colonized many planets during their long history, including Earth and Caralis. On Caralis, only the sea names showed that a Naram civilization had ever existed here. Naram lore did not account for the disappearance of the colony from this planet, but the tank crew wondered if any remnant of that ancient settlement survived.

Sergeant Zomna raised his head above the coaming of the tank's command position and took another look at the damage to his vehicle. The turret-mounted 100mm Gauss cannon had been sheared off just forward of the mantlet, giving the tank a curious, snub-nosed appearance. He'd ordered his crew to stuff pieces from their personal kits into the cannon's muzzle to quiet the ear-splitting howl of the wind roaring across the arctic waters of the southern pole. The Tube or Vertically-Launched Laser-Guided missile racks were empty save for a single shell jammed into the turret's upper right-hand launcher, trapped there when the butt end of the Gauss cannon had smashed the launch tube after taking a direct missile hit.

As Zomna surveyed his crippled tank, Private Coazctal eased himself through the gunner's hatch and crawled over the lee side of the turret. Zomna watched the man disappear over the edge of the TVLG launcher until only the fingers of his right hand, clenched on the scramble rail, marked his position. Then the fingers slowly released the rail and vanished into the darkness.

In an attempt to repair some of the damage to the starboard grav drive, Coazctal had to crawl under the Revo's double hull to reach the engine access ports. The Bata Revo, like most Naram-designed vehicles, had an external shroud covering the armored hull. The shroud protected repair crews from observation and fire while working on the engines in the heat of battle. It also allowed infantry to shelter under the armored skin as they advanced. But the designers had never addressed the problem of maintenance while the vehicle was airborne. The accepted wisdom was that any grav tank needing repairs would have the sense to land. In this particular case, however, landing was impossible.

The Bata Revo belonged to a Cohort of the 2031st Commonwealth Strike Legion stationed on the continent of Rolandrin, the only wholly Commonwealth-held territory on Caralis. The Cohort was flying a routine probing mission against the enemy over Uxmallt, and had made unexpected contact with a Cohort of the Terran Overlord Government. Both forces engaged, but it soon became obvious that neither side would win by staying in the skirmish. A sudden, violent spring storm convinced both Cohorts to break off and make a run for safety. The surviving tanks in the Commonwealth Cohort escaped, but Zomna's Revo had taken damage to its Marshman drive, leaving the tank able to maintain either altitude or velocity, but not both.

The bad weather had probably saved a large part of both Cohorts by breaking off the pointless, minor conflict, but it was now the Revo's enemy. The storm was blowing generally southwest, gale-force winds of speeds up to 150 kph pushing the crippled Bata Revo further and further from land, until all hope of rejoining their unit had been lost. Now the battle was to keep the tank out of the sea.

That had been easy while the power plant was still able to keep the Revo upright and above the waves, but then the temperature began to drop. The Revo's Data Display Panel had no thermograph, but Zomna didn't need the DDP to tell him how cold it was; he could judge the temperature from past cold-weather combat experience. He knew that when water crackled to ice as it struck the ground, the air was at least minus 30° Celsius. When water crackled into ice in the air, it was minus 90° C. At the moment, the water blowing from the wild sea below the grav tank was immediately snapping into ice.

The spray hitting the Revo's hull was quickly becoming a silver shroud that threatened to send the crew to their deaths. The weight of the ice dragged the battered tank closer and closer to the sea's surface, and sooner or later, a towering wave would rise to snatch the vehicle to a frozen death. The crew took turns chipping ice from the hull.

Kneeling on the aft hull, one of the crew would pound away at the spreading ice with a heavy hammer until he broke through to the vehicle's armor. Then the wind would rip the ice from the surface of the tank in huge sheets. The first time they had tried this, the peeling ice had nearly taken Coazctal off with it. They were more careful after that. Zomna experimented with rotating the turret to shed the ice clinging to the tank, but that system only worked after a dangerous amount of ice had built up. The battered vehicle continued to move south.

The only hope for the crew's survival lay in repairing the damaged Marshman drive. Until the grav unit was fixed, they had either thrust or lift, not both, and were at the mercy of the wind. In time, either the wind or the sea would claim the tank. Thus it was that Coazctal crawled over the tank's side to reach the engine access port. This was not an easy task while airborne, but the mechanics of this tank type had long ago found an ingenious way to accomplish it.

Reaching the starboard access required exiting the turret and crawling down to the shroud across the rounded ogive of the hull, which had a series of rails on the upper portion that served as scramble steps for the crew. While hanging onto the last rail, a man with a long enough reach could grasp the beading on the under edge of the shroud. Taking a firm grip on the beading with one hand, the mechanic would let go of the scramble rail and swing under the hull, kicking out against the inner hull as his other hand grasped the beading. From this position, it was possible for the mechanic to use his feet to manipulate the dogs securing the port, reach down to the edge of the opening with one hand, and swing into the engine compartment. The mechanic had to make it on the first try, because this maneuver did not allow a second chance.

Coazctal, the gunner, was the only member of the Bata Revo's crew who had a chance of accomplishing this feat. Private Tenocht, the driver and nominal mechanic, was too small to make the stretch between the scramble rails and the lower edge of the shroud. Sergeant Zomna had the size and strength, but his right hand had been crushed by flying armor from the same hit that had destroyed the Gauss cannon.

"This place is a mess," said Coazctal, his voice crackling in the earphones of the light battle helmet every tank crewmember wore. Hearing him, Zomna breathed a sigh of relief that Coazctal had made the stretch.

"Look for a small coupling on the forward bulkhead," Tenocht told him. To Zomna, the driver's voice sounded weary, as though this was all just an exercise in futility. "There should be one there, probably painted red with lots of wires coming out of it."

In the pause, Zomna imagined Coazctal twisting himself into position to examine the forward portion of the cramped compartment. "I see two connector ports on the forward bulkhead," he said, "but neither one is red. The wires are all burned off the one on top, and the low one near the outside only has one wire on it. Both posts are black."

"Don't touch that wire!" snapped Tenocht. "That's probably the wire that's feeding commands to the lift program. You break that and we'll auger in for sure."

"Great. Thanks for telling me after I climbed over it."

"No prob. Now look at the upper connector. It should be a seventy-two-prong control jack that gives commands to the lateral drive from the TS&R circuitry and the command yoke. Clean it off."

There came another long pause broken only by the sounds of heavy breathing over the headset and the howl of the wind across the hull of the tank. "OK. Done."

"Now we have to see if commands are reaching that jack. I'm going to apply power to my yoke. Take some zip wire—any piece you can find will do—and ground it by touching one end to the bulkhead. With the other end, touch the middle prong of the third row from the top of the jack. Tell me what happens."

Silence reigned once more while the gunner had to be searching the debris in the compartment for a suitable length of wire. Zomna prayed Coazctal was being careful not to make contact with the remaining connection of the lower jack. An amber light flared briefly on Zomna's DDP. "Ux! Damn! That hurt!"

"Hey, we've found the right prong," Tenocht said, sounding surprised.

"What do you mean we, ux-face?" shouted Coazctal. "I'm the one who found it. You could've told me the damn thing would explode in my face!"

"That's enough, you two," Zomna said into his mouthpiece. "Either we all get out of here together, or none of us will make it. Next time, Tenocht, tell him if something's going to snap in his face."

"Sorry. I thought you knew what would happen." Tenocht didn't sound sorry, but

Zomna let it pass. "Now we—I mean you—have to locate the exit port on the inside bulkhead. There are—"

"Wait a parsec, will ya? I can't see a thing in here."

"Okay. Twist around until you can see the inside, then tell me when you're ready."

Another long pause. Zomna knew that the 137-ton mass of the Bata Revo would not be affected by the shifting weight of a 75-kilo Naram soldier, so perhaps it was his anxiety that made the tank seem to vibrate with Coazctal's movement. He found himself willing Coazctal into his new position.

"Goddit. Six connectors on the inside?"

"Right. Count from the rear of the compartment to the third connector. That's the drive circuit. It's a seventeen-prong outlet. The third prong from the left in the fourth row is the one we want."

"Gof ish."

"Coazctal, are you all right?" Zomna broke in. "You sound a little garbled."

"I'm fine, bosh. Jush a li'l' shleepy. Buff I'm warm."

Zomna looked back into the fighting compartment and caught Tenocht's eye. "Make it quick," he mouthed to the driver. Tenocht nodded.

"Take some spare wire," continued the driver, "and connect that first hot prong you found with the connector you located on the inboard panel. Hold the wire in place and tell me when you've done it."

"Ofey, dofey. No prov."

The pause was even longer this time. Zomna was sure he could feel the Bata Revo shudder. Ignoring the instruments, he scanned the horizon from the turret but saw only a blur of mist and spume between the dark sea and the darker sky. The tank definitely shuddered this time. "Give me some lift, Tenocht."

"Right, Sarge."

Zomna was gently pressed back against his seat as the Bata Revo gained a little more height above the water. He tapped the turret-control bar, felt the ice on the hull shatter, and watched the shards whirl away. An unusually high wave caught the windward side of the tank and cascaded over the open turret, drenching the tank's commander. The water on the outside froze immediately, and icy water dripped down into the fighting compartment.

"Govish," came the word from Coazctal in the engine compartment.

"Give it a try," ordered Zomna. Tenocht immediately applied power. The Bata Revo shuddered again, but this time it was from the force of the Marshman drive twisting gravity to provide thrust.

"I've got a red light on the drive."

"Okay, shut it down. We've still got trouble, but at least we've got power."

"Wilco."

"We'll have to take it real easy," said Zomna. "Coazctal, you'd better get back here."

"Buff sharge, thish is the firsh shime I've vin warm in days."

2

1430, 1 Martius 6831—Lieutenant Colonel Stolich Wotan, Assistant Director of Commonwealth Intelligence on Caralis, stared down into the luminescent green liquid that eddied as he twisted the glass in his hand. He always allowed himself one Skuttarran Heartstopper with his meal. It seemed to make his afternoon's work easier and relieve the pain in his right leg. Everything below his knee had been torn off in the disastrous retreat the citizens of Thapsus had forced the Commonwealth troops to make from their planet. The doctors had done their best to replace the missing part of the limb, but their best had not been good enough. The fit between the prosthesis and the living tissue had never been exactly right, but Wotan accepted the discomfort philosophically. Irreparable injury was one of the hazards a professional soldier faced. Wotan was not vain, and so the loss of his leg didn't bother him that much. A compactly built man with average coloring, brown hair, and brown skin that made him look almost khaki, only his eyes, which were the green of his drink, caught more than the casual glance. He shifted the leg to a more comfortable position and looked around the dining room.

The crowd was beginning to thin as the dinner hour ended. Stolich liked to come to Shrak Pivar for dinner because most of the professionals ate elsewhere. He wasn't forced to talk shop while he ate. Only four tables were still occupied, and he knew that the stewards would be anxious to clear the place and set up for the evening meal. Let them wait. He thumbed the controls of the flourodisplay, wiping the fields-and-babbling-brook scene that had been projected on the table's surface. He liked the fields display because it reminded him of his home in Havershom County. He had been away now for almost twenty years, ever since he had signed up to fight at the beginning of the struggle for Shannedam County against the Terran Overlord Government. Both TOG and the Commonwealth needed control of Shannedam County's resource-rich planets and manufacturing capabilities to gain an advantage in the battle for rule of the civilized universe. The metals of Shannedam County were transformed by its primary manufacturing into war materiel, without which the battle could not be waged. Neither side had yet gained a clear advantage; TOG held more planets, but the Commonwealth held vital strategic points.

The screen cleared to reveal the early darkness of a late winter afternoon. A thick snow had fallen in the morning, but now the sky had cleared to reveal Rock Wall, the major moon orbiting Caralis, rising on the eastern horizon. Wotan stared at the giant satellite looming over the city. He knew that Rock Wall exerted a powerful pull; he almost felt drawn to it himself, as though answering the siren call of some inexorable force. He changed the view again and scanned the darkening streets.

Slushy snow was piled along the curbs, and pedestrians had been forced to tramp narrow paths along the icy sidewalks. The street heaters should have melted the snow by now. Perhaps the government's war-ravaged infrastructure was unable or unwilling to deal with a civilian problem while the possibility of aerial attack remained. He watched a man stamp violently through the slush, pounding deep footprints into the snowy crust to reveal the pavement below. Footprints, thought Wotan. Footprints mark the passage of our civilization. (He realized that the Heartstopper and memories of home were making him uncharacteristically philosophical.) We all leave them as we pass through life. Wotan watched the wet gray marks slowly fill with slush. Another pedestrian tramped by, and the first set of prints disappeared under the assault. The new footprints appeared and began to deteriorate as he watched. Our prints don't last long, Wotan decided with his usual practicality. He thumbed the flourodisplay to bring back the fields and brook.

Wotan eased his right leg under his work station. He did no more than glance at his display panel because it showed the same information it had been displaying for the past nine months. Frotik, the largest city on the continent of Malthus, had fallen to the TOG forces almost two years ago after bitter, costly street-fighting. The militia, for all their lack of heavy weapons, had put up a tenacious fight, forcing the TOGs to reduce the city almost to rubble to secure it.

A long, violent campaign followed, and the TOG forces slowly expanded their bridgehead on the planet. The city of Kantara had fallen a year after Frotik, when the TOG Legions broke out of their enclave on Malthus and jumped across the Tutul Xuis to the continent of Alsatia. That move took the Commonwealth commanders on Rolandrin so much by surprise that much of Alsatia's east coast fell to the enemy before the Commonwealth forces stabilized the situation, nine months ago. The campaign had since degenerated into a state of violent attrition as each side fed in reinforcements.

Neither TOG nor the Commonwealth found the stalemate on Caralis to its liking. Both sides wanted this outpost planet, both for its natural resources as well as its strategic position in Shannedam County. The planet's resources were so valuable, however, that both sides recognized limits to what they would do to take the world from the other. Neither side was willing to see the world Buntaried. (One hundred and fifty years earlier, Ivanolo Buntari had blasted Durmella, a populated world, to a glowing cinder as a lesson to the planet's rebels.) Although the TOG leadership nominally revered Buntari as one of the great men of their history, he was also remembered as a wanton destroyer of valuable resources. None of the current TOG leaders wanted to go down in star annals with that kind of reputation.

Wotan posted the latest intelligence on his video map. The changes came up dark blue and red, contrasting with the earlier postings that showed pale blue and pink. He noted the new positions; not much change. The TOG headquarters complex on the southern bulge of Malthus had acquired another support-unit designator. The place was becoming a hive of activity, what those in intelligence would call a "lucrative target." It was also, Wotan could see, a very heavily defended target. The mobile Scipio antiaircraft grav vehicles that had been serving as SAM sites had been replaced by permanent Surface-to-Air Missile installations, and the 1257th TOG Garrison Legion had been posted to the complex.

There was little the TOGs could hide from the LOSATS, the low-orbit satellites used for surveillance, or the COMSATS, used for communications, that constantly orbited the planet. They proliferated like Da'Valk lemurs, cluttering the ionosphere till it was difficult to tell the dead ones from those still functioning. Wotan flicked the command function switch that would show the paths of the current operational TOG and Commonwealth LOSATS. The display blossomed with red and blue dots that raced across the display screen, forming grids like the warp and woof of some orbital garment. Only the poles were free of the woven-light fabric.

The poles! Wotan abruptly sat forward, cleared the screen, and reset the satellite displays, requesting TOG only. He slowed the data, watching the trail of the myriad dots crawling like glowing gnats across the display. He frowned at the screen and cleared it.

Wotan entered a new command, asking the computer to show, second by second, those areas of the planet not covered by the TOG LOSATS. The map flickered with amber patches. He impatiently cleared the screen again. That analysis was useless too.

What Wotan was looking for in the satellite coverage was a pattern showing large gaps in surveillance. He wanted to find a lapse in the TOG satellite coverage that would give the Commonwealth enough time to insert a strike force undetected.

Computers had come a long way since their inception, but they still resembled precocious children. They produced exactly what the user demanded, but the user had to know what he wanted before he asked. The old adage claiming that a machine was only as good as the person running it still held true.

The next program Wotan ran displayed areas free from TOG LOSAT observation for a period of five minutes. This time, the amber patches were much smaller. Wotan let the data run slowly, focusing the display on the area south of Rolandrin. A thin line of amber crawled across the southern ocean toward the south pole, expanding as it came closer to the planet's frozen extremity.

Footprints, thought Wotan again. Each satellite left a footprint like the man in the snow. The print would remain only a few minutes, revealing the activity that produced it. Then, like the footprint of the pedestrian, it would vanish, to be replaced by another print. He reversed the display, slowly tracking back through the recording until a thin line of amber stretching south from Rolandrin toward the pole indicated the lack of satellite surveillance he wanted. He saved the record.

Wotan scrolled forward in time on the display, holding the first line until another track attached itself to the first. He saved it. Time scrolled forward again, and another thin line appeared and attached itself to the end of the growing satellite trail, and was saved. Time scrolled forward. Another mark appeared and was saved. Wotan finally had a thin line of amber, narrow at some points, thicker at others, that reached all the way across the sea to the polar cap.

The computer program developed this series of marks effortlessly. He ran the machine through a month of projected TOG satellite surveillance, watching the amber swatches grow and fade as the LOSATS made their theoretical sweeps through the limits of the atmosphere. He didn't bother to check exit opportunities from the pole. If an attack force could arrive there undetected, the element of surprise in this approach to the TOG headquarters on Malthus would give them a quick victory or an easy retreat. All Wotan had to do was to pick the best date for the operation.

He noted the possibilities, his mind already upgrading the attack from an idea to a planned operation. In order to narrow the field of choices, he rank-ordered the possible dates for the operation based on the widest possible openings as well as the shortest distances through the amber field. The path could not take too long, because the longer the forces were in transit, the better were their chances of being detected. Even with the LOSATS plotted, Wotan knew that some factor unaccounted for could intervene to reveal the force. Quick was better than slow. He worked out the azimuth and speed for each leg of the journey to Malthus for the three most likely dates.

The crossing to the pole would be difficult, and the path would have to be extremely accurate. At times, the force would have to double back on its route to avoid a satellite's sweep. Even altitude would have to be programmed into the tanks' flight computers, because a LOSAT sweeping over the horizon might pick up a vehicle's signature if it were not at a specific altitude. He ran the three proposed plans, watching carefully for problems as each unfolded on his display. It would be a nice touch, he thought, if the force could hide under one of Caralis' many minor moons.

That was something he had left out of his calculations, he realized. Rock Wall, the planet's largest moon at 7,000 kilometers in diameter, produced huge shifts in the planet's surface. The minor moons, named for the Pleiades, had effects of their own. And though they were inconsequential as individual forces, their combined gravitational pull could be spectacular. Wotan plotted the location of the moons into each of the proposed plans, which changed some of the numbers radically. He printed a hard copy and sent the final program into the main computer. The program was securely locked, requiring his own code as well as a random command word generated at the moment of sending to recall the information. The plan was safe from prying eyes until he was ready to present it to his superiors.

Wotan considered the three available operational windows. The first one, opening in just two days, was not really feasible. It would be difficult to plan a strike and organize a force in that short a time. The second window opened in nine days, the third in thirty-five. The thirty-five-day lead time would allow plenty of time to plan and organize the strike force, but it would also give TOG intelligence plenty of time to discover what was going on. Better to go slightly less prepared but with a better chance of retaining the element of surprise. The window in nine days would be best.

He rose from his work station. His next step was to present the operation to Colonel Daubish, Chief of Intelligence, and Brigadier Maxall, Chief of Operations. Wotan saw that the door to the Intelligence shop was open; he thought about proposing his plan tonight, but decided against it. He wanted to get more information to add to the arguments he would use on Daubish. He already knew his CO would object to the plan on at least one count: the current lack of available forces. But Wotan figured there was no need to commit a Commonwealth unit to the task. In fact, he knew none was available. Better to use expendable troops, perhaps a Renegade Legion or part of one. He thought of the battered Renegade Legion presently refitting on Rolandrin, and decided that the 2567th Provisional Renegade Legion was just the unit for this mission.

3

2330, 1 Martius 6831—Sergeant Zomna pulled the thermocoat blanket more tightly around his shoulders to keep out the freezing spray and the inquisitive probings of the arctic wind, but small fingers of cold still reached past the insulating layer to less-protected parts of his body. Even wrapping the long braids of his hair around his neck to add an extra layer of protection didn't keep the wind, which seemed to be blowing straight off the planet's southernmost point, from digging at openings and exploring under the blanket.

The Bata Revo was still being driven south, away from Rolandrin, swept along by a violent storm that had picked up the tank just after Coazctal had jury-rigged the power plant to provide vector as well as lift. It was possible now to give direction to the shattered hull as well as keep it above the huge waves that erupted from the surface of the freezing-cold water. Zomna tried to turn the grav tank north, back toward Alsatia, but the tank seemed to have a mind of its own, and he found himself fighting both the wind and the tank. They had nearly foundered when he fought to bring the bow to the north and east, his heart jumping as an unusually strong gust of wind pushed the left side of the hull into the waves. He righted the vehicle and decided not to try that maneuver again.

Instead, he allowed the tank to drift south, as that seemed to be the direction in which it wanted to head. The gale was dead astern of the tank, driving it at almost 100 kph toward the unknown. The flat stern acted like a sail, and as long as Zomna kept the bow angled slightly upward, the vee-shaped prow acted like a ski. The shattered hatch cover provided Zomna with some protection from the wind.

The DDP at the command station was almost completely dead, having lost too much power and circuitry. On passive sensors the Data Display Panel showed the position of all vehicles within fifty kilometers. "Friendlies" appeared as blue squares for tanks and triangles for fighters; TOG vehicles showed in the same shapes, only red. The DDP also monitored internal vehicle systems. There had been the red light that had flared just after power was restored to the vector control, and then nothing else. Zomna didn't want to remember that light or the sacrifice it meant. Coazctal had wired the thruster, but he had not returned.

Neither Zomna nor Tenocht had had a way of reaching the gunner. It was a poor end to a Naram warrior's life, and Coazctal had not even had a chance to cut his hair. Now Coazctal was dead, frozen in the womb of the tank. By his sacrifice he had bought some safety, however fleeting, for his endangered comrades.

The sergeant lifted his eyes again to the blurred horizon, feeling the ice strike the back of his armored helmet. All he could see was the vast darkness of the sea and sky, merging in a gray crayon scrawl where the elements wrestled for control. He returned his attention to the fighting compartment. Then his head snapped up again.

There, in the distance, within the familiar smudge, he must have seen something different. He strained his eyes against the blackness. There it was again. A plume of icy whiteness against the black horizon. When it vanished, Zomna wondered if it were only an illusion. He looked away into the dimly lit interior of the tank, then raised his eyes slowly to the horizon. It was a casual glance, as though he did not want to startle the distant image by a quick movement. The patch of white appeared again. There was something off the right bow of the tank. Too far away to be recognized, but something definitely solid in the vast expanse of sea and air.

The sergeant reached into his combat station and unsnapped his night-vision goggles, which would enhance any ambient light available in the otherwise stygian gloom. The goggles would not make much difference, but were better than his unaided eyes. He clicked them to the brim of his helmet and looked again.

There, showing as a thin line of white against the dark horizon, was an ice formation. And the presence of ice meant that something solid was present to give it form. Solid meant safety. He scanned the thin line, mentally reviewing what he knew of Caralis' geography and concluding that what he was seeing must be the south pole. He searched for a way onto the ice cap. Even as he watched, huge towers of spray lashed across the formation, outlining a jagged rift of rock and ice fighting continuously for domination. The rocky wall loomed out over the sea, taller even than the giant spouts of water that rose around the grav tank. He needed more power to reach the height of that wall. He spoke into the headset and felt the Bata Revo surge upward in response.

Almost at once the nose of the tank corkscrewed out of control. "Shut down," he shouted into the mouthpiece, but the panicked command was unnecessary. Tenocht, feeling the tank begin to gyrate, had already closed off the vertical thrusters. The tank regained control and steadied on its original course. *This thing has a mind of its own*, thought Zomna. *It wants to stay where it is. Who am I to try to convince it otherwise?* He went back to searching the approaching shore through the goggles.

A double line became visible. The lower one was the waves booming against the icy shore. The upper line, showing faintly against the dark, cold sky, marked the crest of the precipice. A solid wall of rock five hundred meters high stretched across the path of the drifting Bata Revo. The hope of salvation was transmuted into the sure expectation of destruction. Zomna felt cheated. Had he come so far only to glimpse safety, and be denied any chance of achieving it?

Then he saw a narrow cleft in the wall's stony face that angled sharply down from the summit almost to the water's edge. It looked only a few meters wide, but that would be enough. It was slightly to the left of the tank's current path, but Zomna thought he could shift the damaged vehicle enough to reach it. He rotated the turret until the shattered Gauss cannon lined up with the cleft, then switched the driving control from the driver's station to the command. He sensed, rather than saw, Tenocht move in the fighting compartment below him, and he glanced down to catch his eye. With his undamaged left hand, Zomna waved to the driver, grinning down to where Tenocht sat at the now-useless controls. Encased as he was in helmet, commset, and night-vision goggles, Zomna had no way of knowing that what he thought was a grin looked more like a death's head.

Sergeant Zomna moved the steering joystick until it lined up with the gun azimuth indicator. He tapped the power switch and felt the Bata Revo nudge slightly to the left. He braced himself for a violent reaction from the shattered hull, but none came. He tapped the power again, and again the tank shifted to the left. This time he applied more power, testing for the tank's resistance. It didn't come. The tank had evidently decided to make for the cleft. The DDP computer, that entity that lived in the command center, must have decided to survive. Zomna was glad. He applied steady power and pointed the bow toward safety.

The Bata Revo crouched against an outcrop of black rock that protected it from the worst blasts of the storm. With most of the power shut down, the fusion generator was mainly supplying heat to the tank's interior and power to the repaired DDP. The tank had been sheltering here since it had alternately crept and been blown up the narrow cleft that led from the sea. Snow, or, more accurately, slivers of ice blown from the raging waters not too far away, drifted over the sides of the tank, obscuring its lines. Slightly downwind of the hull, a small mound was already completely covered.

The mound was the body of Private Coazctal, late of the Commonwealth army. He would never see his Naram home world again. No tears were shed by either Zomna or Tenocht as they pried the rigid body loose, then lifted it from the engine access port. The Naram culture did not weep for those who had passed beyond mortal control. Furthermore, there was neither time nor energy to waste on sorrow. They laid him in the snow, still crouched, his arms tucked in against his chest as if asleep. A broken piece of the tank's armor driven into the snow marked the grave, should anyone else ever visit the place.

Zomna stood in the fighting compartment, fiddling with the readout dials as he calibrated the emergency-communications sending device. Even damaged, the inertial navigating system continued to function, constantly updating the position of the tank. The only action required was to pulse into the dark ionosphere the coded message that would, theoretically, bring rescue. Somewhere up there, a COMSAT would be passing. Zomna had no idea where it was, but the computer was programmed to locate it and send the emergency message. It was only a matter of time.

The sergeant was concentrating so hard on the task at hand that he almost missed the red indicator flash into life on the DDP, and he almost ignored it. When he looked more closely he felt his heart leap within his chest. The glowing screen clearly showed two TOG vehicles somewhere off in the darkness.

He couldn't tear his eyes from the DDP. The red squares moved slowly across the screen, weaving their way through unseen obstacles. Zomna resisted the urge to press the identification switch that would instantly name and qualify the intruders. To identify the vehicles, the computer would have to cover each with a minute pulse. The intruders would probably not be able to detect him in that instant, unless they already knew he was there, but there was always a chance. He continued to watch. They crept closer. He toggled the identification query.

The DDP immediately identified the red squares as a Cestus heavy ground tank and a Clodius light armored personnel carrier. A tank infantry searching for something; probably them. Zomna looked at Tenocht. The private had removed his combat helmet and begun to cut his hair. The sergeant followed his example.

By the time the TOG vehicles reached the grounded Bata Revo, the crew was waiting for them. They had pried the single TVLG from its launcher and set it up in a ground mount. Tenocht was in position behind the hull, where he could use his Grant rifle after he had fired the TVLG. It would be almost useless against the armored vehicles crawling toward them, but if he could convince the infantry to dismount, he could take some down before they were overrun. Zomna waited in the turret, his left hand on the trigger of the AP laser. It would be as useless against the TOG vehicles as Tenocht's rifle, but he could use the painting laser to help the TVLG hit its target. The enemy tank was well within the four-thousand-meter effective range of the painting laser, and the laser should decode the tank's flicker shields quickly enough to guide the missile through for a hit. Then it would just be a glorious fight. Neither Naram legionnaire spoke of surrendering.

Inside the heavily armored turret of the Cestus, the commander aligned his vehicle so that it would crest the ridge with its hull lasers pointed directly at the stationary Bata Revo. If he could get in the first volley, there would be little chance of the enemy vehicle returning fire. He gave the command, and the Cestus crept over the last intervening outcrop. Behind him, the infantry began to deploy from the Clodius.

4

1200, 2 Martius 6831—The hardpoint on the *Cheetah*'s bow had been modified, and Captain Maria Louisa Cathcart didn't like it. She was perfectly willing to throw herself into combat in a light fighter, but this mission was different. The idea that she should climb into the cockpit of the crowning glory of Renegade fighter craft, and use all that speed and maneuverability to fly into Commonwealth-controlled space and jiggle a satellite to change its orbit, was ridiculous. She sat in the cockpit of the *Cheetah*, waiting for launch, and contemplated the situation.

Some high mucky-muck in intelligence had determined that it was important to get a better view of the southern pole of Caralis. That was reasonable. But a simple command sent to the satellite via telelink would accomplish the mission. It was a waste of resources to send one of Caralis' limited number of air defense fighters to complete the task. Better to let the satellite shift its own orbit. But orders were orders, and she would carry them out.

The initial liftoff forced her against the seat and she felt a familiar thrill lift her spirits. She was angry about being sent on this mission, but she loved flying, no matter what her orders. The glare of the liftoff blast reflected on her cockpit, and she felt the eight-G force squeeze dinner out of her abdomen. This was one way to keep trim, she told herself wryly.

Her orders called for her to maintain full thrust until the fighter was fifteen kilometers from the satellite. The fighter would then drift until it made contact with the LOSAT, and it was this last instruction to which she had objected most. Drifting in space was for freighters. Better, she thought, to power straight to the location, make the change, and run like hell, than to drift with no control toward the destination. But, orders were orders.

Cathcart shut down at the ordered distance and let the *Cheetah* drift. Her DDP was set on "receive only," another agreement with planet command. To ground control stations her ship was nothing more than a piece of space junk, spinning in orbit over the war-torn surface of Caralis. Shut down, with only the life-support systems active, the state-of-the-art space fighter would easily be mistaken for one more load of dead hardware.

The satellite, 56/72/98, appeared on the fighter's DDP as a pale blue square on the right side of the instrument panel. Cathcart watched the square crawl across the display. Nothing to do but wait until the craft and its target made their programmed intersection. A red light flashed.

If it were possible to sit bolt upright while strapped into a cockpit, Cathcart did it. On the extreme lower right edge of the DDP, a TOG *Lancea* had appeared. The DDP tagged the intruder as an enemy and scrolled out the identifying information: Light fighter; Thrust 10;

three hard points; two 5/1 lasers. She relaxed again and awaited developments.

The *Lancea* applied thrust and turned toward the *Cheetah*. The LOSAT continued to broadcast information as if unaware of the danger it suddenly faced. Shut up, stupid, whispered Cathcart, willing the LOSAT to be still, but the chattering satellite maintained its orbit, completely unaware of its imminent demise. She watched the *Lancea* accelerate and bring its bow in line with the satellite.

It was only a matter of time, now. The TOG *Lancea* would close with the LOSAT and destroy it. But the *Lancea* would also pass within meters of the shut-down *Cheetah*. The *Cheetah* would have the *Lancea* in its sights just when the *Lancea* would be in position to destroy the satellite. Cathcart couldn't let that happen. She had no idea if the satellite was valuable or not, but she was in orbit to nudge this tin can, and she would do her job. The stray *Lancea* would not destroy the satellite.

The *Cheetah* was programmed to roll left to align itself with the satellite about now, but Cathcart overrode the preset command to track the TOG craft. By her calculation, which was supported by the DDP, the *Lancea* would pass a few scant meters in front of the *Cheetah*; it was too good a shot to pass up. She waited as the *Lancea* drifted across her sights. She felt the adrenaline surge through her system as the *Lancea* filled her optical sight and then her cockpit window; the TOG ship loomed larger than she had expected. She let the *Lancea* edge its way into the center of the illuminated ring of the targeting system. Cathcart had never seen a target in the manual, illuminated sight. She usually fought using computer targeting and firing, because space combat moved too quickly for Human eyes and reflexes to be of much use. She held her breath and fired. The two EPC-9s bucked, followed by the stabbing, destructive light of the 5/1 lasers. She didn't wait for a damage assessment before she fired the load again.

Lancea 4/892 powered slowly toward the satellite. Keleustes Rodarchus, newly promoted from Junior Grade, watched the satellite move into his sights. His routine patrol over Commonwealth territory had finally produced some excitement. Standard operating procedure was to launch from Malthus and then lie doggo until your orbit decayed to a forced reentry. He had done it dozens of times with no contact with anything Commonwealth. Nothing living, that is. There was plenty of debris up here, and the atmosphere seemed to get more crowded every day. Rodarchus had long since learned to ignore the space junk orbiting in his flight path. Now, here he was, two days after his promotion to Keleustes, with a talkative enemy satellite in front of him. He nudged the *Lancea* until it lined up on the tiny globe.

Standing orders were to destroy anything that moved, but this was the chance of a lifetime. If he timed it right, he could open the underside cargo bay over the LOSAT and snag the satellite from orbit. He smiled to himself; his ranking officer was going to have a fit of jealousy when Rodarchus brought home a Commonwealth satellite. He settled into his seat and opened the lower cargo bay of the *Lancea*. This would be a difficult maneuver, but the constant transmissions of the orbiting LOSAT would make it a little easier. His vision formed a tunnel with the twenty-five-centimeter globe at its center. Closer, closer, closer...

Almost simultaneously, the DDP identified an enemy fighter off his port bow, and the left side of his *Lancea* peeled away under the hammering of an Electron Particle Cannon. Armor vaporized in a heat haze that looked like billions of luminescent butterflies clustering around the almost stationary *Lancea*. Before Rodarchus had time to realize what was happening, two laser cannon blazed through the cloud of debris, punching into the frame of the crippled *Lancea*. A loud hissing told Rodarchus that his life-support system had been breached, and he was galvanized into action. The tunnel vision that had focused on the prize suddenly widened to take in the *Cheetah* that he had dismissed as dead. The lights on the DDP flashed warnings of imminent structural failure, as well as engine damage and life-support systems damage. He shoved the joystick as far to the right as he could and fired the engines. He had completely forgotten the satellite; all he could think about now was surviving. The computer screamed a continuous howl of warning that let him know that the shield generators on the left side were now useless.

As he rolled the *Lancea* to the right, he saw the *Cheetah* fire again. At a range of less than one hundred meters, it couldn't miss. The EPCs dissolved the remaining armor on the left side of his fighter, and the DDP announced that all the *Lancea*'s interior control surfaces were exposed. The last sight Rodarchus saw was the *Cheetah*'s lasers stabbing toward the bare electronics.

Captain Cathcart triggered her second shot as the *Lancea* rolled away. She saw the armor on the damaged side vaporize under the EPC, exposing the entrails of the crippled TOG fighter. For one instant, she regretted firing the twin lasers and destroying the enemy craft, but her reflex was quicker than her mind, and she felt her fighter's energy supply drop as the 5/1s drained the reserves. The cockpit of the *Lancea* went cloudy, a dead giveaway of explosive decompression, and then the pancake-like hull folded in on itself. In less than a microsecond, the *Lancea* was reduced to space junk, consigned to the fate of mere debris in gyrosynchronous orbit around the planet. She switched her attention to the satellite.

The LOSAT had gained position on the *Cheetah*, and so Cathcart accelerated to bring the fighter alongside the small globe. The satellite could have fired its own thrusters, but that was not in the game plan. She positioned the *Cheetah* to catch the satellite in the scoop fitted to the bow hardpoint. By applying thrust, she brought the satellite into a different orbit. At the correct vector, she applied negative thrust and released the satellite from the scoop's gentle embrace. The globe spun off on its new course and was lost to sight. Cathcart continued to mark its passage on the DDP until it was lost to even the low-power scanner. Then she turned to view the wreck of the *Lancea*.

There was no doubt that the TOG fighter was dead. The canopy had blown open, and the fighter pilot hung halfway out of the cockpit. As the *Cheetah* drifted past, the dead man's dangling arm seemed to wave a final salute. Cathcart felt her skin crawl. It was a quick death, but not one she would want for herself. She rolled the *Cheetah* over to the right and applied power; it would be a long fall to the surface.

Lieutenant Colonel Stolich Wotan watched the footprint of Satellite 56/72/98 change trajectory. It had been redeployed to pass more often over the poles. The satellite's new orbit would degrade rapidly, but while it lived, it would transmit crucial information. Wotan knew that elsewhere, frantic orders were being sent from satellite control to try to force the errant satellite back into its original path. Those orders would be futile. Satellite 56/72/98 would pass over both poles for the next few days, and then enter Caralis' atmosphere, where it would burn up; it was a lame duck. But from now until it died, it would report over and over about TOG activity at the south pole.

Wotan did not expect to find any activity there, but a good intelligence officer is both cautious and thorough. No mission was ever launched until every possible scenario had been examined. As the scan of the south pole appeared on his display, Wotan examined printouts of the tortuous formations Rock Wall would create in the sea and on the land. A geologist and an astrophysicist would be in their element. He chucked the first readout into the burn basket and reached for the second.

He looked at the second printout. He was about to throw it in the burn basket when something caught his eye. The pole's center appeared to show the red indicator of a TOG sending unit. Wotan smoothed the crumpled plex onto the desk and lifted the magniglass. His first fleeting impression was right; there was TOG activity at the center of the south pole. It also looked like there was some activity at the ice cap's edge, near Malthus. He quickly sent a new set of commands to the stumbling LOSAT.

A few hours later, on its next pass over the pole, Satellite 56/72/98 was a little more careful about where and what it scanned. On the surface of Caralis, Lieutenant Colonel Wotan waited impatiently for the printout of the latest pass. As each scroll was processed, he ripped the print from the receptor and examined it.

The activity on the ice cap near Malthus seemed to be a pair of TOG tracked vehicles. Analysis postulated a heavy ground vehicle and a tracked APC. That was absurd, thought Wotan. There was also activity around the pole itself that the computer identified as more of the tracked carriers and transports. That identification also was probably wrong.

Any TOG force at the pole would likely be weather people. But the weather this time of year came from the north pole. It would be months before weather was generated by the south pole, making the hypothesis that the TOG force was weathermen highly unlikely. Probably, thought Wotan, the TOGs were just getting ahead of themselves. He considered the printout a moment longer, then decided that this unexpected development was nothing to worry about. He certainly wasn't going to change his plan. He dumped the last prints into the burn basket, swept up the other documents, and went to see Daubish.

When he entered the office of the chief of intelligence, Wotan was surprised to see Brigadier Maxall already in the office. Both men held snifters of Tau Ceti brandy, the orange froth bubbling and clinging to the edges of their glasses. Tau Ceti was best served cold so that room temperature could activate its peculiar qualities.

"Come in, Stolich," said Daubish, beckoning with his free hand. "You look full of important information. But before you give it to us, pour yourself a drink."

Wotan considered for a moment the wisdom of drinking with his senior officers, especially as he had already met his one-Heartstopper-limit for the day. Why not? he finally decided. I'll have finished my briefing before the stuff really takes hold. He dropped the briefing papers on the low table between the two men and moved to the well-stocked bar on the wall. It was possible to program the beverage computer to produce a Heartstopper, but he opted for brandy instead. When he turned back to the occupants of the room, they were already engrossed in his report.

"According to this," said Daubish, looking at Wotan, "we have TOG activity at the south pole." The chief of intelligence fixed him with flinty eyes. "What do you make of it?"

Wotan studied his chief. Daubish wore only the tanker's combat badge on his uniform, but Wotan knew that several lifts of decorations should be below it. Daubish had cut his teeth as an enlisted man, and he was said to have spent as much time behind TOG lines as most veterans had spent in front of them. Another rumor told that his wife, or one of them, had been, or still was, the daughter of a TOG senator. And it was a well-known fact that when his eyes changed from their usual cool gray to the color of steel there was something to worry about. Wotan cleared his throat.

"I believe," replied Wotan, "that the best explanation for the activity at the pole is a weather station. If those are meteorologists, however, they're certainly out early. I have no idea what the activity at the edge of the ice cap represents. Overall, there is far more TOG movement at the pole than I suspected."

Daubish continued to examine the prints Wotan had provided, handing them silently to Maxall when he had finished. Having passed the last document to his chief of operations, Daubish steepled his fingers in contemplation. "The amount of activity at the pole suggests more than a mere weather station, I think. Whatever force you send, Brigadier, I would suggest that it be well-armed and prepared for immediate combat."

Maxall considered the man's words. Seldom did the chief of intelligence make recommendations on operations to his counterpart, but when he did, the brigadier knew from experience to listen closely. Brigadier Bernard Maxall had commanded Daubish at several levels, and he had never known the man's judgments to be far from the mark. He rolled the papers into a tight ball and pitched them into a burn basket. The papers ignited as they passed the rim, reduced to a fluff of spreading ash before they reached the bottom.

"Thank you for the recommendation, Stanley," said Maxall. "I intend to send a strong force into harm's way."

5

1900, 2 Martius 6831—The long line of troops filed slowly past the control officer, presenting their boarding chits as they reached his station near the door of the ship. The line of men somehow seemed unwilling to enter the *Dromedary* Class transport that waited to take them off Caralis. The name *Terpsichore* was stenciled on the hull in block letters, but only someone with a sense of humor could have so named it.

The *Dromedary* Class was designed to haul cargo with the greatest efficiency, whether the load be bulk stores or people. Following the age-old adage that form follows function, the designers had not endowed the ship with any aesthetically redeeming qualities; the transport was simply a huge box with grav drives welded to its sides. It was, in fact, the exact opposite of the graceful muse of dance and song for whom it was named. The men boarding the box knew they were in for an uncomfortable voyage because their orders had been to bring cold weather wear along with other equipment, even though the jump they were making to Rilus V was a short trip.

The *Dromedary*'s heating system was rudimentary, located in the huge bay that hung between the drive units. Those unlucky enough to berth near the heater fried throughout the voyage. Those just a few steps away got no heat at all. That was why the movement orders called for cold weather gear.

The line shuffled forward. The last man to be checked off was still swathed in bandages protecting pink, newly applied plasto-skin. He paused at the top of the ramp clenched between the yawning doors, the last, reluctant departee. Platoon Sergeant Lucifer K. Mullins let his gaze sweep the skyport facilities, then gave a shrug and stepped into the waiting transport. Someone had to bring the replacements forward, he knew, and it was better to send the sick, lame, and lazies to do the job than to withdraw a functioning Renegade Legion. He certainly qualified under sick or lame; he was still recovering from burns he'd taken when his tank self-destructed during a battle two months earlier on Alsatia, part of the ongoing Commonwealth–TOG struggle for Caralis. His Century, part of the 2567th Provisional Renegade Legion, made a successful penetration into, and then behind, enemy lines. The Cohort was on its way back to friendly territory when it discovered nearly an entire community, uprooted by the TOG advance, hiding in a secluded valley. They rescued the civilians, but in so doing, altered the signatures of their tanks beyond the recognition capabilities of any DDP. They were under fire from both sides when the two different TS&R systems that had been jury-rigged into one finally stopped cooperating. His tank crashed and burned, but the cavalry arrived in time to get him out.

Experiences like those were what pulled troops together into a first-class fighting unit. He'd miss the old stomping grounds, but in a month he'd be back, or he'd be somewhere else. The 2567th was his family, and for a while he'd continue to feel loyalty toward it. But if he was transferred to another unit, so be it. The new unit would become his family, and a new loyalty would form.

The loading ramp slid into place under the feor-mesh floor with a shriek of protest. The doors clanged shut, and the sealant pods inflated. Mullins looked across the giant bay, filled eight bunks high with the shattered humanity of war. Plasto-skin and prosthetic devices were much in evidence. Then, slicing through the echoing din of voices and movement, came the quiet tinkle of dice striking a hard surface. Mullins smiled. Perhaps the journey wouldn't be so bad after all.

Stolich Wotan eased himself into the seat in front of the console and called up the tactical display for Operation Gateway. He was sure now that the strike at Malthus across the southern pole would take place. Once a plan had a name, once it was upgraded from "OPLAN XX-XX" to something with a real title, it took on a life of its own. Too many people had too much invested to allow the plan to die. He was satisfied.

At the next console was his counterpart in Operations, Lieutenant Colonel Alban C. Tripp. Tripp was physically very like Wotan, but his features were more defined and more pleasantly arranged. Wotan and Tripp had been counterparts through much of their careers, working together for a time, then leaving for other stations, then meeting again at the same post. In the continual Pendulos games that could be found on any base or aboard ship, they often played together, invariably cleaning up when they partnered. Few teams had a better sense of communication at the table, though an accomplished civilian named Tuituit Keyringorn gave them a run for their money. The huge, bear-like man played slowly, but rarely made mistakes. He was connected with a transport operation on Caralis and tended to leave suddenly and reappear just as abruptly, muttering about crippled drive systems and faulty navigational computers. It would be interesting, Wotan thought absently, to run a check on him. Perhaps after this operation got off the ground.

"Nice plan, Wotan," said Tripp, nodding hello as the intelligence officer sat down next to him. "You always did have a flair for the unusual. How did you come up with this one?"

"I was watching the snow melt."

The operations officer raised his eyebrows. "I shouldn't have asked," he snorted. Alban Tripp scrolled several graphs across the screen and leaned back in his swivel chair. "Yup. A nice plan, but I don't see how we can possibly use it."

"What's the problem?"

Tripp leaned forward again to tap the screen. "Your plan calls for at least a two-Cohort Manus, reinforced, to make the strike. We haven't got the troops available." He swiveled away from the screen. "I just don't see it happening."

"There must be something available." Wotan could practically see his plan arcing through the air to flash on the rim of the burn basket. "Maybe we could use fewer troops."

"You can ask for however many troops you want, but that still doesn't change the fact that nothing's available," Tripp insisted, shaking his head as he returned his gaze to the screen. "That last series of attacks over on Alsatia drained all our resources. Unless you want to commit the clerks and jerks from HQ?" He looked at Wotan sideways and waited for his friend's response.

"That's impossible. Troops are always available somewhere on this planet. In fact, I'll bet there's at least one unit refitting on Rolandrin right now."

"As a matter of fact," said Tripp, "there are two units currently on Rolandrin." He straightened up and pressed a command key. "We have a Legion, the 2031st, almost battle-worthy, and the 2567th Renegade, just beginning to refit. Unfortunately, the 2031st has already been assigned to the line, and our orders are to keep hands off that unit. The 2567th Provisional has been damaged pretty severely, and it will be at least sixty days before they get any replacements."

"Then why not use the 2567th? We've got nothing to lose since their current state means they can't be committed elsewhere. We just task the administration clerks in G-1 to allocate more replacements to account for those troops they will probably lose in Operation Gateway, and send them out. We can make it even more palatable to HQ by cutting the strike force from a Manus to a reinforced Cohort. That should make everybody happy."

Alban Tripp leaned back in his chair and laced his fingers at the nape of his neck. Stolich had a point. Using a Renegade Legion, and a damaged Provisional one at that, made good sense. No one at headquarters could object to sending a provisional Renegade Legion on this mission. Provisional Legions were no more than hodgepodge units consisting of elements from all over Shannedam County. They were assigned together temporarily to accomplish a specific goal. This particular Legion, the 2567th, had successfully held its section of the main battle lines against TOG in its last assignment on Alsatia, but they were still not worthy of note by anyone in power. Their efforts on Alsatia had nearly decimated their ranks; they would have to refit before they could be of any further use in the defense of Caralis, and that refitting would not come for some time. In fact, Gateway should be over before the unit's refitting even began. Tripp rocked forward, releasing his fingers to poke sharply at several keys in rapid succession. "Done, and done, and done!"

Wotan rose from his chair. "I'll notify the 2567th at once." He turned to go, then turned back. "Say, Tripp, have time for some cards tonight?"

The operations sergeant tore the printout from the machine. The tear started on the perforation, then ripped jaggedly across the bottom of the page. The sergeant wondered idly why they bothered to perforate the paper at all; it never tore along the row of holes. The newer printers had cutter bars, but the Renegades seldom got new machines. Every backwater Commonwealth post received one before the Renegades came up on the list. And a Provisional unit like the 2567th Renegade Legion was at the bottom of even the Renegade list. He dropped the printout on the cluttered desk of Legatus Mantelli Lartur, the Legion's G-3 Operations Officer.

"Good news?" asked the legatus, not looking up.

"I don't think so, sir."

"Well, let's see what the tin gods in their ivory tower have found for us to do, then." The legatus pulled the paper toward him and glanced over the instructions. "I don't believe it! This is a warning order for an operation. Most Secret, and all the rest of that garbage. What will they cook up next?" He reached for the commlink on his desk and touched a button. He nearly succeeded in smoothing the irritation from his voice, but a trace of annoyance remained. "I think you'd better see this, sir." He rose from his desk without waiting for a reply.

Prefect NaBesta Kenderson looked up from his paperwork as the legatus entered his office. Compared to the offices of other Legion commanders, Kenderson's was spartan, at best. The regulation, two-pedestal desk was gray. The chair matched it, as did the other two in the room. Behind the desk stood the flags of the Commonwealth and the Renegade Command. There was no Legion flag because the 2567th's provisional status did not merit either a flag or a unit flash.

The legatus dropped the printout on his superior's desk and waited for the prefect to finish what he was doing. Kenderson finally looked up.

"It seems, sir, that the powers-that-be have decided we can do something useful while we refit," said Lartur. "I only hope they've added additional replacements to our list."

Kenderson rubbed his hands across his face as though trying to knead the flesh into life. Legatus Mantelli Lartur was a good officer, except for a tendency to be snide when speaking of his superiors. Kenderson sometimes wondered what the legatus said about his prefect when he was having a few in the club with his peers.

"I'm sure it's important," Kenderson said briskly, though not at all convinced it was. He quickly scanned the sheet of orders. "They only want a reinforced Cohort, so we shouldn't have too much trouble filling this request. Who's available?"

Lartur dropped another printout on the desk. "All ten Cohorts are currently operational, to one degree or another. Of those, six are commanded by a centurion maximus, and the other four by senior centurions. The Cohort Primus is the closest to full strength, but I would not recommend sending that unit. As the backbone of the Legion, it would be a shame to squander it on a mission like this. The most likely units are the remaining five commanded by a centurion maximus. Shall I evaluate each, sir?"

"Shoot."

"Cohort Forblen is at 65 percent strength, but most of his losses were in the maintenance and administrative elements. They were overrun during the last retreat. Cohort Harras is at 65 percent as well, but his losses were spread pretty evenly into his combat units. Cohort Justin is closer to 60 percent strength, but he is not always on top of the Centuries in his command. It may be his fault or a problem with the staff officers; we're still sorting that out. Cohort Martil is between 55 percent and 60 percent, but her troops deserve a rest after the severe pounding they took during the last push. Cohort Vendome is at only 10 percent strength, because they were the first Cohort to be granted leave. Most of them have gone home for thirty days. In my evaluation, Forblen, Harras, and Martil are the best candidates for this mission."

"Pick one."

Lartur considered the three commanders. Forblen had most of his combat strength, but would be forced to fill key staff positions with new people. There would be no chance for a shakedown period, and for a unit operating independently of headquarters, as the warning order required, that was risky. Harras had lost many key commanders as well, but his losses were fairly even throughout the Cohort, and he could replace missing staff from his own command unit. That made Harras a better choice than Forblen. Martil's command was the weakest, and would need the most replacements to reach a full Cohort. Martil was also the most junior of the Cohort commanders. That didn't mean she wouldn't do a good job, only that she was junior, and so probably less experienced. "I'd go with Harras, sir."

"So would I. Notify him of the mission, and ask him to come to my office."

"Yes, sir."

"What do you think, Milt?" Prefect Kenderson leaned back in his chair, his hands braced on the arm rests, his feet on his desk. One of the advantages of a steel desk, he mused, contemplating his shoes, was that foot marks didn't show. Kenderson wondered if the other Legion prefects dared put their feet on their wooden masterpieces.

Milton Harras pushed the warning order away and reached for his brandy. He cupped the glass in both hands and let the fruity fragrance fill his nose before touching his lips to the rim of the snifter. A thin trickle of liquid made its way down his throat. Fine stuff, he thought. Perhaps it was the prefect's way of making the assignment easier to take. "It certainly is daring."

"I know Stolich Wotan up at planetary command, and this has his mark on it. I don't know this Tripp fellow, but if he's a friend of Wotan's, it's likely they're both cut from the same cloth." Kenderson studied Harras surreptitiously. The centurion maximus had many years on the youthful Legion commander, and Kenderson didn't want that to become part of the discussion. It was hard enough having men under his command who had served with his father. "I'll give you anything you want, within reason. But try to stay away from Cohort Primus."

"I wouldn't touch those prima donnas with a ten-foot pole. They think too highly of themselves to be of any real use, as far as I'm concerned," Harras said drily.

"Now, Milt. Just wait until you become the senior Cohort commander and you get Primus. You'll feel differently about those troops then."

"I doubt I'll make Primus any time soon," said Harras, staring into the snifter. Primus, as both men knew, was awarded to rising stars. Harras was a long way from anyone's idea of a rising star.

The prefect groped for something suitable to say, but the moment passed. "So we'll skip Primus Cohort. But you can still take whatever you need. I'll even make sure you keep your current personnel."

"That's something I'd like to talk to you about, sir," said Harras. "I have a decorated centurion in my command that I would like to see boosted to a Manus head shed."

"You're willing to lose one of your officers? Who?"

"Centurion Freund."

"But I thought you just decorated him."

"You just decorated him, sir. Not me."

"Ah." Kenderson paused. "But that's still no reason to lose him. Others have gotten tin they didn't deserve." He tried to make eye contact with Harras, but the older man seemed deeply interested in the last swallow of liquor in his glass. "I'm sure you can keep him, Milt."

Harras finally met the prefect's puzzled gaze. "No. The man makes my skin crawl. I won't dump on his career, but I don't want him around me. Promote him and move him to Manus."

Kenderson looked surprised, but said, "You're the boss, Milt. I'll get him out of your Cohort."

"Thank you, sir. I appreciate that." Harras felt the palpable tension in the room relax. "Any more of that brandy? I feel like imitating the ancients. *Ave Caesar, morituri te salutamus*, and all that." He reached for the new bottle that Kenderson extracted from one of the drawers of the utilitarian-looking desk.

6

1807, 3 Martius 6831—Centurion Maximus Milton Harras checked his Land-Force perscomp. The wafer-thin band circling his wrist usually served to keep track of tau-time, the period a person could remain in T-space before having to spend an equal amount of time in normal space to restore his body to normal. T-space travel took place at such tremendous speeds that the friction of molecules caused matter to disintegrate if it stayed in T-space for more than 30 days. Death by Shimmer Heat—the friction or disharmony of molecules—was a horrible end. T-space travelers spent equal time in normal space to "burn off" Shimmer Heat. But the perscomp also functioned as a diary, notebook, and appointment calendar. The latter was the function he needed now. The calendar was currently set to Caralis time, but it calculated star-time as well. It took Caralis 1,228 days, 22 hours, 44 minutes, and 4 seconds, plus or minus a bit, to orbit Borialis, making its year more than three times the length of a Terran year. The days, in Terran terms, were only 20 hours, 58 minutes, and 47 seconds long. The LF perscomp was programmed to record time in a 24-unit day, with the hours and minutes set slightly faster than Terran time. That small adjustment was an easy one for off-worlders to accept. The year, however, caused problems.

It was no use trying to force Terran months on a year almost four times as long. Instead, the Caralis year was divided into weeks and months that copied the Terran system. Each week was seven days long, a concession to Terran history as well as numerology, but the resulting 175 weeks were divided into 35 five-week months, which included a holiday period of three or four days in the middle of the winter months. The winter holidays were also a concession to Terran history, and were a convenient break for troops made restless by the lack of obvious seasons caused by the minor tilt of Caralis' axis. The LF perscomp kept track of all this information for each planet where a unit was stationed. On command, it would also tell the season. Caralis' land masses lay both above and below the equatorial belt, but the LF perscomp used the current season in Rolandrin, in the northern hemisphere, as its reference point in determining the seasons.

The crystal wafer of Harras' LF perscomp showed the date as (6831)04031807. The year, in star time, appeared within the parentheses; the rest was a straight date-time group. The numbers showed that it was the fourth month (04), third day (03), and seven minutes past six in the evening (1807). That made D-day for Gateway only seven days away. Not much time to plan an operation of this complexity. The one good thing was that the computer had already generated their route, azimuths, and altitudes for the sea crossing. All Harras had to do was organize and command the force.

Harras looked up as a shadow fell across his desk. "Yes, Senior Sergeant?" Standing a few steps in front of his desk, at relaxed attention, was Aktol Graviston, senior sergeant of Cohort Harras.

"Newly promoted Centurion Maximus Alanton Freund to see you, sir." Aktol's voice was usually soft and almost musical, but now it revealed just a hint of sarcasm. He had emphasized the words "newly promoted" as though trying them out for the sound. It was obvious he didn't like the result.

Harras considered his senior sergeant for a moment. A tower of a man, Graviston stood just over two meters tall and weighed 137 kilos, almost bursting the seams of the largest uniform the Renegade Legion quartermaster could provide. And he was as black as the darkness of infinite space. The regulation soft tunic designed to be worn under battle armor revealed rippling muscles covering his chest and arms. A good man to have beside you in a tough spot, thought Harras.

Harras and Graviston had served together when both were newcomers to war. Then they had been Commonwealth soldiers fighting the rear-guard action on Saguntum III. A bond of loyalty between the young Private Harras and the more experienced Sergeant Graviston had been forged in the flame and noise of that long, devastating battle. When Harras transferred to the Renegade Legion, he asked Graviston to come with him. Now they were brothers-in-arms again, truer brothers than blood could make them. Neither had secrets from the other. If Aktol didn't like "newly promoted" Centurion Maximus Alanton Freund, Harras assumed he must have as good a reason as his own.

"Thank you, Senior Sergeant. Send him in." The senior sergeant departed, to be replaced by the centurion maximus, who seemed much smaller. Though anyone would, coming in after Graviston.

"Centurion Maximus Alanton Freund, reporting as ordered, sir."

"At ease, Freund," Harras said. "I hear you'll be leaving us." He almost added, "Sorry to hear that," but was afraid the lie would come through in his voice. He was not in any way sorry that Centurion Maximus Freund would be out of his hair. "A promotion to Manus is quite a career move, and second Manus is a good one." That statement was true enough, especially for those officers who wanted to have the right marks appended to their efficiency reports.

"Yes, sir. I was gratified to receive the opportunity to serve." Indeed, Freund knew it was the chance of a lifetime. His early promotion was probably a result of the medal that Prefect Kenderson had awarded him, and the assignment to such an important staff position was a great honor. He had survived command of a Century, the assignment every officer received first. Now with that safely behind him, his future looked bright. He would be able to put his magnificent talents to full use without the ever-present specter of violent death to haunt him. Freund had once calculated the average life span of officers at various grades and positions, and tank centurions did not last long.

But now Freund was free of that worry. If he could survive the rank of centurion maximus without having to command a Cohort, he would probably be able to retire as a legatus. He felt that a training command deep in the rear echelons would be ideal, but first, he had to get out of the hated 2567th Renegade Legion. That move should be easy. Many staff positions on Caralis were required to be filled by a Renegade officer, and a few words in the right place might allow him to make a lateral transfer before the 2567th was again committed to action.

Harras looked at the man standing before his desk. Freund was competent enough, but something about him always made the commander's flesh creep. The man was strictly by-the-book, but ready to take the credit for everything his unit did right, while quick to point out the failings of his subordinates. It was one of the anomalies of his command that all the successes were Freund's responsibility, and all the failures were carefully documented to fall onto the shoulders of others. Freund had not written a single above-average efficiency report on any of his officers or senior non-commissioned officers during his tenure as Century commander. Every one of his reports had been negative, even downright scathing in their condemnations. Harras had seen to it that these unworthy reports were extracted from the files, and once Freund was gone, he would see to it that the memory banks containing evidence of the man's animosity were carefully erased. It was not at all unusual for reports to be "lost" in this manner.

"I just wanted to wish you all the best in your new post, Freund." Harras felt his stomach clench as he spoke, but he tried to sound convincing.

"It has been a pleasure to serve with you, sir." Freund was also doing his best to sound convincing. His tour with Cohort Harras had been many things, but a pleasure was not one of them.

"Take care."

"Yes, sir." Freund saluted, did a smart about-face, and left the room. The air seemed clearer at once.

Graviston's head reappeared in the doorway. "Optio Roglund Karstil to see you, sir. He doesn't have an appointment."

"Boot his record up on my display, wait one minute, then send him in."

"Right."

The data display on Harras' desk cleared and the service record of Optio Roglund Karstil appeared. Reading through it, Harras remembered why the name had rung a bell; this was the commander of the "Vexillary" on Alsatia that had penetrated enemy lines and rescued civilians, then limped back home, only to be fired on by friendlies. He'd had his command pretty well shot to pieces, and taken several wounds in the process. According to the hospital report, Karstil was on convalescent leave for sixty days. Harras thought it too bad the young man would miss the Gateway operation, because he was the kind of soldier the centurion maximus liked to have backing him up.

"Optio Roglund Karstil, reporting as directed, sir."

"Yes?"

"I'd like to rejoin the Cohort, sir."

"Your medical leave is not over yet, son."

"I know, sir. But I feel fine, and I'd like to get back to my platoon."

Harras knew from the record that there was no platoon to get back to. In its final action some weeks ago, every vehicle had been destroyed. For a moment, Harras thought perhaps he might get this enterprising officer into a platoon and Operation Gateway after all. Then he told himself that, no, the time between now and D-day was too short.

"That's fine, Optio. But there's no need for you to hurry back."

Harris studied Karstil's face. The man stood at respectful attention, but the look he was giving his commander made it clear he knew something big was happening. A general call for replacements for Cohort Harras had gone out, couched in terms that made it look as though Kenderson wanted a functional Cohort, cobbled together from the other units of the command, to act as "school troops" to help train replacements. But Karstil obviously didn't believe a word of it.

"You still have thirty days on your leave, son. You can rejoin us at the end of that time." Assuming, of course, thought Harras, that there's any Cohort left to rejoin in thirty days. "We'll still be kicking around, waiting for fillers."

"I'd like to come sooner, sir."

"There's no need," Harras said kindly. "Come back in thirty days." He nodded in dismissal, and the optio's shoulders sagged as he turned to leave the room. It was too bad, Harras thought, that they'd have to leave one of the live ones behind.

Graviston appeared again. "List of replacements available, sir."

"Punch it up, and I'll take a look." Harras thought the business of getting replacements was the worst part of his job. Vehicles could be examined and found battle worthy or not; with people it was different. Because Kenderson's order requested troops for training, nominally an administrative unit, commanders would not send their best; in fact, they would tend to send their least valuable troops. How could Harras tell from a name and a service number whether or not someone was any good? He had to rely instead on his gut feelings about the commanders who were doing the posting. Scanning the long list of names, ranks, numbers, and specialties, he thought most looked like losers. These were most likely the dregs of all the other units, soldiers they couldn't discipline or who otherwise didn't fit in. Graviston leaned on his commander's desk and watched the names race by.

"What do you think, top?" Aktol, as Harras knew, would be working on gut instinct, too.

"Pretty slim pickings, sir, pretty slim. If we weren't so short on time, I'd can the whole list and start over. Did you notice that there were some names from the 2031st on the list? How could they have been permitted to volunteer?"

"You're assuming they did volunteer."

"I don't understand how a commander could let his people leave just before he was heading back into combat. Either those men screwed up something fierce, or they pushed to get out."

Harras stared at the computer screen as the last of the names flashed by. "Well, take the combat-arms types, no matter where they come from. Take only 2567th people for support." He watched the names scroll past again. Some of them looked familiar, though he couldn't recall where he had seen them. Probably just the same names of his many comrades over the years, only these were of the next generation. The name of an infantry sergeant from the 2031st rang a bell, but Harras didn't know why. He filed "Ross, H.," in the back of his mind, then cleared the screen and returned to his organizational chart.

The biggest problem facing Harras was the organization of his force. The Cohort normally had five Centuries of medium tanks and one of scout vehicles, each Century consisting of nine combat vehicles. But the Cohort for this operation, even reinforced with everything Kenderson could spare, would have only enough tanks for four medium Centuries and six of the usual nine scouts. A force of twenty-four tanks, twelve infantry carriers, and six scouts was not a strong one. He would have to reorganize the Cohort to take advantage of the strengths he had. The easiest thing to do was to go with four full-strength Centuries. That way, he would be able to appoint commanders from inside his own unit, people he knew. The light scouts could have one of the optios as a commander. But the support elements were more difficult.

They would need engineer support as well as support staff for medical, maintenance, and communications. All the vehicles would have to be grav-equipped, because a ground vehicle could never make the crossing from the ice cap to Malthus. There was just not enough support equipment to cover all the bases; they would even be short of artillery support. The nearest thing to actual artillery support available was a Bit `Nak Val, also called a Catapult. But the Catapult lacked thrust for maneuvers. It took forever to reach speed, and once it did, the only way to stop it was to ram it into something solid. Harras would rather leave it behind, but what choice had he? He needed the firepower.

The headquarters element would include the Catapult, a Remus engineer vehicle, and modified light tanks to carry the supporting elements. Most of the support staff would mount Pedden hulls that had been stripped of their artillery pieces to make room for the troops and their equipment. Harras looked at the structure of his reorganized force. It was strong for a Cohort, but he couldn't help wondering if it still might be too few to win and too many to lose.

He could only pray that they could get across the pole and hit the TOGs before the enemy knew they were coming.

7

0950, 4 Martius 6831—The double gold knots accorded a centurion maximus caught the light from the overhead flouropanels. Out the corner of his eye, Alanton H. Freund, newly promoted to that rank, caught the light dancing across the gleaming insignia. He moved his shoulder slightly to send the sparks racing over the gold again. He liked what he saw. It would be a shame, he mused, when the new brightness began to dull. The light would no longer pirouette across the gold the same way, but neither would people be able to tell that he had just acquired his rank.

The cubicle he occupied at the 2567th Renegade Legion's Manus headquarters on Rolandrin was off to the side of a main work area. Many of the stations were empty, their occupants either off on important business or transferred as replacements to Cohorts that had suffered losses. Freund felt a momentary disappointment; headquarters should be filled with dutiful servants of the higher ranks. How could the commanders expect a centurion maximus to get anything done if he were stripped of his underlings? Regulations required that an officer have at least one clerk. The way things stood now, he had to generate his own memos and reports. His first memo had been a request for adequate staff.

At least he had an assistant, albeit a junior one, within the section. Optio Holton Bard had been assigned to the 2031st Legion, but for some reason had not seen much action during the recent campaign on Alsatia. According to Bard, a mix-up in his orders had left him a supernumerary to the territorial headquarters. Bard's story was that he had been left to cool his heels at the headquarters during the action. Now, with his transfer to this Manus, he was anxious to show what he could do.

It was not easy to like Holton Bard on first meeting. His receding hairline, slack lips, and watery eyes, all set in the palest skin Freund had ever seen, gave the initial impression of a man two-days drowned. The impression was even stronger when he opened his mouth. Out came a quavering voice, while he hunched his shoulders and cringed whenever he was spoken to. The Renegade Legion, thought Freund, must have scraped the bottom of the barrel for Bard.

But Bard had been the only one to notice the newness of the shoulder knots on Freund's uniform. He had complimented him on his promotion when they were introduced, and he had been solicitous about making sure that Freund's cubicle was stocked with everything his rank allowed. Somehow, Bard had discovered Freund's penchant for Cream Rollies; not the ones filled with that awful synthetic cream, but the ones filled with the real, thick, white cream that made them justifiably famous throughout the galaxy. The past two mornings, Freund had arrived to find a Rolly, neatly wrapped in a clean napkin, on his desk. When Freund looked around the work area to discover the donor, Bard had caught his eye and given him a shy smile. The new centurion maximus decided privately that this man could be cultivated. Bard also had an uncanny knack with computers, which seemed to come alive under his pudgy, pale fingers. All the more reason to make Bard a friend.

Freund turned his attention back to his work. He had been assigned to the temporary supply section of the Manus headquarters. The Manus normally functioned as a combat headquarters only, with limited supply and administrative functions. This allowed HQ to concentrate on operational tasks while support troops from the Legion did the report-pushing. But when the Legion was placed in refit, much of the administrative work fell to the Manus. Officers in the headquarters were temporarily reassigned, and clerical support needed over and above what the Manus could supply was provided by the Legion. In theory, this allowed the Manus commander, a legatus, to monitor the rebuilding of the Cohorts and Centuries assigned to his command.

The part Freund hated was that some of the officers who would normally be in operations were shunted off to the administrative posts. Such was Freund's lot. As a newly assigned officer from a Cohort of a different Manus, he had won the dubious honor of monitoring the logistical arrangements for his new headquarters. Very little needed to be done. The requests for replacement equipment had been generated even before Freund's transfer, so all the centurion maximus needed do was see that the new equipment was correctly assigned to the requesting Cohort/Century.

Thus Freund spent most of his time browsing through the computer files of the other headquarter units. His greatest coup so far was discovering that the Manus Primus had requested a communicator, vehicular, N/M LCS 625-97, identical to the one his, the second Manus, had requested. Because only one such communicator was available in supply, it had naturally been allocated to the Manus Primus. With the help of Optio Bard, Freund had been able to break into the locked distribution-control files and send the set to the second Manus. He was sure that the legatus would eventually discover that he was the proud possessor of the equipment and reward the centurion maximus accordingly.

The "theft," or as Freund liked to think of it, "the more equitable redistribution of needed equipment," had been a thrilling piece of work. While all the other headquarters were crying for replacement parts, he could just break into the distribution files and divert equipment to his own HQ. Once Freund had discovered how easy it was to get into the system, he spent much of his time shopping among the list of allocated spare parts. He was currently looking for rare equipment to divert to his own Manus. This was going to look very good on his efficiency report.

The list of spare equipment was buried deep in a host of other computer-controlled data. Much of the information he scrolled past was mundane: requests for leave, personnel files, reports of courts-martial, requests for decorations, total items on hand, officer transfers, training problems, Gateway, weather reports, ammunition expenditure by weight and type...Gateway?

Freund rolled the screen back to that single word. He saw that the notation carried the code of a secure-locked program, Eyes Only. Now here, he thought, was someone trying to get a rare item under a specious title. He noted that the code number carried the designator for the Manus Primus, a dead give-away that it was important. He keyed in his own access code and tried to open the file. A warning bell tinkled in the monitor on his desk, and the screen flashed a warning. ACCESS TO DOCUMENT NOT ALLOWED. NEED-TO-KNOW NOT AUTHORIZED. The bell stopped and the warning vanished. Freund glanced around the work space to see if anyone else had heard the bell. Holton Bard looked up from his station and smiled.

Freund knew that Bard's computer, though linked directly with the one at his station, was programmed to filter out all documentation not specific to the second Manus. He would not have seen the "Gateway" notation. Freund smiled back at Bard and gestured for him to approach his superior's cubicle. Bard cleared his own screen and rose to join the centurion maximus.

Holton Bard was not pleased to hear the warning bell from Freund's computer. He was also unhappy at being summoned away from his station. He had been diligently working on a locked file named "Gateway" that he had discovered among more mundane topics. Breaking the computer filter that was supposed to restrict his file access had been a relatively easy process, exactly what his superiors had trained him to do. He had since been reading any generated supply and administrative reports that caught his interest. It was he who had found the communicator, vehicular, N/M LCS 625-97, and prompted it onto Freund's computer. The centurion maximus had snapped at the bait, just as Bard hoped he would. Diverting the communicator had been an easy task, and now he and Freund would be "friends forever." Tying the centurion maximus to the theft of equipment was an even better hook than providing the Cream Rollies, which could certainly be presented to appear as a bribe if he ever needed to discredit the man. That particular bit of information had been provided by a mole and passed down by his superiors after Bard had reported the new officer in his section.

Bard had also taken the precaution of pulling and reading Alanton H. Freund's efficiency reports. Whoever Milton Harras was, he didn't think much of Freund. Although the citations on the awards, the efficiency reports, and the recommendation for promotion were all couched in the most laudatory terms, it was all standard verbiage. The well-trained eye could tell that the man had been found wanting by his commander. The two had obviously had a difference of opinion on a number of subjects, and Harras, in order not to ruin Freund's career, had booted him out of his Cohort and into the Manus. Bard was glad to have Freund around. He could be a valuable tool in Bard's operation. He walked around behind Freund's desk, careful to cringe slightly as their eyes made contact. "You wanted me, sir?"

Freund smiled and leaned back in his chair. He gestured toward the screen, where he had highlighted the word "Gateway." "What do you make of this?"

Optio Holton Bard resisted the temptation to gawk or exclaim. His superior had called his attention to the same file he had been trying to unlock! This was better than he deserved.

Freund did not wait for a response. "Perhaps it is an attempt on the part of Manus Primus to get a specialized piece of equipment," he said with studied casualness. "I just discovered it on my screen and thought you'd like to have a crack at it," Freund said, failing to mention that he had already failed to break the code.

"I'll give it a try if you like, sir. But I'll need your access control number to start."

"I can't give that to you, Holton," Freund said smugly. "You know that it's secret. But I can type it into the computer for you." Freund's access code was just one more of his ways of throwing his rank in the face of his subordinates. His fingers moved across the keyboard, then he placed his hand, palm down, on the recognition panel. The computer acknowledged his presence. "It's all yours, Holton," Freund said, rising from the chair.

Bard had already worked out the first seven numbers of the Gateway access code, leaving only two unknown. He typed the numbers slowly, as though trying to find them. Freund must not suspect that he had already partially broken the code. The last two he knew to be the cube of some number. That number was probably neither one nor two, because that would produce a zero as the second-to-last digit. From experience, he knew that computers did not like to generate zeros as part of a code, because a zero could so easily be confused with the letter "O." A small likelihood also existed of a seven being confused with a one. The most likely number for the last two digits was 64, the cube of four. When Bard reached the eighth number, he tentatively struck the six on the keypad. The computer obediently displayed the number. Then his finger reached for the four key and tapped it.

Immediately the display screen cleared and the order for Operation Gateway appeared. Bard instantly recognized the importance of the document he was seeing. Even without the MOST SECRET: EYES ONLY heading, this was obviously important. Security classifications were routinely assigned to information that people wanted kept quiet, and an MS:EO heading could be slapped on anything, even a request for toilet paper. But this was different. Bard had committed much of the document to memory even before Freund could react.

As the security heading flashed on the screen, Freund seemed unconcerned about the MS:EO heading; it was common enough. Even the presence of the optio at his station did not seem to worry him. He began to read the order, starting with the initiator and working through the addressees. Only when he got to the Mission Statement and Operational Concept did he seem to realize that this was something important. He leaned forward and cleared the screen. "It wasn't what I thought it was," he said, but Bard easily saw through his superior's feigned disinterest. "Thanks for the help."

Bard rose from the chair and caught Freund's eye. It was obvious to both men that they had tampered with a file of the greatest importance, something that should have been out-of-bounds to both. Equally obvious was the unspoken agreement that neither would mention the subject again. Bard nodded at his superior, repressing a triumphant smile, and returned to his station. Freund was his for as long as he wanted him.

After regular work hours, Holton Bard returned to the now-dark work area. He knew his way through the maze of consoles, and made straight for Freund's work station. Not only was the post out of direct line-of-sight from the door, preventing any casual inspection from revealing his presence, but he planned to use Freund's console in case the break-in was ever traced to this area.

He sat down and typed in his superior's access code. Pulling a plasto-skin glove onto his hand, he pressed the recognition panel. Getting the hand print had been easy. He had waited until Freund visited his station, then called his attention to some tiny print on the screen. Freund had been forced to lean forward, supporting himself by placing his hand, palm down, on the only clear space available. Bard had lifted the print, thermograph and all, as soon as Freund left.

The Gateway file opened immediately to the access code. The file was locked against a copy, and Bard did not want to spend the time trying to breach another security lock. He committed the general information to memory, then used an electro-scanner to copy the navigational information. That done, he cleared the screen and erased all evidence of his presence. Of that he was most careful, even wiping clean the finger marks on the back of Freund's chair.

8

1945, 4 Martius 6831—The TOG agent moved carefully past the hutment that housed the Officers' Club and the parking area. The 2031st Renegade Legion was preparing to cross to Alsatia, and their comrades were giving them a raucous farewell party. The 2031st was not the Legion to which the spy was assigned, but he planned to attend the party to try to pick up whatever tidbits of information he could. With enough bits it was possible to create quite a picture, and that picture might fit together with information he had already gleaned from his own assignment. The party had not been going on long enough to generate loose talk, however, and the spy slipped away. He would take this opportunity to do his other secret work.

He had a detailed report to send to his TOG superiors. This was not the first time he had been able to pass on accurate information about Renegade activity. During the campaign on Alsatia some months before, he had transmitted a complete Renegade Legion operational plan. The TOG commanders had not made use of the information, however, and the battle had turned into a fiasco for TOG forces. This time would be different.

Holton Bard was certain that his last transmission had been compromised, so he had spent a lot of time covering his tracks since the failed operation. His current assignment with the 2567th had been a blessing in disguise. The Legion was provisional, which made it easy to infiltrate the command structure. Officers came and went within the Legion's ranks with alarming frequency, while the losses suffered in the last campaign had opened many doors to his personal advancement. Discovering the Gateway operation had been a stroke of luck. The plan was almost certainly genuine; the access code had been too difficult to break for it to be a plant. But Bard's TOG training had paid off, and he now had the memorized plan safely encoded and ready for transmission. He included as hard intelligence the coded navigational information. His superiors on Malthus would be able to analyze the text of the document against the numbers. Even if he had made a small mistake or forgotten something, the navigation code would fill in the blanks for the TOG commanders. He had been forced to send his last transmission from a field headquarters communications center, which was how his message had been interfered with. This time, he planned to send directly from one of the many information-gathering antennae serving the Renegade HQ.

The bank of antennae spread over several hectares of a huge field. Omni-directional parabolic aerials were clustered by type and mission, each trained in a slightly different direction to track a different satellite. Some were idle, awaiting a new satellite to replace one lost or destroyed. (Bard had heard that if brought together, the dead satellites and other space debris would form a virtual ring around the planet, but the gravitational force of Rock Wall kept that from happening. The giant moon of Caralis acted like a vacuum cleaner, sweeping uncontrolled debris out of orbit.) Seeking a specific sending unit, Bard flashed a tiny beam of light on the coded numbers at the base of each mount as he moved through the massive array. He was searching for one that randomly crossed the orbit of a specific TOG unit. He found it near the center of the field.

He checked his LF perscomp. Timing was crucial—in fact, it was everything. The TOG satellite would be within the parabolic sector for a mere 5.73 seconds. The link had to be loaded and powered before the satellite appeared in the window. He would receive no confirmation on the message, because the window was too narrow. He would only have one shot to send this information, because it would be broad daylight the next time the satellite appeared in the arc. Creeping around an antennae field in daylight would not be conducive to his good health or the success of his mission. Bard crouched at the base of the aerial and opened the access panel.

The antenna itself was not powered, and he could not draw power from the base's generating facility. That draw was carefully monitored at the source, and any unauthorized power use would be traced immediately. It could be done, but Bard would do it only in extreme emergency. His TOG instructors had been adamant that an agent's survival was more important than any intelligence that could be sent. The war had been going on for a long time, and it would continue for a long time. New information would always become available, but a new agent could not always be placed in the Commonwealth/Renegade ranks. The only exception to the rule of agent survival had to do with the discovery of a plot against the life of the Caesar. If an agent discovered such a plan, sacrifice was acceptable, even required, to foil it.

The message would require a little power to send, but Bard had obtained a storage capacitor to take care of that. The device was a four-by-four-by-ten-centimeter block that snapped onto the back of his waistband, but the loose-fitting overtunic issued as casual wear hid the bulge it made at the small of his back. He extracted the feed wire from the block and slipped the bayonet plug into the female receptor at the antenna's base. The capacitor would completely discharge its power supply three seconds after the control switch was depressed. He clamped the message-sending device onto the feed wire. When the switch on the box activated the capacitor, power would surge through the message filters. The coded transmission would act as a damper on the power, converting the straight surge into a series of pulses. These pulses, actually four-digit code groups, would be intercepted by the satellite. The final five groups were commands to the satellite itself. The first four designated the addressee, and the last group instructed the satellite to proceed without confirmation. The last group had been inserted to ensure that the satellite did not send a telltale reply back to Rolandrin to be picked up by a counterspy.

Bard watched the seconds flick by on the digital readout of his perscomp. As the satellite appeared in the parabolic window, he depressed the line switch on the capacitor block. He felt the power surge as it left the box. When the satellite had passed beyond the window, he extracted the bayonet plug and let the feed wire snap back into the block. He screwed the access panel back into place. Before he moved away from the antenna, he snapped the message capsule in half and pulled the carbo-silicon wafers from the interior. He carefully crushed each one, letting the fragments fall to the ground. There would be no record of the information he had sent. His task completed, he rose and returned to the club.

As Bard entered the long, low building, he noted the ambulance discreetly parked nearby. These farewell parties had a tendency to become so wild that sometimes a few merrymakers, particularly among the junior officers, required basic medical attention.

Indeed, it happened so often that the headquarters medical staff routinely stationed an ambulance outside the club for these send-off parties.

Inside, Bard blinked against the glare of the overhead flouropanels. The lights glowed at the highest setting to help control the emotions of the officers packed into one corner, the optios of the combat platoons scheduled to depart tomorrow. Soft light seemed only to exaggerate the lunacy that usually held sway at these functions. Bard headed toward the group, intending to join the fringes of the party and try to work his way to the center. He glanced around the cavernous room, checking for any other group that might offer better information. His heart skipped a beat.

Seated in the corner on the far side of the room were the medical orderlies, quietly watching the festivities. In the center of the group was a large man who hunched down in his seat, looking like nothing so much as a huge bear. Bard stepped behind a post, closed his eyes, and breathed deeply to calm his racing heart. Something in his mind had rung a warning bell, and a spy was taught never to disregard a warning. The man's face was familiar, but Bard could not remember where they had met. He forced the sudden panic from his mind and quickly began a mental review of his experiences in the Renegade Legion.

He concentrated on the other man's shape, his presence. Bard was sure that the man was familiar, but not in the setting of a medical corps. His mind drifted back to his first posting in the Renegade Legion, back to the voyage to Rilus V. His eyes snapped open. That was it! The *RLS Maiestas*. He had played cards with this man on the transport that had brought him to Rilus V. His name was Stone, Larry Stone. But he had been an optio then, and here he was a medical orderly. Had he lost rank? Impossible. In the unlikely event that Stone had been busted, he would also have been sent off planet. A broken officer would not remain in his old unit. In any case, the Commonwealth didn't break officers. There had to be another solution.

Another memory nagged at the edges of his consciousness. Bard realized he had seen the man again since arriving on Caralis, but where? He had definitely not been acting as an optio. It had to be something else. A small part of his mind, still occupied with the transmission of his recent discoveries, suddenly clicked into the memory he was searching for. The day he had sent the Renegade operations plan from a communications-rigged Spartius on Alsatia, he had first had to get rid of the insolent communications sergeant. Bard suffered a fresh attack of panic when he realized, with mind-numbing certainty, that that sergeant was one and the same with this medical orderly. Bard's message had been compromised then, and he should have known. A Renegade counterspy had been right under his nose. Sweat beaded on his forehead. He had to escape.

He backed away, careful to keep the post between him and the medical orderlies in the corner. He accidentally trod on the toes of a very drunk centurion, mumbled an excuse, then fled into the night.

Once in his quarters, Bard locked the door and pushed the heavy bureau against it. Still in the dark, he drew the shades, tucking the edges into the cracks so that not even a glint would show on the outside. He knew his behavior was irrational. Anyone who wanted to know what was going on in the room could use an infrared scanner to look straight through the shades. He flicked on the light and looked around. The room must be hiding a miniature scanning device. Even though he swept the room for bugs every time he left it, a passive viewing device might have escaped his attention. He swept the room again, this time with the scanner on high power. Nothing showed up on the sweep.

He would have to get out, and do it quickly. His presence was too well-documented with the second Manus to just vanish; that busybody Freund would send out a search party. Better to use channels and make his departure unremarkable. He'd ask for a transfer to a different unit. Yes, Freund would grant him the request. Together, they had gone too deep for the centurion maximus to create a fuss.

Centurion Maximus Alanton Freund was surprised to find no Cream Rolly on his desk; perhaps the young optio had not yet arrived. He glanced at his in-basket. On the top of the pile rested a gray envelope with printing across the flap. He picked it up and looked at the writing: Centurion Maximus Freund. Most Urgent. He lifted the flap and removed the single sheet of onionskin.

It was a request for transfer from Optio Holton Bard. Freund's dismay quickly changed to anger. The man was trying to escape! So that was why he was conspicuous by his absence this morning. Freund's lips pressed into a thin line. The little fool wanted to get away from him. And after all I could have done for him in this command, thought Freund. He is afraid of me.

I'll show him what happens when someone doesn't play fair with Centurion Maximus Alanton Freund, he vowed silently. If he wants out, I'll send him out. I'll transfer him to the end of the galaxy. He can go to a post he'll hate for the rest of his miserable life. He'll go without a recommendation from me, and I'll make sure he never sees a Human face again!

Freund had worked himself into a cold rage. He keyed up the transfer request on his display. That's right, Bard. I'll have you posted to some dark star covered with ice. The thought made him smile. That ought to make your pasty skin even pastier. There'll be no Cream Rollies for you to give your boss. You'll be lucky to get any food at all.

He searched the postings list for a possible hell to which he could send the unfortunate optio. At the far end of the New Philippines, he found just the distant planet. He posted the assignment on Bard's record. He was just about to save the posting when a smile twisted his lips. A better alternative had just occurred to him, one with all the advantages of the New Philippines but dangerous as well.

Freund cleared the record and began to enter new commands. He would post the optio to Cohort Harras. It was a stroke of poetic justice. Let the man taste some warfare. Cohort Harras was just the place for Optio Bard to reconsider his attitude toward his superior. Freund entered the final data and saved. Then he pushed back from his console and chuckled.

9

0850, 9 Martius 6831—Optio Holden Ventis stood atop the grounded Spartius infantry carrier and let his gaze sweep over the laager. He was glad to be a part of Cohort Harras and the 2567th Renegade Legion. The troops were gearing up to head out of headquarters on a secret strike against TOG headquarters on Malthus. His own Century, made up of two platoons of medium-grav Liberators and an infantry platoon, mounted on his Spartius and two Viper carriers, was arranged around his position. To the right, left, and rear were the other three Centuries of the Cohort. The Cohort was running a Century short this mission, with four combat Centuries rather than the standard five, but all four were at full strength. Their numbers would be reduced soon enough, and it felt good to begin with all the assets in place.

Ventis had been blooded weeks earlier during the near-disaster on Alsatia. His Century had been shot to pieces in a TOG attack, and he had been lucky to escape with his vehicle. Commander of that operation was the recently departed, easily forgotten Centurion Alanton Freund. Freund had torn a strip off Ventis, up one side and down the other, for the losses he had suffered. But Ventis still could not reconcile the chewing-out with the facts. He and the other platoon leaders had been in a no-win situation, faced with overwhelming odds. They had done their best, had come out with more vehicles and personnel than they should have by any calculations, but had not received any commendations. In fact, after the reprimand he had received, he was surprised to be assigned command of a Century, especially a tank Century. Considering his lack of experience, it could only be the lack of officers that had prompted his superiors to give him the position.

Ventis was the only officer in the Century. The platoons were under the command of senior sergeants. As the Century commander, his traditional place was in one of the tanks of the lead platoon. Officers were trained to lead men into battle, which served as a good example and gave the commander better control over the troops. But he was infantry-trained, and he preferred to let the tankers run the tanks. The Century would just have to trust him, because the beginning of a covert operation to be conducted under radio silence was no time for an infantry officer, qualified though he might be, to try to learn tank protocol.

The presence of the Spartius in the infantry platoon was unusual. The standard infantry platoon vehicle attached to a Liberator Century was the light Viper carrier. During the reorganization of the Cohort, Vipers turned out to be in short supply, and the Spartius had appeared as a replacement. Though lacking the 25mm cannon of the Viper, dual 5/6 Herring lasers and a wealth of missiles gave the Spartius plenty of other firepower. It also had a good power-to-weight ratio and armor equal to that of the Liberator, all of which made it a good fit for the medium platoon.

The operations order given by Harras could only be described as interesting. The command was to move south, traversing the expanse of water between Rolandrin and the southern ice cap. The Cohort's course and speed had been carefully calculated to prevent orbiting TOG satellites from detecting its movement. By sticking to the rigid, preplotted schedule of azimuth, speed, and altitude, they should be able to run to the edge of the ice unnoticed. Once there, the command was to make a maximum-power run over the ice to the opposite edge of the cap, south of Malthus. From what Ventis understood, it was pretty much a craps shoot after that, with a high-speed run across the water to Malthus, and then mucking around in the TOG rear area. Survivors would escape back across the water and the ice cap to the friendly side of the planet. Ventis had the sinking feeling that the whole force was expendable, but then, that philosophy fit with the general attitude toward the 2567th.

The support element of the Century had been stripped down to the absolute minimum, with communications, administrative, and maintenance sections represented only by their section chiefs. Other members of support, including the Century clerk, had been spread out among the infantry vehicles and tanks as replacement personnel. They were excited at the prospect of getting into the front lines, experiencing what it really meant to be in the armed forces. Ventis knew that their enthusiasm would overcome many of the difficulties inherent in the transition. Only the medical section was at full strength. It was, in fact, overfilled. The presence of so many medics was reassuring, but extra medical people always meant that hard fighting was anticipated. They had even gone so far as to assign a civilian as assistant to the ranking doctor.

The former Century clerk, Triarii Sevestimus Rollus, was now the gunner for Ventis' Spartius. He had settled into the cavern-like fighting compartment like a dog happy to be home. Tim (no one called him Sevestimus) was full of questions, and Principes Davis Zollach, the driver who delivered the vehicle to the Century, was happy to answer them. Ventis had listened to their exchange for his own education.

"Warning order, sir," noted Tim from his place in the turret. He was monitoring Cohort frequency from the commander's hatch, the usual procedure for the gunner when the commander was away from his position. As Ventis began to climb down into the Spartius, he felt the 189-ton machine rise to the standard one-meter hover above the ground. His heart beat faster in anticipation.

Cohort Harras pulled away from the cantonment area in the combat formation they would assume when they hit the southern ice cap. They were in a diamond shape, each point of the formation formed by one of the Centuries. Across the front and flanks were the light Wolverine scouts, while the center of the diamond was filled by the headquarters and support elements. Harras chose the formation because it allowed for good all-sides defense as well as a flexible response to contact.

Whichever unit made contact with the enemy, front, flank, or rear, that unit would attack immediately. The three unengaged units would face toward the contact. The two Centuries on the flanks would move toward the contact, hoping to envelop the enemy, and the rear Century and the headquarters would become the Cohort reserve. This maneuver had been practiced over and over in the two days prior to the Cohort's departure, and they were supposed to be able to accomplish it with a minimum of orders. It had worked occasionally, but the fiascoes had been spectacular. One time the flank units had become disoriented, attacking in the opposite direction and "destroying" the reserve Century. Ventis had been the contacted Century that time, so he had not shared in the monumental butt-chewing delivered by Harras. He hoped he never would be on the receiving end of such a blistering diatribe.

The Cohort would assume a different formation for crossing the ocean that lay between Rolandrin and the ice cap. In an effort to present the smallest possible profile, the vehicles would be moving in close, almost administrative, column. The light tanks would lead, followed by the bulk of the Cohort in three parallel columns. First and Second Centuries would form the left column, Headquarters the center, and Third and Fourth the right. All vehicles would move at fifty-meter intervals with one hundred meters separating units. The columns would be four hundred meters apart. This formation made the Cohort a prime artillery target, but it also made it an almost insignificant target to the spy satellites.

As the headquarters section rose to a hover and moved to take its position, an Equus grav sled careened into the formation. The driver, with the panache of an expert, swept up to the administrative Pedden and matched its speed. The assistant driver hammered on the port-side door until it opened. "I've got one more for you!" he shouted, pointing to a huddled figure clinging to the cargo rails. "You want to stop, or shall we just heave him aboard?"

The face in the doorway looked blankly at the passenger in the rear of the Equus. The man clearly was displeased with the ride in the sled and the prospect of stepping from the moving sled to the moving converted Pedden. The figure in the doorway of the Pedden waved the newcomer in. The Equus sled continued to match the speed of the Pedden.

On the Equus, the assistant driver indicated to the passenger that he should make a dive for the open door. When the huddled figure didn't move, the assistant picked up the man's kit and hurled it through the door. Then, none too gently, he grabbed the passenger, a Renegade optio, and forced him to his feet. With the man precariously balanced on the sled, he nodded to the driver, who banked the sled sharply to the right. The optio, his equilibrium suddenly upset, had no choice but to grab for the scramble rails on the side of the Pedden. The moment his fingers closed in a death grip around the rails, the driver of the sled dropped away from the Pedden carrier, leaving the optio hanging on the side of the vehicle. The Pedden crew quickly grabbed the struggling officer and roughly pulled him inside. The Equus driver and his assistant laughed all the way back to their post.

Optio Holton Bard had joined his new command.

Thirty minutes later, with the Cohort at TTF, or tree-top flight, and cruising at 240 kph, the lead vehicles of the Scout Century crossed the southern beach of Rolandrin. The scout commander, Centurion Jamie MacDougall, notified Harras, then slid down into the command position of the Wolverine. There was no use staying up, the position he preferred, because there was nothing to see. For the next twelve hours, the only view would be of water and sky, and the navigation of the Cohort was best controlled from the DDP in front of his station. He watched the other vehicles cross the threshold between land and sea.

The beach was just south of the planet's equator, and it was coming on summer where they were. The warm morning sun reflected off the azure sea, spreading sparkles as far as the horizon. The balmy air poured into the open hatch, filling the fighting compartment with the distinctive smell of the junction of land and water. He noted four unidentified objects almost at the right-hand limit of the DDP's range. From their size and speed they appeared to be fishing craft, but they shouldn't have been there. Commonwealth security forces should have swept the beach for one hundred kilometers in both directions of the crossing point as part of standard procedure. It would be foolish for a strike into TOG territory to be spoiled because some civilian talked about what he had seen over his commlink. He thumbed his command net. "Jumbo Basket Three, this is Six. Break right to check contact bearing one-four-hundred relative."

"Basket Three. Wilco."

MacDougall watched the blue square on his DDP representing the investigating scout swing to the right, chasing the unidentified blips on his screen. Printed over the screen was a red line that marked the parameters within which the vehicle must operate to escape detection by the enemy spy satellites. The Wolverine closed at top speed toward the unidentified objects. They were well within the red parameters, permitting the Wolverine to investigate without risk. MacDougall saw the Wolverine's IFF indicator swing wide to the right as it circled the four amber blips. The Information, Friend or Foe system on the DDP identified all craft according to their grav-drive signatures. Civilian vehicles appeared as amber blips, TOGs as red, and definite friendlies, Commonwealth or Renegade vehicles, as blue.

"Jumbo Basket Six, this is Jumbo Basket Three." The headset crackled in the command tank.

"Basket Three, this is Six. Go."

"This is Three. It looks like fishermen having trouble with a net. They look really mad."

"This is Six. Roger. Any sign of comm equipment?"

"This is Three. Negative."

"This is Jumbo Basket Six. Roger, Basket Three. Come on home."

"This is Three. Wilco."

The blue square swept past the amber blips again as the Wolverine roared back toward its unit. The fisherman were well to the rear by the time the scout closed to his assigned position. MacDougall watched the red parameters close down just behind the scout. The hunter had made it just in time.

The rest of the Cohort trailed the scouts across the edge of the water that marked the beginning of their crossing to the south pole. Each vehicle commander felt the same excitement at leaving the known land behind for the unknown sea ahead. Even though the grav tanks were submersible, even though the journey would be but twelve hours in duration, it was still frightening to leave the land behind. Perhaps it was just the reverse of the feeling their long-dead ancestors had felt, when, for the first time, they had left the water to become land creatures.

The fishermen watched the Wolverine whip past, kicking up a giant rooster-tail of water even at TTF level. They waited another half-hour to let the rest of the Cohort pass, then moved the nets off the miniaturized communications set. Aiming the deeply sculpted parabolic antenna along a prearranged vector toward space, the operator keyed the set. In a microsecond, a message flashed into space confirming the passage of Cohort Harras.

10

1500, 9 Martius 6831—It was 8,170 kilometers, as the crow flies, from the southern tip of Rolandrin to the rim of the ice cap marking the south pole. The twisting path of Cohort Harras added almost 50 percent to the total distance they would travel over the ocean, making the trip between the two land masses 12,255 kilometers, more or less. The grav tanks, though traveling at TTF, were not restricted to the 240-kph limit that would have been normal for land. Over solid ground, the twenty-meter altitude of tree-top flight allowed the tanks to clear the tops of trees and small hills. Because some objects and formations rose higher than twenty meters, the TS&R systems allowed for no more than standard safe speed. Travel over the water would be different. Unless the Cohort encountered waves twenty meters tall, they could travel up to the speed of wind-resistance tolerance.

As the vehicles crossed the shoreline, the diamond formation changed. First Century, the point of the diamond, moved in front of Second Century, which had been guarding the left flank. At the same time, Fourth Century, protecting the rear, slid to the right behind the Third. The Wolverines of MacDougall's Century broke into three sections of two vehicles each, one section leading each column. Jamie MacDougall took the center column, the other vehicles forming on him.

Now that they were on their way, the tank commanders and drivers had little to do. The control marks had been downloaded into the navigational computers so that speed and direction were preset. All the legionnaires had to do was keep track of the Data Display Panel, making a constant Human check on the computer functions. The column streamed south under the bright sunlight.

At the first navigational point, the column bore slightly right and began to pick up speed. MacDougall watched the speed bar on the DDP stretch out past the "Safe Speed" tick. He was mesmerized. He had seen the velocity indicator that high before, but never when his Wolverine was this close to the surface. He abandoned the DDP and resumed his favorite traveling position, with his head out of the command hatch. His scarf streaming out behind him, MacDougall enjoyed the blur of shimmering light that the water became at this speed.

Centurion James G. MacDougall loved light tanks. When it came to scout vehicles, he was nostalgic for the time when men rode flimsy craft into the air for the first time. He always claimed he had been born four thousand years too late. Disdaining the standard crewman's helmet, he preferred a bare set of headphones and boom mike. A tight-fitting skull cap, a pair of goggles, and a flowing white scarf completed his uniform. He had passed up many promotions to staff in favor of remaining with the vehicles he loved.

Now he was in his element, the Wolverine screaming across the water at close to 900 kph, the wind tugging at his cheeks. He left the goggles on his forehead until his eyes began to water so badly that he could no longer see. This would be his last command in scouts, and he knew it. A man could duck promotion only so long, and then it was either up or out. Renegade headquarters had notified him that his time as a centurion was over. Either he took the promotion to centurion maximus and got the required staff time, or he would face mandatory retirement. At the centurion maximus level, he would have another ten years in the service, but a soldier was allowed only a certain number of years in the lower ranks. Headquarters believed young men should command units at Century level, because of the physical and mental strain that came with leading men in combat. It was a reasonable policy, but like all policies, it should have exceptions. MacDougall knew he should be one of those.

While this operation lasted, he would relish every part of it. The speed, the power, the flashing waves; he would savor every moment with no thought for the future. If he were lucky, he would face cracking guns and flaring missiles. It would be his kind of hail-and-farewell party. Better than sitting in some club, pounding back the drinks until he got turned sideways and couldn't remember the way out. That was no way to leave a unit.

MacDougall was jolted out of his reverie when the Wolverine made a sharp turn to the left, the tank banking 1400 mils to compensate for the turn. As the Wolverine slowed to its new preset speed, he could feel himself being pressed down into the command hatch and had to brace against the sudden deceleration. This abrupt change was hard on the light tanks, and MacDougall wondered how the larger, less maneuverable medium tanks would take the new course. The Liberators had only two-thirds the maneuvering thrust of the Wolverines, and at 900 kph, the reverse thrusters must have gone into emergency overdrive to slow the larger tanks. Scouts, thought Jamie once again, were the best of the bunch.

They were five hours into the flight before the crews began to notice the change in temperature. It had been getting colder at the rate of several degrees an hour, but the high speed had already made the air feel colder than normal. With nothing to see outside except the rush of sequined blue, most of the crews were tucked inside their vehicles by the end of the first hour. The scouts had been up for most of the journey, watching the horizon darkening to the south. No matter what technology they had at their disposal, scouts were supposed to use their eyes as well as the DDP.

Most tank crews first noticed the temperature change when a film of condensation began to collect on the walls of the fighting compartments. The cooling of the outer hulls created a thin dew on the interior walls from the warm, moist atmosphere. Popping the hatches open to a sudden blast of cold air cleared the condensation, but sent the crews scrambling for gloves and scarves.

As the sixth hour began, those commanders who were standing in their hatches, heavily bundled against the piercing wind, saw Rock Wall rise on the southeastern rim of the planet. The moon was huge against the darkening sky, its pocked face glaring down on any intruder who dared enter its cold domain. The onboard computers, prepared for the arrival of the moon, compensated for the compelling gravitational pull. The endless ocean beneath the rushing tanks felt the attraction as well, surging toward the nightly visitor. The other, smaller moons of Caralis began to appear as well.

Deep in the column of the Third Century, Sergeant Honor Ross found her mind following a familiar train of thought. Ever since signing the request paper, she had been suffering second thoughts about her decision to volunteer for the 2567th. Her unit, the 2031st, had been preparing to redeploy to Alsatia when she heard through the sergeants' grapevine that the 2567th was looking for immediate replacements. Her centurion had confirmed the rumor, but forbidden her to apply. Ross had volunteered immediately, but still did not really understand why. The short time she had spent with the 2567th on Alsatia, after becoming separated from the rest of the 2031st in a thrust through TOG lines, had been interesting. Her makeshift command had been far more exciting than service in her infantry Century had ever been. She had enjoyed the challenge of commanding an improvised unit using half-functional equipment and the responsibility of helping to plan strategy, desperate as it became at times. And she still felt a warm glow of accomplishment at having brought the civilian refugees through to Renegade lines.

She had also liked all the tankers she had met. Karstil, the optio in command of the force, had been a little abrupt, but she had forgiven him because he was so obviously in intense pain from a dislocated shoulder. Mullins, the tank platoon sergeant, had been wonderful, a cross between a father and an older brother. He had been obviously loyal to the optio, and that counted for a lot. She hadn't seen either of them since joining the Century, and she didn't know if they were even on the mission. She had made some casual inquiries, but no one she had talked to knew the whole force.

Now she felt the tank twist under her seat as it felt the attraction of the rising moon, and opened the command hatch of the Viper to watch it. The sea, Ross noted, had lost its deep blue calm and become gray and cold. The waves were no longer long, wind-blown rows, but were cross-chopped and ominous. The wind blowing from the southeast buffeted even the ninety-ton carrier, and the tops of the highest waves were blasted into fragments by its force. The icy fingers of the gale found their way inside her battle fatigues, probing down her back. She pulled her collar tighter around her neck and settled the command helmet more securely over her auburn hair.

She watched as one giant wave rose out of the sea. Its crest, resisting the tearing wind for a time, almost reached as high as the Viper's hull. Then it succumbed to the blast and was torn to fragments. As the spray swept over the bulbous nose of the Viper, it slashed at her face. Ross wiped away the moisture and was surprised to feel tiny shards melting under her fingers. The water was cold enough to make ice. She shivered.

As the Viper continued its plunge to the south, the wind increased and the temperature continued to drop. The towering wave that had first showered the tank with ice became a memory. The waves were even bigger now, some of them looming above the slim hull of the carrier. When a wall of water rose directly in the path of the Viper, Ross flinched as the bow crashed into the falling wave. Her driver wrestled with the controls, the machine twisting against the force of the impromptu waterfall. It was just like fictional descriptions of ancient carnival rides; she felt the carrier drop from under her as the water rushing past her into the command hatch momentarily lifted her from her chair.

Then the wave was gone, leaving the Viper at the bottom of a deep trough dominated by the mountainous seas around it. As the nose of the carrier came up, Ross saw the giant shape of Rock Wall, veiled by the tatters of fleeing clouds, directly in front of the tank. The Viper shot out of the valley, clipping through the crest of another wave. She knew they would have to gain some altitude; twenty meters was not high enough.

"Take her up," she said into the mike. "We need at least forty meters to be safe."

"I can't even get a zero on my altimeter," came the reply from the driver in the forward section of the hull. "You'll have to tell me when we're okay."

The driver, Ross noted, sounded shaken, as well he should. She felt the Viper begin to climb, and she had him level it off just above the tallest visible waves. It was only when she tried to turn back to the interior of the fighting compartment that she noticed her gloves were frozen to the hatch coaming.

Looking down into the turret basket, she could see water rushing across the serrated flooring, while food wrappers and personal kit items sloshed against the sides of the inner hull. Ross cracked her gloves free and dropped down to survey the damage. Millicent Connor, the gunner, was already fishing articles of clothing from the soggy mess. The force of the incoming water had smashed open one of the metal storage compartments, spilling its contents into the tank's interior. Slowly the drains bled off the water, until the floor of the compartment was only damp. Ross noted that the highest level of the water was marked by a rime of ice along the inner hull. She wondered what the infantrymen, sealed in their compartments, must be thinking.

She had begun her career in one of those compartments, and it amazed her now that she had been able to stand it. The Viper was designed to transport a crew of three plus eight infantrymen. The peds were carried in small compartments along the rear hull, two compartments on either side. The cubicles were sealed off from one another as well as from the rest of the carrier to minimize collateral damage from a hit. That was fine for vehicle survivability, but the isolation in the rear sections was frightening. Most of the time the vehicle commander left the doors on the sides of the carrier open; it lessened the sense of isolation and gave the infantry a sense of where they were going. But even this small favor was not possible here. At 900 kph, the rush of wind past the outer hull shield would create a vacuum strong enough to suck the infantry from their holes. And so the peds were locked in, hostages to the expertise of the driver and commander.

The Viper lurched, and Connor crashed against Ross' legs. "It's a good thing you don't weigh much, Millie," she said into the intercom.

"Sorry about that, Honor," replied the gunner. "Blackstone, where did you learn to drive?"

"Any time you want to try this, just crawl down here yourself." Robert Blackstone was a good driver, and he knew it. Controlling the Viper was now a full-time job, and his uniform was wet from perspiration even in the cold. "I've got to get more height."

As if in response to his request, the headset crackled. "Heart Throb, Heart Throb. This is Heart Throb Six. Increase altitude to eight-zero meters." Ross waited her turn and acknowledged the command from the centurion. As the Viper rose higher above the waves, Ross checked her DDP for the other tanks and carriers in the Century. She stared in shock; only one other Viper was left in the formation. The third squad's Viper had vanished, and the thought of the vehicle smashing itself to scrap against a wall of water made her sick to her stomach. If the hull were breached, the crew and its cargo of infantry would not live long in the water. It was no use looking for survivors.

By the tenth hour of the crossing, Ross could hardly stand. She was bruised from armpits to hips from being thrown against the command station as the wind pummeled and beat at the Viper. Ice formed on the hull, but the constant driving spray and the speed of the vehicle kept peeling it away. The upper portion of her battle fatigues were stiff with frost, and she ducked as another sheet of ice and spume slashed past her head. As she beat her hands together to restart the blood flowing, out the corner of her eye she saw another blue square wink out on the DDP. She turned to scrutinize the display more closely. All the vehicles in her Century were accounted for. It must have been someone in the headquarters.

Just after the twelfth hour, a thin line of green appeared on the DDP, and Ross realized they had reached the edge of the ice cap. As the land designation began to creep across the screen, she gave the order to Blackstone to begin slowing the Viper. They didn't want to hit land at 900 kph. Though Ross was confident her driver could handle any emergency, she saw no reason to exceed the safe land-speed of 600 kph. She could see the other vehicles in the Century spreading out into a diamond shape as they crossed the edge of the land. A combat formation would be wiser now that the presence of the enemy was possible.

The command group of Cohort Harras slowed to a hover. Milton watched the vehicles of the four combat Centuries form up into the combat diamond and then settle onto the ice. The Wolverines, like the excitable animals for which they were named, came scampering through the positions to schuss to a stop, throwing snow in all directions. Jamie MacDougall landed close enough to the command Liberator to wave a friendly greeting to Harras.

Harras was not feeling particularly friendly, however. It wasn't MacDougall; he had performed well enough. It was Harras' own performance that had him upset. He berated himself for failing to anticipate the effect Rock Wall would have on the ocean. The sudden appearance of the towering waves had caught them off guard, and the Cohort had suffered losses. First Century reported a Liberator missing, and Third had lost a Viper. But Headquarters had suffered the most. The boxy Pedden carriers had been caught by surprise; the maintenance vehicle snatched from the formation by a giant wave. The communications Pedden almost suffered the same fate, and only a miracle allowed the driver to control the gyrating carrier. In the process, all the antennae were stripped from the tank's roof and sides. These casualties left the Cohort without replacement parts and without communications with its base. They would have to make the journey on what they had and what they knew. They were truly on their own.

Harras struggled from the hatch of the Liberator and made for the communications Pedden. As he approached, the access door on the port side opened to reveal Senior Sergeant Graviston and an officer he had never seen before.

11

1630, 9 Martius 6831—Alanton Freund missed his Cream Rolly. He could always stop by the snack bar on his way to work to get one, but it wasn't the same. To arrive at his cubicle in Renegade Manus headquarters to find the Rolly on his desk, carefully wrapped in a clean napkin, had been a tangible reflection of his status. Getting his own could never be the same. Unfortunately, neither of the two enlisted men currently assigned to his logistical support section had shown any interest in supplying their superior with the tasty treat. Freund glanced longingly at the vacant station, until so recently filled by Optio Holton Bard. He felt a slight twinge of guilt, knowing that the optio was now on the frozen ice cap to the south.

The morning passed, filled with the sibilant whir and click of the computer stations. Freund was tempted to break into some of the locked files that flashed onto his console, but that reminded him of Bard, and so he moved on. When he let his eyes wander around the room again, the sight of an unexpected occupant in Bard's station snapped him out of his reverie. For just an instant he felt his heart skip. The young man had returned. The past had been wiped away and they could begin fresh. Then the surge of emotion faded, and he knew it was a false hope. The man at the station, almost completely hidden by the bulk of the machinery, was not Bard. Freund rose from his chair and went to investigate.

He approached the seated man from behind, making a detour in order to come from that direction. It wasn't so much that he wanted to sneak up on him, but more that he wanted the initial advantage in this encounter. The man wore the uniform of a Renegade officer, but no visible rank insignia. Getting closer, Freund saw that the man was using a device that scanned the station's screen. For some reason, he was recording the work that Bard had done.

"Is there anything I can do for you?" Freund hoped that the icy edge in his voice would rattle the intruder. The man turned slightly to face him.

"You Bard's superior?" The man had not been rattled.

"What is it to you?" Freund said irritably. Up close he confirmed that the intruder wore no rank insignia at all. His shirt, just visible under his tunic, was obviously of civilian cut. The man was probably security, possibly even from the Criminal Investigation Division. Freund felt his face begin to flush at that thought.

"Are you Bard's superior?" The question was more emphatic this time. The man rose from the work station to face Freund. Though only slightly taller than Freund, he had a dominating presence. His hands were large and strong-looking, and the sloping shoulders gave the impression he had no neck. The way he rocked slightly from side to side gave Freund the slightly mad but fleeting impression of a bear searching for honey. Freund took a step back.

"I was. Until two days ago, that is."

"He's gone? Where? When?" Larry Stone took a step toward the centurion maximus.

Freund recovered enough to stand his ground. "I don't know that you need that information. I don't even know who you are."

"There's been some unauthorized activity on your computers. Most of it came from this station."

The change of tactics caught Freund off guard. He retreated another step, and his face flushed even hotter. "I wouldn't know anything about that."

"It has to do with a communicator, vehicular, N/M LCS 625-97. It was supposed to go to the Manus Primus, but it's been diverted to your Manus instead." Stone did not know if the centurion maximus had been involved in the diversion of the communicator, but he had his suspicions.

"I don't know anything about that," Freund sputtered.

His suspicions confirmed, Stone watched the flush on the centurion maximus' face turn pale as he broke out in a cold sweat. This guy kept his entire history on his face. "According to the records, the information was downloaded into your computer," Stone insisted.

Freund looked away from the icy eyes of his accuser, trying to regain his composure. "That doesn't mean anything." Instead of the authoritative tone he wanted, his voice came out a whimper. This man seemed to know everything he had done. "Bard did a lot of unauthorized things on his station. I was constantly warning him about it."

"Are these warnings on record?"

"I didn't see any reason to ruin the man's career by doing that. I would have included them in any written evaluation, however. I can write them up now, if you'd like."

Stone knew Freund's reputation. The officer never missed a chance to write up his subordinates. Freund was lying, and Stone knew it. He glared at Freund's sweaty face. "Gateway."

"It has nothing to do with my Manus."

Suspicion confirmed again, thought Stone. Freund is the leak. He and Bard were in it together. "It was opened on your station."

"How do you know? It was only once, anyway."

"Twice. I checked your station before you got to work this morning."

"How dare you? How could you? That's a breach of security." Freund straightened in righteous indignation, his fear momentarily forgotten.

"We are talking about the breach of Gateway. Why did you open that file? It was secure-locked. It is listed as such."

"It wasn't my idea. Bard did it. I swear it was all his fault. We didn't see anything. Really. And it was only opened once." Now Freund was babbling.

Stone knew there was a grain of truth in what Freund said. If the program had been opened twice, Freund didn't know about the second time. "Don't say anything to anyone about this," ordered Stone, pushing past the trembling officer.

Freund staggered back against one of the vacant work stations as the man he now classified as his enemy passed. He watched the hulking shape cross the work area to the door. His knees felt weak, and he braced himself against the console. He had been so careful! He was a decorated, newly promoted officer. This was wrong! Would he always be surrounded by incompetents and insubordinates?

When his legs felt stronger Freund moved back to his station. He would have to write a report on Bard, predating the evaluation to show that it had been generated before this encounter. That should fix Bard and whoever this man was. The centurion maximus settled behind his console. He felt better already.

An access panel slid open behind the prefect's desk at the same time the lock on his office door silently snapped shut. There would be no interruptions until the prefect released the door. NaBesta Kenderson looked up with mild surprise. He had not expected to see Stone this soon.

"You have news already, Larry?"

"Yes, sir. And it's not good." Larry Stone settled his bulk into one of the steel chairs. "Gateway has been compromised."

"Damn! How did it happen?" Kenderson felt a sudden weight drop onto his shoulders.

"They're already on the ice cap."

"Can we get out a warning?"

"Yes. I don't know what they can do about it, though." Kenderson rested his chin in his hands. "It's not like they can erase the leak."

"As a matter of fact, sir, they could."

Kenderson raised his head to look at Stone. "How?"

Stone allowed himself a grim, stiff smile. "The leak was transferred to Cohort Harras just as they pulled out." Stone watched Kenderson's face brighten for an instant. "It was Holton Bard. The same one who did the deed on Alsatia."

The prefect frowned. "He was off-limits that time, and nothing has changed. Commonwealth command doesn't want him touched."

"But this time is different. He's with the command in contact. He could do serious damage. If they ever do reach Malthus, he could escape back to the TOGs." Stone warmed to his argument. "What happens if Cohort Harras is captured? There's Bard in the prison compound, acting like a Renegade, telling the TOGs everything they want to know about everything. He has to be terminated."

"No," said Kenderson, his shoulders drooping again. "The command ordered us not to touch him, and that's that."

Kenderson stared at Stone, who sat immobile in the steel chair. An awful silence filled the room. Both men were considering the problem, each in his own way groping for a solution. Stone rose to his feet and came to attention. "Sir. I'd like to request thirty days of leave."

"Leave? You've never taken leave while on-planet before."

"Yes, I know. But I'm tired. Brain-dead. I need a break."

Kenderson eyed the centurion. "Not planning anything foolish, are you?"

"No, sir. I'd just like to get away for a while. I have some friends, a friend, who could go with me."

"And where would the two of you be going? Just in case I wanted to get in touch."

"The weather's getting warmer, and I'd like to get in some skiing while there's still snow on the northern islands."

Kenderson knew that Rolandrin had few mountains and even less skiing. "Dress warmly. Your trip could be quite long and tiring."

"I will, sir." As Stone turned, Kenderson thumbed a release button beneath the center drawer of his desk. The access panel on the wall hissed open.

"Let me know when you get back. And good luck." Kenderson almost added "and good hunting," but he refrained. The panel slid shut behind the centurion, and the lock on the outer door snapped open.

***

The Loren grav sled had been so heavily modified that any resemblance to the original was difficult to discern. The 3/6 laser cannon had been removed to make room for an additional power pack. A booster engine had been attached to the normal cargo space in the rear of the sled, increasing its top speed by a factor of ten. The two figures on the sled were not wearing combat suits. Only thin, quilted thermocoats protected them from the cold blast that swept over the vehicle.

The man in the gunner's chair hunched against the wind, his face almost completely invisible under the hood of his cloak. The driver filled his station to overflowing. The blanket was tucked around his multiple legs, and one pair of arms clutched it around his upper body. The other arms held the control wands, and the six-eyed head was completely exposed to the elements.

Larry Stone watched Archon Divxas, his Baufrin friend, struggle with the blanket. Archon, like all Baufrins, was not a great fan of cold weather. The centaur-like spidermen preferred more temperate climes because their chitinous exoskeleton provided little protection from extreme temperatures. Baufrins were a strange breed, and though friendly and intelligent, they seldom became involved with the struggles of individual men. Archon was different. He and Stone had been close friends for almost seven years. Stone suspected that the Baufrin would be an asset once they reached the ice cap. With six legs to support his lower torso, Archon would be stable on the ice. The sharp ends of his legs could act like crampons on the frozen surface, and with two pairs of arms, he could perform multiple tasks. He was glad that Archon had chosen to come.

Stone had not asked the Baufrin civilian to accompany him. He had simply outlined the problem and his proposed action, letting Archon make up his own mind. "I will drive," the Baufrin had said, simply, in response. Stone was glad. Archon was the best grav-sled driver he knew, and his six eyes provided all-round vision that rivaled the sensors. That would be a boon, because they would have to remove the TS&R system to save weight. Even though the Baufrin's eye sockets would have a tendency to ice over in the cold, six eyes were better than two.

"You all right?" mumbled Stone from between numb lips, leaning forward to speak into one of the audio-receptor horns on the side of the spider's head.

The primary eye on the right side of the Baufrin's skull rotated back to look at the huddled Human. It fixed him for a moment before the mandibles clicked a response. Archon could vocalize, but the cold and wind kept him from opening his mouth. The eye rotated forward again and the lower pair of arms clutched the blanket more tightly to his chest.

The Loren grav sled skimmed between the huge spouts of water like some demonic water bug. By using the pairs of eyes sensitive to the infrared and ultraviolet spectrums, Archon was able to detect the rising waves. All he had to do was steer toward less troubled water. It was not a physically taxing job, but it did require constant attention to the task. The Baufrin had no energy left for chitchat with his man-friend behind.

Now their sixteen-hour journey across the southern ocean was almost at an end. The sled had taken the most direct route over the more than eight thousand kilometers of water stretching between Rolandrin and the south pole, unafraid of discovery by a passing satellite. Their signature was so small that a satellite would have to be on high power and looking directly at them to notice the vehicle. The long, thin edge of the ice cap was coming up now, and the Baufrin picked up the change in the horizon ahead with his infrared vision. He clicked his mandibles to attract Stone's attention. The man raised his head and stared into the darkness. He saw nothing.

Half an hour later, the sled, its power supply almost drained, slipped through a narrow gorge in the ice that opened onto the turbulent sea. The sled hovered for a moment beside a towering chunk of black rock, then settled gently to the icy surface. Stone and Archon uncoiled themselves from their seats and stretched. After sixteen hours spent huddled against the wind and cold, they could move only tentatively as the blood began to flow back into their cramped limbs. Archon turned to inspect the sled's system readouts. "Our power supply is depleted. We are exceptionally lucky to have reached our intended destination."

Stone turned awkwardly to face his spider friend. "It was only partly luck. I calculated the power drain before we left. We should have another ten kilometers in the sled, and Cohort Harras is well within that range."

The Baufrin clicked his mandibles in rebuke. "And if we do not? Then what do you have in mind for us?"

"We hoof it if we have to."

Archon clicked his mandibles again. Suddenly, one of his legs broke through the layer of snow and plunged downward. He struggled to free the trapped limb, but his other legs began to break through. He floundered lower and lower in the icy layer.

"What's the matter?" said Stone.

"There is something wrong with my legs. I cannot control them. I am afraid, my friend, that the depressed temperatures have rendered my extremities inoperative."

Stone looked at his friend, floundering in the snow, his belly already against the ice. Baufrins, he knew, seldom voiced personal complaints, and so this admission of weakness was significant. Fortunately, Baufrins, for all their bulk, were not heavy. Stone pulled his friend from the snow and half-dragged, half-carried him to the sled. It took only minutes to rig an emergency shelter and wrap Archon in thermal blankets. But even with the heat turned as high as he dared, it would be hours before his companion would be fit for travel. By then, Cohort Harras would be gone.

12

2330, 9 Martius 6831—Legatus Maximus Antipolous Philippicus was currently out of favor with Brigadier General Drusus Arcadius, the planetary commander for the TOG forces on Caralis. He had, in fact, been out of favor ever since being held responsible for one of the great fiascoes of the current campaign on Alsatia. Only the general's strenuous efforts had averted total disaster. The spy system, of which Philippicus was so proud, had transmitted a Renegade battle plan that was either wrong in its entirety or poorly evaluated. In either case, Philippicus had used it to order troop movements that were ill-timed and ill-advised. He had then committed the reserve Trajan heavy tanks to catch the intruding Renegades, but the Trajans and their support vehicles had been caught in the open and badly savaged before they could break contact.

Now Philippicus found himself in the unenviable position of presenting a second report, from the same source, about another Renegade operation. Like the first, it was full of detailed information that seemed too good to be true. Brigadier General Arcadius surveyed his intelligence chief as the legatus maximus stood at stiff attention before his commander. "Is this information of the same quality as the last transmission?" asked Arcadius, the sarcasm in his voice barely controlled.

Philippicus fought to keep the frustration from showing on his face. "As always, Your Excellency, I do my best." Damn you, he thought. You expect absolutes in combat. If the other officers of your staff did as well as I and my men do, we'd be winning right now. He smiled wanly at the overstuffed brigadier general. If I punctured your bloated hide, you'd burst like an overcooked sausage. "There are ways to confirm the report."

"I know that, Philippicus. I can do your job as well as my own."

Fat chance, thought Philippicus, and he smiled inwardly at the pun. "We could divert a satellite to make a pass over the southern ice cap."

"That would be a waste of a valuable resource, Philippicus." Arcadius laced his fingers across the broad expanse of his stomach. The flouropanels of the headquarters were dimly lit out of respect for the sensitive eyes of the planetary chief of staff. The low area lighting let Arcadius direct an intense light over the area where any interviewee was forced to stand. Philippicus stood there now, skewered by the shaft of light. The intelligence chief, his eyes dazzled by the illumination, could barely discern the brigadier general's face. All things considered, conditions in Arcadius' office made for a daunting interview. "Think of another way to confirm the report."

"It is too late, Your Excellency, to have another agent sent to the area. The Renegades will have reached the ice by now."

"Then you should have thought of that earlier."

"I submitted a request for manpower for such a mission, sir."

"But obviously to the wrong people, and at the wrong time, my dear Philippicus." Arcadius watched the intelligence chief shift his weight nervously. He had received the request for confirmation and allowed it to languish in channels until it was too late, all the while implementing his own plan. His spy had confirmed the transit of the Renegade force as it crossed the southern coast of Rolandrin. Arcadius had the report, and had made his decision, choosing to leave his intelligence chief in the dark. He believed in uncertainty as an effective tool for control.

"I still think we should act on it, sir."

"That, my dear Philippicus, is my decision. You may go."

As the intelligence officer left the room, Arcadius touched his commlink. The wall to his left illuminated to reveal an operations center. The holovid presence of the planetary commander brought the bustle of the place to an abrupt halt as all personnel present rose to attention, their right arms raised in salute. Arcadius savored their response for a moment longer than was strictly expected, then acknowledged their salutation.

"Legatus Cariolanus Camus," commanded the brigadier general, "Have you made your plan?"

"Sir!" An officer in full battledress, his command helmet under his left arm, stepped forward and saluted again. Arcadius nodded a perfunctory response, indicating with a wave of his hand that the legatus should get on with it. "The best plan would be to wait for the Renegade force to cross to Malthus over the ocean from the southern ice cap. The run across the ice and ocean will sap their strength; they will be exhausted and easily defeated. We can wait for them on the promontory south of our present position at Frotik, striking from ambush as they come out of their traveling formation. If we take up positions and shut down on the shore, they will be unaware of our presence, and our satellites will give us ample warning of their approach."

"If I may interject, Your Excellency." Prefect Claudius Sulla, Chief of Operations for TOG on Caralis, and the man who would have final authorization on any plan, stepped from behind the legatus. "It would be better to strike while they are on the ice. In fact, our forces should already have moved to intercept the Renegades."

The brigadier general shifted in his chair. Sulla had been after him for several days to schedule where and when the counterstrike would be launched. Now the same argument would be played out for an audience. "We have discussed this already, Prefect."

"We have, Your Excellency. But the issue is important enough to be aired again. My fellow officer needs to understand the immense value of our operation at the pole."

No, he doesn't, thought Arcadius. He needs to do as he is told, and do it to the best of his ability. He needs to be a good little TOG officer. "The discussion is closed, Prefect Sulla."

"With all due respect, Your Excellency. The station at the south pole is of the utmost importance to the Terran Overlord Government."

"I am well aware of that." But it's not important to me, thought Arcadius. Those scientists poking around in the ice are nothing to me. They use up my food and other resources while they dig holes in the ice cap that have yet to show results. "Their importance does not change my position."

Sulla stepped in front of Camus so that he could speak directly to the planetary commander. "Perhaps, Your Excellency, you should view the most recent data. I have downloaded it to your holographer." Sulla's voice had lost the tone of deference due his superior. His polite request just avoided sounding like an order, and the brigadier general was intelligent enough to catch the implications.

So you, thought Arcadius, are my headquarters spy. Every planetary commander had one, and Arcadius had long harbored suspicions about the prefect's loyalties. Only reports from Grand General Oliodinus Severus Septimus, the sector commander, came by holograph, and the transmissions were always patched through directly to Arcadius' office. It was impossible for Sulla to have intercepted one without the brigadier general knowing about it unless he had access to unauthorized resources. At least, that was what he had always believed. But that was a matter to be dealt with later. The brigadier shut off the wall screen and turned to the holographer. He hated these communications, but at least this one was prerecorded, and the image would not be able to see him.

The 25-centimeter-tall image of his sector commander appeared in the center of the holographic projector. Evidently, Sulla had loaded the program even before this argument had started. That meant the operations officer also had access to his private communications code. He was surely the grand general's spy. On this occasion alone he had given himself away too many times for there to be any further doubt in the brigadier general's mind.

"Brigadier General Drusus Arcadius," rapped out the tiny figure, "it has come to our attention that you have a situation over the south pole. We also have been informed that you plan to do nothing about it until the enemy reaches the southern coast of Malthus." The holographic image gave the brigadier general a withering smile, but Arcadius rotated his chair slightly so that the icy gaze of the sector commander was directed into the vacant space of the office.

"This action does not meet with the general objectives of Caesar. The people at the pole are to receive your complete support. Please see to it. Hail, Caesar!" The hologram blinked out.

Arcadius stared at the empty ions that had represented his commander. So the old man had a personal interest in the activities at the pole. That certainly helped explain some of the directives he had been receiving. This apparently unimportant scientific activity had garnered an inordinate amount of attention from the sector HQ. And Sulla had obviously been privy to the reasons. Arcadius put his feet on the footstool that matched his chair and studied his manicure. It occurred to him that there was a way to deal with all his problems—Septimus, the pole, and Sulla—at once. With any luck, the solution would be to his advantage. He turned back to the wall screen and switched it on.

The figures in the headquarters hadn't moved. Sulla still stood slightly in front of Cariolanus Camus, his eyes riveted to the screen. Arcadius thought he detected a slight smile of triumph flash quickly across his subordinate's face before the man controlled himself. "Was the hologram of any help, Excellency?" inquired the operations officer.

"It has helped clarify the situation," responded Arcadius. And it has, he thought, given me a way to deal with you, you treacherous bastard. "We must certainly move with all speed to see that the force at the pole is supported. Camus, how soon can your force move?"

"We can be ready to lift off in one hour, Excellency, but it would be better for us to delay for at least four. The Commonwealth satellites will give us a clear six hours if we delay, and after that, it will not matter if we are seen. If we leave right away, they will detect us as soon as we clear the hangar area."

"That is unacceptable, Excellency," interjected Sulla, his face clouded with anxiety. "If we wait an additional three hours, our force at the pole will be destroyed."

"Just tell our people at the pole to flee. Any direction will do, and Camus can retake the area as soon as he arrives. Please generate a plan based on a departure in four hours."

"Yes, sir!"

"Prefect Sulla. Have you briefed Legatus Camus on the force he will command on this mission?"

Sulla glared at his commander, barely able to contain his contempt. Even after the brigadier general had had direct contact with the sector commander, he was still attempting to thwart his superior's directives. There would be time after Camus departed for Sulla to file a detailed report on his superior's method of serving Caesar. "I am finishing that now, Excellency."

"Be sure," purred Arcadius, "that you do an excellent job. Many lives may depend on it." He clicked off the wall screen.

Inside the command center, Sulla turned to Camus. This man, he thought to himself, was the perfect combat commander. Camus had a reputation for bold leadership and little imagination. He would do as he was told with unquestioning loyalty. He could also be depended upon to be totally unaware of the more important political considerations of any operation. Sulla knew, even if the brigadier general and the legatus didn't, that this particular operation on Caralis required the use of minimum force. Caesar required victories that continued to inspire the love and respect of the population and the senate. A victory at too great a cost would be unacceptable, but too quick and easy a victory would be dismissed as unimportant. The research station at the pole was searching for a Naram civilization that had vanished more than two thousand years ago. TOG intended to find it and use it to force concessions from the Naram council. That would be a victory indeed. To allow that victory to slip through their fingers because Legatus Camus wanted to minimize the risk of detection was ridiculous.

Sulla permitted himself a tiny sigh, then continued briefing Camus. "The Renegade force is a Cohort-Minus. It has, according to our reports, four combat Centuries and a headquarters Century. Visual reports confirm this. They will be striking across the center of the polar area to appear on the coast at 1200 mils."

"They should be no problem, Prefect. The six Centuries of my full Cohort should be more than sufficient to deal with them. We will outnumber them, and I plan to ambush their force on the ice cap."

This man, raged Sulla inwardly, has no imagination and does not understand the situation. "We must recapture the station at the pole." He needed to explain the mission in terms simple enough for the commander to grasp and make his own.

"That step will follow the destruction of the enemy, sir. Once they have been destroyed or dispersed, we can reoccupy the polar area."

"Fine. How soon can you leave?"

"As I told the brigadier general, we will leave in four hours. It is just a little over thirty-two hundred kilometers to the cap. We can arrive in eight hours."

You had better hope you're in time to save the polar station, thought Sulla grimly. You should have left hours ago. "Very good, Legatus Maximus. Report to the brigadier general."

Legatus Cariolanus Camus stepped onto the signal pad for the wall screen and came to attention. He held that position for a full thirty seconds before the screen activated. "You are prepared, Legatus?" came the inquiry from Brigadier General Drusus Arcadius as he appeared.

"Excellency! For the preservation of the Terran Overlord Government and the glory of the service, I, Legatus Cariolanus Camus, am ready to attack the Renegade Legion!"

"That's just fine," smiled the brigadier general. "I have some good news for you. Because of the extreme importance our revered sector commander and Prefect Claudius Sulla place on this mission, I will allow you to perform this task under close scrutiny." Arcadius looked past the shoulder of the force commander to his operations officer. "Prefect Claudius Sulla, I am placing you with Cohort Camus as my personal observer. Have a good journey." The wall screen went dark.

13

0430, 10 Martius 6831—Holden Ventis wiped the crystalline rime from the face plate of his combat helmet and gazed across the frozen landscape of the south pole. The Second Century vehicles almost looked as if they were hunkered down against the winds that howled over the terrain, hurling clouds of snow against the hull of the command Spartius. He pulled the combat cloak more tightly around his shoulders. The terrain, he thought, never seems to give the soldier a break. It was always too hot or too cold, too wet or too dry, never just right. He dropped back down into the command chair and examined the DDP for the positions of the rest of the Century. The blue squares marking the location of each tank and carrier glowed brightly on the screen. According to the display, the infantry Vipers were close by, but he had not been able to see them through the darkness and the blowing snow. He took a mental bearing on the closest one and poked his head out of the command hatch again.

Carefully lining himself up on the bearing, he peered intently into the darkness, where he could just make out the slanted profile of a carrier. Or it was just his imagination? At three hundred meters, he couldn't be sure. This would be bad when the shooting started.

The electronics of the Viper, Spartius, and Liberator tanks would pick up a vehicle at twenty kilometers, but commanders liked to be able to use their own eyes as a back-up. The designers sitting in their comfortable studios could make all the pronouncements they liked about how this was the age of displays and that men were a mere redundancy in combat. But for the men in the field, eyes and ears told the tale. Not being able to see would make combat even more terrifying than usual.

And when the infantry dismounted, they would face the same problem, magnified by the tearing wind and frigid temperatures. The carriers were heated, as were the combat suits, but the warmth of the suits was minimal compared to the extreme external temperature. An active man would remain warm as long as the suit had power, but a stationary man or one whose suit had been breached by damage would receive the full impact of the cold. Ventis calculated that an hour was the longest the infantry could be expected to remain outside the vehicle before the troops would be too cold to function. He pulled his head back inside the Spartius, closing the hatch against the arctic cold.

"Wobbly Abacus, Wobbly Abacus. This is Wobbly Abacus Six." The commlink of the DDP rattled into life. Wobbly Abacus Six was Centurion Maximus Milton Harras, Cohort commander. No matter what the call sign, which would change every twelve hours, the numeral designator "Six" would always be the commander. Now Harras was calling all the stations listening on the Cohort command net. "Stolid Gateway, Stolid Gateway, execute." The strike across the pole, the "Stolid" portion of the overall "Gateway" plan, began.

Ventis switched to the Century net and repeated the call from Harras. As he finished the message he felt the Spartius carrier shudder to a one-meter hover, felt the accumulated snow scab away from the sides. The blue squares, the DDP's confirmation of a correct IFF transponder in the vehicles of the Renegade Legion, blinked red as the grav drives fired then returned to blue as they attained hover height. All vehicles now showed blue.

The Cohort would move in a modified wedge formation. The six Wolverines of the Scout Century would lead, spread out over a kilometer or more across the front of the formation. Following would be the First Century, its two tank platoons on line and the infantry platoon centered and to the rear. Then would come the Second Century, Ventis', in the same formation. The Cohort headquarters would follow Ventis, flanked by the Third and Fourth Centuries.

This formation was used when contact with the enemy was expected from the front rather than the flanks. The scouts would find the enemy, giving early warning to the First Century. By the time the situation developed completely, the lead Century would be able to strike at the weakest point in the enemy line. The Second Century, listening to the chatter over the command link, would be able to determine which direction it should break to add its firepower to the battle. If the leading Centuries could not overcome the resistance, the reserve Centuries would be available to pile in as the commander directed.

Ventis watched the two tank platoons deploy across the front of his Century. The First Platoon, commanded by Sergeant Kent Narall, was on the left, the Second Platoon with Sergeant Upton Verg was on the right. He would have been happier with another officer in the Century, but no replacements had been available by the time the Cohort was scheduled to take off. He wondered who had gotten the officer who had arrived just as Cohort Harras had departed Rolandrin.

He ordered the Century to maintain a stationary hover to allow the lead command to open a ten-kilometer gap. At 240 kph, the Second Century could cover the ground between the commands in just under three minutes. That would allow Ventis enough time to assess a combat situation and deploy his Century to best advantage. Any closer, and the Century would be involved in the fighting before it found a position. Any greater distance, and the Century might not be able to support the leaders in time. Tank combat was generally very violent and very short.

The Century moved out, picking up speed. Holden Ventis hunched over the DDP to watch the other vehicles. He left the command hatch open, mostly to remind himself of what was happening outside. A constant blast of frigid air blew down his neck as the DDP flashed terrain information across the screen. Red hash marks indicated terrain the Spartius must avoid at its current speed. The infantry carrier was lively, but at their cruising speed of 240 kph, there were gradients that it could not climb quickly enough to avoid disaster. The onboard computer recognized such terrain and fed the information through the Terrain Search and Reaction (TS&R) circuits. All the driver had to do was to steer the vehicle through acceptable ground.

The biggest terrain problem here at the pole was going to be the great towers of ice jutting abruptly from the surface. Some of these monsters rose several hundred meters, sculptured into fantastic shapes by the ever-present wind. Ventis marveled at the contortions they presented.

The southern continent of Rolandrin was not solid ice. The area, volcanic in its dim past, had thrown up a cone some sixteen hundred kilometers in diameter. Parts of that rim still rose above the surface of the surrounding sea. Later in geologic development, another volcano had risen through the cone of the first. This smaller projection was only about five hundred kilometers wide, creating much of what was now the south polar area. The continent thus formed took on the shape of a rock rim with a central pinnacle. The area between the perimeter and the central core was filled with water.

For thousands of years, the central core of this formation had been inhabited, its climate protected and moderated by the buffer of rock that surrounded it. For all the fortunate circumstances of its location, the civilization at the center was doomed. The planet Caralis wobbled slightly, almost imperceptibly, on its axis. As the eons passed, the world's climate gradually shifted from good weather with long growing seasons to a colder clime. Then the snows began to arrive earlier and remain longer until finally, there was only winter. Ice covered the continent, and the civilization died. Of this planetary history, the current residents of Caralis and those who were fighting for it were only dimly aware.

They were also unaware of the unique challenges this frozen void presented to travelers. The landfall on the solid coast was easy enough to cross, if crossing a frozen, gale-whipped sea torn by the forces of Rock Wall could be considered easy. The rim of stone provided a haven for those who survived the first leg of the trip. The polar area would provide another point where the vehicles and their crews could rest. The space between the rim and the pole was the problem.

The sea filled the deep crater formed by the first volcano to a depth of several kilometers. Though Rock Wall exerted its fantastic attraction on this body of water, several hundred meters of ice covered the water. The water, pulled upward against the covering ice, struggled to penetrate the ice. It broke through weak points in the frozen layer in spectacular fountains of ice and liquid that rose several hundred meters above the surrounding land. The local pressure released, the eruption would crash to the surface, freezing upon contact with the snow. The fissure would freeze, and the process would begin all over again.

Optio Holden Ventis, commander of the Second Century, saw his first eruption as a brilliant red dot on his DDP. The display was showing nothing but open ground before the dot flared into existence. He poked his head through the command hatch just in time to see the towering fury white against the frozen air. The base of the upheaval was two hundred meters across, and the top, blasted to crystal fragments by the wind even as he watched, rose more than one hundred meters. Ventis felt his stomach constrict. No vehicle caught in that blast could survive. Both machine and crew would be instantly trapped in ice, frozen forever in its grip. And no TS&R circuitry could react fast enough to plot an escape if an eruption suddenly occurred in front of a hurtling vehicle. The knot of terror in his stomach gave way to anger. It wasn't fair! It was one thing to face death on the battlefield, man against man in a fair fight. You could lengthen the odds in your favor by being careful and smart. The only chance they had against these sudden walls of ice lay in climbing to a safe height, but that would allow any watching enemy to detect them at great distance and engage the thin underarmor of the vehicles. It was as if nature had conspired with the TOG defenders to hold the Renegades helpless.

Ventis gripped the coaming of the command hatch, his fingers rigid claws against the cold steel. He sensed the Century beginning to slow, to climb away from the random, violent death. He should order them to maintain altitude and speed, but the words froze in his throat. A hundred meters on either side of the Spartius, great columns of water and ice thundered upward. He hunched his shoulders against the terrifying roar as the wind tore the exterior and tops of the columns into fragments. Then the Spartius was through the gap, and he turned to watch the tons of water crash down where his tank had been only seconds before. The torrent rebounded from the surface in a cloud of silvery splinters that whirled away into the darkness.

More explosions of ice and water followed. The Century crept higher and higher, moving slower and slower. "Wobbly Abacus, Wobbly Abacus, this is Wobbly Abacus Six. Do not, I repeat, do not slow down. Put the coals to her. We've got to get clear of this area."

Ventis passed the order to his Century and felt his own vehicle begin to accelerate. At one hundred meters, there was little danger of encountering the normal terrain. The vehicles gained speed until the Century was careening over the snow at better than 400 kph. He could see from the DDP that the First Century was also accelerating, and, even at its present velocity, the Second Century was falling behind the leaders. And still the ice continued to explode around and below him. He again felt the knot of terror in his stomach.

"Abacus One-six, this is Abacus Eight-six. Many enemy in contact." Ventis was jerked out of his concentration on this weird alternate reality by the sound of Jamie MacDougall, scout command, calling First Century to report contact.

14

0654, 10 Martius 6831—"Eight-six, Eight-six, this is One-six. Report the direction of the contact."

"This is Eight-six. The enemy is breaking directly away from me at six-two-hundred to two-hundred mils relative. Mostly tracked vehicles. Am engaging."

"This is One-six. We're following. Break. Abacus Six, this is Abacus One-six. Preparing to engage many TOG vehicles."

"One-six, this is Abacus Six. Acknowledge. Break. Abacus Two-six, this is Abacus Six. Support One-six as needed."

Ventis stretched lips frozen rigid to reply. "Abacus Six, this is Abacus Two-six. Wilco." He switched the commlink back to the Century push. "Abacus Two, this is Abacus Two-six. Prepare for combat. Accelerate to five-forty. Engage targets of opportunity." The two tank platoons acknowledged, and Ventis felt the Spartius accelerate as Zollach applied thrust.

"Eight-six, this is One-six. We have contact. Break right and left by sections and engage."

"This is Eight-six. Wilco."

Even over the roar of the rushing Spartius, Ventis could hear the distinctive crack of the Liberator's 150mm turret cannon as the tanks of the lead Century opened fire. The DDP in the Spartius blossomed with the blue indicators of the First Century in action as well as the amber and red markers of the unidentified vehicles and the acknowledged TOGs. The fight was drifting right as the First Century bit into the fleeing TOG units. Some TOGs were sneaking away to the left. "Abacus Two, this is Two-six. Steer five-six-hundred mils relative. Execute." The Spartius swerved left to its new heading as Zollach responded without additional commands from Ventis. Ventis felt an instant of satisfaction. The driver knew his business, was listening to the command chatter, and was responding without hesitation.

"Abacus Two-six, this is Two-one-six. I have targets locked. Am engaging." Kent Narall, commanding the First Tank Platoon, opened on the TOGs in range. A moment later, Upton Verg's Second Platoon followed suit. The brilliant flash of the 150mm cannon illuminated the darkness ahead. Ventis saw both tank platoons bear right in search of TOG vehicles.

"Abacus Two, this is Two-six. Steer five-six-hundred relative." Ventis ordered the infantry carriers to cover the left flank of the formation. He felt the Spartius respond. The Vipers were abreast of the Spartius, four hundred meters to either side, their turrets seeking targets for their 25mm cannon.

"Clodius carrier. Range six-five-double-zero. Bearing five-eight-two-zero relative.

Target velocity three-six. Moving away." The targeting computer had picked up a target at extreme range and was supplying pertinent information in its pleasant, even voice. "Multiple targets. Range six-four-five-zero. Bearing five-eight-two-zero. Target velocity three-six. Moving away." Ventis watched the DDP fill with red and amber squares as more TOG vehicles lit up the sensors of the rushing vehicle.

"Zollach." Ventis switched the commlink to internal and spoke to the driver. "Decelerate. Take her to the deck. We don't want to overrun the TOGs at this height."

"Wilco. On the deck."

Ventis felt the thrusters fire at maximum to slow 189 tons of steel. To brake from 400 kph to a safe 240 kph would take minutes, and the infantry carriers would be within lethal range of the targets before they could reach the surface. The TOGs would be targeting belly armor when the shooting started. Not good. The Viper carriers to the right and left followed Ventis' lead and slowed as well. They were more agile than the Spartius, but even with their better thrust, they too would be at TTF when the range closed. He would have to lead the platoon in a tight circle to bleed off speed.

He opened the comm to the platoon. "Two, this is Two-six. Circle right six-four-hundred mils. Execute." Ventis had left the commlink on internal as well, and Zollach slammed the Spartius hard to the right as the command was given. Ventis felt the carrier turn and the turret swing to the left as Rollus kept the 5/6 lasers trained on the distant targets.

This was a disconcerting maneuver for a commander. The hull was turning hard in one direction, the turret hard in the opposite direction. The DDP reflected the location of targets based on the turret facing. The commander could feel the vehicle turning under him and the turret turning around him, but the DDP remained stationary. Ventis gripped the hatch and lowered his head to watch the DDP. A minute later the Spartius had finished her turn and was back at the original heading, but moving almost 100 kph slower.

"Multiple targets. Range six-four-eight-zero. Bearing five-eight-two-zero. Target velocity three-six. Moving away." The targeting computer, unaffected by the violent maneuvering of the carrier, had been tracking the fleeing TOG force. The Spartius continued to decelerate.

"Zollach, follow the targets."

"Wilco."

"Multiple targets. Range six-four-three-zero. Bearing six-three-double-zero. Target velocity three-six. Moving away." The targeting computer noted that the bearing and range to the enemy had changed slightly. The DDP also showed rugged blocks of terrain that masked the scan ahead. The ground here was solid, with no more explosions of ice and water. The Spartius steadied on the new heading and continued to slow.

"Multiple targets. Range two-four-nine-zero. Bearing six-three-double-zero. Target velocity three-six. Moving away."

"Rollus." Ventis spoke to his gunner. "Pick the biggest target and lay on it. We'll open as soon as we get a lock."

"Right."

"Target identified. Cestus heavy ground tank, range one-nine-nine-zero. Bearing six-three-eight-zero. Target velocity three-six. Moving away. Lock not achieved." Ventis glanced at the target information on the DDP. They rarely fought ground vehicles, which were usually found in TOG garrison legions rather than front-line forces. In fact, he was puzzled as to why TOG would use ground vehicles at the polar cap at all. The Cestus had adequate armor but no flicker shields, making it an easy target for the twin 5/6 lasers of the Spartius. But the Cestus could do damage with three lasers of its own, a pair of 1.5/3s mounted in sponsons on the hull and a single 1.5/4 in the turret. The hull also held a pair of TVLG launchers.

Ventis hit the painting laser treadle. "Target identified. Cestus heavy ground tank, range one-nine-double-zero. Bearing six-three-eight-zero. Target velocity three-six. Moving away. Lock not achieved." Ventis treadled the painting laser again. "Target identified. Cestus heavy ground tank, range one-eight-five-zero. Bearing six-three-eight-zero. Target velocity three-six. Moving away. Lock achieved."

"Identified," called Rollus, letting Ventis know that the cross hairs of the laser sight were on the named target and that the ballistic computer had adjusted for the speed of both vehicles. The gunner's board was green, clear to fire.

"Fire," said Ventis.

"On the way."

Ventis felt the twin lasers power up, saw the muzzles blaze red from the surge of power. Ahead in the dark, the hits glowed on the unseen target. The warning klaxon growled in his ear. The tone was low, telling him the enemy trying to paint his vehicle had not yet achieved a lock. The tone switched to a shrill warning. An invisible enemy's painting laser had deciphered his flicker shields. The twin lasers fired again as Rollus kept pounding the target the guns had locked onto. The target indicator on the DDP blinked to show hits; then it went blank. A kill. Ventis peered over the hatch coaming, searching for the glow of a burning vehicle, but saw nothing. "Switch targets."

The turret tracked to the right and settled on a new red indicator, but before the ballistic computer could identify the target, it too blinked out, a victim of one of the Vipers. The turret continued to traverse. "Target identified. Clodius light ground tank, range one-one-double-zero. Bearing six-three-seven-zero. Target velocity six-zero. Moving away. Lock not achieved."

The targets without flicker shields did not have to be painted. Ventis was only using the painting laser to confirm the lay of the main weapons of the Spartius. The warning klaxon continued to scream in his ear. Whoever had painted them was still on target. As the tank flashed past an outcropping of rock, Ventis glimpsed a group of crouching infantrymen out of the corner of his eye. One of them was holding a TVLG tube, its open muzzle huge against the white of the ice. He instinctively ducked into the hatch as the missile sprang from the tube.

His tank was speeding away from its assailant, but the missile had even greater speed and they couldn't maintain the range. The Spartius had no Vulcan antimissile system, so Ventis could do nothing except brace for the shock of impact. Then the howling wind tore the missile from its course and sent it spinning harmlessly into the night. The wind, an enemy during the attack, had suddenly become an ally. "Target identified. Clodius light ground tank, range eight-double-zero. Bearing six-three-seven-zero. Target velocity six-zero. Moving away. Lock achieved."

"Identified," said Rollus.

"Fire."

"On the way." The twin lasers hummed again, and this time Ventis saw the light ground vehicle in the illumination of the hits. The squat turret was traversed fully to the rear, the antipersonnel and 1.5/5 lasers laid directly on the charging Spartius. The main weapon fired as the ground vehicle died. Ventis saw the sparkle of the laser as it shattered against the Spartius' flicker shields, the broken energy of the aligned light skipping like brilliant sequins thrown into the wind. Then the turret of the Clodius was torn from the traversing ring and the gaping hole in the hull filled with volcanic fire. The burning tank glowed brightly against the blackness, throwing red light across the snow.

He glanced at the DDP. All around him were the blue squares of the other vehicles of the command. His own Century was spread over 15 kilometers, and he could see the vehicles of other commands scattered through his own. To the left and rear, the DDP showed a Viper that was damaged but still underway. He checked; it wasn't one of his. "Abacus Two, this is Abacus Two-six. Status report. Rally on me." He made sure that his IFF signal was functioning. "Zollach. Put her down beyond that last kill. We'll wait for the others." Ventis watched one of his Vipers creeping slowly toward his location. It was the carrier that held the platoon sergeant and an infantry squad. Before he could call it to find out why it was moving so slowly, it called him.

"Two-six, this is Two-three-five." It was Platoon Sergeant Merrian Lut reporting in. Lut was one of the replacement sergeants, detailed from a shattered Manus. Ventis had checked her file on the flight to the pole; she had a good record. Lut had been a platoon commander at the end of the fight on Alsatia and been recommended for a field commission. She was not happy about becoming a platoon sergeant again.

"Two-three-five, this is Two-six."

"Two-three-five, I have dismounted prisoners."

"Two-six. Infantry prisoners are to be taken to the Cohort holding area. The location is on your DDP."

"This is Two-three-five. Roger. These aren't really infantry types. I think you should see them—they look like civilian technicians."

"This is Two-six. Okay, bring them here. And on the way, check for more lurking here." Ventis touched his DDP with a stylus to show the location of the infantry who had fired the TVLG at the Spartius. "They took a shot at me, so they may still be hostile. Be careful."

"Roger, Two-six. We'll be persuasive as well."

Ventis watched the tank platoons come in via the DDP, which showed the tanks approaching in "V" formations, commonly known in the military as vics. The First Platoon, commanded by Sergeant Narall, had no damage, but the Second Platoon with Sergeant Verg, had taken some hits from light lasers. With no armor breached, all tanks were listed as combat-worthy. Irregular movement in the shadows at the edge of the glow cast by the burning Clodius attracted Ventis' attention. A group of perhaps a dozen men, wearing a hodgepodge of TOG battledress and civilian smocks, stumbled into view. Their hands were locked behind their heads, and the strong wind buffeted them as they approached. Behind them was a line of peds, their battle suits attached by umbilical cables to the sides of the Viper. Lut was right. This ragged troop did not look like TOG military at all.

15

0730, 10 Martius 6831—The damaged Renegade Viper shuddered across the south pole's barren ice. A TVLG hit on the right front side of the outer armored shield had caused minor but freak damage. The incoming missile had struck the vehicle at the joint between the inner hull and the outer ogive, and the force of the explosion, directed into the space between the hull and shield, had twisted the outer covering away and down. Now it hung like a great wind scoop.

Under normal conditions, this damage would have been negligible, but the high winds screaming across the ice made handling difficult. Sudden gusts of wind caught the opening and twisted the Viper violently to the right. At 240 kph, the normal safe speed for low-altitude flight, this sudden change of direction could have fatal consequences. The random walls of jutting rock dotting the terrain of the ice cap would be unforgiving. The crew would have to repair the damage or reduce the speed of the vehicle to a crawl.

Sergeant Honor Ross reported the damage to her platoon leader, Sergeant Robert Browning, and he passed it on to the Century. Ross was given three hours to repair the damage or else leave the vehicle behind. She was given that much time based only on the current situation and the need to secure the prisoners taken in the skirmish. Her squad would be spread through the rest of the Cohort if they couldn't repair the vehicle, and because the maintenance section, with all the tools and spare parts, had been lost in the initial crossing, there would be little help from Cohort.

Ross' driver grounded the Viper within the Century perimeter. The sector chosen for her vehicle included one of the many huts erected by the TOG party that had been working at the pole. The larger buildings were within the Cohort position, and were now being used to house the headquarters elements as well as the prisoners taken in the attack. The huts on the perimeter were vacant.

"Bending back that shroud's going to be a real bitch, Sarge." Principes Herman Grold, the first section leader of Honor's squad, was thinking out loud. "Ah, sorry about that." Grold could not forget that Ross was female, even though this was not the first time a woman had been his direct superior. He had been taught at home that certain words were not spoken when the fairer sex was present, and that training, for better or worse, had stuck. He looked to see his sergeant's response. She didn't seem to be offended.

"Anything in the on-board tool kit we can use?" she asked.

Grold shook his head. "That holotorch is designed to cut, not heat, and with this cold, we'd never get the shroud hot enough to bend. Not unless we can isolate the damaged area and keep it from bleeding off the heat."

The other members of the squad stood huddled around the front of the damaged Viper. They were well aware of the situation, and they wanted desperately for the damage to be repaired. They had been a squad for only a short time, since they reported as replacements to the 2567th after the battle on Alsatia, but they were already a family. None of them wanted to leave the unit to become nameless replacements all over again. It was considered a truism of the infantry that the replacements died first in any fight. If collective thought had any strength, the damaged shroud would already have been bent back into shape by pure will power. The wind howled over the side of the Viper and the dejected gathering huddled more closely together.

"There might be something in that TOG shack we could use," mumbled Millicent Connor, the crew's gunner. "And it would be better in there than out here."

The others looked at the shack, each one estimating its size against the bulk of the infantry carrier. "Boost," said Ross to the leader of the second section, "take a couple of your people and check it out." She turned back to the damaged vehicle. As they headed out, the three hunched figures huddled together for imagined warmth. "Act like legionnaires!" she snapped. "That hut hasn't been cleared." Boost chivvied his companions into a line and made for the hut.

It was empty. The ferrocrete prefab panels linked to form a central open area roofed in the same material. The walls and floor were insulated against the bitter cold, and even though the building was unheated, the escape from the wind created an impression of warmth. It took the squad less than fifteen minutes to remove the leeward wall and edge the Viper into the space. The stern of the carrier was still exposed to the elements, but the crew, though cramped between the damaged hull and the rear wall, would have ample space to make repairs. Ross put Grold and the two crewmen to work on the bent shroud, sent Boost and his section to provide local security, and gathered the peds from the first section to explore the rest of the hut.

The shack was laid out as a squat cruciform, with separate rooms extending from three sides. The central area was five meters on a side, and the adjoining rooms extended two meters beyond that. The first two rooms the party investigated turned out to be a bunkhouse for the eight men who had worked there, and the kitchen/recreation/tool storage area. This room was a wealth of resources for the repair team. The pipe stanchions of the bunks proved useful as pry bars, and the kitchen facilities generated more than enough heat to warm the bent plating and yielded additional tools.

The third room was an office that showed signs of hasty evacuation. File drawers had been left hanging opened, the burn basket was almost full with fine gray ash, and the electrotube held a stack of computer chips, all their data erased. The terminals had not been damaged, however, and the keyboards were still operational. A locked closet filled a third of the room. "Unlock it," Ross ordered Brace, one of the three peds with her on the search. The other three stood back, dropping the face plates of their combat helmets, as the legionnaire leveled his Raktarus spike rifle at the locking mechanism. The room filled with a roar and flash as Brace fired a three-round burst at the lock.

The Raktarus was an old design, bulkier and heavier than the newer weapons being issued to Commonwealth forces, but it packed an incredible punch at short range. The three spikes struck square on the code panel. The first one blew the cover and keypad from the door. The second, a fraction of a second later, buried itself in the microchips, which erupted in a shower of sparks and streaming smoke. The third spike smashed through the remaining circuitry and the ferrosteel tab that secured the door. "Locks keep honest people honest," declared Triarii Fredrick Brace, stepping back to view his handiwork. He waited until the last of the smoke had cleared, then, holding the rifle in his left hand, used his right to shove the splintery panel to the left and reveal the interior of the closet.

This was no closet. Ross and her companions faced a cage-type elevator suspended over a shaft that dropped out of sight below the floor of the shack. They murmured in surprise. "Paulus," said Ross, "report to Century that we've found a deep shaft under this building. Tell them that the door was locked. Tell them that we are going into it. Got that?" The triarii repeated Ross' instructions and left for the commlink in the vehicle. The three legionnaires who remained entered the lift.

There were only two settings on the control panel, one illuminated, the other dark. Ross pressed the dark indicator, and the elevator shuddered to life. The overhead flouropanel blinked on, throwing blue-white light over the two-by-two-meter-square area. The cage enclosure dropped away from the upper floor so fast that the legionnaires had to grab for the mesh to keep their balance. The stop was equally sudden, forcing the peds, even in their powered bounce armor, to bend their knees against their own weight. A corridor, cut through ice and rock, stretched away from the elevator into the dark.

Using hand signals to maintain silence and thus retain the advantage of surprise against any unfriendlies, Ross organized the patrol. Brace led, his spike rifle held at the ready. Ross moved second, carrying a Tektara spike carbine, the typical long weapon of a vehicle crewmember. Last came Triarii Ghonathan Grain, also carrying a spike rifle and watching to the rear. The thermographic sensor in their armor's face plates showed the terrain ahead simply as differences in temperature. The floor of ice and the rock above made the corridor an almost uniform temperature, but their instrumentation would pick up whatever differences were there if they moved slowly enough, and they weren't planning to move very fast. Ross' helmet also carried a Basic Lifeform Sensor capable of detecting living targets out to three hundred meters. The high ferrous-metal content of the surrounding strata degraded the effectiveness of the BLS, but then, the probability of engaging long-range targets was minimal.

They crept silently forward, crouched in ready position. The corridor was two meters wide and slightly higher, a machine-made cut through the ice. Reinforcing steel supports were spaced at five-meter intervals. Brace bounded forward, assisted by his bounce armor, from support to support. He kept to the left side of the passage, giving his weapon free traverse across the narrow path. Ross followed on the right side, and Grain completed the search formation on the left side, checking to the rear. Time seemed to slow as they moved, their breathing sounding loud in the confined corridor.

A soft blue blip ghosted across Ross' face plate. "Stop," she murmured into the boom-mike communicator. The patrol froze in its tracks. "I've got a life form ahead. I can't get the range or bearing, just an indication." They peered ahead into the darkness. The blue blip solidified as it moved again. "Got him. To the right. About twenty-five meters."

Brace stepped forward to the next support and took a quick look. "There's a passage to the right. Cover me." Ross came forward until she was abreast of the opening and then signaled Brace to move. He darted across the gap, placing his back against the wall. He peered cautiously around the support and down the gallery.

A great blaze of light filled the corridor, throwing the intervening supports into stark relief. A grinding roar, almost deafening in the confined spaces, announced the piece of machinery trundling down the passage. The light was too bright for the team to see the machine's size and function, but there was no doubt that it was coming right at them.

Brace dropped to one knee, bringing the spike rifle to his shoulder, and opened fire. The blaze of the rifle was puny compared to the arc lights of the vehicle, and the crack of the shots was lost in the cacophony of the charging behemoth. Ross could see the spikes sparking off the front of the machine. Brace was shooting for the headlamps. One of them exploded in a shower of glass that twinkled in the light of the undamaged lamp.

In the reduced light, Ross could see the machine. A pair of huge, rotating drums were set horizontally across the front of the machine. Each drum was set with spikes half a meter long, placed to interweave between the drums. It was the machine that had cut the passage. As it reached each supporting beam, it effortlessly ripped the stanchion from the wall and shredded it between the drums. Brace continued to fire. "Get back," ordered Ross, and the thing continued to approach.

Brace withdrew from the opening of the corridor and flattened himself against the wall of the intersection. Ross and Grain hugged the opposite wall. The crawler erupted from the passage and ground its way across the opening. The passage did not continue on the other side, and the giant mandibles plowed into the wall with a horrendous crash. Great shards of ice spewed from the drums on impact. The articulated body of the machine writhed and jumped as the tracks continued to drive at maximum speed into the solid barrier. A protruding handhold to the left of the power plant caught Ross square in the torso, lifting her off her feet and throwing her backward into Grain. She felt the concussion of the strike, though it didn't penetrate the tanker combat suit.

Grain shouldered past her to open fire on the enclosed control station. The spikes from his rifle blasted through the glazing, shredding the metallic skin to confetti. The machine stopped.

Either it had bitten too much ice for the rotating drums to clear, or the spikes from Grain's rifle had disabled the control system. It didn't matter. From deep inside the hole the crawler had begun to chew in the opposite wall came the reflected glow of the remaining headlamp. It illuminated enough of the intersection that Ross could clearly see the machine and the rubbled remains of the passage. She looked into the control position for the body of her assailant, but the space was empty. The hidden enemy had set the machine to charge them while he fled deeper into the caverns. If he had been a little more patient, or if he had thought to wait for them to enter the side corridor, he might have gotten some or all of them. Ross shuddered. The thought of what those steel teeth and drums could do to a man, even one in bounce infantry body armor, was not something she wanted to contemplate. You won't get away, she thought. I know you're here, and you're mine. She signaled Brace down the ruined passage.

Almost immediately the blue blip of a life form appeared on Ross' BLS. Her enemy was moving rapidly, using his knowledge of the subterranean maze to his advantage. But Ross had a trump card of her own. His movement was creating heat, and the BLS was getting a firmer lock on his exact location. His body heat was also being reflected off the walls of the labyrinth, and that thermal difference was revealed on the face plates of the other stalking legionnaires. The target was exposing his position even as he fled.

Ross directed the patrol on the target's trail. The blue blip had become solid and easily tracked. Now the problem was obtaining a clear shot. The web of corridors was so intricate that even when their adversary was a mere ten meters away, they couldn't get line-of-sight. Then the blue ghost stopped. Ross halted the patrol. The thermographic terrain displays revealed that the quarry had reached a blind corridor. He was trapped. The patrol crept forward. Grain and Brace led on either side of the gallery. Ross followed, centered in the corridor and several meters behind. Her BLS showed her the positions of both men in her patrol as well as the enemy.

"He's ahead about ten meters. Crouching." She felt the boom mike against her lips. Her eyes never left the target indicator. "Brace. Stop. Get ready. He's beginning to move toward your side. Grain. Move up a bit. Stop there. Both of you, stay low. I can shoot over your heads." The patrol froze. "Wait. I'll illuminate. Open on my command."

Holding the carbine in her right hand, the butt firmly settled against her right shoulder, she raised her left arm toward the target. One of the advantages of the vehicle crew armor was that a small light source was affixed to the back of each hand. This allowed crewmen to work in a dark area with a steady source of light that illuminated the fingers; it also made a convenient flashlight. Ross closed her fist and the light came on.

Caught in the glow, a TOG soldier stood starkly silhouetted against the dark wall. He was partially uniformed, only his torso protected by body armor. He was wearing a heavy combat helmet with extra cables that attached to a large backpack. The man was startled by the sudden glare, frozen like an animal caught in oncoming headlights.

"Drop your weapons," said Ross in a loud, even voice. "Drop them or we'll shoot."

The enemy remained still for a moment, and then his arms slowly descended, his hands twisting outward to show empty palms. Ross felt the tension lift from her shoulders. As the soldier's left hand reached the level of his belt, he snapped it behind his back. Before Ross understood what was happening, he was holding a Marcus 12mm submachine gun. The wire brace stock of the weapon was folded over the barrel. Ross watched the muzzle rising toward her.

"Don't!" she shouted. "Fire!"

All three Renegade weapons opened fire simultaneously. Grain and Brace had their rifles on full automatic. A steady, double, converging stream of spikes slivered into the torso of the TOG soldier, slicing through the body armor. He was thrown violently against the rearward wall, his own weapon releasing a stream of 12mm slugs into the ceiling. The body crumpled into a messy heap. Chips of ice continued to fall, moving like minnows through the steady stream of Ross' hand light.

16

0930, 10 Martius 6831—The screaming wind tugged at the edge of the emergency shelter's holotarp, making the thin material roar like a wounded lion. Under the camouflage material, a thermal blanket protected Stone and Archon from the pole's punishing weather. The swirling ice had built a rime of frost along the leeward edges of the canopy, crusting the tarp to the surrounding ice. Any movement within the shelter cracked the layer of frost, and the wind flung the shards away into the pitch-black sky.

Inside the shelter, Larry Stone crushed a tiny capsule that immediately began to glow. The light grew brighter as the chemicals within the blister mixed, giving a blue-green luminescence to the shelter's interior. Stone rolled out of his own thermocoat and examined the Baufrin lying crumpled under a second thermocoat. The alien's exoskeleton had regained its normal emerald-green coloration, a welcome change from the pale pea-green it had been some hours before. Stone reached out and brushed his hand over the nearer ear-horn. His friend reacted at once.

Archon Divxas opened all six of his eyes and inspected his Human companion. "In answer to your unstated question, my friend, I am feeling much better." Divxas shifted slightly, tentatively flexing his multiple legs. "It was good of you to delay your journey on my account."

Stone snorted. He found it difficult to accept thanks. Emotional response of any kind upset him; it was probably the only thing that frightened him. He preferred to be in control at all times, and emotions, in his opinion, were nothing but a loss of control. Statements of friendship or love or admiration were the worst. He never knew quite how to respond to them, so most of the time, he did nothing. He had never learned how to say "thank you" to a compliment. It made for a self-contained, if lonely, existence. This occasion was no different.

"I can see," continued the Baufrin, "by the charge indicator on the control panel that this time was not completely wasted. The batteries have had an opportunity to recover somewhat."

Stone looked at the control panel. The Baufrin was right. During the five hours they had spent huddled under the thermal shrouds, the power pack in the sled had recovered some of its punch. The green bar now extended well across the charge indicator. Stone made a quick mental calculation, and decided they had perhaps four hours of flight at low-power drain. He got to his feet, careful not to shake the tarp too violently, then crawled into the command seat of the Loren grav sled. The Terrain Analysis System on the DDP showed their sled's location on the edge of the ice cap. He switched to high resolution, and the TAS displayed the entire cap. Stone traced around the edge of the continent to the point where the Cohort was expected to exit the ice for the final leg toward Malthus. The exit point was well within the range of the sled. With a little luck, they would be able to catch the Cohort there.

"Let's go," he said, rising to his full height under the twin tarps that had protected the pair from the elements. Their icy shroud shattered and vanished. Stone staggered against the blast of the wind.

"You do things with such aggressiveness, my friend," chided Divxas, scrambling to save the tarps. "Perhaps a word of warning would be in order the next time."

"He who hesitates is lost, Archon. Up and at 'em."

"A little hesitation may have been in order in this situation. We came close to losing the tarps, which, I might point out, will continue to be important accoutrements unless it becomes much warmer in the near future." Divxas gave Stone the look that passed for a sarcastic smile among members of his race.

"Close only counts in holopitch, hand grenades, HELL rounds, and dancing." Stone began to pack their small store of essential equipment. The Baufrin abandoned his attempt to chastise his friend and followed suit.

Larry Stone indicated the Cohort exit point on the rim of the ice shelf with a light pen on his display. The TAS recorded the information and plotted the intercept course to that location. By cutting across the chord of the arcing path, rather than following the perimeter, the grav sled would be able to reach the exit point with a little power to spare. The DDP power analysis always figured a 5 percent reserve into all calculations, but Stone preferred to add another five, just to be on the safe side. He confirmed the chord as the course.

The sled rose to a one-meter hover and moved off on its journey. Divxas drove again, and Stone occupied the gunner's seat. The wind would blow straight into their faces for the entire run. As they left the limited shelter of the outer volcanic rim, they faced the full blast of the frozen wastes. Stone pulled the thermocoat blanket tightly around his body until he resembled a poorly wrapped mummy. He left the smallest possible opening for his goggles, and even that tiny space allowed the stinging ice to work its way under his coat. He felt ice melting off his chin to flow in frigid fingers down the front of his throat and chest.

Archon Divxas did not have the benefit of goggles, but by opening and closing alternate pairs of eyes, he managed to keep a clear view of the DDP. The wind forced him to keep his head low, but with nothing of interest beyond the edges of the sled, this did not concern him. When the DDP flared to life showing a scarlet blot directly ahead of the sled, the first ice column explosion caught him completely by surprise. He looked up quickly, but already the tower of ice loomed above the sled, tearing itself to shreds under the howl of the wind. He ducked, trying to avoid the wave of shards battering against his chitinous exoskeleton like hail on a tin roof. The sled roared over the boiling remains of the spout.

"That was an interesting phenomenon," commented Divxas. "Do you think that it was representative of the conditions we will encounter during our journey?"

"How would I know? I've never been here before. I don't even know what it was." Stone unsuccessfully tried to keep his momentary panic out of his voice.

"That, my good friend Lawrence, is a pity. It would be quite anticlimactic to have come so far only to be devoured by the ice before we make contact with your Cohort."

"Don't be sarcastic. It doesn't become you," mumbled Stone.

"Sarcasm is a tool best used in polite conversation. A keenly ironic utterance could not be fully appreciated in this situation."

"You're being sarcastic now."

"My abject apologies."

Another spout erupted well to the right of the sled, its presence marked by another scarlet blot on the DDP. The pair gazed in awe at the fury of nature exploding in the air.

"If one of those gets us, we'll never know it."

Divxas nodded absently, giving careful attention to the DDP. Another scarlet blot appeared. The Baufrin looked up to watch the water and ice shoot from the frozen surface. He slowed the sled to a crawl and stared into the darkness, completely disregarding the DDP. Stone peered over the Baufrin's shoulder to view the display. A scarlet blot appeared well ahead, so far away that the column was invisible in the darkness.

"I have it," Divxas stated triumphantly. "I can see them before they erupt."

"How?"

"As you know, my race is superior to the Human race in a number of ways." Divxas had given this lecture on the superiority of Baufrins over Humans many times. Stone had heard it all before, but he knew better than to interrupt.

"With our triple-eye system, we are able to detect light over a greater range than the simple white light you perceive. As a result, we can see in what you call the infrared as well as the ultraviolet spectrum. The eruptions generate heat as they rise under the ice cap. No, that is a slight misstatement. They create an absence of the extreme cold that is the ambient situation within this precinct. I can see that change. If I disregard the Data Display Panel, allowing the sled to steer itself on the predetermined course, I can make the minute adjustments to the azimuth that will allow us to avoid this interesting hazard." The Baufrin crackled with delight.

"You mean you can steer around them?"

"Precisely."

"Why didn't you say that?"

"I believe that is exactly what I have just said."

Stone groaned silently. It was no use beginning a conversation with a Baufrin unless you had plenty of time for verbiage. "Do it."

"With pleasure and alacrity."

In the hours that followed, Divxas stared fixedly into the darkness, blinking constantly to clear his vision as the ice built up on his eyeballs. He could have used help from Stone, but the Human of course lacked the ability to detect the slight shifts in thermal imagery that presaged the eruption of the ice. As the sled continued on its course across the ice, he began to feel the cold more intensely. With ice forming more quickly on his infrared, he was tempted to lower his head under the thermal blanket for just a moment, anything to clear it from his eyes. His thoughts turning more and more to the warmth of the thermocoat and away from the danger posed by the shifting ice, Divxas began to lose his concentration.

It was just such an intense reverie that made him miss the boiling column of ice and frigid water that exploded almost directly under the sled. The shock of the blast lifted the sled clear of the column and hurled it, stern over bow, to one side. The sled, caught broadside to the wind, flipped over on its long axis as it inverted. Stone, in the rear seat, was thrown clear by the initial thrust, his body snatched by the wind and dashed to the ice. Divxas was not so lucky.

The extended panel of the Loren sled's control station was intended to cover the legs of the operator. The Baufrin, with six legs to fit into a space designed for two, had had to wedge his limbs under the DDP. When the blast threw the sled over on its bow, he was trapped. The wind caught the sled as it inverted, twisting it sharply to the side. The Baufrin's two right rear legs were jammed under the panel by this sudden motion. As the bulk of his body rolled clear of the sled, those two legs were wrenched across his back. His body cleared the sled and like Stone, he slammed into the ice.

Stone saw the sled and its driver crash down well away from where he had landed. As soon as he caught his breath, he crawled toward his friend. The sled lay on its side, the miniature Marshman grav drives glowing in the darkness. He crawled around the sled into the minimal protection its bulk offered against the unrelenting blast. Archon Divxas lay there, totally still. Stone saw immediately that the Baufrin's injuries were grave. The middle leg on his right side was bent completely across the back of his torso. The rearmost leg wobbled slightly in the gale, obviously no longer under control of the alien's brain. Stone dropped to his knees beside his friend.

Fearful of what he would find, Stone gingerly lifted away the Baufrin's thermocoat, which had been blown over his head. All six eyes were tightly closed, the mandibles gaping open. A rivulet of drool trailed from the lower opening. Stone stared at his friend, silently cursing himself for allowing Divxas to come at all.

"Damn!" he muttered. "Damn, damn, a thousand times damn!"

"Cursing will do nothing to alleviate the intense discomfort I am currently experiencing." The Baufrin's eyes snapped open, his jaw snapped shut.

Stone fell back in surprise. "Hey! I thought you were—"

"A completely understandable assumption on your part, I am sure," Divxas cut in. "I reiterate my previous statement concerning my acute discomfort. You will please take appropriate steps to solve the problem."

Stone was deeply concerned. He had thought Baufrins incapable of rudeness, yet Divxas had cut him off in mid-sentence. His friend's pain must be unbearable. "What can I do? I don't know anything about Baufrin physiology."

"The simplest solution to the problem is to remove the affected appendage above the source of the discomfort."

"Cut it off?"

"You have a quick appreciation of the correct course of action."

"You're being sarcastic again. And to think I was worried about you." Stone mocked his friend in intense relief.

"I am humbled."

Stone drew his laser stiletto. "Where do I cut?"

"Just place your incision through the first joint from the body. That is the first one to have suffered appreciable trauma, and you might as well remove all of the damaged parts rather than attempt to save anything."

Stone gripped the lower portion of the leg and double-clicked the control button on the hilt of his laser stiletto. The weapon was designed to pierce rather than cut, but Stone found that by placing the burning force at the six-centimeter range, the power of the aligned light sliced through the damaged tissue. Stone had to activate the blade three times before his task was accomplished. His hand became so rigid with tension that he had to pry his fingers from the haft when he was done. He was tempted to hurl the stiletto into the darkness in his rage against circumstances, but rejected the futile action. Theatrics were good for the theater, but he had no audience. He sheathed the weapon and turned to face his friend.

Divxas was hurt. The pain from the original wound and the additional damage from the amputation had left him weak and shaken. There was no chance of him driving the sled. He would need a warm place to recover his strength.

"Do not worry, my friend," Archon said. "I have five other legs, and although this represents a loss of sixteen point six-six-seven of my lower appendages, upon recovery, I will have lost a much smaller percentage of my motive ability."

Stone bundled the Baufrin in the remaining thermocoat and dragged him to the sled. The

Loren was so light that he could right it with little difficulty before setting his wounded friend in the gunner's seat. The DDP was undamaged, the coordinates of the rendezvous still firmly implanted in its memory. Stone fired up the drives and moved out.

It was immediately apparent that Stone would have to travel higher than the sled's normal one-meter flight level, because he could not sense the building force of the explosions. The first one to burst near the sled again warned him of the danger. The second convinced him that safety would only be found in altitude. He pulled back on the control wand and climbed. At just above normal tree-top flight, he found that most of the explosions didn't reach the sled, and those that did could be avoided. He was careful not to twist the sled too violently for fear he would dump his wounded comrade from the gunner's seat.

Stone did not notice that the eruptions had ceased as he approached the rendezvous point. He was aware only that the wind continued unabated, grasping at the sled, continually threatening to twist it out of his control. Then the DDP blossomed with myriad red designators coming in from the north. Stone stared in shock. Red meant TOG vehicles, and these were skimming toward the pole from Malthus.

He reacted instantly, thrusting the control wand forward and diving for a rock outcropping that seemed a likely shelter. He grounded the sled as close to the rock as possible and then shut down cold, taking the chance that he wouldn't be able to get the Marshman drives to fire again. As he snapped the holotarp over the sled, the high-pitched scream of multiple grav drives rose above the howl of the wind. Looking up, Stone saw multiple vics of Horatius tanks and Romulus infantry carriers roar overhead at TTF altitude.

The sound and the sight transfixed him. Stone remained staring upward at the impressive array of enemy machines, almost not daring to breathe, until the last one had passed and the air was still again.

17

1145, 10 Martius 6831—Legatus Cariolanus Camus raised the face plate of his combat helmet and bared his face to the wind. All commanders should feel this, he thought, as he watched the other vehicles of his Strike Cohort cross the north edge of Caralis' southern polar ice cap. In close column, the Horatius heavy grav tanks skimmed the towering shafts of ice that rose along the littoral, kicking up huge plumes of snow from the ancient rocks.

Camus knew he was too senior to be commanding a Cohort. A legatus deserved a Manus, but this had been his Cohort for three years. Even though he had been promoted out of the command, he had volunteered to come back for this mission, and with the assigned commander on his annual home leave, Camus was the best choice. Camus was pleased with himself. Cohort commanders seldom had the opportunity to play an independent role in battle, and he had refused to allow a centurion maximus to steal his chance. If he performed well here, and he had little doubt that he would, it could mean early command of a Manus.

He ran through the simple mission plan in his mind. The Cohort would land on the cap's central plateau, directly on the Commonwealth force's route. Shut down, and using only passive sensors, his Cohort would be practically impossible to detect. They would wait until the Commonwealth Cohort entered their killing zone and then spring the trap. The entire battle should take less than five minutes, and they would probably take a few prisoners as well. Camus knew that it was a good plan.

In twelve years of service to TOG, life had lived up to his every dream and expectation. Though he had begun with garrison duty, his promotion to centurion had sent him into combat on many planets.

Garrison life had been dull, of course, except for that uprising, but it had lasted barely long enough to try his abilities. Civilians were really no match for armored vehicles and antipersonnel lasers. The rebels who had poured into the streets had been easily swept aside and the leaders sent off to a penal mine. It was too bad that his wife had been involved, but a spouse's secrets was one of the imponderables in any relationship. She had been captured and deported with the rest of the troublemakers, and only the strenuous efforts of the planetary governor kept the file on his marriage from official notice. Camus had felt no sense of loss then, and had almost forgotten her since. Two years was time enough with any woman; he had been ready to move on. Any woman was interesting for a while, but personal ties were restrictive to a soldier with ambitions. And Camus was ambitious.

His promotion to centurion was his reward for his part in putting down the rebellion, bringing with it his transfer to a Strike Legion. Three years an optio, five a centurion, and then four as a centurion maximus, promoted ahead of schedule in every case. Life was good, Camus thought. And now, he had seized the chance for an independent command under the direct observation, but not control, of an important member of the planetary command staff. And the mission's success was assured. Life was indeed good.

Word of the Commonwealth attack on the polar station had arrived when his Cohort was still over the water, halfway to the edge of the south pole. Camus was expecting this development. The planetary command had told him that Commonwealth forces would attack the pole, and the original plan was to try to forestall that attack. But politics at planetary headquarters made that plan moot. For some reason, the planetary commander and the operations chief were at odds about the value of the work being done at the polar station. Camus normally paid no notice to these petty quarrels; this one only came to his attention because he was involved in the operation to save the project.

Prefect Sulla had a watching brief for the mission, and was even now somewhere in the headquarters element of the Cohort. Camus felt a twinge of worry. The headquarters had lost at least one vehicle to those monstrous waves that seemed to rise from the very bowels of the polar sea. The combat Centuries had taken losses, too. He shrugged mentally, knowing such losses were inevitable. Combat was a risk, and soldiers expected to die. No one was going to get out of this life alive, and when fate pulled your strand of the skein, you went.

Camus watched the reinforced Cohort clear the edge of the ice cap. He mulled over his two options for the location of the ambush. He could await the arrival of the enemy force on the ice's edge, or he could catch them on the plain that extended from the rocky cliffs toward the pole. Setting up on the edge would provide cover for his forces among the pinnacles of rock that marked the continent's perimeter, but that same cover would permit enemy survivors to escape detection if the first volley did not kill them all. The battle would degenerate into an infantry fight, peds stalking the grounded vehicles. His standard medium-grav Cohort gave Camus only six platoons of infantry. Even the reinforcement of the two additional platoons attached to headquarters did not make the TOG advantage strong enough. Better, he decided, to meet the enemy on the open plain. With his forces shut down and the infantry deployed in missile ambushes, they could easily pick off the Commonwealth troops. The plain it would be.

Camus gave the order, and the Cohort drifted down from tree-top flight to the one-meter altitude of normal flight. He did not order the drop to normal-flight altitude made because he feared detection; his prey could not possibly know that this force was on the continent. Camus was merely listening to his TOG grav-vehicle commander's common sense, which told him not to cross potentially hostile terrain at anything higher than normal-flight mode. As his Romulus tilted down into a gradual dive for the surface, he gave another brief command that spread the Cohort out into a basic combat formation.

The three medium Centuries led in a shallow vee formation, followed by the light Centuries in an identical vic. The headquarters, with the additional infantry, was positioned between the two. When they reached the ambush location, this formation would be reversed. The three medium Centuries would ground in a shallow vee formation, the arms extended toward the enemy. The three light Centuries would pass the first vee, the flank Centuries extending the arms of the formation. The middle Century would spread out between the arms of the vee and bury themselves in the ice. They were set to provide early warning, and they would attack from the rear when the mediums opened on the enemy. Headquarters would set up at the base of the vee to act as a reserve and dig out any Commonwealth survivors who went to ground. Commlinks would be on listening silence until Camus gave the command to fire.

The Cohort members went to ground in their assigned positions once they reached the predetermined ambush site. Digging cannon fired into the ice to provide suitable craters for the tanks and infantry carriers, silvery shards of ice exploding from the holes in fragmented rainbows that quickly dissolved in the fierce wind. The drives of the settling vehicles blew the rest of the ice splinters from the depressions.

Those commanders watching their DDPs during the grounding saw a scarlet blot appear on their displays beyond the left arm of the vee. Those who looked out their hatches into the snow-filled light beheld a tower of ice and water, torn by the wind, crash down onto the frozen surface just beyond their position. Those who saw the explosion felt a sudden sense of foreboding, but none reported the phenomenon to Camus. Camus, busy with routine control of the Cohort, did not see it for himself. The infantry deployed from the Romulus and Lupis carriers and began to emplace their TVLG systems in preparation for the expected Commonwealth arrival.

Sergeant Haverford Westan grounded the Romulus medium infantry carrier in the crater he had just blasted into the ice. His position, in the middle of the left arm of the vee, gave him a sense of security denied others in his Century. Those farther forward would be the first to engage the enemy. The Century headquarters was there too, which meant the commanders would be under direct scrutiny of the centurion. The vehicles farther back along the arm, toward the base of the vee, would be seen and checked on by the Cohort commander himself, Legatus Cariolanus Camus. An interesting fellow, Westan thought. He was too high in rank to be commanding a Cohort.

The internal commlink in the Romulus chattered. The infantry, unenthusiastic about deploying in the frigid temperatures and the icy blasts of the wind, wanted to remain within the heated confines of the carrier. Westan checked the DDP for adjacent vehicles and intervening terrain, and discovered he was completely hidden from his neighbors. He contemplated the possibility that his deviation from the operational plan would be observed, decided that it wouldn't, and allowed the infantry to remain safely tucked away within the armored shell.

On the opposite side of the ambush site, the infantry deployed as ordered. The terrain was completely open here, and none of the squad leaders or carrier commanders was willing to risk their defiance being observed. The Third squad of the Second Century deployed in front of the rest. The squad leader, envying the vehicle commander's warm position, deployed his men into the individual craters the vehicle had blown for them. On the right flank of that squad, Triarii Bradford Harnd settled down to watch and wait. The cold and wind and darkness thrust themselves on his mind, creating the terrifying impression of complete isolation. But legionnaires endure; his TOG training had taught him that. He let his attention wander, conjuring heat and light within his mind. He was home again, sitting on the steps of his family's villa in New Rome. The warm summer sun baked the steps, and he could feel the residual warmth on his buttocks. Slowly, that warmth spread upward into his torso. It felt so good.

In his mind, he looked up to see his brother standing in the street in front of him. Wallen, four years older and already six years dead, was smiling at him. He opened his arms and stepped forward, gesturing to Bradford Harnd to join him. Harnd stood on the steps and felt the sun on his face. His brother approached, arms still open wide, and the triarii held out his own arms to welcome his kin. Their fingers touched.

The wind piled small bits of ice against the huddled soldier. The creases of the trooper's uniform filled first, the glittering shroud growing like moss over the rest of the uniform. The last feature of the silent sentry to succumb to the wind-driven particles was the face plate of the combat helmet. By the time the snow began to pack across its surface, the inside of the mask had frosted over.

Sergeant Westan saw a scarlet blotch appear on his DDP to the left of his position and well out of visual range. Almost immediately, a cloud of ice shards rattled over the carrier. The sergeant pulled his head inside the command hatch, relishing the vehicle's warmth. Tiny rivulets of water streaked down the vertical surface of the coaming to form tiny drops that held onto the edge for a moment, then dropped away to spoink softly on the extruded surface of the fighting compartment. Westan settled back in the command chair and stared out of the open hatch. The infantry access doors were cracked open to prevent them from freezing shut, but the heaters in the Romulus would keep the infantry cells warm enough. He propped his feet on the DDP and stretched.

Even if Westan had been paying attention and had seen the telltale change of color on the DDP as the shaft of water exploded under his position, he wouldn't have known what it was, and he would not have been able to react. The blast engulfed the entire crater holding the infantry carrier, dumping it onto its side in the first rush of icy water. The troops on the down side of the Romulus were immediately thrown from their compartments into the icy liquid. Those on the high side were crushed against the interior, and blacked out. Westan was knocked to the floor of the fighting compartment. As he looked up, the command hatch filled with a torrent of icy water. He opened his mouth to scream, but the sound was drowned by the rush of water.

The towering shaft of water and ice crashed down, the base of the eruption suddenly liquid and seething with huge icebergs that ground violently together. Then the wind sheeted the surface and the liquid, already well below the freezing mark, became solid again. Deep under the ice, a soft light glowed for a few moments, flickered, and went out. The wind swept over the vacant position. Nothing remained to mark the existence of the infantry vehicle, her crew, or the squad of men who had once held that spot for the Terran Overlord Government.

18

1500, 10 Martius 6831—Optio Samuel Rand peered over the shoulder of his communications section chief as the sergeant probed into the mysteries of the CC/T 528 commlink. When a massive wave of water tore the antenna from the outer hull of the converted Pedden carrier during the crossing from Rolandrin to the south pole, it did collateral damage to the commset. Now Sergeant Shawn Arsen was attempting to repair the mischief, but he was not having much luck. The miniscule probe he held delicately in his right hand sparked and hissed as the sergeant moved deeper and deeper into the innards of the set. Beads of sweat stood out on his forehead despite the chill that penetrated the interior of the Pedden.

Arsen was an experienced comm tech. He had graduated from that specialty repair school at the head of his class nine years earlier, and his talent was confirmed in the work he had done since. But he was aware that the talent he possessed was just that; he had a feel for electronics, not a knowledge of the intricacies of the systems. He tried to relax. Just let your fingers do it, he told himself. No use trying to think your way through this one. He was tempted to close his eyes so that what he saw would not interfere with his intuition, but he knew that the officer hovering over his shoulder would not understand his method. Another spark sprang from the set.

"Making progress?" inquired Rand, staring into the maze on Arsen's lap.

"Not much, sir," he said, not turning his head. "The quick-release must have been frozen when that antenna ripped away, because the leads tore right out of the system. The water did the rest of the damage." He shook his head. "At least no one was transmitting when it happened. The damage was bad enough on listening silence. If the set had been under full power, the whole thing would have fused."

Rand straightened and looked around the Pedden's interior. They had used personal gear and clothing to plug up most of the leaks caused by the external damage, but water still dripped onto the non-conductive flooring that covered the steel deck. Rand was a recent graduate of the Officers' Training Program. He had never been to specialty school. He was commissioned in the signal branch, but what he knew about commlinks would fit in a thimble. He glanced at the other officer in the cramped carrier. "Excuse me, sir. Do you know anything about the CC/T 528?"

Optio Holton Bard sneered at the young optio. These Renegade officers, he thought, were poor specimens of military men. They would never survive in a TOG program. Most of them wouldn't even be good enlisted men in the army he served, and they treated their peds with unnecessary respect. "I am a qualified officer," he said primly. "Of course I can help. I can fix the set myself. But that is not my job. You are the optio in charge here. Get the job done." He turned away and folded his arms. Two incompetents, he thought, leading each other in circles.

This whole expedition was incompetent, Bard decided. If the operation had been well-planned, they would never have been caught unprepared by the sea's reaction to the rising of the moon. He shuddered, remembering how one of the gigantic waves rising unexpectedly from the polar sea had pitch-poled the comm Pedden. In one terrifying instant, the carrier had rolled stern over front. The lights went out and bits of the hull were ripped away. The crew had been hurled about like rag dolls, crashing into the comm equipment, the stools, and the sides of the tank. One of the operators had struck a console with so much force that it broke his neck. The other operator broke both arms and three ribs. When the Pedden finally righted itself, all communications had been lost.

"We're moving out, sir," called the driver in the forward compartment.

Optio Rand grunted in reply. The Pedden lifted off the ice and turned to take its position within the headquarters Century. It accelerated gently as the Century began to move, the driver careful not to apply too much thrust too soon. Sergeant Arsen was grateful that the driver was cautious; a sudden jump, and he would lose all the work he had done on the commlink.

Centurion Maximus Milton Harras shifted his DDP scan to extended range to cover the entire Cohort. The accuracy of range and bearing would be degraded in extended mode, but all the IFF signatures of the vehicles would appear on the screen. Let the combat units deal with the minor stuff; Harras was more interested in pushing the commanders. He watched as the Cohort formed an inverted vee and began its trek across the ice toward the exit point for Malthus. They assumed the same formation they had used to approach the pole, and Harras knew that it was standard policy to rotate the lead and trail units. He decided to make an exception in this case and keep the organization the same, rather than require the commanders to adjust to a new scheme. They had enough to deal with under the current situation.

The communications loss was what concerned him most. With the communications Pedden out of action, he had been unable to reach his headquarters on Rolandrin, and Harras had a feeling of impending doom. The TOG force at the pole was much larger than intelligence reports had led him to believe. In fact, the principle information supplied to him for this mission had suggested that the enemy outpost was nothing more than a weather station. Instead, they had encountered what looked like a garrison Legion. The Cohort was now saddled with thirty prisoners and was leaving behind a virtual junkyard of destroyed vehicles. And he couldn't report it to headquarters.

The DDP showed the Cohort streaming across the packed ice. Though the formation showed holes left by casualties from the fight at the pole, their fighting strength was not seriously damaged. The Scout Century was still at full strength, so at least there would be no gaps in the Cohort's screen. The Second Century was down one Viper, which had been left to guard the prisoners taken at the pole. That was another problem of the inaccurate intelligence. If the TOG installment had been a weather station, the few TOGs manning it would have been carried along as prisoners with the column. But thirty enemy soldiers was too many for Harras to drag along.

No communications, more prisoners than he wanted, more TOGs at the pole than he had been told about, and now the TOGs on Malthus probably knew of his planned attack. Harras thought there were too many questions for which he had no answers at the moment. Would the TOGs send a relief force? If they did, when would it leave Malthus? Should he expect to engage the enemy on the ice, at sea, on his arrival at Malthus? Lack of communications was not his only problem. Time was his enemy as well. Communications could be restored, that he did not doubt. With enough time and effort, they could repair at least one of the major commlinks, but by then the entire mission might be compromised. And that was another problem. If the mission *had* been compromised, Harras had no way of knowing if it were to a point where they would do better to cut and run. He hated the thought of abandoning the strike against TOG headquarters on Malthus. It was a good idea, and the enormous dividends certainly outweighed the costs, even if his Cohort were destroyed in the process. No, Harras decided. They would not turn back. They would keep on going, according to plan.

As the Scout Century cleared the edge of the polar escarpment and began its trek across the ice plain that separated it from the outer rock rim, the Wolverines rose to TTF altitude. Centurion MacDougall had no intention of allowing his light tanks to be caught in the water spouts. Tree-top flight made his units more vulnerable to detection and attack, but if they met the enemy on the ice plains, their vehicles would also be at tree-top altitude, so he didn't worry about the disadvantages. The Wolverines spread out across the front and flanks of Cohort Harras.

The LOSAT began to tumble as its orbit collapsed. The ground controllers had predicted the event when it had been deliberately sent off-course, and now they smiled at one another with smug I-told-you-so expressions. They had long ago stopped trying to explain the theory of rotational ballistics to high-ranking officers, because they couldn't or wouldn't understand. Those officers were also ignorant of the complications and costs of getting a LOSAT into orbit. No matter that the equipment was styled as "low cost satellites"; anytime an organization is operating on a limited budget, nothing is low cost. Now the controllers were going to lose a satellite for no good reason, which meant having to procure and launch another in its place. That would take time and money.

This petty bickering did not affect the satellite, of course. Having been nudged from its equatorial orbit to track across the southern pole, its useful life span had decreased. As it dropped lower and lower toward the thin upper edge of Caralis' atmosphere, it began to accelerate. The LOSAT's first passes over the pole had been at daily intervals; now it was crossing every four hours. But the increasingly frequent passes did not mean that it gave more accurate information about activity on the pole. As the satellite began to fall planetside, it also began to tumble. At first the surface handlers could control the oscillation of the viewing port. But as the wobble became more pronounced, it was obvious that the LOSAT did not have enough power on board for its handlers to control every pass.

The ground control decided to let it tumble, accepting whatever information it could send back. This would be the satellite's last useful pass over the pole. The control station fired off the remaining charges in the stabilizing thrusters and steadied the satellite for one last look at the polar cap. Its eye peered down through the windswept atmosphere at the tiny activity of mankind. Every six seconds it told its receiving station what it saw. It passed beyond the commlink horizon and began the automatic shutdown procedures for self-destruction, which would prevent the enemy from recovering anything of interest or use. By the time the LOSAT skipped across the outer edge of the atmosphere, it was an empty box. Minutes later it struck the atmosphere again, now at a steeper angle. This time it didn't bounce, but plowed straight in, reaching incandescence in seconds. Then it was gone.

Principes Rosco Warton lifted his eyes from the adventure magazine and watched the printout of the satellite scan slide out of the machine. He wasn't supposed to be reading civilian material on duty, but sitting at a printer all day was the pinnacle of boredom. He checked the code number that indicated which LOSAT had sent the information and stacked it with the appropriate file. The code printed across the bottom of the scan indicated that this was the satellite's termination scan. Warton felt no remorse for the loss of the satellite. Having served with the Commonwealth forces for almost twenty years, he had become inured to the destruction of expensive and valuable equipment. He had also been promoted to sergeant seven times and demoted to triarii the same number. Officers, especially those who read the scan prints and pontificated about their significance, were all dweebs. He had told them so a number of times; seven, to be exact.

Rosco noted that one stack of prints was coded Category A/Rush. So what? Every officer wanted his stuff first. He stacked the distribution packets and resisted the urge to put the Cat A/R packet on the bottom. When the duty messenger came by, he pointed to the Cat A/R on the top. He didn't tell the triarii to deliver it first, deciding he had done his job by pointing out the important packet. Then he went back to his magazine.

Legatus Mantelli Lartur, Operations Officer of the 2567th Renegade Legion, broke the seal on the Cat A/R distribution packet. He resisted the urge to snarl at the triarii who made him sign for the documents. The wad of prints was thick enough to indicate that they should have been distributed at least once earlier. Do not confuse the message with the messenger, he thought. This kid was just doing his job, but somewhere else in the Commonwealth bureaucracy on Caralis was a man who didn't care. Lartur knew that man would never be found, and would probably finish out his career with a commendation he would hang on the wall of his retirement home and show proudly to his friends.

Lartur spread the prints across his desk in chronological order and began to evaluate them. Some prints were a dead loss; they showed a clear, sharp picture of a broad expanse of stars. Others had been shot at such an oblique angle that it was hard even to tell where the satellite had been. He discarded the useless prints and re-sorted the rest. Some of them were quite good; he could even see on one the streaks of ions released by Marshman grav drives at full power. That would be Cohort Harras attacking the TOG installation at the pole. The battle showed quite a few footprints of TOG tracked vehicles, and Lartur's brow furrowed as he counted them. A lot more than he would have expected, given the official theory of a TOG weather station. Curiosity prompted him to reexamine the less-clear prints. Having discovered one unexpected thing, he wondered what else HQ might have missed.

Something caught his eye on one of the blurred prints showing the littoral south of Malthus. There, just on the edge, were what looked like the telltale streaks of grav drives. He slipped the print into a magnification panel and looked again. No doubt about it. The satellite had seen grav vehicles moving south from Malthus. He spread over his desk the prints generated before and after the one showing the drive tracks. The last one showed the same streaks, but this time they were short and sharp; the TOG vehicles had gone to ground. He counted the streaks, tracing their formation. More than sixty vehicles had grounded on the ice field in classic ambush formation.

The TOGs were on the ice cap in force.

Lartur hit the call button to Prefect Kenderson's office as he rose from his desk. He didn't wait for a reply, just opened the door and entered his commander's office.

* * *

Kenderson worked to stay calm. He tried to remember that these officers were not Renegades, but they should still feel some responsibility toward the Legion he had sent to the pole. "We have to do something," he said, emphasizing the "we."

"I understand the way you feel, Besta," replied Lieutenant Colonel Alban Tripp, Assistant Director of Commonwealth Operations, "but we've tried over and over to contact the Cohort, and we just can't raise it." He looked at Colonel Holcomb Daubish, Chief of Intelligence, for support.

Daubish nodded his head. "There's nothing we can do. Your Cohort is hanging out to dry, and we have no way of letting them know or of getting them back." He slumped in his chair and stared at the ceiling. He hated this, hated it with all the passion in his soul. He had begun his career in a Naram Special Forces Regiment, one of the few non-Naram ever admitted to those ranks. The driving precept of that unit, and all Naram units, had been that no one, under any circumstances, was ever left behind. It didn't matter what the risk, you always went back for your people, even if you were convinced they must be dead. No one was left behind. It was a kind of loyalty that could not be taught. It just happened.

Now, a Renegade Cohort was about to be slaughtered on an ice cap two thousand kilometers away, and Daubish raged at his inability to prevent it. His hands gripped the stylus he had been using, and slowly bent it double. The others in the room stared at his hands in amazement. The stylus was designed to be indestructible. Daubish, however, had a reputation for immense strength. These men had just seen it proved.

Tripp rubbed his jaw as he pondered aloud. "We don't even have a relief force available. And even if we did, they wouldn't do any good. They couldn't get to the cap before the Cohort hits the ambush."

"I could put one together," said Kenderson, hope coloring his voice.

"You haven't got the troops available, Prefect," stated Tripp flatly. "All you have is parts."

"You're right. But those parts could make a unit."

"They still wouldn't get to the cap in time."

"That's true," Kenderson agreed. "But if I know Harras, he won't get caught in the trap. A relief force will give him the materiel he needs to survive and break away. He'll go to ground and fight it out. The relief force will tip the balance in his favor."

"We've at least got to try," said Daubish, as he rocked his chair forward and landed with a bang. "NaBesta, put out the word in the 2567th. The unit has to launch in two hours. Take any one who volunteers. We'll organize it as we go."

Prefect NaBesta Kenderson rose to his feet and smiled grimly. "Done. I passed the word before I came to see you."

The organization was confused, at best. The force was more than a Century in strength, but less, much less, than a Cohort. Nine Liberator medium grav tanks, two Spartius infantry carriers, three Vipers, and a Wolverine had assembled. All the tanks were fully manned, but the five carriers had only half a squad each. Four optios had volunteered, but no officer was senior enough, or experienced enough, to take command. A search was instituted for a likely candidate from headquarters.

Optio Roglund Karstil dropped into the command hatch of the Liberator. The call for volunteers had not specified that they couldn't be on convalescent leave, so when they didn't ask, he didn't volunteer the information. Now he was back where he wanted to be, in the turret of a Liberator.

All over the cantonment area troops were running toward vehicles. Karstil took command of the two Liberators nearest his own and moved them closer together. He wanted to talk to the commanders as soon as possible and appoint one of the sergeants as his second in command. He didn't really care who was going to give him his orders; that would be determined soon enough. He wanted to know who was under his control.

The commlink crackled in the turret. "Abrasive Mandrake, Abrasive Mandrake. This is Abrasive Mandrake Five. Vector two-eight-double-zero. Prepare to move." Karstil noted the "Five" designator of the call sign. That meant that the executive office was still in control. Evidently no commander had yet appeared. He passed the order to his tanks and received affirmatives. They were on their way.

The approach to the ice cap would not be by stealth for this force, because there was no time to plot a path. The unit would form on the move, crossing the ocean at low-altitude flight. The extra height would permit the commander to herd his charges on the run, unaffected by weather. It would also allow the vehicles to reach their theoretical top speed of 900 kph. The force would vector in on the pole moving fast, arcing down from eight kilometers to strike at the landing zone. This high altitude, high angle of attack-approach would plunge the relief force straight into the combat, preventing some of the casualties typical of a conventional break-in. At least, that was the idea.

"Abrasive Mandrake, Abrasive Mandrake, this is Abrasive Mandrake Six. Maintain course. Break. I am in Spartius FERRAX REGAL four-four-two."

Karstil heard the "Six" designator and knew the commander had arrived. The voice was familiar, but he was too busy to place it at the moment. The name would come to him later. Ammunition and maintenance reports were still arriving from the other two tanks in his platoon. He was trying to take command on the move, and it demanded all his attention.

In the command Spartius, Centurion Maximus Alanton H. Freund wiggled himself unhappily into the command seat. Snatched from his safe position at Manus headquarters, here he was in command of a mob, headed toward some unknown destination, their mission to relieve a disaster.

19

1730, 10 Martius 6831—The giant moon of Rock Wall was hidden behind the bulk of the planet, but the vehicles of Cohort Harras were not taking any chances. Nobody could forget the instant ice columns that had devoured vehicles on the run in. Harras knew that it would be dangerous, if not impossible, to hold his formation at normal flight, so he ordered the vehicles to tree-top mode. The storm that had been howling over the ice cap since their arrival had died down and the clouds had passed. A hemisphere of sable pinpointed by silver stars now enclosed the surreal landscape of twisted ice and jagged rock. So intense was the dark that even the coils of the Marshman drives reflected a deep blue against the white of the ice below. The air was filled with the boom of grav drives straining to hurl tons of titanium, steel, and ceramic across the icescape.

Cohort Commander Harras could see most of his command from his hatch. The reflection of the stars and the grav drives provided just enough light for the leaden hulls of the tanks and infantry carriers to glow against the ebon sky. The aura of tranquility about the scene tugged at his heart; his world, if only for the moment, was at peace. Peace. The word echoed around inside his brain. For most of his adult life Harras had known only war or the prospect of war. Perhaps someday he would be able to turn his thoughts and talents to something else. He snapped his attention back to the ice cap. This was no time to be woolgathering.

Far ahead of the main force the scouts of Jamie MacDougall ranged. The six Wolverines spread their sensor net across the front of the formation, darting through the ice spires that had frozen in pinnacles above the wind-combed surface. Like a litter of happy terriers, the tanks investigated the domes and turrets, and then, seeming to lose interest in what had caught their attention, scurried away on some other private errand. MacDougall watched his brood on the command DDP, smiling at the apparent exuberance of their antics. Like Harras, he was mesmerized by the stillness, the grandeur, the sense of infinity about the landscape that lay before him. The passage of the arctic storm had left a purity and stillness that he was loathe to violate with machines of destruction. Also like Harras, he did not linger in such thoughts. He pulled himself up short; daydreams were not appropriate for a man hurtling over rugged terrain at 200 kph, entrusted with the welfare of hundreds of others.

"Unidentified activity. Range five-zero kilometers. Bearing six-two-hundred mils relative. Target stationary." The warning voice of the onboard computer murmured in MacDougall's ear at the same time an amber blip appeared on the upper limit of the screen.

MacDougall stared hard, willing the clouds obscuring the unknown object to be stripped away. He considered sending a recognition code to probe the mystery, but if it were hostile, it would be able to home in on his sensor. Too risky, he decided.

"Activity lost." The DDP sounded upset, but perhaps it was only his imagination. To anyone who spent enough time in a tank, the disembodied voice of the computer seemed to take on the personality of a sentient friend. Right now, the DDP voice sounded frustrated at losing the target. MacDougall had dealt with this voice for six years, and he had grown accustomed to her. (At some time in the far-distant past, the designers had decided that computer voices should be female. That decision had become the standard for all computers.) Their relationship had developed to the point that Jamie even imagined how she looked and what were her moods. She would definitely be annoyed at losing the target.

"Tha's a-right, lassie," he said softly to the DDP. "You'll find it soon enough again. 'Tis no trouble." False readings appeared from time to time, and they usually turned out to be ghosts. But he felt the hairs on the back of his neck rise, and he knew this blip was trouble. He was tempted to notify the Cohort commander, but what would he say, that he had some kind of premonition? Better to get additional information. He pointed the nose of the Wolverine toward the ghost and accelerated.

"Unidentified activity. Range five-zero kilometers. Bearing nine-five mils relative. Target stationary." MacDougall waited. He was aimed directly at the place the DDP had identified as the location of the first ghost, so the bearing should still be centered or left of forward if the "unidentified activity" was moving. This new target was to the right of center. He waited. "Activity lost," the DDP said once more.

Well to the right of the Wolverine, MacDougall saw the ice break away in a boiling mass of snow and spume. Even from the other side of the planet, Rock Wall had enough gravitational pull to disturb the substrata. MacDougall wanted to believe the ghosts were the boiling mass; it would be a satisfying explanation, if not a comfortable one. He slowed his Wolverine and allowed the rest of his unit to roll past.

Legatus Cariolanus Camus scanned the dormant DDP in search of the approaching enemy. If the initial intelligence reports were correct, the center of the Renegade force would fly right into the waiting arms of the ambush. Because the DDP was not actively searching, but merely waiting to receive the signal of any activity, it would take a significant electronic pulse to activate the screen. But sooner or later the enemy would arrive, and the DDP would tell him once they entered long-range detection. He leaned back in the command seat, pressing the small of his back into the lumbar support.

Only a faint green glow on the DDP revealed the vehicles of his Cohort, the slight bleed-off of energy from the power plants clearly visible on the screen. He could see the base of the ambush as well as the reserve vehicles that would provide the assault force once the trap was sprung. He thought there should be more vehicles on the right arm. They must be hidden by intervening terrain or else their drives were running cooler than usual. The storm that had raged when they reached the cap had abated, the howl and buffet replaced by an almost deathlike stillness. Camus tapped the side of the fighting compartment to maintain a sense of reality.

A soft bell tone sounded in his helmet, followed almost immediately by the voice of the DDP. "Many targets. Range five-five kilometers. Bearing six-three-hundred mils to one hundred mils. Closing. Estimated speed two hundred plus. Estimated time to engagement one-five minutes." Camus glanced at the DDP and saw multiple symbols coalescing and spreading across the top of his screen. In time the images would solidify, but for now it was enough. He blew softly into the commlink. If his vehicles were on listening silence, and they had better be, that soft, rushing sound would alert them.

More images grew on the screen behind the first line. Camus watched them stream down the display. They were close together, much closer than he could have hoped. Perhaps the Commonwealth commander was so confident that he hadn't bothered to spread his force into a battle formation. Either that, or he was planning to use the Cohort like a phalanx, counting on weight and speed to overwhelm the ambushers and break out before they could close the trap. Self-doubt suddenly soured the legatus' stomach. With an observer from planetary command staff in his headquarters Century, it would be better not to fail. The reserve force should be called up at once. He decided to transmit the change in plan immediately. If he waited too long, the enemy forces might be able to pinpoint the transmissions. He spoke into the lip mike.

"Single target; hostile commlink transmission. Range five-zero kilometers. Bearing five-zero relative. Stationary." Perhaps, thought MacDougall, the ghosts had been real after all. This was probably a stray from the fight at the pole, escaping toward the coast and safety. He switched the DDP information-transmit switch to the "Download" position and rebroadcast the target-acquisition intelligence to the other commanders of the Cohort. He added his evaluation to the end of the transmission, then, without further delay, sounded "tallyho" to his troops and accelerated. The chase, for what it was worth, was on.

The other Wolverines heard the call and followed their leaders toward the distant mark on their screens. They were hounds hunting an injured fox across a treeless expanse. "Spotless Poacher, Spotless Poacher, this is Poacher Six. Pin with the left and sweep with the right. Poacher Six will mark and pin. Normal flight at twenty klicks." MacDougall broadcast his tactical plan and waited for the other units to roger. "This is Spotless Poacher Six. Execute."

"Target identified. Horatius tank. Range four-zero kilometers. Bearing six-three-five-zero. Vehicle stationary and transmitting." A fat target, thought MacDougall. A lone Horatius was a significant event for a Wolverine, but this would be like dogs baiting a bear. With any luck, most of his scouts would be able to close with their 100mm cannon and tear the Horatius apart before it could get off more than a few shots. It would call for all the tactical skill the centurion could muster, but MacDougall was ready for the challenge. He checked for the Liberators of the First Century closing from behind. If his troops couldn't handle the target, the First Century could. They were close enough behind. With luck, the Horatius would become completely involved with the scouts while the mediums crept up on him.

Legatus Cariolanus Camus watched his DDP in amazement. The Commonwealth force had turned directly toward his vehicle and was coming straight in. This was better than he had hoped. The entire unit would be within the arms of the trap when it closed. He practically bounced up and down in the command seat. He stared at the DDP, wiping his moist palms on his trouser legs in anticipation. Come on, he thought. Just a little closer, a little closer. The lead Commonwealth vehicles were still closing. The DDP identified them as Wolverines. Target identifiers continued to spread across the top of the screen. He had the entire Cohort. His field of vision narrowed until he saw only the tiny red squares hurtling down the screen toward his position. At the top of the screen, unnoticed by the TOG commander, the flanking Centuries of Cohort Harras were well down the display. Unlike the scouts rushing forward, the flanks were well spread out in their vics, echeloned almost to the outer arms of the ambush site.

* * *

Honor Ross felt her Viper turn slightly to the left as Blackstone twisted the light carrier to avoid an immense ice cone. He had been letting the infantry vehicle drift lower and lower as the calls from Spotless Poacher had come over the auxiliary commlink. Their vehicle, like the others, was on listening silence, and so the receiving computer constantly scanned the frequencies for traffic. Ross heard MacDougall make the first contact and felt the Viper begin to sink as the possibility of contact neared. She let her driver do as he liked. Blackstone was good, and she preferred not to interfere unless he strayed too far from the rest of the Century.

The DDP in the Viper flashed red across the entire screen; the alarm klaxon exploded in her ear. "Horatius tank. Range five-zero meters. Bearing three-three-double-zero mils. Stationary." Ross blinked. Surely the information was wrong. The Horatius should be at the opposite bearing and at a much greater range. The DDP said it was to the rear and within 100 meters. "Blackstone. About turn. Get low and find that contact."

20

1900, 10 Martius 6831—"On the way. Hope it's wrong." The Viper slewed around to the left in a gut-wrenching turn that threw the crew and the surprised infantry against the unyielding sides of the hull.

"Horatius tank," came the call from the DDP as the Viper turned. "Range one hundred meters. Bearing five-eight-hundred, increasing. Moving." Ross didn't wait. She believed the DDP. Toggling the infantry deployment switch, she felt the peds blow from their cocoons. The next instant she opened a comm channel to all units within the Cohort. "Glassy Relic. Glassy Relic. Ambush. Ambush. Ambush. This is Glassy Relic Three-three-three. Ambush. Ambush. Ambush."

The Viper carrier was lucky. When it passed over the grounded Horatius, the TOG commander was as surprised as the Renegade squad leader. The tanker was lying in his blasted hole, his main gun just above the rim of the crater. The fixed main gun was unable to bear on the carrier as it screamed overhead, and by the time the turret began to rotate, the Viper was in a tight turn away from the Horatius. Without waiting for the painting laser to decipher the flicker shields, the TOG gunner fired the 3/6 laser. The stern shields of the Viper took the full force of the hit, becoming bathed in shattered light. An APDS round from the 50mm cannon hit square on the carrier's stern, blasting the auxiliary power-supply condenser from its mount. Then the Viper was around and closing.

The enemy infantry tumbled from the open doors almost on top of the grounded tank. Suddenly the TOG commander had too many things to do, too many options. He had no orders to fire on the enemy. To the contrary, he had been emphatically warned that weapons control was tight. No one was to fire without permission. He had also been told to engage the Commonwealth Liberators as the priority target. Now he had violated both directives. He had a moment's desire to reverse time, gain a chance to redo the last few minutes of his life.

With a Viper carrier about to cross the stern of his Horatius, infantry dropping to the ground around him, and Liberator tanks all over his DDP, he needed to notify his commander of the situation. Then he saw the TVLG launchers on the Viper's bow enveloped in the telltale blast signature of a launch. He froze.

Infantry section leaders Grold and Boost had their people on their feet the instant they hit the ice. The first men out brought their painting lasers to their shoulders and fired. With the painting laser from the Viper helping to decode the flicker shields, there was virtually no chance they would fail to decipher the code. They didn't.

Without waiting to hear that the rear shields of the now-rising Horatius had been decoded, Ross triggered a pair of TVLGs from the racks and followed with a HEAP round from the turret-mounted 25mm cannon. The squad loosed two TVLGs as well, one from each section. The Vulcan antimissile system sensed the threat in the air and spun to engage. It didn't make it. Whether it was because the turret had been traversed in the opposite direction, or because the system paused with the tank commander, or because it was too cold to operate efficiently on such short notice, became academic. All four TVLGs slammed into the stern of the Horatius.

The rear armor absorbed the TVLG damage, but the 25mm HEAP round found one of the holes blasted by a missile. It burrowed into the armor, burned through the ballistic protection, and smashed into the thrust controls. The Horatius, its thrusters at full power, spewed incandescent flame into the darkness. The tank staggered, swung sideways, then continued to rise. Before the TOG commander could retaliate, the Viper and the infantry squad fired again.

As the Horatius began to swing away from Ross' grounded Viper, she knew she only had one chance to strike a killing blow. Ross fired an SMLM at the stern, and hoped for some help from the 25mm Gauss cannon, which was just better than useless against the TOG medium tank. Even firing HEAP, the Viper's best penetration, the cannon would need to land at least three hits against the same location before doing any real damage. Millicent Connor kept the Gauss' firing pedal depressed and let the tiny cannon hose down any exposed surface. The squad's TVLGs struck again.

The aft end of the Horatius was gouged by the impact of the missiles. Huge slabs of titanium armor blew away from the battered stern, scything toward the infantry, who scattered from the path of the flying metal. The SMLM would have destroyed the back-up thrusters as well as the stern shields, but the missile never struck. The Vulcan antimissile system had finally responded to the threat and engaged the incoming projectile at the last moment. The missile exploded like a giant marigold against the night sky. The Horatius settled on the edge of the crater facing the Viper.

The squad, its TVLGs expended, paused for a moment in grim anticipation. Then training and desperation took control. Alcyone and Grain of Grold's section raced for the Viper's open infantry bays for more ammunition while Grold and the members of Boost's section charged the grounded vehicle. The anti-personnel laser on the turret of the crippled Horatius sensed both movements. For some reason, the ballistic computer evaluated the running men as the greater threat and fired on them as they reached the protective shroud of the Viper. Grain made a final, successful leap for sanctuary; Paulus Alcyone was not fast enough.

The AP laser struck him cleanly on the back of his combat helmet. In a microsecond, the aligned light burned through the plastic laminate, vaporizing his brain. The man's body crumpled, the upper portion hissing as it struck the snow. Grain pulled three more TVLGs from the internal storage racks and turned back toward the rest of the squad. He did not stop to consider that the AP laser might be waiting for him. But it had turned on the squad moving toward the shattered stern of the tank and was engaging that threat. Grain slipped easily from under the carrier's shroud and crossed the snow in a single, powered leap.

The main gun, centered in the lower hull of the 273-ton Horatius, was pointed directly at the vulnerable infantry carrier. The TOG tanker lost no more time in making multiple decisions. He had notified his commander, been given permission to fire. The 150mm Gauss cannon flashed death.

The HEAP round struck the Viper opposite the targeting computer on the front of the turret. As the explosive charge ripped into the glacis, the entire vehicle was bathed in flying shards of titanium and ballistic protection. The force of the explosion slammed the carrier backward with such force that Ross and Connor were thrown from their seats and the turret spun like a top. Even with the hatch closed, Blackstone, crouched in the hull below the commlink station, felt the suction of the shell's burst. He threw the Viper into full reverse, hoping that the next shot would catch the tank's front rather than the turret. The heavy TOG cannon tracked the ruptured turret.

Grold and Boost had reached the stern of the Horatius, and huddled there under the dubious protection of the crumpled armor. They were too close to risk firing into the dangling shards of the stern, but backing up to acceptable firing range would give the AP laser a clear shot. It hunted for them like a nanny relentlessly rounding up some recalcitrant brood. Grain reached the squad with the TVLGs.

When the Horatius' main gun cracked the clear night again, Blackstone juked the Viper sideways. He was almost good enough to dodge the hit, but not quite. He was, however, good enough to catch the shot on an undamaged portion of the turret, so that the main force of the explosion dissipated on already damaged equipment. The right side of the turret glowed and sparked, a shattered wreck of electronics. The 25mm cannon was out of action, one trunnion sheared completely away and the muzzle sagging across the upper plates.

From the rear of the Horatius, Infantry Section Leader Principes Massai Boost saw the imminent destruction of his vehicle. He was momentarily stunned into immobility by the ferocity of the combat he had just witnessed, but his training quickly took over. Gently he pried the three TVLG launchers from Grain's clenched arms and stepped away from the stern of the Horatius.

Turning his back on the grounded tank, he took five steps, counting each one. Five paces was the minimum arming range for the TVLG. Reaching the designated distance, he turned to face his adversary. The AP laser sensed his presence and fired. The first shaft of energy passed by his shoulder, striking the ice in an explosion of ice and steam some twenty-five meters away. Boost raised the first TVLG to his shoulder and fired. The missile sprang from its launch tube and buried itself in the battered wreck. There was no explosion.

The enemy AP laser fired again.

Had Boost been erect, in position to fire the second TVLG, the beam of energy would have caught him full in the chest. Because he was bending down to arm the second missile, the bolt of light only creased the back of his armored suit, splitting the protection from nape to buttocks and inflicting deep burns on his dark skin. He brought the second missile to his shoulder and fired. The TVLG leaped from its tube and buried itself, the rocket motor still burning, in the hull of the Horatius. The members of the squad, still huddled around the crater, suddenly realized what was happening and bolted away from the intended target.

Some technician at the TVLG assembly plant that produced these missiles had decided that the four and a half meters represented by five paces was not a great enough safety margin to protect the person firing the missile. He had reset the fuse mechanism for a slightly longer range. This alteration was not a significant difference in a missile designed to fire at ranges of up to twelve hundred meters, but for men in close combat, that minute adjustment could mean life or death.

Massai Boost reached for the last TVLG with his left hand. The AP laser caught him, attracted by the flash of the armored glove. The hand took the force of the energy. One moment the hand was there, a living extension of the arm and the man. The next instant it was gone. It vaporized, leaving the wrist cauterized by the laser.

Without missing a beat, Boost brought his right hand down on the arming loop and pulled it free. He lifted the tube, turned his back on the grounded tank, and took three more steps. His eyes filled with pain and he stumbled over an ice shard in his path. He dropped to his knees.

Steadying the launch tube with his left arm, he swung his body toward his adversary and depressed the firing switch. The AP laser fired with the blast of the launcher. Section Leader Principes Massai Boost never knew if the third TVLG hit its target. For the AP laser, the third time was a charm. The bounce-infantry combat suit was designed to withstand extensive damage, but not to take a full laser blast at pointblank range. The laser burned through the center of the laminate cuirass, exploding lungs, heart, and spine. The legionnaire's body collapsed hissing into the snow.

The last TVLG buried itself in the shattered stern of the Horatius tank. The officious technician had recalculated the safe arming distance as ten meters. From the rear of the tank to the front of the tube was just under that distance. But the existing damage to the stern had extended the range from launch to impact to just greater than that distance. The TVLG slammed into the rendered stern and ignited. The force of the blast propelled the two dormant missiles into the fighting compartment where they, having reached their arming point, exploded as well.

A horizontal sheet of flame sprang from the lower hull of the TOG tank. Titanium will burn if its molecules are sufficiently excited. The titanium protecting the Horatius vaporized. The infantrymen, face down in the snow, face plates lowered, their eyes crimped tight, still saw the light from the blast. The concussion wave struck an instant later, lifting them from the ice and hurling them almost a hundred meters before they stopped bouncing. Darkness descended again.

In the center of the ambush site, Cohort Harras was fighting for its life. Sergeant Ross had sounded the warning just in time, and instinct and training overcame the initial surprise. In fact, the Renegades fired the first shots in the battle. MacDougall immediately grasped what had happened and ordered the Wolverines to break left. Copan's First Century, following close behind, broke to the right. The other Centuries, depending on how badly they had been entangled in the arms of the ambush, either fought lonely actions like that of Ross' platoon, or sliced through the sides and away.

Harras committed the Headquarters to cover the withdrawal of those too deeply enmeshed in the center of the killing zone to break out. The Catapult, its low thrust proving to be as much a liability as Harras had feared, could not be extracted. With regret, the Cohort commander sent it forward into a maelstrom of fire. It grounded, missiles arcing over its flaming hull, firing its 200mm cannon at any TOG vehicle foolish enough to expose itself to the crew's fury.

The survivors scattered across the ice. Harras called his fragmented force together on the run, heading toward the pole to regroup and reorganize. There was no convenient place short of the center of the ice cap to sort out the pieces. The dispersed legionnaires vectored on the pole, applied full power, and fled.

Legatus Cariolanus Camus surveyed the burning wrecks dotting the ice field ahead. The ambush had not been the overwhelming success he had anticipated, and he wasn't quite sure who to blame. The Commonwealth forces had broken through the arms of the ambush in several places, and the vehicles that should have been defending those locations had never answered his call. Investigation revealed that the vehicles had vanished. Perhaps they had fled toward Malthus at the first opportunity. He should have detected their desertion. In any case, the names of the missing crews would be posted as cowards; their families would suffer for their failure.

Damage reports streamed into his headquarters. Prefect Claudius Sulla stood in white-faced silence as the assessments were made. It was strange, thought Camus, that this man who was supposed to be watching everything, commenting on everything, said nothing. Perhaps he was just awaiting his moment. Camus shrugged it off. He had too much to do to worry about the odd behavior of a headquarters stooge. Fifteen minutes after the last report was logged, Camus formed the Cohort and began pursuing the remnants of the Commonwealth force.

21

0130, 11 Martius 6831—First Century and the scouts had taken the brunt of the fighting in the ambush. MacDougall brought back only one of the Wolverines he commanded besides his own. Copan's First Century totaled one Liberator and the administrative Pedden; the Century commander had died almost as soon as the battle began. The Second Century, Optio Holden Ventis commanding, was down to three Liberator tanks, his command Spartius, and a Viper, plus the administrative vehicle. The Pedden was heavily damaged but still mobile. In the final break through the TOG lines, the Pedden's commander had stopped to pick up the remnants of an infantry squad and the driver of a destroyed Wolverine.

The Third and Fourth Centuries were not in much better shape. Only six Liberators and three Vipers had escaped the debacle, enough to form one full-strength Century. All the administrative equipment from those two Centuries had been lost. Harras' Headquarters Century had made it out with the fewest losses. The Catapult had been destroyed, but the Remus engineer vehicle was only slightly damaged, as were the medical vehicle and the crippled communications vehicle. Things might have been worse, but Harras wasn't sure how.

The real difficulty, as far as the Cohort commander was concerned, was the lack of command and control personnel. The Cohort had begun the mission short of officers, and fighting their way out of the ambush had reduced that minimal strength even more. Centurion Uxmail Copan, the Naram commander of the First Century, had died in the ambush. Ventis, the junior optio commanding the Second Century, had survived with a slight wound. Fagan Walker, a senior optio and commander of the Third Century, had survived, as had his very junior optio. The Fourth Century had lost all its officers and the senior sergeants in the headquarters section.

The Headquarters Century was in the best shape. Centurion Sedden Matruh, the headquarters commander, still had his Viper available with its full complement of troops, although they were not experienced combat peds. The Cohort staff vehicle had also survived, a Pedden commanded by Centurion Moldine Rinter, the operations officer, assisted by Aktol Graviston, senior sergeant of Cohort Harras. Both were dependable officers. Rinter had been with the Cohort since its inception, and Harras both liked and trusted her. She had not held a command for quite some time, because her administrative talents were so great that no commander was willing to spare her for combat duties.

The new organization for the depleted Cohort slowly took shape as the survivors rallied at the pole. The First Century was eliminated because too few vehicles were left from its original organization to rebuild it. The Second Century retained the three Liberators, the Spartius, and the Viper with which it had escaped the ambush, and Ventis remained in command. Fagan Walker's Third Century also maintained its structure with four Liberators and a badly damaged Viper. The Fourth Century was cobbled together from parts of the old Fourth and the remnants of the First, three Liberators and two Vipers. The Fourth was given to Optio Rand, of the useless communications section, to command. A new Century, designated the Reserve Force, was established under Centurion Rinter. She would command the remaining two Wolverines of the scout section with MacDougall in charge, the engineer Remus, and two Peddens, which would act as battlefield taxis for the headquarters peds. Centurion Matruh's Viper and two Peddens would serve as the Cohort headquarters as well as the last reserve unit.

Harras was satisfied with the organization. He hated to give up Rinter's advice to combat command, but she had earned the right to her own Century. If the Cohort had to go down fighting, and there was every indication that it would, she deserved to go out as part of a combat unit. After all, she was only as far away as the commlink, and he could reach her if he needed to. The only part of the reorganization that worried him was that he was forced to put the officer Bard in command of the communications section. The section was basically useless, at least for the present, but the man would also serve as Matruh's deputy. Bard had not inspired much confidence, even though he talked like he knew what he was doing and had a good grasp of the operation. But Harras couldn't shake the sense that something about the man was not on the level. Whatever the problem was, however, he hoped it could wait. It would have to.

The three combat Centuries set up in a loose circle around the pole, surrounding the Reserve Force and the headquarters. Harras placed his own Liberator in the center. Then they settled down to await the arrival of the TOG forces. They didn't have to wait long.

The Renegade and TOG positions were reversed. Now the Renegades were laagered in, their equipment shut down and all but invisible. The TOG Cohort, on the other hand, was well-illuminated by its own drives, distinct targets to the watching DDPs. The approaching TOG forces appeared on the Renegade screens at fifty kilometers. The defenders waited.

Holden Ventis saw the TOGs approaching on the DDP of his Spartius command carrier. His infantry had deployed right and left of the vehicle, well away from the hull so that if the tank took a catastrophic hit, the infantry would not be destroyed. The lead infantry section was more than two kilometers forward, in place to paint any oncoming TOG vehicle well before it could engage the hull-down Spartius with anything but lasers or the heaviest Gauss cannon. The Spartius' twin 5/6, turret-mounted lasers would savage even the heaviest tank before it could get off an effective shot. That was the plan.

Holden was worried about the two men in the forward post. He didn't know either of them. Kallach, the squad leader in the Spartius, had vouched for them, but Kallach didn't know them that well either. So the optio had been forced to send two men he didn't know but had to trust forward to occupy the most important position in the Century. Now they were two thousand meters away in the cold and dark, facing the onslaught of the TOG attack.

The Century was deployed in a ragged line. Hull-down in craters, two Liberators were on the left, followed by the Spartius with Ventis. The third tank was on the right. The Viper, the weakest vehicle in the command, was positioned on the far right and slightly to the rear of the line of medium tanks. The Viper's infantry were also deployed well away from their vehicle, scattered in two-man positions around the Viper and the Liberator on the right.

"Target identified. Horatius tank. Range four-five-zero-double-zero. Bearing six-two-double-zero. Speed one-eight-zero. Target closing." Ventis felt the turret shift slightly as Tim Rollus laid the twin lasers on the approaching target in response to the DDP's information. Holden knew that the tanks on the left would probably take out the enemy long before the Spartius' lasers would engage, but he didn't bother to tell Rollus. Targeting incoming enemies would keep the young gunner busy and his mind off his nervousness.

"Multiple targets identified. Horatius tanks. Range three-five-zero-double-zero. Bearing six-two-double-zero across one-double-zero. Speed one-eight-zero. Targets closing." Ventis watched the display. Multiple blips appeared at the top of the screen and streaked down toward his position. To the right and left he could see other target indicators, but they were out of his arc of opportunity; let the Third Century deal with them. More red squares were appearing behind the Horatius tanks, and the computer identified them as Romulus infantry carriers.

The Romulus was a brute of a vehicle. Designed as support for TOG infantry breaking into Commonwealth defenses, the armor had been boosted to impressive levels. The turret and front armor were heavier than that on the Horatius tanks accompanying them, and a high flicker-shield rate made the Romulus impervious to most missile and laser shots. One of the reasons Ventis had positioned his infantry so far forward was to attempt to decipher those shields at extreme ranges.

"Multiple targets identified. Horatius tanks. Range two-five-zero-double-zero. Bearing six-two-double-zero across one-double-zero. Speed one-eight-zero. Targets closing." Ventis often felt the waiting was the worst part of any battle. The DDP constantly updated the enemy's position, and the defenders just had to sit tight. Ventis sometimes wished the sensors were not quite so good; too much information only made the anticipation worse. He wondered if they would be better off not knowing what was coming. He scanned the DDP for his other vehicles. With the drives shut down and all other systems passive, the blue squares indicating friendlies were only blurs, even at close range.

The tank to his left was a scant five hundred meters away, the next one the same distance beyond, but with their IFF transponders shut down, they were almost invisible. The red squares kept coming, almost as though they were unaware of the Renegade positions. "Multiple targets. Horatius tanks and Romulus carriers. Range one-five-zero-double-zero. Bearing six-three-double-zero across zero-five-zero. Speed one-two-zero. Targets closing." The TOGs were slowing down now, searching for the Renegades. On the far left, in the Third Century's sector, the enemy tanks were almost within range. I wish that were me, thought Ventis. At least the waiting would be over.

"Glassy Relic. Glassy Relic. This is Glassy Relic Three-six. Engaging." Against the raven sky of the polar night, 150mm Gauss cannons flamed in golden halos above the hidden Liberators, the sharp crack of the shots ringing against the snow and rock.

"Glassy Relic Six. This is Glassy Relic Three-six. Am engaging multiple targets. Many burning. We have close action."

Ventis listened to the disembodied, dispassionate voice of Fagan Walker on the commlink. The commander of the Third Century sounded in total control of the situation, unflustered and unhurried. He watched the DDP showing the outer limits of the Third Century's positions. Even as he watched, the red indicator of a Horatius blinked out, appearing on the DDP as a broken square. The sky to Ventis' left was a dancing blaze, the cannon-shot reports beating like slow drums. More red squares showed broken. The sky stopped flickering and began to glow, a borealis of leaping light.

"Multiple targets identified. Horatius tanks. Range one-five-zero-double-zero. Bearing six-three-double-zero across one-five-zero. Speed two-four-zero. Targets moving left."

Ventis had been almost mesmerized by the light of the battle and the soft, repeating voice of the DDP, but the new information from the DDP jerked him back to his own situation. The TOG forces to his front were accelerating, swinging toward the fight in front of the Third Century. They were pivoting on their own right, allowing the flanking units to cross almost directly over the hidden Second Century.

"Multiple targets identified. Romulus carriers. Range five-zero-double-zero. Bearing six-one-double-zero across one-five-zero. Speed two-four-zero. Targets moving left." The Romulus infantry carriers continued moving left, crossing closer and closer to the Second Century. TOG was planning to strike at the Third Century on what they thought was an open flank.

"Multiple targets identified. Romulus carriers. Range five-zero-double-zero. Bearing six-one-double-zero across one-five-zero. Speed two-four-zero. Targets moving left." In just moments, the TOG vehicles would be within range of the Second Century. Ventis would make his tanks hold off a little longer, just until the TOGs were fully committed to the attack. Then they would savage the TOGs with flanking fire. With the sensors still passive, there were no target locks, but that could wait. He was ignoring the voice of the DDP now, watching the red squares cross the stadia lines on the screen. Almost. Almost. Almost. He toggled the active sensor switch.

"Multiple targets identified. Romulus carriers. Range three-zero-double-zero. Bearing six-one-double-zero across one-five-zero. Speed two-four-zero. Targets moving left. Romulus locked." A blinking red square indicated the target the DDP had chosen. Blue squares bloomed to the right and left as the Liberators fired up their power plants.

"Glassy Relic. Glassy Relic. This is Glassy Relic Two-six. Engaging." Ventis switched to the Century frequency. "Glassy Relic Three. This is Glassy Relic Three-six. Fire at targets of opportunity."

"Target identified. Romulus carrier. Range two-five-double-zero. Bearing six-one-double-zero. Speed two-four-zero. Target moving left. Lock achieved." The turret hummed as it traversed to find the carrier. Ventis could hear Rollus' heavy breathing in the intercom.

"Steady, gunner, steady. Wait for the paint."

"Yessir."

Ventis felt his stomach churn. The infantry in the forward observation post should have a target by now, but there had been no indication they were even alive. "Target identified. Romulus carrier. Range two-four-double-zero. Bearing six-one-double-zero. Speed two-four-zero. Lock achieved. Target painted." They had him.

"Gunner. Hit the Romulus carrier at two-four hundred with the laser."

"Identified."

"Fire."

"On the way."

Ventis felt, rather than heard, the high scream of the twin lasers as aligned light sliced toward the target. He looked up from the DDP in time to see a distant glow as the energy struck the side of the enemy carrier two kilometers away. The side of the hull glowed briefly then vanished. It was no use looking for the enemy, he was invisible in the gloom.

"Lasers recharged." Rollus notified him that he was ready to fire again.

"Hit the carrier again."

"Target identified, locked, and painted."

"Fire." The lasers cut through the blackness once again.

Ventis looked up from the DDP to see bright spots appear in the dark ahead of him, and saw two fiery trails as TVLGs launched. The infantry positions, two kilometers ahead of the carrier, had fired, well within range of the TOG machines sweeping down on them. The Vulcan antimissile system on the Romulus knocked one down, but the other TVLG burst full on the turret.

The warning klaxon ripped through the calm of the turret, telling Ventis that his vehicle had been painted. He looked back at the DDP and saw that his adversary had traversed his turret to lay on the command Spartius. He knew his crew could do nothing to avoid the shot, so he leaned forward against the padding above the DDP and waited for the laser to hit. He wasn't worried, the shot wouldn't penetrate on the first hit. The Spartius had enough armor to stop an initial laser hit, but anything more would cause serious trouble.

"Lasers recharged."

"Hit the carrier."

"Target locked and painted."

"Fire."

The turret filled with the sticky-sweet smell of vaporizing ballistic protection. Ventis jerked back in his seat, his eyes searching for the telltale blister on the tank's interior that would show where the laser had struck. The center of the headrest over the DDP was smoldering. He felt sick to his stomach. He leaned away from the charred mark, as though to escape the realization of how close he had been to his death.

"Lasers recharged."

"Just shoot!" Rollus was clinging to the by-the-book firing commands for the twin lasers, using the routine to stay calm, but Ventis didn't care anymore. He wanted the gunner to shoot and keep shooting. To hit and keep hitting. He pressed the treadle for the painting laser so hard that the bar began to bend under the force. "Just shoot!" he shouted.

"Target destroyed."

"Keep shooting!"

"The target's destroyed, sir."

"What?"

"We got it, sir. It blew up."

Ventis looked out over the coaming of the command hatch. Two kilometers away a Romulus infantry carrier was spouting flame. An expanding circle of snow around the burning vehicle glowed blood-red. He looked back down at the DDP. Broken red squares littered the screen within the stadia lines. Across the top other red squares fled upward and out of range.

"Glassy Relic Three. This is Glassy Relic Three-six. Cease Fire. Report status."

The other vehicles of his Century reported no casualties. The Third Century had also escaped death; Ventis heard that report just before giving his own. He sank back in the command chair and stared at the charred smudge on the padding in front of him.

22

0730, 11 Martius 6831—His Imperial Majesty's Ship *Gradior* broke out of tachyon space, the dimension that allowed faster-than-light travel, well short of Caralis because the captain had fudged the coordinates just to be on the safe side. Breaking out over a contested planet was extremely dangerous. If the Commonwealth had fighters up, or if a battle was taking place, the heavy transport ship would wallow like a fat pig in a slaughter pen. She was armed well enough to defend herself against most fighter squadrons, but a capital ship of any size would rip the *Gradior* apart. And so the captain had chosen to fall a bit short. He could always blame the helmsman if anyone ever criticized the deviation from the set coordinates.

The *Gradior* was far enough away from the planet on the TOG side to keep from startling any Commonwealth units in the area. A startled Commonwealth pilot was a dangerous Commonwealth pilot, the skipper always said. Never mind the garbage fed to the civilian populace of TOG, the enemy pilots were no slouches at fighting. The sky over the planet was clear, however, and the captain let his ship coast toward the distant speck that was Caralis. As the ship orbited the planet's southern rim, the sensors picked up signs of activity on the surface.

In the command center for the combat unit that *Gradior* was delivering to its new assignment, Commander Legatus Maximus Rocipian Olioarchus of the 356th Penal Auxilia listened to the communications traffic on the planet. A fight was in progress near the south pole, and the reports indicated the TOG forces were not doing well. He turned to the hololink that had been established planetside and switched it on. It crackled once, hissed light, and then the figure of Planetary Commander Brigadier General Drusus Arcadius glowed to life. Olioarchus stood at stiff attention.

"With all due respect, Your Excellency," began the regimental commander, "I beg to report the arrival of the 356th Penal Auxilia at the Caralis combat zone. The 356th is prepared to undertake any mission you wish."

The tiny hologram stared at the regimental commander standing rigidly under the brilliant light of the flouropanels. "It is unusual for a regiment to report directly to the planetary commander. I appreciate the opportunity to see you so promptly." Arcadius had the feeling that this new Auxilia commander wanted something more than just to pay his respects. He waved at the commander to continue.

"As a newly reorganized Penal Auxilia, the 356th requests permission to be inserted into the conflict at the first possible moment."

"I understand that the regiment has just returned to full strength, and that you are its new commander," said Arcadius thoughtfully. He was stalling, trying to determine what this new man wanted and what he could already know. His forces were losing the fight at the pole; perhaps Olioarchus had intercepted that comm traffic. The legatus maximus probably wanted to be sent into that fight. Arcadius hated penal regiments. They were made up of the scum of the galaxy, and they had those awful Ssoran guards. Those semireptiles made his skin crawl. The pole might be just the place for them. "I have no mission for you at present, Legatus Maximus. I will deal with your request as soon as your transport reaches a suitable launch point."

"I am honored, Your Excellency."

"As you should be." The hologram flickered out.

Larry Stone watched the last of the TOG vehicles lift from the ice and vanish into the darkness. The horizon had sparkled with combat for several minutes, then fallen silent once again except for the crackle and pop of burning equipment. The flaring light slowly died away. When the ice was dark again, the remaining TOG vehicles rose and ghosted away in the gloom. Creeping down from the jutting rock where he had lain and watched the destruction, Stone joined his Baufrin friend beside the grav sled.

"My friend," said the Baufrin, "you look gravely worried. I think that what you have seen has not pleased you."

"Not much. It looks like the disaster we came to prevent happened anyway."

"That is quite distressing news. I do not suppose that our continued presence in this terrible place can be of any use."

"Maybe you don't," snorted Stone, "but I'm not going back until I get what I came for. There's the little matter of a spy I have to deal with." Stone began to load the remnants of their meager supplies onto the sled. "If that little bastard is still with the Cohort—which I don't doubt—I need to reach the troops if only to blow him away."

"This attitude is understandable, if slightly manic. Yet I believe there might be a more reasonable approach to the difficulty than merely barging in and killing the spy."

"Really?" Stone turned savagely on the alien. "Go up to the top of that rock and take a look out on the ice. With your better-than-Human eyes you should still be able to see our burning tanks. At least a dozen are out there. Each one represents at least three good men dead, maybe more if they were infantry carriers. Burned or frozen, all of them. Go look at that and then come back and talk to me about a more reasonable approach." Stone hurled a thermocoat onto the rear seat of the sled.

"My dear friend," said Archon Divxas, ignoring his companion's outburst, "I did not mean that you should abandon your quest. Far from it. What I suggest is that we, and I wish to stress the 'we' portion of that, go a bit more cautiously."

Stone stared at him, then finished loading the sled. "Rock Wall isn't due to reappear for an hour. If we hurry, we can reach the pole before it comes up." He climbed into the command seat. "You can drive."

Divxas scrambled into the seat and wedged his legs under the DDP. He knew that Stone was asking him to drive, not as a show of superiority, but because the alien was the better man for the task. He applied lift to the grav sled and let it drift forward while he checked the instruments. "The power pack indicates we will just make it to our destination, and then only if we are careful."

* * *

The Renegade relief force reached maximum altitude over the small island off the southern coast of Rolandrin. The circling climb had kept the force hidden as long as possible from known TOG LOSATS. At an altitude of eight kilometers it turned south and began its 900-kph run toward the pole. It was eight thousand kilometers to the edge of the ice, and another one thousand kilometers to the pole. Even at full speed, the run would take ten hours.

The force had been loosely organized into a unit. Alanton Freund, the force commander, had arranged the column into three over-strength platoons consisting of three Liberators and a Viper each. He had explained this organization as due to a lack of officers. He needed one of the four optios in the command to supervise the headquarters element, which meant no officer would be available to command a fourth platoon. He kept as part of his command section the two Spartius carriers, with their heavy lasers, and the Wolverine.

Century Freund formed into a close column. Two tank-infantry platoons led, followed by the headquarters and the third tank-infantry unit. The formation was good for headquarters control, but it had no combat strength. Most of the headquarters' fire was masked by the other units, and the HQ was so far back in the column that the leading units would be entangled long before the rear elements could be strategically committed to the battle. As the run began, the headquarters element managed to drift so far astern of the leading platoons that there was soon a thirty-kilometer space between them and the rest of the Century. The leaders were still within commlink range of the command Spartius, however, and even though the force was supposed to be on listening silence, the platoon leaders were bombarded with advice from the commander.

Roglund Karstil, commanding the second tank-infantry platoon, listened in growing frustration to the stream of messages from Abrasive Mandrake Six. Call signs, he knew, were randomly assigned, but this one seemed chosen especially for his force commander. He had served under Legatus Maximus Alanton Freund before the man's promotion, and even then they had not worked well together. Karstil always seemed to do or say the wrong thing to Freund, and, in fact, suspected that his superior had occasionally conspired to make him fail or commit some error. Karstil knew Freund must be competent, or he wouldn't be here and in charge, but he wasn't happy about a possible repeat of his first combat experience. Listening silence meant that he couldn't even reply to the tide of advice and orders from the commander.

He wished he could at least leave the command hatch open on the Liberator, but at such extreme altitude and high speed, it was impossible. The moment Karstil closed and dogged the hatch, a wave of claustrophobia swept over him. Like most tankers, he wanted to be able to see the sky, to use his eyes in addition to the electronic sensors that displayed the world to him. He let the command chair drop into the fighting compartment and shuddered. The smell of fresh paint over charred ballistic armor was overwhelming in the sticky warmth. The gunner, Triarii Spentling Crowder, looked up from his sight panel and smiled. Behind both of them the driver, Triarii Charles Boutselis, studied his control display.

"Weather front ahead, sir," offered Boutselis, without lifting his eyes from the glowing green screen before him. "I think it's too high to go over and too wide to avoid."

"It shouldn't be a problem, Triarii." Karstil turned in his seat to face his driver. "I'd like to call you by something other than your rank. It's a little formal for people who are going to live together in these cramped quarters. What do people call you?"

"Most call me Boots, sir." The driver leaned back in the padded seat and stretched his legs. "They call me other things, too, but I guess I answer to Boots best." The driver nodded toward where the gunner sat hunched over his sight. "Ask Spent why they call him that."

Karstil turned toward the gunner. "I assume it has something to do with your first name. Am I right?"

Boots chuckled. "You'd think that, sir, but ask him anyways. Go ahead, Spent, tell him."

The gunner squirmed in his seat. "It's just my name, sir."

"Ri-ight!" Boots was grinning. He leaned forward and crossed his arms over the top of his DDP. "It also has to do with three young ladies at a certain spaceport."

"It was only the other guy's word against theirs." Spentling Crowder's face was a deep shade of red inside his combat helmet. "The girls didn't complain!"

Boots threw his head back and roared with laughter. "It's not a bad name, sir. As a matter of fact, it was a compliment. But it gives Crowder something to live up to in every canteen between here and home."

Karstil looked at the gunner. The blush was still on his face, but the look in his eyes was one of triumph. Karstil nodded in appreciation. "Do you mind if I call you Spent? Or would you rather it be something else?"

"Spent will be fine, sir." The gunner turned back to his sight, making an obscene hand gesture to Boots as he did so.

Karstil thumbed the food processor switch and waited for the unit to heat a ration. "It'll be a long trip to the pole, so we'd better eat while we have the chance. You eat first, Spent, and then you can spell Boots at the controls while he eats. You'd also better get some rest. From experience, I can tell you that once things start happening, there'll be damn little of either." He heard himself talking like a hardened veteran. The other members of the crew looked at him almost in awe. Neither of them had ever seen a shot fired outside the practice range.

Karstil swung his chair back to the DDP to check on the other vehicles in the platoon. He was leading the diamond formation with his second tank on the left, commanded by Sergeant Marshall Bartlett, and his third tank on the right, commanded by Sergeant Mark Goodwin. He hadn't met either one so far; they were just voices and names that came over the commlink. Both were experienced tankers, having served in Liberator platoons on Caralis and other planets. The infantry Viper in the rear was another matter altogether. The commander was Sergeant Johnny Parnell, newly promoted from principes in an administrative section. Someone had decided he was good enough to be a ped sergeant, but they had probably expected him to have some shakedown time before he had to leap into combat. Well, thought Karstil, that couldn't be helped. The man would just have to do the best he could, and Karstil would watch out for him if he got the chance.

"Abrasive Mandrake Two-six." It was Freund again on the commlink. "This is Abrasive Mandrake Six. You are drifting out of formation. Please correct your flight path five-zero meters to the right."

23

1730, 11 Martius 6831—Legatus Cariolanus Camus watched the status display. As the Centuries of the TOG Strike Cohort reported in, their status was noted on the board. Camus was not pleased. All units had suffered in the attack, some of them quite grievously. What should have been a decisive victory against the Renegade Cohort, weakened by losses in the ambush, had come off as only a qualified success. The Horatius Centuries had taken the worst beating because of their more aggressive attack at the pole. Of the eighteen Horatius tanks assigned to the Strike Cohort, only ten had survived. The nine assigned Romulus carriers were down to four. The Aeneas Centuries were in better shape with a total of twelve tanks and six carriers. The two Romulus platoons had suffered one destroyed and one damaged each.

Centurion Marmoreus Patrius, operations officer of the Cohort, watched his commander study the DDP. Patrius had been born Georg Hammelschmidt, but had taken a Roman name upon becoming an optio in the forces of New Rome. The Hammelschmidts were tenant farmers on the lands of one of the great senators of the new empire, the family destined to spend their lives in humble servitude. But Georg was given the opportunity to enlist in the TOG army during a crisis, and had leaped at the chance to escape his destined drudgery. A bright young man, he had been chosen for Officer Candidate School. Graduation with high honors brought him a new name and the command never to acknowledge his patrimony. A detailed false background and heritage were developed for him, and only the original processing officer would ever know of his less-than-exalted origins.

Camus turned away from the status board as the last reports appeared. "Ops. We have two choices, as I see it. We can break into the Commonwealth lines and rub them out, or we can begin siege operations. Your evaluation, please."

Patrius covertly studied his commander. A legatus did not usually ask a centurion to evaluate a plan unless he had already made his decision. He knew how the system worked. The commander made his plan, then asked his staff or advisors for their evaluation. It was a test. The staff offered their comments, and if they got it right, they were praised. If they got it wrong, they were corrected, and if they got it wrong too often, they were gone. This was one such test. Patrius searched the face of the legatus, looking for a clue to what he had decided.

"Sir." Patrius stepped forward to give his evaluation. "A siege is a long, drawn-out operation that leads to ultimate success. An attack would give a quick victory but at a heavy cost in equipment and lives. The basic question is whether we have the time to spend in a siege. I would recommend immediate attack. With a good plan, we should be able to inflict as many casualties on the Commonwealth as they inflict on us, and ultimately there are more of us than there are of them. In addition, a siege will not quickly weaken the enemy. I think we must assume that the enemy has the same food and other supplies as we do. The immediate attack is preferred."

"A well-reasoned evaluation," said Camus, folding his arms. "But I fear, my dear Centurion, that you have not correctly assessed the overall situation. A siege is not a passive measure. We would push the enemy force from all sides, inflicting casualties as we go. They would not be able to resupply their units, but we would. Replacements could be brought in as we tightened the knot. Eventually, they would have to die or surrender. It would be a cheap victory."

"I understand the reasoning behind a siege, sir." Patrius spoke respectfully, watching his commander. Prefect Claudius Sulla of the planetary command staff had just entered the converted Pompey artillery vehicle that served as the operations center for the Cohort. Even the arguments propounded by the legate could be part of the test. "I believe we should not waste time with this tiny Commonwealth unit. Planetary command surely desires a quick, overwhelming victory here, and the return of the strike Cohort to the main battle area on Alsatia."

"You forget your place, Centurion Marmoreus Patrius," the legate snarled, glaring at his operations officer and forcing him to step back from the plotting board. "You have no right to include the name of planetary command as a part of your argument. They have given me special command of this Cohort. We are completely independent of the needs of the forces of New Rome on Alsatia. Planetary command is me, and I am planetary command." There was a slight hiss in the background as Prefect Sulla vacated the operations vehicle.

Patrius understood. The legate had lost his nerve. The unexpected casualties suffered in the first attack had rattled him far beyond what he would admit. He opted for a siege because it would give him time to recover. It would also give planetary command (and no matter what he said, Patrius thought grimly, the legatus didn't speak for that headquarters) time to either withdraw the Cohort or reinforce it to overwhelming strength. Legatus Cariolanus Camus was no longer a rising star to which a man could attach himself. Patrius bowed his head, acknowledging the reprimand. "I spoke wrongly, sir. Your plan is the better one. I will support you in every way." Like hell I will, thought Patrius. You'll be crushed by your cautiousness, and I will not stay to be destroyed with you. I am rid of you.

Five hundred meters away, Prefect Claudius Sulla slipped into a second converted Pompey vehicle being used as the communications center. The enlisted men rose from their seats as he entered, standing away from the commlink when he moved to the console. He dropped into a chair and tapped a frequency into the system. He slipped a coded wafer into the access port and began to key in a message. The commlink absorbed the entire dispatch, transferring the plain-text message into a series of numbered groups. When the prefect was satisfied with the report, he struck the command key. In a microsecond, the commlink transmitted a single screech to the COMSAT hovering on the horizon.

The Loren grav sled drifted slowly through the towering pinnacles of rock and ice. The two figures occupying the seats huddled together as though for warmth, but shared body heat was the least of their concerns. Both studied the DDP, its luminescence muted to give off the least possible light, as they tried to find navigational points. The Data Display Panel showed dull red indicators marking enemy vehicles. So many appeared on the screen that further progress by sled seemed almost impossible.

"I think, my good friend," whispered the Baufrin in the driver's chair, "that we have reached the limit of our journey. Any further traverse of this terrain will increase to unacceptable limits the possibility of our being detected."

"You're right. Ground the sled." Larry Stone leaned back in the gunner's seat and reached for the light combat helmet behind him. He winced as he pulled the plasto-laminate covering over his head. It had been impossible to cover himself with the thermotarp while wearing the helmet, so the helmet had been consigned to the cargo area for the journey. It had reached the ambient temperature of the surroundings; seventy degrees below water's freezing temperature.

"One of the significant advantages of the Baufrin race over you less-developed Humans is the ability to dispense with the obligatory display accouterment. Our eyes do it all."

"Archon, I don't need the we-are-better-than-Humans speech right now," said Stone through teeth clenched to keep them from chattering. He knew his comment was wasted, but he wanted to deal with the TOG forces, not enter a no-win discussion with his friend.

The Baufrin shrugged off the comment as he let the sled crunch softly onto the ice. "I suggest that we cover the sled with the holotarp. There is no point in letting our TOG enemy know of its existence."

"Do it. I'll get the weapons ready." Stone pulled a pair of Sabre-Cut laser rifles from the rear sponson box and laid them on the gunner's seat, checking to see that they were fully powered. The Sabre-Cut allowed only twenty shots before it would need to be recharged, but Stone didn't plan to become involved in an extensive firefight with TOG troopers. Virtually silent and without recoil, the rifles were good for clandestine missions. The laser rifles were joined by laser pistols. Stone and Divxas strapped the weapons on in silence.

In spite of the Baufrin's claims of superior abilities, Stone was the reconnaissance expert, and he led the way. Crouched low against the snow, he picked his way forward toward the unseen Renegade lines. To his right and left, the Head-Up Display of the combat helmet showed thermographic imagery of legionnaires and vehicles. The Basic Lifeform Sensor detected life, but even the BLS could not identify what type of life form it had detected. Until each figure could be visually identified, all forms were to be considered hostile. Stone and Divxas crept on.

Stone's strategy was to approach targets until he could identify them. This method allowed him to choose the time and place of contact. If he had instead avoided each life form detected, he would be reacting to circumstances rather than choosing his course. He, as always, preferred to generate the action, and so he encountered each head-on. Stone and Divxas, moving slowly and protected by Ranger stealth suits, were almost invisible. Only someone searching especially for the two could have detected their presence. No TOG legionnaire was so occupied.

Cariolanus Camus ground his teeth as he read the message from planetary command. The tissue-thin flimsy had been handed to him by Marmoreus Patrius, and the Cohort commander thought he could detect a supercilious smugness in the operation officer's posture. The message ordered him to attack the entrenched Commonwealth forces at once. It stressed that the recapture of the polar station had highest priority at planetary command and that reinforcements would be sent if needed to accomplish this mission. The tone of the terse order had implied that if Camus were not capable of accomplishing his task with the forces at hand, the relief force commander would be given the honor of the victory. Camus understood: do the job or be relieved.

He turned to the centurion, who had remained at attention in his presence, awaiting the orders he knew the legate must give. "Alert the Centuries to prepare for an immediate attack. Lead with the peds on foot. Once the break-in has been made, we'll push into the breach with the 'vehicles."

"As you wish, Commander." You wimp, thought Patrius. You are still trying to avoid attacking these miserable survivors with your tanks. We'll do it your way this time, but wait until the relief force arrives. He snapped a salute and left the command vehicle.

From the top of a low outcropping, Stone and Divxas surveyed the area to their front. Several Romulus and Horatius vehicles were scattered over the area in individual craters. The crews were out servicing the tanks and carriers. Stone laid the Sabre-Cut on the snow and aimed it at one of the groups of figures. Depressing the trigger to the first detent activated the targeting system built into the combat helmet. The readout that appeared on the HUD indicated that the target was almost two thousand meters away, the theoretical extreme range for the weapon. Stone held the trigger at the stop, and the target system began to magnify the area within the sight scan. The magnification began at x05, and the power increased the longer the switch was activated. At x50, the sight had reached its full magnification, and the target stopped growing on the face plate. Stone watched the men working on the Romulus.

The full infantry squad was deployed around the vehicle, but they weren't in their craters. Instead, they huddled close to the rear of the carrier beside the open ramp that gave access to the interior. The men were all wearing extra protective gear, including combat smocks and camouflage tarps. At first he assumed that they were trying to keep warm, but then he realized that a figure, probably a sergeant, was issuing extra pouches of hand grenades and rifle magazines. These men were preparing for an infantry probe.

Stone signaled Divxas to retreat, then followed the Baufrin down the slope of the outcropping. Because the TOG legionnaires were busy preparing for an attack, their security would be minimal. This was their first decent break of the journey. It was time to move and move fast. The two figures darted from outcropping to outcropping, passing through the TOG Century. Only once did they come close to discovery, but the TOG legionnaire was more interested in delivering his weapons cargo than investigating a fleeting image on his BLS. They kept moving.

Within minutes, they had passed beyond the limit of the forward TOG positions. This would be the most dangerous part of the maneuver. Between opposing lines, both sides would tend to shoot first and ask questions later. Stone didn't want to become a casualty to friendly fire. The BLS indicated a line of emplacement to the front. Stone studied the indicators. They were strong emitters, but he was suspicious. If the Renegade forces were showing that much electronic pulse, they would be easy targets for the TOG legionnaires. Scanning the twisted terrain carefully and slowly, he eventually discovered the almost invisible forms of the infantry in their positions. The Renegades had taken the time to plant dummy emitters. Good plan.

Using hand signals, he pointed out the real positions to Archon Divxas. The Baufrin nodded. The creature knew his part in this plan. Slipping behind a volcanic flue, he shed all the gear he had been carrying. In the intense cold, he knew that he would only be able to function for a few minutes. That would have to be enough time to accomplish their purpose.

The pair hoped that the Renegade sensors were set to register only Human life. The BLS would thus not recognize the Baufrin's cardiovascular system and might ignore him until he was close enough to attract attention without being shot. Divxas set out, Stone following the soft blur on his own BLS.

The alien crept forward on his five good legs, his torso low to the ice. The anatomy of the Baufrin was a distinct advantage here, because he could move at full speed even when his body was only millimeters from the surface. He stopped occasionally to use his six eyes to establish reference points along the trail. He had pinpointed the location of a Renegade soldier, but wanted to approach the legionnaire without alerting those around him. He passed the imaginary line that marked the extreme border of the Renegade lines. The outpost's position was now to his rear. That was safer, but not safe enough. He crept closer and closer to the soldier. He could tell that the figure was watching something to his front, and hoped that that point of interest was Stone. Their plan had been for Stone to move around enough to activate the sentries' BLS. Then, with their attention riveted to the front, the Baufrin would be able to creep up on them from the rear. He could see the jaw plates of the sentry's combat helmet quiver; he was speaking to someone. With great care, Divxas stretched out along the snow, extending one arm toward the sentry. He tapped him on the shoulder.

The reaction was more violent than he had expected. The soldier sprang straight into the air, turning to bring his slug rifle to bear on Divxas. For an instant, the Baufrin wavered between grappling with the soldier or springing back. He chose to back away, rising to his full height as he did. The finger of the sentry jerked on the trigger. The shot went wide, tearing a drift to powder.

Before the soldier could fire again, he made sense of the Baufrin's up-raised arms. The soldier, still covering the alien with the rifle, gestured the creature forward. Larry Stone and Archon Divxas had made contact with the Renegades of Cohort Harras.

24

1830, 11 Martius 6831—Eight kilometers above the ocean, and just short of the ice cap's edge, the relief force finally caught up with the weather front that it had been following for the past several hours. Huge, billowing clouds stretched from horizon to horizon, blotting out the sea below. The coming night colored the underside of the clouds an evil black, while the lingering rays of the planet's sun, Borialis, painted the cloud tops shades of violet and mauve. As the column passed into the solid wall of boiling vapor, it was engulfed in instant and total darkness.

"Abrasive Mandrake. Abrasive Mandrake. This is Abrasive Mandrake Six. Close up the formation. Close up the formation. You are too spread out. Close up the formation."

Roglund Karstil, leading the second platoon of the relief column, spoke into the internal commlink, and Boots Boutselis began to slow the Liberator. The violence of the weather front forced the driver to pay strict attention to the controls, for even though the Liberator tipped the scales at 273 metric tons, the forces of nature were unimpressed. The velocity indicator dropped below 800 kph as the tank twisted in the force of the blast. "I hope this blows itself out before we get to the pole, sir," Boots muttered into the commlink. "It'll be hell trying to bring this thing down in this weather."

"You'll do all right," said Karstil, hoping that Boots got his wish. Karstil had had a rough drop from altitude when he first reached Caralis, and one hot jump, descending from altitude under attack, was enough for any man's career. He thought back to his crew for that drop; Duncan Spint, posthumously promoted to sergeant after the recent fighting on Alsatia, and Quentain Podandos, his right arm replaced by a prosthetic device as a result of the same running battle. It all seemed so long ago.

"I've been on a hairy drop before," Karstil said. "Reaction and training take care of most of it. Just drive the thing by the seat of your pants, and you'll do all right."

Karstil glanced back at the driver's station to see Boots wrestling with the controls. "I have faith in you. I always figure that the driver wants to live at least as much as I do." He nodded toward the gunner. "And remember that there are three young ladies at the canteen at Alabaster who really want Spent back." That made Boutselis smile, finally, and Crowder blushed again. The Liberator shuddered.

"Abrasive Mandrake. Abrasive Mandrake. This is Abrasive Mandrake Six. This weather is worse than we expected. We may have to turn back. Report status in turn as I call your units."

Karstil rubbed his temples. He had long ago abandoned feeling frustration with his commanding officer, for fear had begun to set in. They were supposed to be on listening silence for the entire run to the pole. They would be easy enough to detect without the constant commlink chatter, and the commander kept breaking all the rules. They knew the enemy was out there, and Karstil was pretty sure that, by now, the TOGs knew they were on the way. But no matter how severely they were battered by the weather, and what was in store for them up ahead, there was no need to turn back or even talk about turning back. A relief unit was not an optional maneuver—these were desperate measures for desperate times. When his unit reported status, he added, for Freund's benefit, that he was experiencing no difficulties.

"Abrasive Mandrake Two-six. This is Abrasive Mandrake Six. I will make the decisions about the conduct of this force. What I need from you is information, not opinions. Abrasive Mandrake Six out." The Liberator lurched again.

"How you doing, Boots?" Boutselis had the only important opinion at this point, and Karstil wanted to include him in the decision loop if possible.

"I think I've got the hang of it, sir. You were right. If I just let the tank drive itself while I feel the motion, I think I can control it on the drop."

"Good. We're going in when the time comes."

The intercom was silent. Karstil had just told his crew that they were going to the pole no matter what the commander said. The tension in the tank radiated silent approval.

The TOG legionnaire plotted the intercept on his status board. According to the vectors, the source of the commlink traffic was at the edge of the ice and very high. The direction indicated a relief force from Rolandrin, but nothing else about this formation agreed with that assessment. A Commonwealth relief force should come in at the lowest possible altitude to avoid detection. This blip was flying too high and making too much noise. But this legionnaire believed in reporting everything to the staff and letting them deal with it. Enlisted personnel, no matter how experienced, were not allowed to make judgments. He turned to the optio in the commcenter and signaled for his attention.

Two minutes later Centurion Marmoreus Patrius posted the plot in the command center to reflect the probable intercept. He brought the information to the attention of Legatus Camus and Prefect Claudius Sulla, who were examining the progress of the Cohort.

"Is it possible, Cariolanus Camus," asked Sulla, "that the Commonwealth would try to slip a relief force in over the top of your cordon?"

"That would be unexpected from them. But if they were trying such a maneuver, they would surely maintain commlink silence until they arrived."

"Perhaps the high-altitude force is a diversion. The main force may be coming in on the surface."

"That sounds more like the Commonwealth." Camus turned to the operations officer, who had remained at his elbow. "Patrius. Redeploy the Horatius tanks to the threatened sector. The Romulus and Aeneas tanks will cover the high approach. Do it."

Centurion Marmoreus Patrius nodded, saluted, and left to issue the appropriate orders. Within five minutes the tanks and carriers of Cohort Camus had been set in motion. Fifteen minutes later they lay in wait for the approaching relief force.

They had made it through the worst of the weather front, or at least so it seemed to Karstil. Boots had the Liberator under control, and though it still was prone to lurch and dive suddenly, those sudden shifts were decreasing. All other things being equal, their force would not have to worry about the weather on their descent to the surface.

"Abrasive Mandrake. Abrasive Mandrake. This is Abrasive Mandrake Six. The weather has taken a turn for the worse. Prepare to operate independently." Centurion Maximus Alanton Freund's transmissions were beginning to break up. Either the weather was beginning to affect the signal, or the sender was having trouble getting the words out.

"Abrasive Mandrake. Abrasive Mandrake. This is Abrasive Mandrake Six. Conditions are too adverse for a drop to the surface. Return to base. Follow me."

Karstil stared at the commlink in disbelief. He switched his attention to the DDP and saw the Spartius carrier designated as the headquarters turn sharply to the right and accelerate. The other vehicles of the headquarters did the same. The Third Platoon followed the leaders. As he watched, the right-hand tank of his own platoon veered away as if to follow. The range opened, and then, the tank, evidently seeing that his leader had not changed course, swung back. The Viper carrier had also dropped behind on the orders to withdraw, thought better of it, and closed on its assigned station.

The lead platoon was in complete disarray. The lead tank, commanded by Greenhill, was still on course. His wing man, the tank to the left, was still with him, but the right-hand Liberator and the infantry Viper had made a sharp turn. With the lead of the column still vectoring toward the pole at 700-plus kph, and the others retreating at 800-plus kph, the distance between the two groups opened rapidly. Soon the six vehicles were alone.

"Mandrake One-six. This is Mandrake Two-six." Karstil called the lead platoon, or what was left of it. "You lead in. I'll follow."

"Two-six. This is One-six. Roger."

"Boots, we'll follow him in. Run the speed down to less than four hundred klicks. Make sure you're at least forty klicks behind the lead platoon when it dives."

"You got it, sir."

Karstil watched the plot plan indicator of the DDP. The red dot that showed his position crawled toward the circle that was the location of the pole. The grid reference numbers on the digital readout rolled over as they matched the grid reference numbers of the pole. Any minute now the DDP would see the Renegade forces at the pole, if any were there. Karstil was assailed by a sudden wave of doubt: what if no one was there? Headquarters had been unable to contact Cohort Harras since the force had left Rolandrin. He was going into this situation absolutely blind. The dot that was his vehicle crossed into the red circle of the pole.

"Two-six. This is One-six. I'm going to circle down. I'm moving too fast to dive straight in." Greenhill had already made the same decision Karstil was reaching: 400 kph was too great a speed for the tanks to nose over for a power dive toward the surface. The velocity increase of the dive would make their speed impossible for the grav drives to overcome when they reached the ice cap. Better to approach the pole in a shallow dive than to risk making a mistake at zero altitude. The lead platoon began a wide turn, shedding altitude and speed.

"Orbit over his position until he's well clear, Boots."

"Got it, sir. We'll let him get clear."

"Unknown vehicles. One-zero-double-zero. Directly below at six kilometers. Stationary." The voice of the DDP sounded in Karstil's ear. That's a relief, he thought. At least someone is home. The voice continued to update the information, the altitude steadily dropping as the platoon orbited lower and lower toward the pole.

"Horatius tanks. Directly below at four kilometers. Stationary." The DDP had achieved extreme range to identify the vehicles on the ground. Karstil was annoyed. The least they could do is set up a landing beacon to give us a hand, he thought. Harras must have identified them by now. Even with communications destroyed, which he assumed had happened, it would be easy for one of the Liberators to fire up a painting laser to guide them.

He suddenly realized that the DDP had said Horatius. But Harras had not taken any enemy tanks with him. Could the DDP have mistaken the IFF response of a Horatius for a Liberator? He overrode the DDP cycle and requested the surface information again.

"Horatius tanks. Directly below at three kilometers. Stationary." The warning klaxon whooped. "Horatius tanks and Liberator tanks. Directly below at three kilometers. Stationary. You have been painted." The DDP blossomed with red and blue indicators.

Karstil's heart stopped. There was someone home after all, he thought. Everyone was home. The DDP showed two ragged circles: a large red one that indicated the location of the enemy tanks, and a smaller blue one, about 40 kilometers in diameter, that was Renegade-held.

"Spent—shoot anything red, and keep shooting. Boots. Get us down as fast as you can. Aim for the center of the blue circle. Don't worry about making a fine approach, just get us down." He switched from intercom to platoon push. "Second Platoon. We're going in. Shoot everything red and don't forget your smoke. Follow me!"

The Liberator rolled onto its left side and nosed over, a classic split-S maneuver. Classic for a space fighter, that is, but not for a 273-ton tank. With its nose pointing straight at the ice below, the tank was falling completely out of control. But the unexpected maneuver gave the crew a few moments of breathing space. The ballistic computers on the Horatius tanks far below had been calculating the flying tank's possible future locations in order to take their best shot. Their weapons, except for the 150mm main gun fixed in the hull, had been tracking the lead Liberator. Based on a best-guess solution, the weapons were laid on a spot the computer had decided the tank must cross. When Boots pulled the snap roll-and-dive, the computer was completely fooled. A stream of 50mm shells arced into the empty sky.

Technology was on the side of the diving tanks. Actually, it was a lack of technology that was keeping them alive. The TOG forces at the pole had not included antiaircraft artillery vehicles in their organization, and the vehicles they did have had limited targeting elevation. The interior turret weapons in the Horatius had a standard maximum elevation of 800 mils. The external weapons, such as the TVLG and SMLM pods, could go vertical, but the targeting system, also mounted internally, could not provide terminal guidance at that elevation. The designers had not planned for grounded vehicles to operate as anti-air platforms.

The angle-of-attack warning light on the DDP glowed. Under normal conditions, the light would flash as the angle of attack increased. The higher the rate of flash, the greater the danger of losing control of the vehicle. The best angle of approach was about 200 mils, when the light would flicker at about the rate of a normal heartbeat. At 400 mils, the light would pulse as fast as the heartbeat of a running man. At 1,600 mils, straight down, the computer was unable to calculate the danger, and the light burned like a fibrillating heart. Right now, the light was a steady glow.

Karstil felt the Liberator plunging toward the surface. He was only marginally aware of the repeated shocks of the main gun firing, but it had not painted any targets. The DDP was calling off enemy vehicles, friendly vehicles, ranges, elevations, bearings, painting laser warnings, and velocity in such a cacophony that nothing made sense. He was aware only of the dive, and the surface of the ice coming closer too fast for comprehension or thought. His hands clutched at the cushioned grips on the sides of the DDP and his feet crushed the painting laser treadle. He pressed back into the command chair. He was hypnotized by the steady light of the angle indicator.

The DDP showed an angle of attack of 1,600 mils. The number flickered; 1,500 mils. The tank was pulling out. 1,400 mils. A change of 200 mils is hardly noticeable, but Karstil would swear he felt it. The change, however slight, meant that there was a chance that the tank would be level when it reached the surface. There was hope. 1,200 mils. There was hope. Be 1,000 mils, he willed the DDP. If we can get to 1,000 mils there'll be a chance. 1,000 mils. Karstil felt the blood surge through his limbs, felt his heart begin to beat again. 900 mils. He looked at the altitude indicator. 1,000 meters from the surface. Too close.

"Put it in a tight turn, if you please, Mister Boutselis." His voice was not completely steady. "A tight turn to slow her down."

From deep in the bowels of the Liberator came a grunt of reply. Karstil felt the tank turn to the right, the bank pressing him against the seat of the command chair. 600 mils. Almost there.

The crash warning went off in his ear, ringing through the titanium hull like a death knell. The Terrain Search and Reaction warning flashed across the DDP and the voice of the computer spoke softly in his ear. "This vehicle has exceeded safe operating speed for this altitude. The recommended course of action is to reduce velocity." Boutselis applied full reverse thrust. The angle-of-attack warning light flickered, matching Karstil's heartbeat. The TS&R system spoke again. "This vehicle has exceeded safe operating speed for this altitude. Reduce speed at once. Solid object approaching."

Karstil focused on the DDP panel for the first time since the dive began. The DDP showed the long line of a ridge extending across the entire front of the vehicle. The height indicators showed that it dwarfed the surrounding terrain. The Liberator was going straight in. If the tank had been in level flight, there might have been a way to climb over the obstacle, but the Liberator was still nose-down. It was gaining control over the dive, but there was no time left to level out and climb. The angle warning light went out; they were level at 360 kph.

"Traverse right." Even as he gave the command, he overrode the gunner's station and swung the turret. The 150mm gun seemed to hesitate for an instant and then began to turn away from the wall of ice looming up in front of the tank. The turret had completed half a turn and was facing full to the rear when the vehicle struck.

One instant, Karstil was screaming across the surface, facing forward, at 360 kph. The next instant, he was facing backward and going the same speed. The mind understood, but the intestines did not. He felt as though his stomach had turned around inside his body. Then the Liberator struck the wall.

On the surface, the fighting had stopped. There had been few targets available, and those targets still operational had gone to ground. Both forces were enthralled by the spectacle of a Liberator hurtling across the ice at almost 400 kph. The grav drives tore great chunks of ice from the surface, sending them spinning aloft in clouds of white that glowed against the inky sky. The reverse thruster, firing continuously, glowed an evil red. Just before the tank struck the ice rampart, its turret swung rearward.

There was a shattering crack as the thundering tank hit. Shards of ice as big as the tank itself exploded from the surface, hurled away by the force of the impact. A great ripping sound filled the night. Those stationed on the opposite side of the ice wall, unaware of the true scope of the drama, felt the ice and rock shudder under the hammer blow. Then the ice on the opposite side gave way and the Liberator, clothed in white, burst from the surface.

The rear grav coils had been torn away from their mounts. The forward sponsons had been crushed, bent back over the hull like wet tissue paper. The Vulcan mount on the top of the turret had vanished. But the tank still flew. It swept around in a tight circle to the right, fired its digging cannon, and then settled to the surface. Optio Roglund Karstil had arrived.

25

2300, 11 Martius 6831—The Renegade officers crowded into the converted Pedden. The atmosphere was thick with expelled breath and sour sweat. The air conditioning was on low power, serving only to circulate the little fresh air available in the enclosed space. Air conditioning had been included in the normal equipment for the Pedden, based on the assumption that the tank would be operating mostly in temperate climates. No one had expected that these maneuvers would turn into extended operations at temperatures of 70° C below zero. And the temperature was still dropping. With the passing of the recent storm, the brilliant, clear skies were cooling the southern polar cap even more. The only good thing was that the wind, at least, had gone with the storm. But everyone in the Pedden knew it would return.

Centurion Maximus Milton Harras waited for the last of the officers to settle in. The interior of the command carrier was crowded, even though the faces looking at him were fewer than before. Harras cleared his throat. "We appreciate the efforts of those of you who broke into our perimeter a few hours ago. I am still not clear on why there were so few of you, but I am sure the force commander made the best decision he could at the time. Nice to have you." He surveyed his officers again, their faces pinched by the cold. They all looked older. He rubbed his own cheeks, which felt stiff and numb. And rough. He realized that he hadn't had the chance to shave in four days. Hadn't had the chance to bathe, either.

The briefing began. The logistical section reported, as did operations and the combat Century commanders. It was not an upbeat meeting. The logistics were bad. Ammunition stocks were at acceptable levels; there had been a lot more casualties than actual expenditure. Most tanks were reporting nearly 90 percent of ammunition available for the cannon and the missile racks, and the infantry carriers also had plenty of missiles. Food was not yet a problem, but the situation certainly could and would get worse. The logistics sergeant recommended rationing the troops to two meals a day.

Moldine Rinter, acting as both reserve commander and operations officer, summarized the situation and the plan. "The reinforcements to our perimeter include three Liberators and two Viper carriers. The sixth tank, one of the Liberators, was shot down during the approach, and only the driver survived. Our total combat force comprises thirteen Liberator tanks, a Spartius infantry carrier, and six Viper carriers. The headquarters element includes the two remaining Wolverine scout tanks, the engineer vehicle, and five Pedden command carriers, two from the Centuries, the communications Pedden, and one each from operations and the hospital. The Century Peddens will be used as infantry carriers with the reserve force.

"Cohort Harras will defend our position at the pole with a loose circle of three combat Centuries. The organization of the force will be as follows: Second Century, three Liberators, a Spartius, and a Viper. Third Century, four Liberators and the Viper from the relief force, which we will exchange for the damaged one. Fourth Century, two Liberators, plus one from the relief force and their two Vipers." The main beneficiary of the arrival of the relief effort was the Reserve Century under Rinter. It gained two Liberators and a Viper, as well as the damaged Viper from Third Century that would be used to plug holes in the outer edge of the defense perimeter.

"The defense zone is ten kilometers in circumference, about three in diameter. The reserve will set up in the center, in order to be able to travel the two kilometers to any threatened point on the line in less than a minute. This force can hold out for a while, barring a disaster, but we're working on a plan for a break-out. Okay, that's it, people. Let's get to work."

Honor Ross instructed her driver to ground the damaged Viper inside the reserve-force perimeter. The main gun was completely worthless, and her first job was to get the wreckage cut away so that it would not interfere with the operational SMLM launchers remaining. She was helpless to fix the casualties in the squad, but she did appoint Triarii Barstow Drinn, promoted to acting Principes, as the second section leader to replace Boost. Blackstone set the Viper down without firing the digging cannon. Only four charges were available, and with none in reserve, he didn't want to waste them.

The crew dismounted and stretched. Every legionnaire attached to the Viper had bruises and scrapes from the battle. Most personal armor was undamaged, but slamming around inside a titanium hull, even in battle suits, was hard on the body. Ross let the peds talk among themselves for a while, releasing the tension of the battle and flight, and then set them to work. She knew that legionnaires needed time after an action to decompress. She watched, and listened for the war stories to change to morbid remembrances of the casualties. That was the point at which she would set the team to work in earnest.

The peds gathered in clumps by sections, the vehicle crew excluded from the conversations. Those who fought from inside the Viper had a sense of isolation from the rest of the force. Only ground troops understood the terror of careening into battle in the cocoon of a hull, hostages to the skill of their tank crew. They were dumped into combat without warning or orientation, faced with instant, violent, solitary death. When the threat passed, the peds gathered to talk, excluding the vehicle crew that they looked upon as turnkeys of their fate.

Ross, by virtue of her position as the squad leader, was tolerated in the ped groups; Blackstone and Connor were not. The vehicle crew took no offense at their exclusion because they considered themselves superior to the infantry. Besides, they had enough to do caring for the machine. In their opinion, unless troopers were very lucky, all crew started out in the titanium cells within the body of the Viper. If you were good enough, you were set free to become part of the crew. Blackstone and Connor set about doing what they could for their damaged carrier.

The titanium armor, smashed so easily by the HEAP round of the TOG tank, was unyielding to the torch. Even with the cutting laser on full power, Blackstone had to cut slowly to make any headway carving away the damaged 25mm cannon mount. The snub ogive of the SMLM missile was solidly butted up against the damaged armor, and even though the SMLM could not be detonated by heat alone, the driver was careful about where he aimed the cutting tip. He was a skilled cutter, good enough to be on the maintenance team, but he preferred to stay in the carriers and do his cutting only when needed. After clearing away the jagged damage, he went back over the cuts to smooth the contours. Then he carefully heated patches of titanium to fit over all the holes where the ballistic protection had been exposed. In an hour he was finished.

Ross waited until the peds started to talk about their lost comrades before she intervened, suggesting that they set up section and squad fighting positions. Although Ross was the squad leader and a professional, she preferred to lead by suggestion and direction, rather than to rule by fiat. The Commonwealth Armed Forces and the Renegade Legion made no distinction between men and women in command positions, so it was not her sex that made her leadership style different. It was more a result of her successful upbringing in a family where suggestion was the method of control. Family discussion produced general decisions, but the individual members were allowed to make their own choices, suffering any consequences of those choices. Military structure did not allow that measure of freedom, but Ross liked to lead by consensus whenever possible. The squad members had more confidence in her decisions if they could see the reasoning behind them. Her usual style of command also gave Ross instant, unquestioning response when she cracked the whip.

Slowly, the squad shook itself out into defensive positions. The two sections were down from eight to three members each, and they had to decide between developing section positions or going with fewer peds in each hole. Ross went with three-to-a-hole section positions. The squad wouldn't be able to cover as much ground, but individual holes were too dangerous. Peds alone were hostages to their own fears. And peds alone had a tendency to fall asleep.

The three-ped positions allowed camaraderie to develop; the members of the section would fight to defend one another. The three-ped positions would also allow one member at a time to return to the vehicle to warm up and use the sanitary services. The squad hadn't had a bath for five days. Though bathing was not a necessity, Ross knew it would be good for morale. The men also wanted to shave, a ritual that seemed to serve more as a reference point for normalcy than fulfill a real need. Ross found men's dependency on that small, private ceremony interesting.

Explosions shattered the stillness as the sections blew their initial holes in the ice. The individual cratering charges got the positions started, then the peds would resort to stoop labor with hand-held equipment.

"Sergeant," Section Leader Principes Herman Grold called from his position. "You'd better take a look at this."

Ross joined the section standing around the crater blasted in the ice. The force of the cratering charge should have excavated a pit three meters across by one and a half deep. The force of this explosion, following the path of least resistance, had broken through the surface to reveal a cavern below. "It looks like the same thing we encountered before," said Ross, as she knelt at the edge. She stood and scanned the area for the remains of a shed, but there were no structures to be seen. "I wonder where this one was going?" she mused out loud, more to herself than to the peds around her. She addressed the section leader. "Grold, move your section over fifty meters and prepare another position. I'll report this to Century."

Glassy Relic Regal (the Reserve Century had been given a name rather than a number) acknowledged Ross' information and told her to secure the area. They would send someone down to deal with it. The voice of the tank commander who spoke to her on the commlink seemed familiar, but she put the sense of recognition down to fatigue or unconscious familiarity with the other Renegades' voices she had heard over the past days. Yet she had a nagging feeling that she would recognize the voice in another context. Fifteen minutes later, her mind dismissed the voice to deal with the people from headquarters, who arrived at her position in an Asinus grav sled. They parked next to the Viper and dismounted.

Ross was surprised. She knew no out-worlders had made the crossing with the Cohort, but she had heard rumors about some strangers arriving earlier. Now she had confirmation that something was going on. The man in the command chair was large, but common enough. The driver of the sled, however, had a spider-centaur-type body, and could only be a Baufrin. She had seen Baufrins before, but only at a distance. This would be a new experience. She waited for the two to approach her.

"Stone," said the man, and then indicated the Baufrin behind him. "This is Archon Divxas."

"Good to have you." Ross silently acknowledged that the man had not given either his first name or his rank. She had been in the Commonwealth forces long enough to understand that when a man gave only his name, he probably didn't have to give his rank. In any case, she was more interested in the Baufrin.

"My friend is not a paragon of manners," began the Baufrin. "I am indeed Archon Divxas, originally from the planet you call Shannedam IV. That, of course, was many moltings past. More recently, I have lived on Caralis where I have—"

"She doesn't need a complete background run-down, Archon," the man broke in. Ross considered herself a fair judge of character, and decided almost at once that these two were friends. Stone interrupted the Baufrin with the air of one used to stemming a flow of conversation, but with the affection usually accorded a favorite but talkative relative.

"I was only attempting to be polite and to assuage any misapprehensions she might have experienced based on the abruptness of your introduction."

Ross smiled. This was going to be great. "If you gentlemen would walk this way." She indicated the section's blast crater almost a hundred meters away. Stone moved off immediately, but Archon waited for the sergeant to begin walking before he fell into step beside her.

"You will have to forgive my good friend for his rudeness, Sergeant," chattered the Baufrin. "He has come many kilometers to meet your troops, and he feels he is a man with a mission. This current exploration, unfortunately, is not a part of that mission." Archon turned to watch Ross' reaction to that information, but with the face plate down it was difficult to see what she was thinking. He could only tell that she was still smiling.

They reached the hole and stared down. "I don't do holes," announced Stone, turning to Archon. "I think that this is more your speed."

The Baufrin peered into the blackness, made darker by the whiteness of the snow around it. "If the good sergeant can spare me one or two of her men, I would be more than willing to explore the labyrinthine passages that seem to be indicated by this chamber."

"That's all right with me," said Ross. "I'll give you Grain from the first section and Calvert from the second. I'll go with you as well."

"That will be most acceptable. I appreciate your willingness to accompany me. Some of your race would be less willing to join a stranger on what could become a dangerous mission." Archon dropped into the crater, caught himself on the lower edge of the hole, then dropped the last three meters into the pit below. He immediately began to examine the sides of the excavation, searching for signs of the way it had been made.

Ross shook her head. This alien may be an expert in tunnels, she thought, but unless he learns something about security, he'll be dead before he finds anything interesting. A quick call on the commlink brought Grain and Calvert on the run. "We're going to explore the area under the snow. There's a Baufrin, a spider-type, with us. He's already down there." Grain and Calvert looked surprised. "Yeah, he knows less about security than you and I were born knowing. We'll have to look after him, or he'll get us and him killed. Let's go." She slid down the side of the crater, caught herself at the edge, and dropped in. The two peds were right on her heels.

26

0145, 12 Martius 6831—The gallery was a smooth cut through the solid ice of the polar cap. By the time the three legionnaires joined him, Archon had already determined that the machine that had cut this opening had been a relatively simple auger that had transported the spoil to the rear by means of a flexible conveyor. There was no sign of the machine itself, and from the deteriorating condition of the walls, he guessed that the gallery was already several months old.

At first, there seemed no pattern to the gallery and the intersecting shafts radiating out from it. The side corridors were smaller than the three-meter-high main gallery and branched off at irregular intervals. A large room, like the one uncovered by the cratering charge, appeared every two hundred meters along the corridors. These rooms showed signs of human habitation.

It soon became clear that the diggers had moved with a plan. For every five hundred meters of corridor, there was an opening to the surface for disposing of the ice rubble excavated from the galleries. When the horizontal shaft had been driven far enough, another opening to the surface was made and the last one closed off. Side shafts near the openings to the surface allowed spoil to be removed in the most efficient manner. The side shafts curved away from the galleries like giant petals extending from the center of a flower.

The explorers discovered a problem almost at once. Archon could see in the infrared spectrum, but below the ice cap there was almost no heat to be detected. The BLS in Ross' HUD did not show her the passages because it detected only life forms, not geologic shapes. The thermographic sensors in the combat helmets were designed to detect only thermal differences as well. The patrol was operating blind.

The solution turned out to be white light. Each combat helmet was equipped with a short-range illumination device that allowed the wearer to see up to fifty meters. The lights would allow the patrol to see both ahead and behind, but the illumination also made their presence known to anyone or anything lurking in the tunnels. It was a choice between going in blind or alerting a possible enemy to their presence. Ross decided to use the lights.

The shaft drove on into the darkness ahead. The glaring white of the ice reflected the headlamps, making the sides of the gallery glitter and twinkle as the peds probed forward. The main gallery sloped gently downward into the deep ice below. Almost imperceptibly, the color and texture of the ice began to change. The brilliant, crystalline luminescence gave way to yellow and then to ochre. The ice became denser, pressed down by the immense weight of the layers overhead. Occasionally, the ice groaned under the pressure. Archon, in the same way he had been able to sense the eruptions of the geysers on the ice field, could sense the minute shifts caused by gravitational pull even meters under the surface. Large chunks of ice, loosened by the tiny movements, crashed down from the low ceiling, making the soldiers jump. They traveled deeper.

"This formation is quite unstable for the depth we have reached." The Baufrin was examining a part of the ceiling that had just dropped a big section of ice. "I can sense the movement of the ice generated by the attraction of Rock Wall, but there is no reasonable explanation why the moon's gravitational pull should affect the ice at this depth. It is all very strange."

"Is this going to collapse on us?" Ross was still in the lead, followed by Archon, but she was aware that both Grain and Calvert were hanging further and further back. She motioned them to close up ranks. "If the roof collapses, you two, we'll be better off together." The two triarii crept quietly up to where Ross and Archon were examining the walls and ceiling of the tunnel.

"There is no way of determining the future condition of the gallery with absolute certainty," Archon stated, rubbing his head with two of his four hands. He thought for a moment, then continued. "But still, there is something unusual about this place. As I said, I can feel the attraction of Rock Wall on this ice, but at this depth, the attraction of the satellite, even one as massive as Rock Wall, should not affect the ice." He paused again. "The only possible explanation for the phenomenon is that the ice is not solid. And the excavation we have uncovered is not extensive enough to cause this reaction."

The three legionnaires huddled around the Baufrin as he talked. Triarii Dorothea Calvert would have liked to echo Stone's sentiments on tunnels, but she was not senior enough to voice her preferences. At seventeen she was the youngest member of the squad. Her combat experience, and even her time away from home, had been limited. She was glad that she was in Ross' squad. Her leader reminded the triarii of her older sister, and she responded much better to Ross' leadership style than she had to the drill sergeants during preliminary training. She watched Ross unobtrusively, carefully emulating her stance and hoping to gain her composure.

"I don't understand what you're telling us," said Ross.

"It is quite simple, and at the same time, quite inexplicable, Sergeant Ross." Archon considered how to word his explanation so as not to sound as though he were talking to a Human three-year-old. "I have examined the striations and fissures appearing in the ice that forms the strata through which these tunnels have been bored. If you will examine them as well, you may note that the fissures on the right side of the tunnels are smaller than the fissures on the opposite wall. If the strata were of uniform density, these fissures would be of uniform width. Thus, it would appear that the fissures in fact radiate from an area to our right. Because the fissures demonstrate this uneven radiation, it can only mean that there is a rather large opening somewhere to our right." He waited for Ross to indicate that she understood.

"So there's a hole, a big one, to the right. Why didn't the people who were looking for it find it?"

"I do not know. The fissures have actually developed rather recently, perhaps as a result of their tunneling. The others may not have seen them, or, if they did, they took no notice."

"Let's take the next side tunnel to the right and see where it leads us."

They turned down the next right-hand passage. They traveled less than forty meters before Ross, who was in the lead, held up her hand to signal a halt. Ahead, in the glow cast by her headlamp, she could see an object blocking the path. The patrol moved forward cautiously, Ross remembering her last encounter with mining equipment under the ice.

Chunks of the ceiling had broken loose and crashed down on the tunneling machine, and ice rubble was piled almost waist-high in the corridor, more detritus than they had seen anywhere else in the underground labyrinth. The rear of the machine was a long, flexible conveyor that rode on independent tracks. The side panels had been bent almost in half by the falling debris. As they rounded a corner, the cab of the machine came into view. Ross stopped and leveled her carbine at the back of the cab and signaled Grain to proceed. He squeezed himself against the right wall and moved toward the control house.

Seconds later, Grain snapped his rifle to his shoulder and fired a three-round burst at the machine. The explosions startled all four of the members of the patrol, and the concussion brought more slabs of ice crashing to the floor of the passage, forcing the peds to dodge out of the way. Archon hunched down, letting the falling shards rebound from his carapace. As the echoes died Grain looked back at Ross and gave a sheepish shrug. "Thought I saw someone. Sorry."

"Better safe than sorry." Ross motioned him forward. Grain moved over the debris toward the back of the cab. His first instinct had been right. Ross could see a figure in the control seat. But this person was harmless now, and it had nothing to do with Grain's quick reaction. The operator had not appeared on the BLS or been detected by Archon because he had been dead for a long time. The digging must have triggered some fault in the hairline fissures in the ice. The ceiling had collapsed, and it looked like the operator had panicked and tried to escape from his seat under the armored roof of the machine. A slab of ice had caught him on the temple as he bolted out of the control house, crushing his skull like an eggshell, and the force of the blow had thrown the operator back into his chair. The extreme temperature froze the body at the height of rigor mortis, and it was that shape that Grain had seen silhouetted against the glare of the headlamp. Grain had killed a corpse.

The patrol crawled past the machine and the ice rubble in which it was buried. Archon led the way, his physique allowing him to move more quickly through smaller areas than the peds could move in the bulky bounce suits. He reached the limit of the gallery and began to examine the face of the ice. The others crawled to where he was probing the wall.

"This ice is decayed much beyond any we have seen so far. I believe there is something here worth investigating." Archon tested a section of the wall, and a large chunk of ice came away. "Ah. We should be able to easily clear away some of this wall." Archon began to push loose chunks of ice aside and pry others from the face of the gallery. Ross and her team moved the loose ice out of the way, clearing the area around the Baufrin. "There is something here, I am quite sure. Please increase your efforts." The alien's voice actually conveyed excitement. He felt sure he was near the end of his search. The others were also oblivious to their surroundings, unaware of any danger that might lurk nearby. They were caught up in the Baufrin's excitement, riveted to the spot in anticipation.

"We have found it!" Archon turned to his companions with a dramatic flourish of all four arms. "See! There is something here!" He pointed with one arm at the glistening surface revealed under the ice. "That is not a natural substance. It is not ice."

The others pressed forward. There, just visible through the ochre slabs of ice, was a pearly shell. It looked like the curve of a giant egg hidden under the snow.

"The open area we seek must be behind that shell." Archon turned and struck the shell with one of his claws. "It does not sound hollow, but I am also sure that there is nothing behind it. The substance seems quite thick." He turned to Ross. "We must break through the shell."

Without a moment's hesitation, Ross reached for her laser stiletto. The shell was tough, but it had not been made to resist this technology. The burning tip carved into the strange substance without difficulty. The knife's power supply was almost exhausted by the time a square opening had been scored on the shell. Ross kicked at it with her armored boot.

The searing pain that coursed up her leg reminded her that she had been below the surface more than two hours, and that it had been even longer since she had been completely warm. Her foot was numb. She realized that there were two others in the same shape, and assumed the temperature would affect Archon, if it wasn't already. She should probably get back up to the surface. She almost voiced her concerns, but the pull of the discovery was stronger than even her desire for comfort. "Too tough for me. Someone else try."

"I think that my lower arms may be able to move it. Even though I am of significantly less mass than any of you, I have greater strength. Let me try." Archon took Ross' place in front of the score marks on the shell. Only Stone would have recognized how focused he was on getting through this mysterious shell—the Baufrin had failed to elaborate on Baufrin superiority over Human physique, his favorite theme.

He braced himself against the ice with his lower legs and slid his long, thin claws deep into the fractures left by the stiletto. With one violent heave, the cut portion of the shell tore free. The patrol stared.

In front of them was a black opening. The light from their headlamps shined through the square space, but there was no reflection. Archon picked up a chunk of ice and dropped it through the hole. More than three seconds later, they heard it strike.

Ross finally stirred, shaking off the sense of blank wonder the whole patrol was feeling. She knew it was time to let the Cohort commander know what was happening. Normally, she would have reported her situation to her platoon leader, but this patrol was a Century function, so she called Rinter's designation on the commlink. "Glassy Relic Regal Six. This is Glassy Relic Regal Two-two-six. Sitrep."

"This is Regal Six. Go ahead."

"This is Regal Two-two-six. We have found a cavern under the ice. We will investigate."

"This is Regal Six. Affirmative. Keep us informed."

27

0300, 12 Martius 6831—The headlamps provided no clue to what lay below in the mysterious blackness. The thermographic imaging system on the combat helmets also showed only the void; whatever was below the patrol was at a constant temperature. The patrol was completely unaware of what awaited them below, but each member was ready to be the first to discover it.

The Human race has always preferred the known to the unknown. They like riddles only in the abstract, not in their daily lives. One of the many reasons Humankind went to space was to answer its riddle. But even space was not a complete unknown; they knew where they were going because they could see the stars. The immense distance was less frightening because they knew their destination. The basic Human need to know now drove this small party of explorers.

Humanity's long string of amazing scientific advances did not change the fact that the patrol was still looking into a fathomless void, unknowable by any other method than direct exploration. It both repelled and attracted their Human and Baufrin souls. If any of the patrol had considered their feelings about the adventure lying before them in a rational manner, they would have been able to examine the phenomenon of curiosity. Not one considered leaving the opening unexplored, but each was grateful for the others' presence. The unknown territory the team faced held the fascination of standing at the railing of the balcony of a tall building. The empty space drew them forward, but warned of danger.

Ross broke the spell. She unsnapped the hand torch from her belt and thumbed the function switch to full power. Elbowing her way past the two still-stunned peds to the opening, she leaned in as far as she could without losing her balance. Waving the torch around in the darkness provided no further information. She switched the illumination from white light to infrared. Still nothing. She tossed the torch underhand as hard as she could. The heat source scribed an arc across her HUD, hit something solid far below, bounced twice, and came to rest. Ross watched a series of solid, rectangular shapes begin to form around the light source. "There's something large and squarish down there," she announced. "The HUD says the torch fell 154 meters away. Your bounce packs will get you down, but I'm not sure how we'd get you back. This is a pretty small hole to aim for."

Archon rattled his mandibles, the Baufrin equivalent of a Human clearing his throat. "There are a number of advantages we Baufrins have over the Human race. The primary superiority, in Human opinion, is our advanced ocular acuity. This ability is important, but is only given primary consideration by Humans based on their own, limited abilities. You may have noticed that we Baufrin have four working arms on our upper torso, and six motive legs on the lower torso. On my lower torso, of course, there are only five, but that is the result of an unfortunate accident in the recent past."

Ross began to understand why Stone had been so abrupt with the Baufrin. She wanted to interrupt his lecture, but she didn't want to be rude. She let him rattle on, hoping that eventually he would make his point.

Archon went on to describe the accident that had cost him his leg and the emergency surgery that had followed. "But I digress," he finished, flashing Ross a smile. "We are, after all, basically spiders as far as our physiology is concerned. This has certain advantages as well as disadvantages. One of the great disadvantages is our susceptibility to extremes in temperature. This cold is significantly degrading my reactions, and perhaps that is the reason I was so slow to solve our problem of entering this excavation. But again, I digress."

His three comrades were more than ready to hear his solution. Calvert looked blank, as if she had let her mind wander from the Baufrin's dissertation. Grain was poking at the edges of the opening. Only Ross looked like she was still listening, and even her eyes were a little glazed, as if even she was beginning to wonder if the speech were ever going to end.

"Being blessed with the attributes of a spider, I have the innate ability to spin a web."

Now he had Ross' full attention. Of course, she thought. The spider could drop into the opening and return on his own web. And if the strands were strong enough, the whole patrol could use it.

"With that ability, assuming I can find a satisfactory anchor for the filament, I should be able to excrete a fiber that will support my weight as I descend into the cavern below. Because my mass is significantly less than yours, I would have to lay several strands in order to support one of you. This would take some time, but, based on the current situation, we have plenty of time available."

"Great. Do it."

"It is odd, Sergeant," said Archon. "But your speech patterns more closely resemble my good friend Stone's the longer we are together."

The patrol regrouped at the base of Archon's multistrand web line. Ross set up a relay retransmitter at the edge of the opening in the dome before dropping through, just to be sure they would be able to transmit to the surface from inside. The light Ross threw in earlier provided an infrared source to guide them on the descent, and the white light of the headlamps soon illuminated an awe-inspiring scene.

They had found a fantastic city, a place unlike anything they had ever seen or dreamed. The patrol stood at the foot of a stepped pyramid, its pinnacle vanishing in the gloom, out of range of their lamps. The stone risers were five meters high, and they could count ten risers within the range of the circle of light their lamps cast. A set of stairs centered on the face of the pyramid led upward into the darkness.

Broad avenues rimed with ice surrounded the pyramid, then stretched away to vanish in the cold dark. Frost coated the stones of the plaza, showing every contour of the structure in soft relief that glistened under the harsh white of the arc lamps. The sheer, unexpected grandeur filled the intruders with awe; they stood silent and open-mouthed in wonder.

Ross signaled, and the others followed as she led off, her combat boots crunching on the frost. The internal mapping system in each ped's suit began marking the path the team took. They spread out into the standard formation for investigating unexplored territory, Ross ahead and in the center, the two legionnaires flanking her ten meters away on each side.

Archon brought up the rear, his pointed feet cutting through the frost to the stones below.

They moved away from the pyramid. An obelisk, two meters square at the base and fifteen meters high, appeared in the pool of light they cast before them. The sides of the stone were heavily carved with humanoid forms that sat cross-legged on sculptured stools. The figures wore fantastic headdresses that looked like huge, upturned bowls decorated with enormous feathers. Prominent glyphs proclaimed the importance of the representations, but none among the intruders could decipher them. Ross stepped closer and directed her light onto the face of the monument. She rubbed her hand over the stone, brushing away frost in a silver shower. "Look at the hair," she said softly. "They're all wearing their hair long."

"Naram," said Archon immediately. "I have seen such items before, but only in repositories of cultural artifacts. These are certainly quite ancient, and they bear a marked resemblance to the relics so dear to the Naram population." Archon Divxas fell silent again.

"Glassy Relic Regal Six. This is Glassy Relic Regal Two-two-six. We've found something you're not going to believe."

Centurion Moldine Rinter spread the sketch map on the illuminated table in the operations Pedden. Parts of the underground city were still missing from the map, but enough of it had been sketched in to reveal its extent. The preserved area was two and a half kilometers in diameter, covered by a dome several hundred meters high at the center. The dome was a tough, thick plastic that supported the tons of ice that had formed over it. Four entrance arches stood on the perimeter, sealed by massive doors that were in turn sealed by the ice. The ice had broken through the dome in several places, but the ice and snow that had fallen covered only small areas of the city.

Centurion Braxton Sloan, the engineer officer assigned to Cohort Harras, studied the sketch. Sloan was a specialist, and well aware of his special status. Engineers, as he and his peers were quick to point out, trained as tankers or infantry, but they could do constructive jobs in addition to fighting. Unit commanders leading troops with engineers among their ranks tended to try to protect them. If an engineer could survive his initial combat assignments, he was almost guaranteed a long life and safe berth. Promotion among the upper ranks of the engineers was slow, but the lower-ranked officers usually achieved higher rank rapidly. Braxton Sloan had made centurion in two years, but he had maintained that rank for the next twelve. Slow promotion had its advantages: engineer officers were fully qualified in a number of tasks, and they knew everyone in the corps. But complacency also made engineers less responsive to new situations. When an officer knew that how well he did in a given task would have no direct bearing on his prospects of promotion, the competitive edge disappeared, and so did the innovative solutions to complex problems that kept one military force ahead of another.

Sloan struggled to overcome the lethargy of stagnation that had dulled his mind. In his fourteen years in the Commonwealth Armed Forces, he thought he had seen every engineering problem, but this was a new one. He was supposed to advise the Cohort commander on how best to defend an ancient domed city against TOG attack. He studied the sketch on the flourotable. The people who built the dome knew what they were doing. The arc of the shell was perfectly calculated to carry what they must have known would be a great weight. Parts of the dome had been ruptured, but not through any structural fault. That damage could only have been caused by significant and unforeseen seismic shifts.

The city covered by the dome was equally impressive. The central plaza was several hundred meters on a side, surrounded by what were obviously municipal buildings. Some of these structures rose as high as eight stories above the plaza, with wide flights of steps leading up to the doors. Every structure was built with the same volcanic stone, which would have been very difficult to work with primitive tools. Beyond the municipal area lay houses constructed from the same volcanic material. The ancient race that built this city had built it to last forever, and so it had.

"What we've got here," said Sloan, beginning his analysis, "is a basic Class A/2 urban area. The streets away from the main square are random-dense, and buildings are located close together along the edges of narrow, winding streets. That is the Class A urban area classification. The type-two construction indicates what we call masonry construction, characterized by thick exterior walls of natural stone. Interior walls and floors in this construction type are generally thinner and may be a fire hazard; however, in the buildings I have examined, the interior construction appears substantial.

"The A/2 pattern is an excellent one for defense. The narrow, winding streets limit attackers' observation and fire opportunities, and, in turn, permit the defense to develop ambush sites and kill zones that become apparent only after the attacker has committed his forces. In addition, the masonry construction gives the defenders good protection. Communications within buildings is good because it is easy to generate mouse holes for movement. The attackers must use heavy charges in order to breach the exterior walls. Overall, the defenders have a strong position."

Rinter listened to Sloan's lecture on defense of urbanized terrain. She had heard it all before at General Staff School, but it was nice to have a refresher. She addressed the engineer. "Can we hold the place with the force we have? Will the dome stand? How difficult will it be for the TOGs to break in?"

"I cannot predict whether or not we can hold the city for ourselves. We will certainly give better than we get in this setup, but as to holding, I don't know. The dome is sound. Of course, the TOGs will be able to breach it as easily as we did, but we will be able to hear them coming, which gives us an advantage. If we have time, the engineers can rig some nasty surprises for the TOGs. Our only alternative is to defend our position on the surface, and we already know the problems we'll have doing that."

Rinter stared down at the map. Sloan was right about the situation on the surface. The wind had picked up again, making the wind-chill factor newly dangerous. The Centuries were already reporting cases of frostbite, and at least one death was directly related to the freezing wind. The medical section had already requested a warmer place for the dressing station.

"I'll take your advice to Milt," she said. "I think he'll agree that you're right. We'll have to go underground. Normally, I'd be worried about whether this move would cut our communications with Rolandrin, but we haven't talked to headquarters since we left for this godforsaken spot, so what's the difference? I say under the ice is our best chance for survival."

28

0700, 12 Martius 6831—The excavator Ross' team had found partially buried under an ice fall in the corridor near where they discovered the dome proved a blessing. Sloan and his fellow engineers had it backed out of its cave and running within hours of the decision to go under the south pole. One of the ruptures in the dome was near where the Renegade Cohort headquarters was set up, and Harras decided to use that break as an entrance instead of making a new one or digging out one of the doors. Digging through the ice far enough to clear one of the doors would be too time-consuming, and would create a significant activity signature that would likely be read by the TOGs.

Sloan's first task was to cut a passage from the surface to the dome, which were separated by less than ten meters of ice. The spoil created by the excavation went into one of the main existing passageways. This cut would be used only as an entrance, supporting foot and grav vehicle travel, so there was no need to make the slope a gentle one. When the engineers reached the surface with the machine, they turned around and cut away the ice that had extended from the fracture down into the city. A simple hole would suffice here, also.

When the initial tunnel was finished, the engineer corp widened it so that the larger vehicles could be brought into the city if necessary. The result was a passage eight meters wide and four meters high that started at the surface, descended in a steep incline to the level of the broken dome, then turned at a sharp right angle toward the dome itself. Conventional wisdom dictated that a straight passage was undefendable, so the turn served as an ambush site. From the right-angle turn, the tunnel ran to the fracture. The break in the dome was narrower than the initial cut Sloan made, just wide enough for a Liberator to scrape through. Once inside the dome, the passage broke through the sloping surface of the ice. From there, it was just a matter of negotiating the glacis down to the floor of the city. Sloan's team was finished less than two hours after they dug out the excavator.

The Cohort began to evacuate even before he was finished. The headquarters section went into the hole first under the control of Centurion Sedden Matruh, whose primary function within the Cohort was to establish the jump command post. The operations sergeant went with him to set up the light commlink equipment. The medical section, led by Dr. Kelton Hess, and the communications team accompanied Matruh into the city.

The city was immediately familiar to Hess. He had served as a Renegade legionnaire for almost 30 years, joining as an enlisted man in 6801, before the fighting even began on Caralis. He accepted an honorable discharge when his initial enlistment was up, and spent several years crewing around on freighters, first visiting the star systems of the Orion arm of the Milky Way, where his home world was located, and eventually traveling to other parts of the Orion galaxy and Naram space. He found the Naram fascinating.

This tall, olive-skinned race developed in much the same stages as the Human race, and it was difficult for the doctor to see them as anything but a branch of Humanity. He worked for a year as a common laborer for a Naram cooperative, learning the Naram language and absorbing their culture. He embraced their philosophy of reverence for life and the importance of altruistic endeavors, and so turned to medicine. He returned to his home world and applied to medical school.

Older, and perhaps more serious, than his peers in the university, Hess excelled at his studies while neglecting to make friends. He graduated with high honors and quickly established a flourishing private practice, but Hess found that this way of practicing medicine did not fulfill the Naram philosophy he had accepted as his own. Something was missing. He was fast becoming a society doctor, which was not the turn he wanted his life to take.

Hess sold his practice and rejoined the military. Too old to be accepted as a neophyte surgeon by the Commonwealth forces, he joined the Renegade Legion. He enjoyed his initial assignment to a Cohort dressing station, and had resisted promotion to a field or surgical hospital. Hess was happy with the smaller units.

Entering the city brought back a flood of memories. The great plaza with its towering municipal buildings reminded him of Copan, his favorite Naram city. Privately naming this ancient site Copan, he wandered the central plaza from the beautifully carved perimeter stelae to the base of a great acropolis. Even in the darkness, penetrated by only his hand-held torch, the dimensions were impressive. Hess found the side streets leading away from the plaza area equally fascinating.

The homes were of the same Naram design with which he was familiar. The buildings showed a solid front to the street, but the interiors were complex systems of common and private rooms. The typical building opened on a large area, usually the height of the building, called a "hutch" by Human anthropologists. The exterior walls surrounding the common area were filled with "dens," accessible through a complicated series of stairs and balconies. The headquarters section set up in a hutch, and engineering bored holes through the walls of adjacent buildings for the medical and communications units. It was one of the best field hospital arrangements Hess had ever had.

The central area of the building set aside for the hospital was established as a receiving center and triage. The lower-floor rooms were set aside for living quarters for the staff of three enlisted corpsmen, a nurse, and Hess. The surgery was organized in the room adjacent to the doctor's living quarters, and there was enough additional space for four wards. The building was completely furnished with the habiliments of a Naram home, including a well-equipped kitchen. It also held the dead.

Discovery of the first inhabitant was a shock. She was found sitting in a chair in the central hutch of what became the headquarters building. Dressed in a fine, linen cloak embroidered with flowers, she sat as if awaiting guests. On her lap was a feathered headdress of gold and jade, the feathers so brittle from age and cold that they snapped off when touched. The legionnaires spoke quietly and respectfully around the woman, as though afraid of disturbing her vigil. The body was too rigid to be laid to rest, so the chair and its occupant were moved to an empty room off the central hall. The others found in the same house were placed there as well. By the time the advance element had fully occupied the three buildings, they had moved a total of seven bodies, all women or children.

With the new command post established, the Cohort began to plan how to move to its subterranean base. Two basic ways to break contact with the TOG forces were commonly used: assume that there was no contact and bug out by unit or section-sized groups, or assume that a disengagement was required, and retire by smaller groups. The TOGs had been quiet, except for occasional, ineffective sniping, but Harras still had to decide how to withdraw.

The Cohort commander faced one major problem. Though the tanks and carriers currently occupied hidden positions with their power plants shut down, making them almost completely invisible, the TOGs would be able to pinpoint their location as soon as the machines powered up. Dummy transponders, or even the IFF units of the vehicles, could be placed at the Renegade positions when the vehicles retreated, but the Marshman grav drives emitted such a strong signature that their ion cloud could not be disguised. The TOGs would pounce as soon as they discovered that the Renegades were moving.

The solution to the problem was a hybrid. The first vehicles to retreat would follow the example of the advance party, moving individual tanks and carriers to thin the lines. The designated vehicles would pull back one at a time from their positions, the most forward first, to the bolt-hole. This part of the plan would proceed for as long as the TOGs were quiet. Once the retreat was discovered, and the Renegade positions came under attack, the unengaged elements would break for the tunnel. Those in contact would retire by bounding overwatch, with each unit falling back to a defensive position to cover the withdrawal of the more heavily engaged vehicles. The unengaged units' retreat would have to be tightly controlled because there was only one avenue of withdrawal once the vehicles reached the gallery. Any crowding at the surface would lead to chaos, and the same was true of any vehicle damaged while in the passage. A jammed Liberator at the edge of the dome would be a disaster.

The Reserve Century, closest to the hole, moved first, leaving Jamie MacDougall's Wolverines and Sloan's engineers to cover the hole. The Wolverines were small enough that they would be able to make a quick dash through the tunnels, and the engineers had to stay to keep the opening clear in case of trouble. Sloan drove the tunnel cutter into a side passage and left it ready. Ross' Viper squad went down to cover the break into the dome, and their Viper set up on the floor of the city, its SMLM missiles trained on the opening. Ross stayed at the breach.

Based on their proximity to known TOG positions, Fourth Century moved first, followed by Third and Second. Ventis, with the heaviest defensive force, would be the last to move. All his vehicles dumped their IFF transponders just to keep the TOGs confused for as long as possible about what was really happening. Fourth Century pulled out.

    Centurion Marmoreus Patrius watched the illuminated plot plan of the Renegade positions. The enemy had been dormant for hours, and he was worried. Legatus Camus had executed an attack on these positions simultaneous with the entry of the Renegade relief force, but had done nothing since. And that attack could not be judged a success. Most of the small Renegade reinforcement force had been able to break into the perimeter, and pushing infantry against the Renegade position had proved they were still full of fight. Legatus Camus had requested reinforcements from Malthus, artillery as well as air-defense units. They had arrived after the attack, immediately accepting orders and establishing target reference points.

    Patrius was unhappy about the presence of the artillery. He felt sure Camus would rather pound the Renegade positions for the next millennia than commit his combat forces. The present situation did not call for a formal siege. Patrius was even more convinced that what was needed here was a sharp attack and a quick victory. Standing around like this only allowed the Renegades to seize the initiative.

The plot flickered, and Patrius watched the red indicator of a Renegade vehicle move within the lines. He had been seeing significant movement now for some time. As he watched, the vehicle moved toward the center of the Renegade position. Then the symbol stopped and began to fade. It moved slightly and faded again. This signature was completely consistent with a driver shutting down and letting the Marshman drive bleed off power so that his location would be hidden from sensors. The trick would do him no good, however. The computer of the Plot Plan Indicator would remember where the vehicle had cooled and re-post its last known location as required. He let the image fade completely, made a quick ten-count, then asked the PPI to re-post all moved vehicles. He stared at the screen. The computer was telling him that all the vehicles he had seen moving were co-located.

Patrius blanked the screen and asked the computer to re-post all moved vehicles again. The same overlapping group of red indicators appeared. The Renegades were making a move, and he had missed it. He cursed. Camus would have his rank for this. He toggled the alert switch, calling himself a fool. Camus walked through the anti-flash curtains separating the operations section from the command post. "What is the alert, Patrius?"

"The Renegades are moving, sir. It just started." Patrius pointed to the cluster of red indicators. "They're up to something. We should attack at once!"

Camus pushed the curtains aside. "Gunner," he said to the artillery commander. "Alert your units. Prepare to commence firing on my command. Compare target data."

"Sir," repeated Patrius, "we should attack at once."

"Patrius," said Camus coldly, "we attacked without artillery before, and we have the bodies to prove the folly of that approach. This time we will do it right." The cannoneer approached and spread the fire scheme across the PPI. All three officers compared the numbered crosses with the current location of the Renegade vehicles. "Shoot groupings DEBEO REGAL eight-two-one and one-one-seven."

"Roger," replied the cannoneer. "We'll use HAFE. The ice will create extra fragments."

"Shoot for three minutes and then be prepared to lift one-one-seven. We'll have assault troops move on that area."

"As you command." The cannoneer departed.

"Now, Patrius, we will launch our attack. It will take three minutes for the Second and Third Centuries to mount and move, and the artillery will prepare the way."

"It will also tell the Renegades where and when we will attack. Sir." Patrius added the final "Sir" as an unmistakable insult. The two officers glared at each other. Patrius had overstepped his bounds, and it was only a matter of time before Camus took up the challenge.

The first HAFE rounds dropped into Ventis' position just as his flanking infantry squad began to move. The peds were up and out as the first round burst over their position. The first section was partially shielded by the bulk of the Viper carrier and had not been as quick to move on command. As a result, it lost only one man. The other four-man section was fully exposed, though, and the round burst directly over the section leader. The survivors saw the principes vanish under the flechettes. Even his armored, insulated boots were reduced to fragments.

At the bolt-hole the deadly darts expelled by the HAFE rounds scythed across the opening, ringing off the sides of the Wolverines. Jamie MacDougall shouted a warning before the round exploded, and so all the scout vehicles were buttoned, the flechettes rattling off the armor. The Wolverines dashed far enough down the tunnel that they suffered no damage, but any vehicle near the escape hole would take the full force of the blast.

The artillery pounding continued as the two Pompey vehicles saturated their target areas with rounds. The HAFE ammunition did not need a painted target to hit, just an observer. The bursts over the bolt-hole were targeted by computer-generated data, spreading the pounding over a wide area. The artillery targeting Ventis' Second Century did not have that disadvantage. They were using a forward observer, who could see the entire target area and make trajectory corrections after each round to walk the fire back and forth across the targets. All the tanks and carriers in Ventis' position took damage.

As the three minutes of "softening up" ended, the observer shifted the fire deeper into the Renegade perimeter, Horatius tanks and Romulus carriers sweeping past him as the last artillery round burst over the enemy location. Even as the observer called to shift the fire, the main guns of the tanks opened on the cloud of ice and snow marking the shattered Renegade position.

29

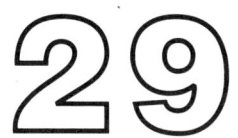

1100, 12 Martius 6831—Optio Holden Ventis saw the last HAFE round burst well away from his Spartius. Knowing the TOG artillery would only lift if ground troops were being committed, he alerted his Century's surviving vehicles. He had no time to take casualty reports, which would be a pointless exercise anyway. If a vehicle didn't report, it was either dead, or too busy fighting its way toward the escape hole in the ice cap. Either way, it didn't matter. His own DDP would tell him where the enemy had broken through.

Unless the enemy came in at tree-top flight, Ventis knew that intervening terrain would block his line-of-sight to the TOG vehicles until they approached to within three kilometers. It wasn't likely they would attack at TTF, however, because the TOGs had taken a beating for staying at that height too long in the first attack. The second TOG attack had used infantry supported by mortars, and it had been equally unsuccessful. The TOGs had failed to press their assault, and their peds had gone to ground well short of effective infantry range. But this time was different. This time they were using artillery.

The computer spoke in his ear. "Many vehicles. Horatius and Aeneas tanks, Romulus and Lupis carriers. Range five-zero-double-zero. Bearing five-eight-double-zero to eight-double-zero. Velocity one hundred. Closing. Targets not acquired." The DDP had picked up the approaching TOGs, but the terrain was obscuring a lock-on.

Ventis thumbed the commlink to the Century. "Glassy Relic. This is Glassy Relic Two-six. Fire at will. Am withdrawing to position two now and will cover." He switched to internal. "Davis," he said to the driver, "Get to the next position marked on your screen."

"Roger. Moving now."

The Spartius slid backward down the rear slope, spun around at the foot, and began to move the eight hundred meters to the next position. Ventis would liked to have pulled back farther, but eight hundred meters marked the next good defilade for covering the other three vehicles in the Century. He watched the DDP for activity from his Liberators.

"Many vehicles. Horatius and Aeneas tanks, Romulus and Lupis carriers. Range four-zero-double-zero. Bearing five-eight-double-zero to eight-double-zero. Velocity one hundred. Closing. Targets not acquired." The TOGs were still coming, still blocked by the terrain.

The middle Liberator of his Century glowed on the screen. Ventis could tell that it, too, was moving now, but toward the approaching TOGs rather than away from the attackers. It rose from its crater and slowly accelerated across the brow of the hill blocking the enemy. It turned to track across the front of the Century's position. Ventis heard the 150mm cannon crack, followed by the sharper report of the 50mm. The DDP showed smoke blossoming between the friendly and hostile lines. Ventis smiled. The Second Platoon leader, Sergeant Kent Narall, was giving the TOGs something to think about. The two cannon on the Liberator continued to fire, throwing clouds of smoke at the attackers.

"Many vehicles. Horatius and Aeneas tanks, Romulus and Lupis carriers. Range three-five-double-zero. Bearing five-eight-double-zero to eight-double-zero. Velocity six-zero. Closing. Targets not acquired." Narall's smoke had slowed the TOGs. They couldn't see beyond it, and they didn't want to chance bursting through the shroud into the massed fire of hidden Renegade tanks. Ventis' Spartius turned to face the TOG lines as it reached the secondary position and crept up the hill until the turret cleared the edge. Ventis heard his gunner and driver talking as the carrier went into turret defilade. His infantry bounded back past the carrier, moving toward the higher ground in the rear.

A kilometer behind the Second Century's new position, the HAFE rounds continued to burst over the bolt-hole. Ventis felt sick to his stomach when he contemplated the final run. The enemy artillery pounding their escape route would make the final jump dangerous. He forced himself to think instead about the TOGs in front. Let the future take care of itself.

"Many vehicles. Horatius and Aeneas tanks, Romulus and Lupis carriers. Range three-zero-double-zero. Bearing five-eight-double-zero to eight-double-zero. Velocity one-zero-zero. Closing. Targets not acquired." The TOGs had picked up speed again. The DDP's voice continued to update the target information. "Many vehicles. Horatius and Aeneas tanks, Romulus and Lupis carriers. Range two-eight-double-zero. Bearing five-eight-double-zero to eight-double-zero. Velocity one-zero-zero. Closing. Targets acquired and locked." The TOGs had maneuvered through the smoke layer. The line of hills in front of Ventis flashed with fire as all three of the Liberators opened on the advancing enemy at once.

"Tim." Ventis spoke to the gunner. "Pick a small one. Try for an Aeneas or Lupis. Leave the big ones for the tanks."

"Roger. Tracking." There was a pause while Tim Rollus scanned the enemy, picking his target. "Got one."

Ventis treadled the painting laser. "Target identified. Lupis carrier. Range two-seven-double-zero. Bearing four-zero-zero. Velocity one-zero-zero and closing. Target locked." Ventis hit the painting laser again. "Target identified. Lupis carrier. Range two-six-double-zero. Bearing four-zero-zero. Velocity one-zero-zero and closing. Target locked and painted."

"Gunner. Hit the Lupis carrier at two-seven-double-zero with the laser."

"Identified."

"Fire."

"Done."

Ventis glanced at the DDP to evaluate the effect of the lasers.

"Lasers recharged," said Rollus over the commlink.

"Gunner, the Lupis is still up. Hit it with the laser again."

"Target identified."

"Shoot."

"Got it."

The Lupis identifier blinked and became a broken square. "He's dead," said Ventis. "Switch targets." I can't do this, Ventis told himself. I can't run this Spartius and command the Century. "Tim. Go to local control. Pick and paint your own shots."

"Local control. Roger. I have it."

Optio Ventis scanned the DDP for his command's three Liberators. Narall's tank, off to the position's right flank, showed as a solid square. He was still engaging. The center Liberator indicator was blinking. Dead. Ventis tried to remember the commander's name, but he couldn't. He couldn't even remember what he looked like, what he sounded like over the commlink. "Regal Two. This is Two-six. Forward elements withdraw to next position." The acknowledgement was interrupted by the whine of the dual Herring lasers as Rollus fired at another target. The DDP blurred as the two remaining Liberators covered their withdrawal with clouds of high-density smoke.

The TOG vehicles were close. Ventis didn't need the ballistic computer to call off the ranges; he could see the tanks and carriers himself. The Liberators roared past him, their grav drives kicking up huge clouds of snow as they took up positions closer to the bolt-hole. The paint warning klaxon howled in his ear; it was almost time to go. The twin lasers whined again. "Incoming rounds. Vehicle painted." He looked out over the coaming of the command station. The sky sparkled with glowing trails as missiles left their launch platforms. The Vulcan antimissile system whirred over his head and two of the incoming TVLGs burst like small suns against the night sky.

The Spartius shook with the impact of the remaining TVLGs. The carrier's left front vanished under the multiple hits. Ventis ducked as a wave of titanium and ballistic shielding fragments washed over the turret, sparking off the TVLG housing on the left side. A blinking light on the command console reported that the port-side Terrain Search and Reaction system was destroyed. The fighting compartment filled with the familiar, sticky-sweet smell of vaporized ceramic shielding. The Liberators' 150mm cannon cracked overhead.

"Zollach." Ventis spoke calmly into the commlink. "Get us out of here." The Spartius reacted at once. Davis Zollach had almost anticipated the command, and the pummeling the glacis had just taken inspired his driving. The carrier turned so violently that Ventis was thrown against the side of the turret. The gunner triggered two smoke canisters to cover the withdrawal, and the paint warning klaxon stopped shrieking.

The Spartius ran out of cover after it leapfrogged past the two Liberators covering its retreat. HAFE rounds continued to burst steadily over the escape hole and Ventis made a quick decision. "Take her to tree-top flight and hover."

"Tree-top?" Zollach sounded unhappy.

"Roger. Tree-top," repeated Ventis. "And try to stay away from the HAFE rounds." At TTF, the Spartius could fire over the terrain as the Liberators withdrew. He switched to external comm. "Glassy Relic Two. This is Glassy Relic Two-six. Move."

The two Liberators backed away from their positions, and Ventis realized he had lost the Viper carrier in the confusion. He scanned the DDP, searching for the carrier's signature, but it was nowhere to be seen. Either it had made the withdrawal safely to the bolt-hole, or it had been pounded to slag in the first attack. He didn't have time to search for it. Below him, he could see his own peds streaking for the safety of the hole. They passed from his field of vision. More HAFE rounds exploded to the rear.

"Many vehicles. Horatius and Aeneas tanks, Romulus and Lupis carriers. Range one-zero-double-zero. Bearing six-zero-double-zero to five-double-zero. Velocity one-two-zero and closing. Targets locked."

The DDP lit up with target indicators as the TOG vehicles cleared the smoke. "Get on 'em, Tim."

"Painting now."

"Target identified. Horatius tank. Range one-zero-double-zero. Bearing six-three-double-zero. Velocity one-zero-zero and closing. Target locked. Target painted." The lasers fired. Ventis stuck his head up above the coaming and saw the glow of the laser hits. The

Horatius tank shimmered with light, illuminating the other TOG vehicles emerging from the smoke thrown by the Liberators. The smoke reflected the flash of the TOG vehicles' weapons fire.

Below and to the right a Second Century Liberator had drawn the attention of the advancing enemy. The tank was accelerating toward the safety of the escape hole, its stern to the enemy. Ventis saw the armor go molten under repeated fire. The vehicle yawed wildly as the driver tried to maintain control. Grav coils spewed from the shattered stern, ricocheting off the ice like powered springs. The tank buried its nose in a jutting pinnacle of ice that exploded under the impact. The tank spun, and the left side crashed into an ice hummock, burying itself to the turret. Smoke and flame gushed from the damaged stern like a torch, vaporizing the snow to instant steam. The burning tank glowed through the steam, creating an eerie effect of living fire.

The other Liberator raced for safety. The Horatius tanks finished destroying the dying Liberator and turned their attention to the Spartius. The paint warning klaxon screamed as Ventis saw a tank directly in front of him shift slightly to bring its 150mm main gun to bear. The muzzle looked huge as it trained on the hovering carrier. Rollus fired the twin turret lasers. The stern of the enemy tank absorbed the hits, but the muzzle never moved. A gout of flame sprang from the black hole. The impact was instantaneous. The Spartius leaped backward, slamming Ventis' helmet forward onto the hatch coaming. Stars flashed across his vision.

The Spartius carrier, even at 189 metric tons, could not resist the momentum of a 150mm APDS round. Zollach fought to bring the gyrating carrier under control. Another round smashed into the underside, and the driver's control station spewed smoke. Red warning lights flashed. "Grav drive system failure," Zollach shouted. The Spartius fell at sickening speed.

The carrier hit the ice and rebounded. Smoke was pouring from the underside. "Davis. Tim. Get out. I have the lasers!" Ventis took control of the turret and turned it on the nearest Horatius. He treadled the painting laser and fired, not waiting for confirmation. The twin Herrings blazed coherent light. Ventis attempted to fire the rest of his missiles, but the DDP showed the left-side hull launcher as inoperative. He switched to the right and fired a pair of TVLGs. Tim was standing on the top of the turret pulling the driver through the escape hatch. Zollach was doubled over, his body wrenched by violent coughs as he tried to clear his lungs. Fire burst from the sides of the stricken carrier. The lasers blazed again.

Ventis saw the DDP flash a series of warnings across the screen, each one blinking "SYSTEM FAILURE," and knew it was time to go. The fighting compartment glowed; waves of heat engulfed him. He was warm, really warm, for the first time in days, and he enjoyed it until the soles of his boots began to burn, and the pain shocked him into action. He thumbed the firing circuits one more time. A single TVLG shot from the rails, but the lasers refused to fire.

The Spartius was surrounded by fire and steam. Ventis leaped from the turret, trying to clear the ring of flame. He was surprised when he hit water, then realized the Spartius was melting into the ice. He splashed away from the burning carrier, warm water pouring through the joints in his battledress uniform. Clouds of steam made it hard to breathe. His feet slipped on the surface beneath the melting ice. It was colder away from the vehicle. Then he was clear of the smoke, able to see his location.

The bolt-hole lay less than twenty meters away. He could see the rim, smooth from the passage of the other vehicles and men. A Wolverine stern protruded from the hole, great slabs of armor torn from its side. Enough space remained for a man to pass between the dead scout vehicle and the edge of the hole. Ventis staggered to his feet and made for the rim. He slipped, slamming to his knees in the water-covered ice. His thighs were cold and he couldn't feel his feet, couldn't get them to move on his command. He stumbled again as he tried to gain his feet.

Optio Holden Ventis dropped to all fours. Once again, he willed his legs to carry him toward the opening in the ice that meant safety. The space between the Wolverine and the ice blurred. A HAFE round burst overhead, blotting out feeling, and sight, and life. The Wolverine began to burn.

30

1330, 12 Martius 6831—Sergeant Terrance Kallach, the assistant squad leader of the Spartius commanded by Optio Holden Ventis, stumbled over an ice outcropping in the rough tunnel the Renegade engineers had cut from the ice cap's surface to the city below. He gave in to momentum and sat down, his whole body aching from constant collisions with the ice. His HUD was practically useless in the frigid darkness, and he lifted the face plate out of the way. The other members of the squad stumbled over him and cursed, but he was too tired and too cold to curse back. The last dash for the escape hole had been through ankle-deep water, and some of it had gotten into his boots. He could barely feel his toes, and he wiggled them to help the blood flow.

Discomfort and disorientation were new to Kallach. He liked the security of being attached to an infantry carrier, knowing that his world had a constant reference point. The carrier not only provided power to the bounce suits the peds wore, it was home. He, like most infantry, didn't like to ride the carrier into battle, but it was a nice place to come back to after a fight. He had become especially fond of his carrier during the current operation, because, above all else, it had been warm. The titanium cocoons were heated, and the peds had been able to heat their combat rations. Chipping a meal from its plastic sleeve was a trial, and trying to choke down the frozen food was more trouble than it was worth. Now the Spartius was gone, trapped above by the ice and the TOGs. He rose and stumbled on ahead of his squad.

At the base of the long incline they met their guide, a triarii from another infantry Century, who led them into a city that rose in spectral grandeur before them. They walked in silence as the triarii gestured with a torch, pointing out various unit areas, kill zones, and headquarters locations. Kallach could not pay attention. He was too tired and cold for any of it to make sense. He followed the guide down the street and into a huge building.

The other members of Cohort Harras were in much the same stunned, weary condition. The retreat to the city had been more successful than any of the commanders had hoped. They had taken casualties, to be sure, but the TOGs had been slow to react to their withdrawal. The Reserve Century, as well as the Third and Fourth Centuries, had escaped with most of their vehicles intact. The Second Century, the last to retreat, had been caught by the advancing TOGs and the artillery. Only a Viper and a Liberator from the Second had made it, but the peds from the command Spartius had reached the hole, even though their carrier was lost topside. Jamie MacDougall's scouts had been reduced to only the command vehicle.

Harras and Rinter began to reorganize the defense.

The total Renegade force now comprised eleven Liberators, seven Vipers, and a Wolverine. Additional troops, mostly surviving crew from destroyed vehicles, made up two full infantry squads. The real problem was the limited number of officers left to command the force. Only three centurions remained: Rinter, the operations officer, Matruh, the headquarters commander, and MacDougall, the scout commander. Four optios had survived: Walker of the Third Century; Rand, the former communications officer and commander of the Fourth Century; Karstil, who had come in with the reserves; and Bard, now in charge of communications. Doctor Kelton Hess of the medical section had the experience and rank to take a unit, but could not be used as a combat leader. His position as a non-combatant was sacrosanct.

Harras divided the remaining troops into three Centuries. Jamie MacDougall commanded the First from his Wolverine with Optio Samual Rand as his second. The First Century was made up of four Liberators and two Vipers organized in two equal platoons. The peds from the Vipers were dismounted to act on defense, and the vehicles were to be used as counterattack forces. The Second Century was commanded by Sedden Matruh from the headquarters Viper. His second was Fagan Walker. This force also consisted of four Liberators and two Vipers, divided into two platoons. The peds were deployed in the buildings, and the vehicles were set up for counterattacks.

The Third Century served as the reserve under Moldine Rinter. She had commanded the reserve earlier while acting as the operations officer, and she continued in her dual role with Optio Roglund Karstil as her executive officer. The reserve had two Liberators and two Vipers, along with the engineering vehicle and two Peddens to transport infantry. The final grouping was the Cohort headquarters, now under the control of Optio Holton Bard. It included the useless communications Pedden in addition to the medical and operations sections' carriers. The only combat vehicle in the Headquarters Century was Harras' Liberator.

It was not the perfect unit with which to defend a city. Commanders given the mission of defending built-up areas preferred to be infantry-heavy. Tanks only got in the way in the streets, were easy to spot on enemy DDPs, and easy to ambush if they didn't have good infantry support. The tank's primary role in city fighting was as mobile supporting artillery, for tank guns did not throw a large enough high-explosive round to be a significant asset. Harras, like every other officer defending a city, would have preferred something like the Kershaw Special Artillery Platform available to the TOGs. But Harras had to use what he had, and what he had was a tank-heavy Cohort.

Legatus Cariolanus Camus stood in the command hatch of his Romulus carrier, peering into the dark arctic night lit by the burning hulks of Renegade vehicles. Aeneas tanks and Lupis carriers prowled the area, searching for their own survivors. They also hunted down Renegade survivors, and found some hidden in the crags and pinnacles that jutted like ragged teeth from the surrounding ice. One Renegade Viper and its squad put up a desperate fight, dodging from crag to crag and sniping at the TOGs. The squad was finally cornered in a blind canyon. With no way out except up, they tried to escape over the chasm's rim. They might have made it if not for a Scipio antiaircraft vehicle lying in wait. Just as the Viper cleared the rim, the Scipio hit it with two missiles to the underside, scattering pieces of the Viper for a hectare in every direction.

As the operations Pompey pulled alongside the Romulus, the side door slid open. In the dim light of the interior battle lanterns, Camus could see the silhouettes of Centurion Marmoreus Patrius and Prefect Claudius Sulla. He thought for a moment about using the antipersonnel laser on the turret of his carrier. One short burst would get them both, and his immediate problems would be solved. He could always claim that it was a computer malfunction. He pressed the activating mechanism with his knee and let the mount swing toward the operations vehicle. Then Sulla threw him the Terran Overlord Government's fisted salute, and Camus took his knee from the power switch.

Sulla gripped Camus' right forearm as the legatus climbed into the command Pompey. "You have done well, Legatus Camus," the prefect pronounced. The man was trying to be dignified, but betrayed the jangled state of his nerves by spraying spittle over the front of Camus' uniform. "This victory will go on your record."

"Thank you, Prefect. I am your humble servant."

"With all due respect, sirs," Patrius broke in, "there seem to be very few vehicles destroyed for the reported size of the Renegade Cohort. There must be many more in hiding."

"I am sure Legatus Camus' troops will find them." Sulla sounded less confident than his words. He peered out into the night, then shifted out of sight of the open tank door.

Camus eyed the prefect. The man was obviously a nervous wreck. Even three kilometers from the perimeter of the fighting had been too close for him. The legatus half-expected to see a telltale sign of moisture on the legs of the prefect's combat uniform. He stole a quick glance downward, but the dim light in the Pompey made it impossible to tell if the man might have wet himself. "Does this evaluation mean we will return to Malthus right away?"

"Not just yet, but very soon," replied Sulla. "We must wait for the replacement scientific, I mean meteorological, team to arrive. They are already on their way."

"With all due respect, sirs," Patrius repeated insistently, "the Renegades who occupied this position must still be taken care of. The number of destroyed units surrounding us is too small to account for what was posted on the operations screen. Too many of them are missing. We should conduct a search."

"Nonsense, my dear Patrius. You are just nervous. We have seen with our own eyes the destruction of the enemy Cohort. I, Prefect Claudius Sulla, have seen it, as have you. It was a great victory."

Optio Holton Bard sat in his Pedden and waited for the crash of the TOG forces breaking into the city. He couldn't understand why they were waiting so long to pursue their advantage. It was standard TOG military strategy to maintain pressure when the enemy was on the run. It should have been inexcusable that the Renegades be allowed to reorganize their shattered forces in this underground city. The only possible explanation was that the attack force commander was a total incompetent. Even with a depleted force, the momentum of a TOG attack was usually maintained. What could the man be thinking? Maybe he didn't know where the Renegades had gone. Bard sat up abruptly in his chair. That was the answer! It probably looked as if the Renegades had disappeared without a trace. The TOG commander needed to be told the Renegade location before he simply abandoned the area. He must be notified at once.

Bard took three quick steps and slipped into the communications console chair. He could easily broadcast on a power band that would be read by the TOGs above. Any message, even a simple administrative directive, would be enough to bring them down on the Renegade position. The commlink hummed to life under his fingers. He had to make this quick. He typed in a message to all TOG units, set it on cipher, and waited for the green light to indicate the system was ready to send.

"System's broke, sir." The voice of Communications Sergeant Shawn Arsen shattered the stillness of the commcenter.

"What?" Bard spun in the chair to face the intruder. "What do you mean?"

"I'm sorry, sir. The system is still down. And we shouldn't be transmitting on that band down here anyway." Arsen reached past Bard and turned off the set. "What with all your other responsibilities, it must have slipped your mind."

"I didn't forget," snapped Bard, rising to his feet. "I assumed you would have the system operational by now. I have no idea how a man as incompetent as you ever became a sergeant." He opened the door of the Pedden and climbed down, stomping away from the vehicle. The cavernous hutch of the building echoed to his footsteps. He was furious. Furious with himself for forgetting that the set was not working, and furious with Arsen for catching him at the set. Now he would have to find another way to get the troop and strength information to the surface. He just would have to do it himself.

As the acting headquarters commander, he was privy to all operational information on the Cohort. He couldn't remember the exact location of every vehicle, but his memory was well enough trained to remember where the headquarters and lead tanks were set up. He also knew how weak the command actually was. The information he carried in his head would be enough to give the TOGs the final advantage. The breach exposed by the engineers would be well-guarded, but it should be easier to slip out through the opening cut by that infantry sergeant. If he could escape through that entrance, he should be able to reach the surface. That was his plan.

Bard paced as he thought. Now that he had formulated a plan, adrenaline pumped through his system, clearing his thoughts and charging him up for the task ahead. Perhaps it was that surge that heightened his senses. As he crossed the open space of the hutch toward the opening, a shadow briefly darkened the door. It was just one more shadow among all the other strange shadows cast by unfamiliar surroundings, but this one froze the blood in his veins. He instantly connected the hulking shape of the shadow to a bear-like apparition that still haunted his dreams. Bard ducked into one of the side doors of the hutch and stared fixedly at the opening. When the shadow did not reappear, Bard moved silently to the street door. He looked out. The shadow was gone, but he knew it had been real. Bard knew he had been found.

31

1500, 12 Martius 6831—Lieutenant Colonel Alban C. Tripp wiped the data from the screen in front of him. The harsh lighting of the Renegade headquarters on Rolandrin etched deep creases in his face, making him look like a predatory bird. Rubbing his chin wearily, he stared at the blank screen with equally blank eyes. He had examined the satellite report for hours, looking for conflicting data, but the report said it all. Now he had to tell Kenderson.

Tripp stood and stretched, and the pain in his leg suddenly reminded him how long it had been since he'd slept more than a few hours at a time. The leg was stiff with fatigue, and he had to rub feeling back into his thigh. But he was procrastinating, and he knew it. He reached over and ejected the two-centimeter chip from the console, slipped it inside a protective sleeve, and reset the console's combination lock. He would hand-deliver the report to Prefect NaBesta Kenderson. It was better that bad news come from him than from some anonymous clerk.

Legatus Mantelli Lartur was already with the prefect when Tripp knocked on the frame of the open access panel. He could tell by the expressions on the other officers' faces that they already at least suspected that the news was not good. "Final report from the pole, sir." Tripp's voice revealed his agitation.

"Is it that bad?" asked Lartur.

"I'm afraid so. I brought the latest scan."

Kenderson indicated the port on the console, and Tripp snapped the chip into the opening. He punched in his combination and access numbers, and the screen filled with the grid indications of a satellite picture. "This scan," he said, pointing to the terrain that appeared on the display, "was taken by LOSAT number 3475/A1 as it passed within range of the pole. The resolution is not the best, but it's all we have at this time. There is no indication of friendly activity." The three men scrutinized the screen as if trying to negate the information displayed. "As you can see, the only identifiable signatures are from TOG equipment."

"This isn't a full view," Lartur complained. "It's only a partial. Friendly units may be hiding in the mountains."

Tripp looked across at the operations officer. He could tell by the tone of the man's voice that he was still hoping, trying to convince himself that all the evidence was not yet in. But Tripp knew better. Granted that the satellite had not passed directly over the pole, granted that this was only a limited scan of the frozen continent, even granted that Renegade units could be hiding on a different side of the ice cap, Tripp knew any hope for their survival was a false hope. He had put his best intel people to work on the scan. They had identified every visible drive unit. Previous scans had been analyzed, and every Renegade signature plotted. All were accounted for.

The most damning evidence was the analysis of enemy activity, which showed that the TOGs were no longer conducting combat operations at the pole. Had there been Renegade survivors, the TOGs would be hunting them down, and that activity would appear on the scans. No. The Renegade unit had ceased to exist.

"We've made a complete review of this and previous scans, sir," said Tripp. "It's as if the Renegade vehicles fell through the ice. They can't be found, which means they must've been destroyed. I wish I could believe otherwise, but it's all over."

"It can't be!" exploded Lartur, leaping to his feet and striding across the room. He turned back and threw out his hands. "We can't just write them off without absolute confirmation."

"This kind of behavior isn't helping matters," said Kenderson in a low voice. "Listen to what the colonel has to say. He's the expert."

The operations officer glared at the two men standing behind the console. "No!" he blurted, then turned and fled the office.

"You're sure there's no hope of any survivors?" Kenderson asked again.

"Statistically, sir, there is no such thing as an absolute. But the chance of the unit's survival is so small that it's no longer statistically significant. I'm sorry."

The prefect studied the scan. Using an electronic probe, he increased the magnification of part of the trace. He increased the same area again. "That looks like a couple of ours."

"Yes, sir," agreed Tripp. "A Spartius and a Wolverine. Both destroyed."

"Pretty close together, though. I wonder why."

"A last stand, maybe. Magnify that again, sir." Tripp pointed to the screen. "Notice how the vehicles are sunk into the ice. They must have burned pretty badly to melt that ice. That's probably why we see so little wreckage."

"There must be a way we can confirm our guesses. How about sending a satellite to pass right over the pole?"

"We could do that, sir. And I would have suggested it myself if I thought our intelligence pictures left any room for doubt. To get the scans we want, we'd have to jiggle 3475/A1 out of its standard orbit. That would mean eventual loss of the satellite, unless we wanted to launch a fighter to save it. The last time we sent a fighter to bump a satellite, it nearly didn't come back. And that's not the only problem. There's a TOG ship in orbit approaching Malthus right now. Sending a fighter to move that satellite would almost surely provoke a TOG reaction."

"But what if the TOGs are up to something at the pole?"

"If the TOGs do anything strange, the other satellites currently in orbit will let us know."

"But is their coverage of the pole good enough?"

"We could beef it up. We have fighters patrolling south of Rolandrin supplementing our LOSAT coverage. We could divert a fighter occasionally to take a closer look. A stray bird now and then probably wouldn't worry the TOGs too much, and even if it did, the fighters would be in and out before they could react." Tripp noticed he was feeling less tired. "That way we'd know for sure."

"And we could keep a better eye on TOG activity." Kenderson brought the plot back to full scan. "I never trust the TOGs. Not even when it seems like they're not doing anything. *Especially* when they're not doing anything."

"I'll take care of it, sir," Tripp said smartly. "I've got a friend in fighter ops. He'll talk to the squadron leader for that sector." He cleared the screen and retrieved the data chip. "I'll keep you informed. And as far as I'm concerned, there's no need for either of our headquarters to get involved in this operation. Not unless something develops."

"Thank you, Tripp."

The wind began to rise again, whipping shards of ice across the cap. The TOG headquarters vehicles were circled near the shattered and partially sunken hulls of the Renegade Spartius and Wolverine. The light from the Pompey cast livid shadows of those inside against the icy terrain. The guards patrolling the perimeter of the headquarters pulled their cloaks higher about their necks.

Inside the Pompey, Centurion Marmoreus Patrius watched the other two officers. He had decided that Sulla, as a member of planet command, was a man with whom he could deal. The prefect would be able to help Patrius' career. Legatus Cariolanus Camus, on the other hand, had made enough mistakes to mark himself for elimination. But with the present situation far from resolved, Patrius knew better than to cut himself off from his commander until the time was right. The centurion smiled at both men. "I salute your victory." He lifted his glass.

The TOG legionnaire on patrol turned his back to the wind again and glanced toward the command vehicle. Officers always seemed to get off easy. They were in the Pompey toasting each other, probably with some fine liquor, while the common legionnaires got to fight the battles, then stand around in the cold. The triarii kicked in frustration at the ice around the stern of the dead Wolverine. A chunk broke away and was snatched by the wind. He watched it bounce over the ice, appearing and vanishing as it passed through the illumination thrown by the drive windows of the Pompey. It rolled beyond the light. The legionnaire, amused by the ease with which he could loosen parts of this apparently solid continent of ice, kicked again.

This time, instead of breaking free and rolling, the ice chunk crashed downward into a hole. The triarii kicked harder, and another chunk broke free and dropped into the hole. The legionnaire hunkered down and hammered on the ice with the butt of his Manticore spike rifle. This was the first hole he'd seen in this wasteland that wasn't a crater, and he wanted to see where it led. He seemed to be making some headway with the rifle. The ped enjoyed using the rifle as a hammer, because it was worthless as a shoulder weapon. The weapon was designed to paint targets as well as cut down enemy infantry with slivers of plastic shredded from a solid ammunition block and fired at high velocity, but when switching back to firing from painting, the weapon lost power. Maintenance claimed that the fault had been corrected, but he hadn't seen proof yet. When hammering stopped loosening the ice, he rose to his feet, pointed the muzzle at the ice, and fired a long burst.

The stream of spikes smashed into the ice, spraying a shower of fragments against the side of the dead Renegade Wolverine. The ripping sound crashed over the desolate plain to rebound from the towers of ice and rock.

The mastati who was acting commander of the guard shot from the shelter of the dead Spartius and ran toward the triarii, cursing as he came. By the time he reached the Wolverine, the ice had settled around a hole large enough for a man to drop through. The triarii was on his stomach, only his backside and legs visible above the ice. The mastati planted his heavy boot where he thought it would do the most good, and the triarii jerked up out of the ice.

Although the mastati would never be called imaginative, he was astute enough to understand that the hole was something that bore investigation. He lay down beside the Wolverine, hanging headfirst over the edge of the hole. The triarii resisted a momentary urge to plant his own boot in a vulnerable spot, then went to report the discovery to the guard sergeant.

By the time the sergeant arrived, the mastati had dropped completely into the hole and begun to explore the ice cavern below. As other members of the guard force fired their own spike rifles into other areas around the two dead Renegade tanks, it became apparent that this area of the ice cap was traversed by a network of galleries. Ricocheting spikes filled the air, picking up additional force from the wind and making movement in the area dangerous. More galleries were discovered.

The three officers in charge of the Cohort were not pleased by the overwhelming evidence of a large-scale Renegade escape. With so little wreckage and so few dead, they had suspected that all was not right, but preferred to ignore the implications. Now their suspicions were confirmed, and they knew where the Renegades had gone. The easy explanation was that the enemy had escaped into the tunnels and were using them to evade the TOG forces. But the galleries in this icy warren were not wide enough to accommodate vehicles. And if Marshman grav drives had been running under the surface, the DDPs in the tanks and carriers on top of the ice would have picked up the signature. The easy explanation wasn't the right one, but they knew the Renegades were under there somewhere.

The Cohort commanders ordered troops down to explore the galleries in force. In less than an hour, they discovered entrances into the dome below. In one place, the damage looked recent, as though the Renegades had cut an entrance and then closed it behind them. A Lupis carrier went down to run a passive sensor check, and its DDP showed Renegade vehicles through the rubble. The enemy force was definitely there.

The searchers also found a Human-sized opening in the shell, and the thermographic sensors in their combat helmets showed movement below. It was a perfect opportunity to take out a few of the enemy with a couple of free shots, but cooler heads convinced the others to preserve the element of surprise. The sergeant in command posted a guard at the hole and reported to his centurion.

The Cohort officers decided on a simple plan of attack. As Sulla put it, the Renegades were "trapped like rats in a hole," and it only remained to exterminate them. The plan was to bury several demo charges in the ice at the large fissure near the dead Spartius and Wolverine. When all units were in place, the charges would blow, knocking out the Renegade defense at the breach. The moment the blast began to settle, a force of Aeneas light tanks would pour through the crack to set up covering fire for the infantry, who would follow, attacking on foot.

At the same time, a full infantry platoon would drop through the small breach with bounce packs. If the TOG troops could catch the enemy from two sides, the Renegade force might fall apart. Both footholds would receive reinforcements as required. It was a perfect plan.

The commanders chose to ignore the fact that the attack required two forces, attacking from opposite directions against an unknown enemy, to act in concert. The TOGs were also counting on the Renegades being taken completely by surprise.

32

2100, 12 Martius 6831—A line of Aeneas tanks hovered near the dead Wolverine. The Renegade tank had been pulled clear of the opening to the main breach, and the smashed borer had been extracted. The only thing still standing in the way of the main TOG attack was a solidly packed pile of ice blocking the crack in the dome. The tank commanders closed their face plates, dropped into the tanks, and sealed the hatches. Fighting from an exposed position would gain them no advantage, and when the charges went off, the ice fragments sent into the air would have the force to kill.

At the instant of detonation, the light tanks would burst through the exploding ice and ram any part of the ice still blocking the breach. The shock of the explosion should rattle any defenders beyond the ice fall, and the light tanks should send the enemy into panicked retreat. By the time the Renegades realized what was happening, the infantry would be in place, giving the TOG forces a foothold. The light tanks, carrying 100mm Gauss cannon, would be adequate support for the infantry in the close combat that would ensue.

The engineers lifted the cratering charges, actually artillery crater rounds with special fuses, into the 25-centimeter holes bored in the frozen rubble. The rounds slipped easily into the openings and settled gently against the face of the bore holes. The engineers stretched the detonation antenna clear of the bore-hole openings, and packed ice fragments from the drilling against the charges. The depth of the holes and the packing would direct most of the force of the blast down and in, clearing the blockage. The sergeant in charge checked the connections one last time, then quickly made his way clear of the gallery. He gave a thumbs-up signal to the engineering optio as he passed up onto the surface.

When Patrius got the ready signal, he made a quick commlink check with the patrol at the other entrance. The infantry there reported ready. The first section of the assault force had been reequipped with Divider spike carbines, a smaller, but equally powerful weapon that would make it easier for the peds to drop through the narrow opening prepared to fire than if they were carrying the larger Mantichore rifles. Once the first squad hit the floor of the gallery, the second squad, still armed with Mantichores, would drop through.

The ops officer nodded to Camus, and the legatus acknowledged the signal. He silently counted to five, taking the pause to make it patently clear that he was the one making the decision, not the operations officer. His five-count completed, Camus nodded to Patrius. The ops officer thumbed the button on the commlink. The blast was instantaneous, and the first ped dropped through the smaller opening.

* * *

The Renegades guarding the rubbled bolt-hole had reported the TOG activity to Harras. Guessing at the TOG's plan, the Renegade troops were ready for the blast, and were also monitoring the gathering force at the other opening. Harras had hoped that the TOGs would not discover the smaller breach, but accepted the inevitable and deployed his forces accordingly.

At the main breach the defending infantry had been pulled well back, because there was no way to determine in advance the force of the blast concussion. The peds dug into the buildings at the foot of the breach or took up stations on the upper floors, prepared to fire down on any targets that appeared. Jamie MacDougall, the commander at the breach, placed his four Liberators on side streets, where they would have a good field of fire.

The small opening was nearer the center of the city, so the responsibility for its defense fell to the Reserve under Rinter. She deployed a single, full-strength infantry squad to hold the position, sending the damaged Viper with the squad. In its present condition, the tank was not much more than a battle taxi, of little value in a mobile action, but for the squad at the small entrance, it would function well as static defense. Sergeant Honor Ross had command of the position. Two of her peds had been lost in the surface action, but the squad was returned to full strength with a driver from a dead tank and Archon Divxas, the Baufrin civilian who had joined the Cohort's position on the surface. Because Ross and the Baufrin had worked well together in finding the underground city and seemed to get along, Rinter had added him to Ross' squad.

When the blast at the main breach shattered the centuries-old silence of the hidden city, the Renegades were ready. Four Liberators engaged the first Aeneas to appear out of the blast cloud even before the ice had settled. The 150mm main guns fired first, followed by the 50mm cannon. The moment the Aeneas cleared the cloud and gave the painting lasers a clear field, the 5/6 lasers opened as well. The Aeneas went incandescent, the turret melting under the impact of the combined fire of the four medium tanks. With all the controls shot away, the light tank crested the edge of the ice rubble, teetered there for a moment, then tumbled down the slope to rest against a building. The titanium burned off in a brilliant, blue-white flare that cast leaping shadows against the surrounding walls.

Meanwhile, more TOG tanks had made it through the breach. Because they were hull down, even at close range they were not automatic hits. The Liberators pounded away, but the TOG tankers had survived this long for a reason. Crafty positioning gave them an advantage. The crater was above the Liberators by fifteen meters, and the Aeneas tanks had only to back away from the edge to be completely under cover. They dodged around, screening themselves from the Renegade tanks and trying to concentrate on one enemy at a time. Then the TOG peds broke though to join their armored support.

The TOG infantry crept through the shattered ice to take up positions in the crags and cracks. From here, they could paint the Liberators in relative safety for easy targeting by the TVLGs. The peds had at first tried firing their mortars from the breach, but the first round to strike the top of the dome created an avalanche of the artificial shield and ice. They didn't try it again. The TVLGs, on the other hand, could be fired at a trajectory low enough not to hit the protective dome. The black sky around the fight was soon streaked with the exhausts of the missiles.

The Liberator's major flaw for use in close fighting now became obvious. The commander could fire on any infantry he spotted, usually after they had fired on him, but the Liberator lacked an AP laser with which to engage the enemy. The only weapons available to the commander were the heavy guns. They got the job done, but it was a little like killing ants with a sledgehammer. The other problem was that if the gunner was engaging the infantry with his main weapons, it meant he wasn't shooting at other tanks. The Aeneas scouts quickly began to get free shots against the harried Liberators, which also lacked infantry support.

The Renegade infantry moved forward over the rooftops and parapets of the surrounding buildings. They had abandoned their positions prior to the blast for fear the explosion would destroy the buildings, but they had underestimated the strength of Naram construction. Seeing their emplacements undamaged, the infantry quickly set up their weapons. The TOG infantry, believing that the Liberators were unsupported, had by now exposed their positions. The Renegades waited for the command and then opened fire together.

The TOG peds, caught in the open, scrambled back up the slope, hurried along by spikes from the Renegade rifles. The hidden infantry followed standard target priority and picked off the sergeants and optios first. As soon as they determined who was giving orders, they quickly cut those troopers down with multiple streams of spikes. With their leadership destroyed, the survivors fled back to the surface past the supporting Aeneas tanks, allowing the Renegade peds to bring their own TVLGs to bear on the exposed scout vehicles. It was no longer safe for the light tanks to drift around in craters waiting to jump an isolated Liberator. When two of the scouts went up in blazes, the survivor followed the infantry up and out of the city.

At the smaller hole, Ross had deployed her squad in a rough semicircle. She did not surround the opening for fear that, in the excitement of combat, her people would shoot each other across the battlefield. She kept Archon near her, as well as Hamilton Hull, the tank driver who had lost his vehicle. Both these men were about to be initiated into infantry combat, and she wanted to be able to control their movements. She was oddly distracted by the thought of calling the Baufrin a man. She knew that Baufrins were not considered either gender until late in life when the mating process began. Only during mating did their gender become known, even to them. Ross decided that she should probably think of Archon as "it" rather than "him," but all that did was muddy her already chaotic thought processes. She returned to thinking of him as male. The other three-ped sections she spread to the right and left. As the explosion at the bolt-hole echoed over the city, the sky above her position was blotted out by plunging bodies.

The roar of the bounce packs was deafening in the confines of the dome. For an instant Ross was transfixed by the sight of the TOG peds descending on streams of fire and steam. Half the TOG section was on the ground before she recovered herself and gave the order to fire. More TOGs came pouring down from the opening.

Deployed in the buildings, the Renegades had the advantage. The TOGs were caught in the city's central plaza with no cover, their only hope to overcome the defenders by sheer firepower. Bodies crumpled to the ice, their armor shredded by dozens of spikes. The second line of troops huddled behind their dead and fired back. The TOG troops threw themselves into the battle, testing the theory that they could win because they had more bodies than the defenders had bullets. At a pause in the firing created by the Renegades charging their spike rifles with new polymer blocks, the TOGs took advantage of the respite to rush one of the positions. They hugged the walls for protection and blasted their way through the stone with demo charges.

"Ross. This is Grold. They're inside." The commlink in Ross' helmet confirmed the worst-case scenario.

"Right," said Ross. "If you need help, let me know."

"You got it."

"Drinn," she said to the other section leader on the commlink. "Try to cover Grold's position. The Toggies will try to put more people into that hole."

"Right, Sarge. I'm moving people now."

Ross' BLS showed that Drinn was moving someone to the right to get a better line-of-fire. From his new position the ped had a clear shot at the breach in Grold's building. The next rush of TOG infantry paid the price of that repositioning, but two of the four made it through the hole.

"Ross." It was Grold. "I need some help. Brace is down and Grain is surrounded."

"Right. I'm on the way." Ross motioned to Archon and Hull to follow and headed toward the mouse hole that had been blown into the side wall of her building. She ran through, followed closely by the Baufrin. In the dust that hung over the fighting positions, she lost sight of Hull.

Grold was crouched behind a rock barrier in one of the dens off the main hutch, the air swirling with dust from the grenade explosions. The section leader pointed toward a small hole in the side wall and held his hand palm-down. Just as Ross and Archon quickly dropped low, a stream of spikes erupted from the opening and ricocheted off the back wall.

Archon sprang across the room and flattened himself against the side wall near the TOG's firing port. When the muzzle of a Manticore spike rifle poked through the hole and fired again, Archon kept his own carbine in his upper arms while grabbing the offending weapon with his lower ones. The great strength of those appendages was more than the unfortunate TOG ped could overcome. Archon jerked down on the enemy muzzle, snapping the stock up against the ped's chin. When he felt the weapon come free, he drove the muzzle back into the hole, striking something that gave way. Then he dropped the muzzle and raised his own carbine to the hole. Careful not to allow the muzzle to clear the opening, he fired the full block of flechettes into the other room.

Ross leaped for the door of the den, but her Thermographic Imaging System showed no life forms in the hutch. She dropped to her knees and crawled to the next den, where her TIS outlined three TOGs. She readied her carbine. Sensing movement behind her, she assumed Grold was backing her up.

The TOGs in the den broke for the door. Either they didn't have a TIS system available, or they thought they could overcome what they saw. The first one caught the full burst of Ross' weapon. The first spike glanced off the face plate. The second one buried itself in the plasto-shield cuirass, but the ped was still moving forward, propelled by those behind him and dying as he emerged from the den.

The body dropped on Ross, the impact carrying her to the floor of the hutch. As the other two TOGs made it out the door into firing position, Ross twisted free of the death grip of the first ped and came face to face with the muzzle of a spike rifle.

She felt movement behind her again and saw a claw-like hand reach over her and wrench the rifle away. The flash of the weapon blinded her at first, even through the face plate, and the next few seconds seemed like a slow-motion drama. The TOG ped had begun to fire before losing control of the rifle. Ross saw the barrel warp under the force of the Baufrin's claw, saw the breech blow back under the built-up pressure of the trapped rounds. The bolt flew back, smashing into the helmet of the ped. The face plate collapsed under the impact of the titanium shard and she had a split-second vision of surprised eyes, a gaping mouth. Then the bolt struck square between the eyes and the man went down. Archon ripped the useless rifle free from the lifeless hands, swung it over his head and brought it down across the fallen ped's helmet. The straps of the heavy combat helmet ripped free and rolled away into the darkness.

The third ped fled back into the den and out the breach in the exterior wall. Grold took a snap shot at him but missed. The building was silent for a moment, then they heard the TOG run a few steps. "Damn," said Grold. "I missed him." His words were lost in the sound of a shot ringing out.

"I didn't." It was Hull. He hadn't kept up with Ross' first change of position, but had managed to make Grold's original position and bring down the fleeing TOG legionnaire.

Ross checked her BLS and TIS. Assuming that Drinn's section was still in place and alive, she scanned for the members of Grold's team. She could find only one other life form. Brace was dead at his position, but he had died hard, judging by the spike marks on his battle suit and the number of dead TOGs around him. Grain was alive, but had taken hits also. Physically, he was unhurt, but his armor had been shattered, and that was a problem. With below-zero temperatures, any break in the armored suit created the risk of frostbite. Grain needed new armor, and he needed it soon.

The Renegade *Cheetah* arced over the pole, its infrared and radar sensors pointed down. The pilot glanced at the screen as it plotted a series of TOG vehicles. The brief had said there might be some surviving Renegade positions on the surface, and the fighter was to try to locate them. Watching the surface stream past, the pilot spotted nothing to report. He rolled the fighter into a tight turn and fled for home.

33

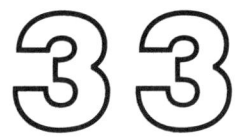

0500, 15 Martius 6831—In the TOG Pompey carrier, Legatus Camus stared at the report and then looked up at the sergeant standing before him. He wondered if the sergeant knew, or even wished to know, the meaning of the numbers in the message. The reported casualties were devastating. Three infantry platoons had attacked the Renegade positions below the ice, but there were not enough survivors to form even a single full squad. An entire Century of infantry had been destroyed in this operation. Of the eight full platoons assigned, barely four remained. Even the elite legionnaires of a TOG Strike Legion could not sustain casualties at that rate. Camus knew what effect this would have on morale among the peds. No one would complain out loud, because legionnaires never complained, but little things would start to go wrong, jobs left undone or done poorly at best. Nor could he attempt to hide losses this great. Even reorganization would leave gaping holes. The tanks had also taken heavy losses.

The Renegades had savaged the six Aeneas tanks sent into the breach. The only one to make it back to the surface was virtually useless. With its main gun inoperative and its front armor destroyed, the tank could be used for spare parts for other vehicles, but it had seen the last of combat. The other tank platoons were in only slightly better shape. The original complement of eighteen Horatius mediums was down to eight; thirteen tanks of the original thirty-six assigned to the Strike Cohort remained. Camus clutched his head in his hands, having completely forgotten to dismiss the enlisted man who had brought the report.

In another Pompey carrier, Centurion Marmoreus Patrius and Prefect Claudius Sulla had just finished evaluating the same report. The implications were clear: disaster was imminent. "There have been some serious miscalculations made." Patrius spoke his thoughts aloud.

Sulla pursed his lips and stared at the ceiling of the carrier. "The commander is responsible for all his unit does"—he paused for effect—"or fails do to. How would you rate the progress of this operation so far?"

Marmoreus had expected the question. It was a double-edged sword that could be dangerously sharp if gripped the wrong way. He studied the prefect's face, trying to guess what his superior officer wanted to hear. As the operations officer, Patrius was responsible both for the training of the unit and the development of the tactical part of the operation. At least some of the blame for any failure could be laid at his feet. But Sulla was right; the success or failure of a mission was ultimately the commander's responsibility. He made up his mind. "As I said, there have been some problems. May I speak plainly and off the record?"

The question was just part of the ritual, the game Patrius was caught up in. No one ever spoke "off the record" to a prefect. The request to "speak plainly" translated as meaning that he planned to criticize his superior. Sulla smiled, enjoying himself, his eyes crinkling shut as he examined the centurion over his steepled fingers. He nodded. An ambiguous response. He did not ask Patrius to say anything, had not given his permission. He would test this officer. If he were willing to criticize Camus, well and good. But this conversation did not constitute a contract between the two of them. Nothing prevented Sulla from using Patrius' statements to his own advantage at a later date. The prefect smiled again.

Patrius saw the gaping trap opening before him. It was now or never to take the gamble. He drew in a deep breath. "Legatus Camus has been less than aggressive in his conduct of this entire operation." He watched the prefect's expression, but it didn't change. "I believe we should have been more aggressive at the initial ambush and that we should have attacked again as soon as we reached the pole. The two attacks we made here were weak, allowing far too many Renegades to survive. You may remember that I recommended just such a course of action at the time."

Sulla continued to gaze at the centurion. "Do you recommend that your commanding officer be replaced?"

Patrius shifted involuntarily in his seat and retreated from honesty to comfortable false modesty. "I am not qualified either by placement or by rank to make such a recommendation. That decision must be made by those more knowledgeable than I."

"Well said." Sulla rose from his chair. "I have some work to attend to in the communications center. Perhaps we can speak again later."

Honor Ross stretched out in her fighting position. She was still sore from the struggle with the dead TOG legionnaire, still haunted by the memory of the spike-rifle muzzle looming in her face. She tried to fall asleep, pulling the thermocloak tightly around her shoulders. She finally drifted off, only to face the muzzle again, drifting out of the fog. She jerked awake, drenched in perspiration.

She stared into the darkness around her. On the other side of the den she could hear Hamilton Hull breathing. He had the first watch and was wearing the BLS normally carried by the squad leader. Ross felt naked without it, but it was of more value to the watch than to her while she was asleep. She rolled over again and willed herself to sleep. It came as she replayed the fight with the TOG bounce infantry in her mind. Then the spike rifle came back to jolt her awake. She threw off the thermocloak and stood up. Might as well check the squad's deployment and be useful rather than thrash around on the floor.

Hull was awake and alert, and she left the BLS with him. She didn't need it to check the positions, which she knew even in the dark. Left through the mouse hole, fifteen steps down the corridor of rubble to the hutch. Then across the open space for twelve paces till she reached the wall. Right five steps to the mouse hole to Drinn, Calvert, and Tscholmankia. The den was filled with the rumble of snoring, and she had to listen carefully to distinguish the shallow breathing of the sentry. She crossed to where the sentinel watched through a firing port blown in the outer wall.

"Evening, Honor," said Dorothea Calvert without turning her head. "You were pretty noisy getting here."

"How did you know it was me and not one of the TOGs?" Ross was miffed that she had not been challenged, and angry at herself for making enough noise to alert the triarii to her presence.

"I can tell your step anywhere. Call it instinct."

"Bunk!"

"That's your opinion."

"Perhaps you two ladies should speak more quietly and pay closer attention to your surroundings."

Archon's voice made both of them jump.

"Damn thermographic sensors!" muttered Calvert. "You don't show up on the thing."

"One of the many advantages of my species. You Humans persist in believing that you are the only important life form. What will you do when you reach an environment populated exclusively by Kessrith, Ssora, and Baufrin? You will be in a constant state of surprise." Archon picked his way across the room to where the two women were sitting. Ross moved over to give him space by the firing port. He settled down with a faint rattle.

Ross realized she felt better now, but she wasn't quite sure why this alien creature, this civilian, should inspire such a sense of security. With him near, she felt warm, really warm, for the first time since they hit the pole. She felt her muscles begin to relax, and soon her head dropped forward onto her chest.

Dorothea Calvert unfolded the thermocloak she had rescued from her damaged carrier and wrapped it carefully around the shoulders of her sleeping sergeant.

Moldine Rinter placed the last of the glowing marks on the map unfolding on the display in the command Pedden. Braxton Sloan kept posting more and more information to the diagram of the city. He seemed to be in his element. The engineer had taken the cartographer's job seriously, and he and his two enlisted assistants had been hard at work since the Cohort came underground. The map of the city became more and more detailed, and an equal amount of detail was gathered on the condition of the protective dome.

The breach the Renegade Cohort had used to reach the floor of the ancient city was not the only one in the dome. The mapmakers had found four others, two of them of significant size. It seemed unlikely that the TOGs knew about the other breaches, and so the command was not yet too concerned about defending the new discoveries. A guard was posted at each opening, but no further reinforcements would be added until enemy activity was detected. Seismic sensors had also been buried in the ice near the openings, and the sentries' helmets were equipped with BLS systems. The BLS was exchanged when the guard changed. There was no chance of a surprise attack.

The breaches used by the TOGs in the last attack were more carefully watched. Because the possible entry points of the TOGs were limited so far, most of the force could be deployed in those areas. The main breach was defended by MacDougall's Century, well dug in with tanks supported by infantry. The rear breach was held by Rinter's Century. Matruh's Century was given as much rest as possible. The surviving mess sections were set to heating water so that the troops could bathe and shave. The brief respite from the threat of attack was a welcome relief.

All three Century commanders as well as the vehicle commanders needed to know where the breaks had been discovered, and so Rinter made chip copies of the engineer's map for each vehicle's DDP. The map would help the tanks navigate through the city as quickly as possible. In addition, as defensive positions were established, the new information could be downloaded instantly to all maps. She looked for a sergeant to deliver the chips.

"I'll do that for you, ma'am," said a voice behind her.

Rinter turned to see the communications optio standing behind her. It was the new man, the one who had loaded just as they left Rolandrin. She couldn't remember his name. "Excuse me?"

"It's Bard, ma'am. I'm the communications officer. Since none of my commlinks are working, I guess it's my responsibility to deliver communications from the headquarters to the lower commands."

Rinter studied the officer, an unimposing man who seemed genuinely anxious to help. The delivery job should have been a task for an enlisted man, but this officer was obviously feeling useless with his equipment not operational. "All right. Go ahead and take these to the vehicles. The ones marked red on the edge are for the Century commanders. Do you know where to find them?"

"Yes ma'am. Their positions have been marked on the map in the ops shed. I'll find them." Bard held out his hand for the chips.

As he left the hutch where the Pedden carrier was concealed, Bard glanced up and down the street. The afterglow of the combat at the breach had died down, but the level of Renegade activity was enough to slightly displace the blackness that blanketed the city. He would be able to find his way without the thermographic designator in the helmet. Though the helmet would give him a better view of the terrain, he preferred not to wear it because its narrow field of sight restricted his peripheral vision.

The first vehicle was around the corner, and Bard crept along the side of the building to reach it. His caution was not entirely prompted by the general need for security. He had seen the shape of the bear in the door, and he was taking no chances.

Arriving at the command Pedden just as that woman finished copying the maps had been a stroke of luck. These people were so easy to manipulate. All he had to do was behave as though he really wanted something to do, and no one questioned his motives. He had approached the Pedden hoping to pick up some valuable information to give the TOGs when he escaped, and it had been handed right to him. The best part was that now he had an unimpeachable reason for being away from his post. He would deliver the chips to the nearest Century headquarters, that of Centurion Sedden Matruh. His delivery route would then take him past one of the newly mapped breaks in the dome, one not yet discovered by the TOG troops above. Bard had found this particular breach most interesting.

A recent seismic shift had broken open the dome and dropped ice into the city. The breach had also cracked open a narrow fissure leading to one of the mined galleries. If he could reach that breach and slip through the crack, he would be able to gain the surface undetected. Using one of Rinter's chips, he could deliver the entire Renegade deployment into the hands of the TOG troops. That information would allow the TOG forces to quickly annihilate the enemy. He was so pleased by the prospect of his own escape and the destruction of the hated Renegades that he didn't see the large shadow detach itself from an alley and follow him.

34

1000, 13 Martius 6831—Optio Holton Bard reached the first Liberator and climbed the scramble rails on the left side. The command hatch was open and the soft, red light of the interior battle lanterns cast a welcoming glow against the Vulcan antimissile system's laser-transparent dome. He was not challenged as he climbed to the top of the turret and looked in. It took a moment for his eyes to adjust to the light and even longer to spot the crewmember inside.

When he finally saw a figure crawling from the driver's station in the rear of the fighting compartment, Bard cleared his throat to attract the crewman's attention. Glancing toward the hatch, the triarii nodded to the officer, then began rummaging through his kit. Bard cleared his throat more forcefully, but the young legionnaire ignored the optio, intent on ripping open an emergency food pack he had unearthed from his personal gear. The package open, the man rocked back to sit cross-legged on the floor of the fighting compartment and began to eat.

Bard stuck his head and shoulders into the turret. "Legionnaire! Get on your feet!" His voice cracked with anger. "Is that the way you behave when an officer is present?" This man, thought Bard, was a typical slovenly Renegade soldier. He did not even think of the man as a legionnaire. That would be giving this poor excuse for a soldier too much credit.

The tanker triarii looked up at the turret. He struggled slowly to his feet, assuming a kind of half-crouch to face his visitor. "Sorry. Didn't know you were still there."

"Sir!" prompted Bard.

"Sir."

"And put that food down when talking to an officer." Bard dropped into the turret. He regretted it at once. The fighting compartment had seemed spacious from the outside, but now its actual dimensions became painfully apparent. In order to face the soldier in the rear of the tank, Bard had to stoop slightly and angle his shoulders to the left. If he tried to stand at attention, his face was half-hidden by a portion of the Vulcan control system that hung from the turret roof. It was very undignified. "You people think that just because you are in tanks you can act as you please. This is a military organization, and you need to understand that. We would never tolerate this kind of behavior."

The soldier looked at him strangely. "I thought we were all in this together…sir."

Bard's mouth clamped shut. He stared at the soldier with one eye. The other eye was blocked by the apparatus of the Vulcan system. "Of course we're in this together. What do you mean?" He was confused. He tried to remember what he had just said. What could have alerted this simpleton that there was something different about the optio in front of him? He suddenly felt as if he had lost the initiative in this encounter. He changed tactics. "I have an important chip for the tank commander. Where is he?"

"Dunno, sir. He went off to have a bath, I think. And to get some rats for the tank."

"Rats?" Where, thought Bard, would a man find rats in this frozen city? And why? Then he realized that the soldier meant rations. He switched to the attack again. "Your sergeant left his command to a triarii in order to get rations? Absurd!" Bard had always had a hard time dealing with the fluid leadership style of the Renegade Legion. "He should be here. You should have gone for supplies. What's his name? What's your name?" Bard fumbled in his pocket for his pad and stylus, remembered that he would never be returning to headquarters, and remembered that time was his enemy now, not this insubordinate Renegade soldier. "Never mind." He thrust the chip toward the soldier. "Give this to him when he returns."

Bard crawled out of the command hatch and turned to scramble down the side of the Liberator. He stopped. He couldn't resist the urge to take one more shot at the soldier. "Tell your sergeant that I'll be back to discuss his leadership style." But the triarii had already returned to his meal and didn't even look up at the voice of the departing officer. Bard was furious.

The next vehicle was the Century commander's Viper. A group of people stood around, clad in armor covered by thermocloaks. They paid scant attention to the approach of the optio, and Bard was beside himself at their lack of courtesy and respect. After no more than a cursory search for the centurion, he gave the chip to a sergeant who promised to see that it was delivered. Bard was increasingly aware of the urgency of his mission, and though he longed to give someone a thorough chewing, it would be a waste of valuable time. He asked directions to the next vehicle, a Liberator, and set off into the darkness.

He moved down a twisting side street until he was out of sight of the crowd, then stopped. It was past time to clear his trail. He cursed himself silently for allowing the slipshod attitude of the Renegades to overshadow the importance of reaching the surface. Knowing he had wasted time and energy, now he focused his mind firmly on his mission. He pressed back into a vacant doorway and scanned the street.

His combat helmet lacked the Basic Lifeform Sensor system routinely issued to officers in a leadership position, but the thermographic imaging system standard in every helmet was enough to give him the information he needed. All he really wanted to know was whether any heat source existed in the area, and the TIS would tell him that. If a heat source moved, it was probably alive. He scanned the Head-Up Display.

In the extreme cold of the city under the ice, heat sources stood out in bold relief on the helmet's transparent face plate. Even the group around the Viper, completely blocked by the intervening buildings, was clearly outlined. He saw that several people had joined the group, probably the Century commander and some of his cronies. Bard shuddered at the thought. The concept of officers making friends among the enlisted ranks was beyond his imagining. He pushed the thought from his mind.

He began to turn his head, concentrating on one 600-mil arc at a time. Scanning this way was a time-consuming process, but he knew it was better to be careful than surprised. He noted a heat source directly ahead across the street, but it was at some distance and so appeared quite fuzzy. That was probably another fighting position. His headset did not have the capability to load one of the chips Rinter had given him, and so he had to try to recall the layout he had seen on the plot plan in the command vehicle. He thought hard for a moment, but couldn't be sure that the heat source conformed to the plot. He stored the location of the heat source in his mind for future reference.

Completing the sweep, he moved out again. If he had calculated correctly, the breach in the dome he was seeking was at the end of this alley. When he reached the edge of the built-up area, he scanned again. The TIS showed the same heat sources. He unfolded the holotarp he had stolen from the headquarters Pedden and draped it around his shoulders. The tarp would leave his head unprotected, but it would disguise most of his body-heat emissions. Bard moved into the darkness, his right hand gripping the butt of his Hornet spike pistol, his left arm extended in front of him. Shuffling slowly forward, he had not taken more than a few steps before his feet struck the talus of ice that had tumbled down through the crack. So powerful was the wave of relief and exaltation that he sagged to his knees. He was on target!

He tucked the edges of the holotarp into the front of his battle armor, and using both hands to support himself, clambered up over the ice. The crevice he was looking for was very small, and so he made for the general direction of its location. Again, luck was with him. Finding it on the first try, he slipped in, his shoulders parallel to the crack. Because it was so narrow, he had to force himself through the last few meters to the edge of the dome. Feeling the smooth sharpness of the break, he heaved himself over the edge. He had come to the opening that led to one of the galleries—and to freedom.

Larry Stone quizzed the group around the Viper. They all agreed that an optio from headquarters had been there, but they couldn't remember his name or what he looked like. It wasn't that they were unwilling to deliver the information, they just hadn't paid him any attention. He had seemed angry, they remembered, but cold and hunger and fatigue had dulled their senses. All they remembered clearly was that he had been there and had gone. Stone quickly searched the surrounding streets, then headed for the next Liberator in the Century.

He made a cursory search of the area around the next narrow alley, and was turning to go when the soft blur of a heat source appeared on his thermographic sensor. He turned back down the street, moving with more speed than caution. At the edge of the built-up area, he actively scanned again. This time he found two heat sources.

One indication was high up against the dome, and it vanished as he watched it. The other, stronger image was approaching from the right, moving to a position directly below the first, vanished source. The first target must be his quarry. He moved rapidly toward where it had vanished.

The rubble of the breach caught Stone by surprise, making him stumble against the crusted ice. He fell, but caught himself on his hands, glancing to his right to see if the other heat source had noticed him. The image had stopped, coalescing into a solid blip, like that of a kneeling man. It was a sentry. Stone rolled left into a crevice to hide his own heat image, covering himself with the holotarp he had salvaged from the sled he had abandoned after reaching Cohort Harras. Keeping low, he crawled upward on the ice slope.

The climb was hard and draining, the cold seeping in through his body armor and gauntlets. His fingers were numb and even his limbs felt as though the heat was being sucked from them. Despite the cold, he willed himself to concentrate on the task at hand. After ten minutes of steady movement, he stopped to check on the sentry to his right rear. Edging above the side of the crevice until his face plate registered the guard, he saw that the man hadn't moved. As Stone watched, the figure of the sentry rose from his kneeling position and followed Stone's trail. He knew that it was only a matter of time before the sentry saw him and challenged him. When that happened, Stone knew he had two choices. He could give himself up, abandoning his search for the spy, or he could make a run for it. But where would he run? He dropped back into the crevice and crawled.

The crack he was traveling in became deeper and leveled out. Movement was easier now, and when he glanced back to check on the sentry's progress, Stone discovered that he was surrounded by ice. He was safe in here, at least for the moment. He rose to a crouch, his knees protesting the prolonged exposure to the subzero surface. The crevice became tall and narrow, and he had to wedge himself forward. His bulk, an asset in most cases, was working against him. Even the holotarp was too cumbersome. He let it slide off, rolling it and stuffing it into his belt. He struggled forward for several meters, then the ice gave way with a rush, and he found himself in a wide gallery.

His TIS was useless here. The cold was so intense, so universal, that the sensors were overwhelmed. He raised the face plate and reached for the hand torch on his belt. He switched it on and light flooded the area, reflecting off a cut chamber that extended away in two directions. He directed the light down both tunnels. The right tunnel slanted down slightly, the left rose. If Bard were in here he would be headed up and out. Stone turned to the left and began to climb.

Optio Holton Bard made good time up the tunnel. His climb was made easier by the light of the torch, but his sense of urgency had dropped away. With success at hand, he no longer had need for any incautious haste. He turned off the torch and waited for his eyes to adjust to the darkness. For almost ten minutes he stood without moving, leaning against the side of the gallery and attempting to calm himself by concentrating on slowing his racing heartbeat. Just as he decided to move again, a soft light appeared up the corridor behind him.

Bard looked away and then back, just to make sure the light had not been an illusion. It was still there. His heart began to beat frantically again. He knew without seeing that his enemy had followed him. It could be no one else.

Bard stretched his arms out to his sides, searching the walls for a place to hide. Without taking his eyes from the approaching light, he moved cautiously up the passage. A few paces later he found his spot. The cutting machine that had carved the tunnel had dislodged a small avalanche of loose ice from one wall, partially blocking the passage. He scuttled behind it and drew the spike pistol from its holster.

The range was impossible to determine, but it would be pointblank. He drew the holotarp over his head, leaving only the smallest portion of the combat helmet exposed. He dropped the face plate, and at once the heat source appeared. It was a man. The heat from his hand torch stood out like a beacon. Bard thumbed off the safety on the side of the pistol, clicking the selector to full automatic, and steadied it over the top of the ice fall. On full auto, the pistol would discharge the entire magazine of five hundred 2mm plastic spikes in a single one-second burst. The twenty-five-round magazine would empty in less than five-tenths of a second—before the recoil was even noticed. He tightened his finger on the trigger as the light approached.

The thermographic display recorded only heat, not intervening structures. Between Bard and his enemy, the gallery made a slight turn, blocking the line-of-sight down the passage. But Bard, his face plate down to take advantage of the TIS system, could not see the cover provided by the ice bending the corner. The display on the HUD showed only the clear impression of the man and the torch. When the light of the torch flashed across his face shield, he aimed the spike pistol at the center of the mass shown on his HUD and fired.

The reflected flash from the muzzle was so intense that even the suppression function of the face plate was overloaded. Bard could not see the effect of the blast, but he could tell that the man went down hard. Before the echoes of the shot died away, Bard was on his feet. He glanced down the corridor at the fallen man, took one step toward him, and then changed his mind. No use dealing with a dying man. He turned toward the surface, snapped on his torch, and jogged up the passage.

* * *

Stone's vision cleared. His hand torch lay on the floor of the gallery, the lens directing the light toward him. He couldn't feel his left arm, and he looked down to see if it were still attached. An oozing line of blood ran down the arm from the shoulder to the wrist, turning dark as he watched. With the fingers of his right hand he felt the armor of the stealth suit he wore. The cuirass was shattered, a neat line of spikes splitting the breastplate from armpit to armpit. A useless weight now. The armor on the left arm was also destroyed, and one of the spikes had buried itself deep in the deltoid muscle of his shoulder. He grunted as he pulled it free and examined the wound.

The damage didn't look too serious. The spikes had impacted as if they had been deflected; a quick patch job would stop the wound bleeding. The emergency packet issued with the suit and the extreme cold would see to that. The armor was another matter. Its ECM ability was gone, and so was the suit's internal heat source. Stone decided to discard the broken half of the suit. Inoperative, it would do more to chill his body than to protect it. The armor clattered to the floor. He picked up the torch and continued up the corridor.

35

1300, 13 Martius 6831—Brigadier General Drusus Arcadius, planet-side commander on Caralis for the forces of the Terran Overlord Government, was very unhappy. Legatus Maximus Antipolous Philippicus, his intelligence officer and acting operations officer while Prefect Claudius Sulla was gone, had brought him more bad news. The simple operation of trapping an under-strength Renegade Cohort on the planet's southern ice cap had gone from a misadventure to a disaster. The most recent report from the pole indicated that Cohort Camus was in danger of being destroyed by the Renegades.

First, the Cohort had reported that a foolproof ambush plan had been, at best, a qualified success. Then Sulla had requested artillery and anti-air assets to finish off the enemy, so Arcadius had sent what he could spare. The combined artillery–ground attack on the Renegade defense was declared a complete success; there had been no survivors. That was the good news. The bad news had arrived shortly afterward. Cohort Camus reported that the Renegades had in fact retreated under the ice to a hidden city. Now Camus was saying that he did not have the strength to dislodge the enemy and had suffered grievous casualties in an assault against the dug-in Renegade defense. He needed reinforcements before he could attack again, perhaps needed them just to hold his position. A complete disaster.

The casualties were bad, but that was not the worst of it. Camus claimed they might have to destroy the city to rout the Renegades, the very city the TOG scientific team had been there to find. Their presence was what had started this mess. The TOG government gave high priority to the mission to find the city at the south pole; now it had been found, and the high command certainly didn't want it destroyed!

The portal slid open to reveal Philippicus requesting permission to enter. Brigadier General Arcadius irritably gestured him forward. The intelligence officer approached the console, stood at attention, and cleared his throat. "What is it, Philippicus?" Arcadius hated the way the man procrastinated. Why didn't he just get on with it? "What is it now?"

"Your Excellency." Philippicus kept his eyes firmly riveted on a spot just above the brigadier general's head. "I know we have no troops available on Malthus to send as reinforcements to the pole, but there is a Penal Auxilia currently in orbit. Perhaps they could be of some use."

The brigadier general's day took a decided turn for the better. Of course, he thought. The penal infantry were the perfect troops for the ice cap. He should have sent them earlier. Better to use them as fodder in a difficult fight than to have them running around loose on Malthus or Alsatia. They and their abhorrent Ssoran guards could join the battle at the southern ice cap. With any luck, they would take devastating casualties and have to be evacuated off the planet. As an added bonus, the warm-blooded Ssora would hate the cold. Yes, let them deal with the Renegades. "I have been considering that option, Philippicus. But it was correct of you to mention it." Arcadius felt more relaxed than he had in days. "Notify the Auxilia commander to launch his men to our Cohort's location in assault boats."

Arcadius had learned in TOG training that the reptilian Ssora had reached other worlds through T-space travel long before any other race, but that their exploration was driven by the need for new worlds to accommodate a growing population, not a desire for conquest. Arcadius had a hard time understanding that motivation, which he felt showed a lack of ambition. The Ssoran's unique philosophy also slowed their relations with other races. Lying, cheating, and manipulation are the heart and soul of Ssoran interpersonal relationships, and the most successful Ssoran negotiation is the one in which the Ssoran never mentions the object of his desire; it is offered without ever being named. Arcadius despised the Ssoran race for their alien physiology and their unenlightened moral attitudes, but he had to admit that their unshakeable belief in absolute order in the universe made them good soldiers. They obeyed orders unquestioningly, expected instant obedience from those ranked below them, and delivered completely evenhanded punishment.

"If I may make a suggestion, Your Excellency. Rather than sending them on a straight drop to the pole, we could park them in a holding orbit around Rock Wall. That way they could approach the pole without risking detection by the Commonwealth forces."

"Well done, Antipolous." The general used his intelligence officer's first name as a sign of approval. "Have the necessary orders sent at once. Tell them to assume orbit around Rock Wall and hold until further notice."

"One other thing, sir." Philippicus still stood at attention, but his spine became straighter each time his superior praised him. "At least one unit should come straight in to Malthus. The Renegades must be expecting the deployment."

"Quite good. Quite good. I think a Cohort would do, don't you?"

Klaxons sounded throughout the *IMS Gradior*, sending the penals and their Ssoran guards scrambling for the debarking stations. The reptilian Ssora used prods on the legs of the men to inspire them to move more quickly. The penal legionnaires, their weapons safely locked in racks on the assault boats, just turned their backs on the lizard men and moved as fast as they could. Any thoughts of rebellion had been beaten out of them at the holding stations and training camps.

Legatus Maximus Rocipian Olioarchus, commander of the 356th Penal Auxilia, watched the activity from his command station. Final mission orders would come later, but the unit was finally going into action. The last two days of waiting had been almost more than he could stand. He had found the slow drift toward the planet since they had exited T-space galling. The skipper of the transport had no sense of urgency, and the transport positively crept toward the planet. The man was obviously trained as a merchant captain. Any halfway decent TOG officer would have applied maximum power as soon as possible and closed with the planet. To be ordered to drift around in space while battle was imminent was insufferable. At last, though, it looked like they would see some action.

The guards crammed the last of the legionnaires into the assault landing craft that had been carried outboard on the *Gradior*. Each boat was large enough to carry a full thirty-three-man platoon made up of three ten-man squads and the platoon headquarters. The guards sealed the doors, trapping the troops inside until a coded combination was broadcast over the correct commlink channel. The doors were locked only to remind the men inside that they were still in a Penal Auxilia, not because the troops were likely to blow the doors in an escape attempt while in orbit around Rock Wall or during the drop.

With the penal legionnaires safely stowed, the Ssora boarded the larger transports that would carry their tanks to the surface. The Ssora's vehicles were specially converted Nisus light grav vehicles. The original design was an attempt by TOG designers to develop a powerful, well-armored, and inexpensive light scout vehicle. They only achieved inexpensive. With its weak armor and minimal firepower, the Nisus proved to be a battlefield liability. But the TOGs' philosophy of never throwing anything away converted the Nisus to a military police vehicle. Two AP laser systems replaced the 50mm cannon and 1.5/5 laser, and the new configuration was designated the Nisus-S.

The 129-ton Nisus-S tanks left the transport in small carriers designed to bridge space for the Nisus-S from the transport to the atmosphere, where the light tanks were released. The tactical plan called for the Ssora to follow the penal landing craft to the surface and provide covering fire as the infantry deployed. Because this combat insertion was to an engaged unit, the standard ground vehicles usually assigned to the regiment would be landed later on Malthus and transferred to the pole.

Olioarchus and the command staff boarded their landing craft last. Although the command vehicle was the same class craft as that occupied by the penal infantry, the similarity ended with the outside configuration. The craft Olioarchus rode in was fully heated, and there were bunks along the rear bulkheads. The midsection was filled with a small galley and head, and the front area served as a lounge. The pilot and navigator sat forward. The legatus maximus walked through his command post, approved the accommodations, and strapped himself into one of the lounge chairs. When the other three members of the staff were settled, he nodded to the command pilot. The launch sequence began.

    Stone and Bard were an even match in the galleries below the ice. Bard was unhurt but lost, his trip to the surface a series of fits and starts. He had to stop at each branch in the maze of tunnels, checking each one to determine which was most promising, and this made his progress slow. Stone, hurt and fighting a losing battle against the cold, moved more slowly. His advantage was that Bard, trying to cover as much ground as possible, did little to cover his tracks. Stone unerringly picked up Bard's trail at each new tunnel.

    Bard knew, more by instinct than anything else, that Stone was alive and following him. He could only keep moving or stand and fight. He knew he would not get another opportunity for an ambush. Stone was too crafty to fall for that twice. And time was working against him. Sooner or later, the TOGs on the surface would attack again, and without the information he possessed, the TOG forces would be slaughtered. He had to keep going.

    A dispassionate observer would say the race was between the tortoise and the hare. Bard gained ground on the straight-aways but lost it in the turns. Stone moved slowly and steadily forward. The same observer would also say that Bard's searches where the galleries branched wasted a lot of time quite unnecessarily. If Bard had used his head and looked a little more carefully, he would have discovered that the correct path was fairly obvious. The distance between the two narrowed inexorably, but Bard was almost to the surface.

    Gasping for breath, the TOG agent crawled upward into complete darkness. It was the first time during his flight that his torch had reflected no light, and he knew this breach must lead to the surface. He had reached the surface. He stumbled out of the gallery into intense blackness. The sudden transition from dazzling light to total dark was so overpowering that he staggered, completely disoriented. He dropped to his hands and knees to regain his balance. He felt giddy, unable to control his limbs. He hung his head down and closed his eyes, forcing himself to calm his nerves and collect his thoughts.

His first task was to get well clear of the opening. Somewhere in the frozen bowels of the ice cap, his enemy was closing in on him. Better to get away from the opening and have some warning when the other man emerged than to wait to be stumbled over. He counted a hundred steps forward, bearing slightly to his right. The feeling of urgency was strong again. He had to communicate with the TOG command.

Somewhere in the darkness around him was a TOG commlink to which he could transmit the Renegade's position. But where? He had no idea if the receiving station was even within range of his transmitter. The tiny commlink he carried under his belt had a range of only three kilometers and required a thermal-generator power supply. The commlink would also operate on a power pack, but all power packs emit a constant signal. Intelligence agents were normally issued a thermal generator designed to convert body heat to energy so that even the minor emissions of a power pack could not be detected by the enemy.

Bard lowered the face plate of his combat helmet. The built-in perscomp was capable of detecting commlink emissions out to ten kilometers. If a TOG station was transmitting within that range, he should be able to locate it. He switched the frequency from the narrow band used by Cohort Harras to wide scan. He knew that TOG and Renegade forces operated on different frequencies within the commlink spectrum, even using different command frequencies, by what amounted to mutual agreement. Some overlap occurred at the end of the spectrum, and Bard could only hope that the TOG stations were within that blanket. He knelt again and waited for a signal to appear on his HUD.

Stone saw the black hole above him and realized he had reached the surface. Satisfaction and fear swept through him. He was satisfied to have made it this far, but now he faced two possibilities: he would be too late to stop Bard, or the spy lay in wait in some concealed position above him. Up to now he had just kept plodding forward, trying to shorten the distance to his enemy. He had not worried about Bard setting a second ambush, trusting to his senses to keep him alive. Now, with success so close, it would be stupid to stumble into a trap. He would have to be cautious.

His left arm was numb and hung uselessly at his side. He switched off the torch, tucking it in his belt. With his good hand he drew the laser pistol he had carried from the Loren sled. It was not his weapon of choice for killing a man, but it was all he had. His weapon powered up and at the ready, he crept slowly toward the opening.

When he reached the edge of the surface he paused. He knew Bard was somewhere in the darkness, and he would be able to scan for the spy as soon as he cleared the crevice. He had kept the helmet from his armor, even though the rest of it had been destroyed. The sensing devices in the face plate should reveal any heat source in the area, but the damage to the rest of the suit had degraded the helmet's capability. Stone wasn't sure it would work.

He was tempted to just stick his head above the rim to make a scan, but if Bard were still in the area it would give him a perfect shot. Coiling himself, he sprang forward over the rim and rolled. His left arm was no longer numb. Pain sheared through his brain as he rolled, and a red haze swept across his vision. He felt himself falling slowly through space, and he fought against it. Slowly, his vision cleared. He realized that the silence had not been broken by the sound of a shot.

Larry Stone stood, careful not to step in the direction from which he had rolled. The thermal imaging in the helmet did not show the contours of the ice, and he didn't want to stumble back into the crevice. He made a slow traverse of the area. Halfway through the sweep, the thermal sensors detected a heat source. Stone knew it had to be his quarry.

He moved cautiously for the first twenty paces, and then, certain that he was no longer in danger of falling into the breach, began to move more rapidly. The thermal image became steadily sharper.

The TOG transmission signal flared to life on Bard's HUD. The dot marking the TOG base showed up near the inner edge of the range radius designator; Bard figured he was about two kilometers away from the base, well within his transmission range. He fumbled for the transmitter in his belt, extracted it, and connected the thermal generator. He felt a tightness in his chest and fought to control the panic that threatened his mission. He knew Stone must be very near, and he was torn between the desire to complete his assignment and to get away from the man stalking him.

He was fumbling with the chip. The cold had numbed his fingers to the point that he couldn't handle the tiny piece while wearing his protective gloves. He raised the face plate and bit down on the ends of the fingers of his right glove, pulling it from his hand with his teeth. He took off his other glove, but still couldn't get the chip out of the case. He finally turned on the hand torch, placing it carefully on the snow in front of him. The light revealed that the safety catch on the chip carrier had been bent. He pried the clip away with his fingernails and shook the chip out onto his palm.

Holding the transmitter in his left hand, he inserted the chip into the access port. Switching the transmitter to his right hand, he stood and aimed it directly toward where the HUD showed the TOG base was located. With his left hand he began to massage the thermal generator. He waited for the green light to illuminate on the transmitter. When it winked on, he squeezed the push-to-send switch.

The torch flared like a beacon in Stone's HUD, almost blinding him. He lifted his face plate and saw a man standing less than thirty meters away. He was facing away from Stone, the light at his feet silhouetting him against the black void of the sky. Bard's right arm was raised, pointing into the distance.

Stone felt his consciousness slipping away again. Now he saw two of Bard, now three. The air between Stone and his target seemed to shimmer. He became aware of his harsh breathing, the fresh blood oozing down his left arm. He could see his legs trembling in the scant light cast by the distant torch. He dropped to his knees, only his right hand keeping him upright. He lifted his head.

Bard was still standing there, pointing into the distance. And there was only one of him. Stone knew that this was his last chance. He raised the laser pistol, thumbing the select switch from single pulse to continuous beam. He pushed the toggle one more notch to the overload position. One shot would empty both the onboard power supply and the reserve. The gennium-arsenic crystal would also burn out, but Stone didn't plan to use the weapon again. He aimed the pistol at a point just below the spy's combat helmet and pulled the trigger.

Bard never felt the hit. The combat armor he wore was built to stop most hits, but the designers could not make it proof against all assaults. The back of the helmet could not be made to fit flush against the rear back plate of the infantry suit or the wearer would not be able to move his head. Because there was little chance of an attack from the rear, the designers allowed for a gap in protection at the base of the skull. The aligned light of the laser pistol struck through that opening.

In an instant the skin on his neck burned away. The laser penetrated into the skull, and the cortex flashed into steam. Bard stood for a moment, his nerves sending messages to a brain that no longer existed. Receiving no answer, all the muscles relaxed at once, and the body crumpled, smoking slightly, into the snow.

Stone remained kneeling, the laser pistol glowing as the gennium-arsenic crystal cracked under the strain of overload. He dropped the useless weapon onto the ice, where it hissed and crackled as it cooled. Then the red mist swept across his eyes once more. He sat back heavily on his ankles and then toppled slowly backward.

36

1900, 13 Martius 6831—The assault landing craft of the 356th Penal Auxilia drifted clear of the transport *Gradior* as their pilots jockeyed the barges free from the mother ship. The craft were stored in three tiers, and so launching them was tricky. The course to the drop was preprogrammed, downloaded from the main computer on *Gradior*, but breaking away was completely under manual control. The one hundred and five penal barges, in addition to the Ssoran and headquarters craft, created quite a traffic jam around the flanks of the transport.

The ether filled with cross-chatter from the commlinks as the pilots nudged their bulky craft into drop formation. The Cohorts formed in columns, the five Centuries of each Cohort taking up wide vee-shaped formations, each Century's platoons stacked behind its respective Century headquarters. The pilots were experienced, and the whole process took less than ten minutes. When the last craft signaled that it was in position, Legatus Maximus Rocipian Olioarchus initiated the drop sequence, and the 356th Penal Auxilia began to fall toward the planet's largest satellite.

The commander's orders were to put the bulk of his Auxilia into orbit around Caralis' moon, but they also needed to make a drop toward the surface for the benefit of the Commonwealth forces on Caralis. The Commonwealth must have seen the *Gradior* hanging in orbit, and they would be expecting the deployment of the TOG force. Letting them see a decoy force was part of the operational plan. The fifth Cohort was chosen for the move toward Caralis. Olioarchus was not pleased to be losing 20 percent of his force even before he landed, but aside from the pilots, only penals would die. He shrugged it off.

The formation banked left toward the looming bulk of Rock Wall and plunged down, the pockmarked landscape of the giant moon appearing in the forward windows. The computers calculated the necessary angle of approach that would bring the craft within the satellite's gravitational pull. The formation would orbit past the face of Caralis so close to the planet's surface that they would fool all surface sensors. Accelerating all the way, the formation would whip around the equator, then using that velocity, break away again toward space. The planet's gravitational pull, first used to speed the approach, would slow the escape. As they reached the limit of their initial orbit on the far side of Rock Wall, hidden from the surface of Caralis, they would slow even more until the gravity of the giant moon drew them back.

Falling toward Rock Wall, their elliptical orbit would bring them past the surface of Caralis once more. This time, instead of going into another long orbit to change direction, the gravity of Caralis itself would warp their flight path. As they broke past Rock Wall, their trajectory would bend toward Caralis. It would then be a minor matter for the maneuvering thrusters of the assault landing craft to direct that warp toward the southern pole. Their approach would be at such a high velocity that even if the enemy fighter squadrons detected the approach, they could not deploy in time to intercept it. There was only the small problem of slowing the craft as they struck the atmosphere. Some of the craft would surely be lost, but the command was willing to pay that price to maintain the advantage of complete surprise.

Inside one of the landing craft, Optio Asinus Strovasi looked toward the front to watch the sweep toward Rock Wall. Four longitudinal seating sections filled the craft. Each row held nine seats, the outboard ones facing inward, the central ones facing outward. The legionnaires sat facing each other in double rows, the knees of the penals in one row alternating with the knees of those in the opposite row. It was a tight fit, but on the order to rise for debarkation, the seats would drop into the deck, leaving plenty of space for the troops to exit the craft. As platoon leader, Strovasi sat in the second row with the rest of the headquarters unit. From his seat he could see the pilot and navigator/engineer at the command console, and in front of them, the windows revealed the approaching bulk of Rock Wall.

Strovasi was fat, even for a TOG garrison legionnaire. He claimed his excessive bulk was a result of glandular dysfunction, but the only one of his glands that dysfunctioned was his salivary gland, and it worked overtime; he liked to eat. The penal units had a strictly limited caloric intake, and he used his position as platoon leader to requisition additional rations from the peds. He was always the first of his platoon to go through the chow line, and then he positioned himself so that the other penals were forced to pass him as they reached the end. He stabbed one item off each legionnaire's plate as they filed by, but there was no grumbling, at least within his hearing. Any complaint met with instant and cruel discipline.

He shifted his bulk to get a better view of the moon, elbowing Platoon Sergeant Lisectus Barcus in the process. The sergeant leaned away. The three members of the headquarters platoon were assigned an extra seat each for the additional gear they carried, and Strovasi overflowed his allotted space. Barcus eyed his leader with undisguised contempt. The optio was a bully, and an incompetent one at that. Sergeant Barcus had been assigned to the penals as punishment for defending his platoon against stupid orders from his centurion, and he was convinced that his current superior officer was no improvement over his last.

He had been charged with insubordination, and Barcus knew it was true. He should have obeyed his leader and led his platoon to certain death; that was the way of the Legion. But he had objected, and so had been arrested and court-martialed. Only his long and glorious combat record saved him from the usual sentence of execution. True, that same list of decorations and commendations had been deleted from his file, but he had retained his rank, if only to serve with the Penal Auxilia. In the end, another sergeant had taken command of the platoon he had tried to save. That sergeant executed the disputed orders, and every ped in the platoon died. His protest had been a futile gesture.

Sitting next to Strovasi gave Barcus a safe opportunity to examine his optio unobserved. The platoon commander was turned so that his back was to the sergeant, the folds of fat at the back of his neck flowing over the stiff collar of the combat armor. The man's jowls looked like the rubber tires of an Aclys, the standard wheeled APC of penal infantry. He thumbed the safety catch of his Mantichore spike rifle to the off position. His optio would be a small loss if the weapon "accidentally" misfired. Unfortunately, the weapon was not loaded. Ammunition would be issued after they reached the surface. Barcus craned his neck to see past the pyramidal bulk of the optio.

The long TOG assault formation swung toward Rock Wall. Commlink traffic was light, consisting mostly of grunts and short commands. The pilots had done this many times, and they knew their business. The Auxilia bent like a giant snake around Rock Wall, and Barcus could see the surface rushing past, fascinated by the pockmarks of aged craters. Something flashing past the upper left corner of the windows caught his eye. One of the landing craft was breaking toward Caralis.

"Command. This is Cohort Quintus." The commlink came to life as the commander of the Fifth Cohort called Auxilia command. "We have broken out of formation."

"This is command. What's the problem, Quintus?"

"This is Quintus. Our helm does not answer. The computer has taken command of the craft."

"Understood, Quintus. Command out."

"This is Quintus. We are dropping too fast. We will strike the atmosphere of Caralis." Barcus heard the voice on the commlink crack. The man speaking was afraid.

"This is command. Quintus, the computer will take you in. It's part of the plan." The soothing voice of Auxilia had an odd edge to it. Frantic chatter came over the commlink as too many people tried to talk at once. "Steady now, Quintus." Auxilia broke through the noise.

"Command, this is Quintus. Wings do not deploy. Our angle of approach is too steep." The disembodied voice was practically shouting. Barcus could see them now, a vic of landing craft plunging straight toward darkside and Caralis' atmosphere. The heat of re-entry made the landing craft glow against the somber silhouette of the planet. The point of the vee flashed into a drifting cloud of sparkling specks. The others followed in rapid succession. A voice screamed "We're burni..." and then the commlink went silent.

Strovasi turned away from the flight deck and fixed his piggish eyes on his platoon sergeant. "*Dulce et, Ave Caesar*, and all the rest of that. Better them than us." He smacked his lips. "Any emergency rations back there?"

Barcus shuddered. He understood the purpose of penal infantry; it was generous and practical of the Terran Overlord Government to give its soldiers a chance to redeem themselves. But the penals who had just been incinerated had also been men. Even penals deserved better than that. The 560 officers and peds of Cohort Quintus had been a diversion; a decoy for those on the surface to record while the rest of the regiment hid behind Rock Wall for the next several hours. "I hope it was worth the cost," he muttered.

"What did you say, Sergeant?" asked Strovasi, staring at his platoon sergeant.

"Nothing, sir."

"It had better be nothing, Sergeant. Talk like that was what got you into this outfit. If you keep it up, you'll find out how lenient the government will be next time around."

The Renegade patrol worked its way along the frozen gallery, weapons at the ready. The signs of the ambush had been their first real clue that they were tracking more than an illusion. The expended ammunition would have been a clear enough sign, but the bits of broken armor and the blood also stood out against the white of the passage under the ice. The patrol was investigating the section sentry's report. He claimed to have seen someone or something moving on the ice fall at the breach in the dome of the abandoned city. The sentry's report didn't make sense. His superiors assumed that fatigue had created an illusion of movement, but they wanted every incident checked out, and now the patrol knew the truth. Two people had found the crevice in the ice slope and headed toward the surface. They had fought, and both had survived.

The seven men crept up toward the opening that showed the blackness of the sky against the surrounding ice. The sergeant positioned his men, and on his command they broke for the surface, flopping down to cover the entire perimeter. Silence and darkness greeted them.

The surface of the ice cap presented the patrol with different problems from those encountered in the gallery below. Though the tunnel was an excellent place for an ambush, at least the patrol knew which way its quarry was moving. On the surface, there was no way for the patrol to stalk its prey. The sergeant dropped his face plate and activated the TIS on the off chance that there was a life form within its three-hundred-meter range. He scanned the area in a slow sweep.

The TIS recorded a weak signal barely a hundred meters away. Too faint to be the thermographic signature of a Human, it still deserved exploration in an area where nothing should be alive. The sergeant gave two quick hand signals, and the patrol moved off toward the signal.

The TIS in the sergeant's helmet led them right to the bodies, but they never would have found them without it. The first man was covered so deeply by the drifting ice that he was all but invisible. His damaged ranger stealth suit, combined with the cover provided by the ice and his dangerously low body temperature, simply did not show up on the standard thermographic system of the patrol's combat helmets. As they prepared to move the injured man, one of the patrol stumbled over the second body.

The whole situation looked strange. The dead man was a Renegade optio. And the first man had obviously shot him in the back. The sergeant ordered the patrol to carry back both the dead and the dying man.

37

2200, 13 Martius 6831—Dr. Kelton Hess cut the blood-soaked tunic away from the left shoulder of the wounded man. He saw that the deltoid muscle was completely severed from the bones along the anterior portion. The posterior section of the muscle was still attached to the humerus, but the man would not be able to use his arm for some time. Had Hess had access to a fully equipped medical facility, he could have repaired the damage quickly, but he lacked a baking system and the necessary adhesives, so he'd have to do it the old-fashioned way. Hess was impressed by the fact that the man had been able to continue to move after suffering the wound, and concluded that much of the associated damage had occurred after the initial injury.

Larry Stone regained consciousness as the doctor extracted a final fragment of bone from the laceration, but he didn't move. Only his eyes followed the doctor as he probed the wound, cleaning bits of armor and fabric from the ragged opening. Hess saw that his patient was awake. "You've taken quite a whack, young man."

Stone grunted in reply.

"There're a few people outside who'd like to talk to you about how you acquired this beauty. Do you feel strong enough to answer some questions?" Hess closed the wound and sprayed plasto-skin over it. "I'll have to put that arm in a sling and secure it to your chest. You'll heal, but you'll be out of action for awhile." The doctor stepped back to view his handiwork, and Optio Roglund Karstil and Sergeant Shawn Arsen, communications chief, appeared at the doctor's elbow. "This gentleman would like to have a word with you," said the doctor, indicating Karstil.

Karstil moved around the doctor and stared at the patient. The haggard face of the wounded man stared back. Karstil did not recognize the man as his sometimes partner in the games of Pendulous played to while away the time on the RLS *Maiestas*. The trip from Windsor to Rilus V was six months in the past, and even though Karstil had seen Stone once since then, he didn't connect the man on the stretcher with the sergeant in the tank bone-yard, either. "It's about the other man," he said abruptly.

"Bid aggressively, double more often," replied Stone.

"What?"

"Wasn't that your philosophy of Pendulous on the *Maiestas*?"

Completely at a loss, Karstil looked more closely at the wounded man. "Stone?"

"In the flesh. Look, Karstil. Can we talk for a minute in private?"

"I'm supposed to be taking your statement and having it notarized," Karstil said stiffly.

"Yeah. Fine. But I'd like to talk to you alone first."

Karstil hesitated, then nodded to the sergeant. "It's all right," he said. "I don't think I'm in any danger from Stone, here." He was not convinced his last statement was true, particularly because of what he suspected of Stone. He turned to watch Sergeant Arsen leave the room with the doctor, and turned back to find the patient standing beside the operating table. He almost shouted for Arsen to return.

"Here's the straight scoop," began Stone. "Bard was a spy. I've been on his trail for almost two years. He sent a message to the TOGs on the surface before I could stop him. Tell Harras, and then send him to see me. Better yet, take me to him now."

"You want to see the Cohort commander?" Karstil was still a little off-balance from surprise at what Stone was telling him. "What makes you think he'll see you? He doesn't even know you."

"Wrong. Harras and I go way back. We worked together on the *Tacitus*. By the way, you nearly blew that one wide open."

Karstil remembered the gloomy equipment bay on the transport. Remembered the dim shapes he had seen crawling over the Liberators. At the time he had thought there was something familiar about the pair, and now he understood what it was. He had believed he was seeing the saboteurs responsible for the frequent, random accidents plaguing the 2567th Renegade Legion, but now he knew what he had seen was Stone and Harras checking the tanks for more of the insidious time-release traps. "Right. Let's get you out of here."

The TOG penal formation made the turn at the apogee of its orbit and began its run back toward Rock Wall. Crammed into the landing craft, the peds felt the increased gravitational pull that followed the momentary weightlessness of the turn. Unheated, poorly ventilated, and virtually uninsulated, the assault landing craft were rapidly becoming minor hells. Not designed to spend much time in space, the ships were ill-equipped to deal with the needs of passengers. When the pilot and his navigator had noticed the instruments becoming blurry about an hour into the trip, they had gone on oxygen. For those in the rear of the ship no such luxury was provided.

Men began to doze off, slumping against their fellow peds. At first, those still awake objected, but they soon lacked the energy even for that. The mission strategists had calculated exactly how much oxygen the peds crammed into the craft would need to survive, and each ship had been issued one oxygen bottle to be opened four hours into the journey. That little boost was calculated to get most of the men to the surface alive.

The 356th Penal Auxilia was at full strength, providing nearly twenty-five hundred combat soldiers for this operation. More than five hundred of those soldiers had burnt up in the atmosphere, sent as a diversion to deceive any unfriendly observers on the planet below. Of the two thousand troops remaining, the operations officers had estimated that sixteen hundred would be enough to deal with the enemy hidden below the surface of the ice cap, which meant they were willing to accept 20 percent casualties on the run in. Because the commanders expected the landing to meet no resistance, the 20 percent losses normally taken from enemy fire in a hot drop could be absorbed by attrition in orbit. The oxygen-reserve figures were reduced accordingly, making the insertion a basic cost–benefit equation.

The barge pilots were another matter altogether. These men were part of the fleet services, highly trained experts not to be wasted without good purpose. Those destroyed with Cohort Quintus in the diversionary tactic represented a significant but acceptable loss. But the operations officers did not plan to lose any more pilots than necessary. They were provided an oxygen supply exclusive of that provided for the penal troops.

In Assault Landing Craft 332, which carried the Second Platoon, Third Century, Third Cohort, Platoon Sergeant Lisectus Barcus watched the platoon leader crack open the oxygen bottle held between his legs. The fat man took a deep breath, then gently screwed the valve shut again. The optio looked around the cargo compartment furtively to see if he were being watched. His greedy eyes locked with those of his platoon sergeant. The optio gave him a tight-lipped smile.

Barcus was too far gone to care. He knew that the men in the rear of the barge would never get a breath of that oxygen. They would breathe whatever air was left, and soon that would be none at all. He turned his head slowly to look aft and saw that some of the sleeping men in the cargo bay had blue lips. He turned back to stare at his optio.

Barcus struggled to force his oxygen-starved brain to make sense of the situation. He was loyal to TOG, believed in them implicitly. Since birth, his parents, teachers, and friends had assured him that the rule of the Terran Overlord Government was the last, best hope for mankind. The destruction caused by the terrible wars with the Kessrith and the noble sacrifices of all those who had gone before him had been drilled into his very consciousness. New Rome had risen from the ashes of the past to become the foundation upon which all civilization now stood. The Commonwealth and its Renegade mercenaries were bent on destroying that foundation. Barcus had willingly dedicated his life to their extermination. It had been an unspoken contract between him and history: he would do his best, and TOG history would crown him with glory.

Now he was trapped in an assault craft, watching his platoon slowly suffocate. Somehow the contract he had so willingly signed was being strained. Perhaps the contract already had been broken.

Harras was in shock. Hammered by the cold, the fatigue, and the hunger cramping his belly, he found it difficult to comprehend the magnitude of the damage one spy had done. Stone outlined the extent of Bard's treachery, reminding Harras of other treacheries that had occurred not so long ago: the accelerator coils that had been tampered with, discovered while on the *Tacitus*, the finger-bombs on the control cables of the front-line tanks on Alsatia, illicit and damaging transmissions made from command headquarters. Why had the spy not been eliminated when they'd first discovered his identity? Harras demanded an answer. Why had he not been informed of the spy's presence in his Cohort?

The patrol had carried back everything they found on the surface near the men. The computer chip displaying the layout of the city and the openings in the dome, and a demonstration of the transmitter and the thermal generator had removed all doubt. Harras contemplated the disaster he was facing. The TOG forces on the surface now knew everything about the Cohort's defense. They would be able to attack at every breach, and he didn't have enough troops to cover all the approaches.

When the enemy knew of only two places to attack, the Renegade forces stood a chance. Now there were four more entry points to be protected, and two of them were large enough to admit TOG vehicles. If Harras deployed his three Centuries against the largest breaches, that would leave him nothing in reserve. But the breaches as well as the three smaller openings, which provided good access for infantry, had to be covered. Fortunately for Harras, the TOG troops above were short on infantry and long on tanks.

Harras called together his command staff and rearranged the defense assignments once again. Each Century would defend one of the large openings and an adjacent infantry-sized approach. The centurions left the headquarters with a grim determination to redress the damage the spy had done. The leaked information was a bad enough blow, but the Cohort had suffered an even greater loss. The knowledge that one of their own had betrayed them created a nagging doubt that still another spy might exist within their ranks. Everyone would have to be watched. The breakdown of trust between soldiers was one of the worst disasters that could strike a unit. Even at the best of times it was imperative that each man be able to rely on the trooper beside him. For Cohort Harras, that bond of trust had been destroyed.

As the other officers were leaving the briefing, Harras signaled for Stone and Karstil to remain. "You two have performed an invaluable service," he began, "and I hardly know how to thank you. Larry, you and I go back a few years. I thought I had seen the last of you and your kind when I joined the Renegade Legion, but, fortunately, I was wrong. You have done me and the Renegades a great service, more fully appreciated because you are not one of us." He turned to Karstil. "And you, young man, have been a nuisance to me ever since I took command of your unit. Even so, I thought I saw something in you that could be of great value to this Legion, and now I am gratified to see you prove me right."

Harras shifted his weight, unwilling to begin his next topic. "It is still difficult for me to believe that a member of my command was a spy. I won't say he was disloyal, for he never really was loyal to us. No. He was always a spy for New Rome. We can't be certain that he was working alone, however, and so I need your help more than ever. Please keep your eyes and ears open. If anything at all strikes you as odd or strange or suspect, let me know immediately."

Karstil and Stone looked at one another, then back at the Cohort commander. Each man nodded an acknowledgment, and then the pair left the tank without speaking. Outside the command vehicle, Karstil touched the other man's arm, stopping him from leaving for a moment. "One of these days, Mister Lawrence "just-call-me-Larry" Stone, you've got to tell me what that was all about."

Stone smiled and nodded. "After we get out of here."

The assault landing craft lurched as they struck the upper limits of Caralis' atmosphere. At almost the same moment, the TOG pilots fired the reverse thrusters. The sudden deceleration threw the men in the cargo bays forward against their restraining harnesses. Many of them regained consciousness at the shock, struggling to clear their heads in the airless environment.

The second deceleration shock was even stronger. The landing craft were entering the atmosphere at too steep an angle. The approach from Rock Wall to the pole required emergency re-entry procedures, and the pilots continually fired their reverse thrusters in an attempt to slow the diving craft. The small ships began to corkscrew as they dropped, bouncing and twisting the peds strapped in the seats. The noses of the ships began to glow from the intense heat of re-entry, filling the barges with the acrid smell of burning paint.

Assault Landing Craft 332 fought to maintain formation within the Century and Cohort. Violent rocking forced the pilot to fire the lateral thrusters, which slammed the ship sideways. The drifting smoke inside the ship reduced visibility and burned the throats of the already miserable peds. When some of the men became nauseous, they couldn't avoid vomiting on their mates. All of them were too weak to care, and the smell of vomit mixed with the stink of smoke. Platoon Sergeant Barcus watched Optio Strovasi suck the last of the oxygen from the reserve bottle. The optio's eyes, no longer tiny dots in his bloated face, stared wildly from his ashen forehead. Great beads of perspiration coursed down his cheeks. The barge lurched again.

With a stomach-churning drop, ALC 332 leveled out and slowed. The heat glow vanished from the forward bulkhead. The navigator reached up and thumbed a switch that opened the ventilation ports on the forward ogive, and a blast of frigid air swept through the cargo bay, clearing out the smoke and stink. The penals felt the freezing blast strike deep into their sweat-covered bodies, but the cold air was a welcome relief from the suffocating, oxygen-poor interior. The reverse thrusters fired again.

Through the forward canopy, Barcus could see a vast expanse of white illuminated by the landing lights of the barge. Then, with a grinding crash, the landing craft struck the surface. "All right, you penals!" shouted the pilot, as the rear clamshell doors popped open. "Get out of my ship!"

Sealed containers beside the doors broke open to disgorge a cascade of polymer ammunition blocks. The penals gathered them up as they stumbled from the assault craft.

38

0330, 14 Martius 6831—Legatus Cariolanus Camus wasted no time on finesse. The transmission of the map giving the Renegade's defensive positions and the location of all known breaches in the dome, not to mention a complete map of the city under the ice, had seemed to come out of nowhere. The legionnaire who brought it to his attention was agog with excitement, but Camus had refused to satisfy the man's curiosity, simply accepting the message as if it were expected. He had checked the transmission authorization codes with his intelligence people, and they confirmed the codes as belonging to an active agent behind Renegade lines. How the man had managed to obtain the information and transmit it, or even if he had been caught and killed in the process, was unimportant. Camus intended to make use of his good fortune as quickly as possible, perhaps even before the Renegades realized their plans had been compromised. As the TOG penal troops staggered from their assault craft, they were rounded up by his own legionnaires and assigned to tanks and infantry carriers. Others were herded into the tunnel complex and toward the small hole through which the infantry had previously attacked. Their Ssoran guards had little to do but fall in behind the assault force.

The penal infantry were not allowed to ride inside any of the vehicles. They fought in the tradition of tank marines of ages past, riding the vehicle hulls into combat and dismounting at the objective. It was a crude form of mechanized infantry, and the penals would take heavy casualties, but those losses were acceptable; they were there to pay with their own blood for their misdeeds. The first of the Horatius tanks mounted its assigned squad and headed for the main breach.

Even under their shroud of ice and the protective dome, the Renegades could sense the movement of the enemy forces overhead. The DDPs in Karstil's tank platoon, assigned to the main breach, blossomed with red indicators showing TOG movement. The two Liberators were deployed near the breach in the same positions occupied earlier by MacDougall's vehicles. The TOGs would know where to find them, but they were set up in the best positions available.

Centurion Moldine Rinter was in a command Pedden close to the front lines, determined to add its limited firepower to the battle if needed. The two infantry squads assigned to the Century were positioned in the buildings on either side of the main street that led away from the breach toward the central temple and Cohort headquarters. Now the Renegades waited for the first enemy vehicle to break through the ramshackle ice wall built across the opening. They didn't wait long.

Roglund Karstil was oblivious to the cold that stung his cheeks. He was halfway between the open hatch and the command DDP, unwilling to devote his complete attention to the electronic data that would be his only source of information until the fighting started. Burning tanks had cast plenty of illumination on the last fight, and he knew he would see more from the open hatch than the DDP could tell him once the next fight began. Karstil, along with most other tank commanders, considered the DDP fine for raw data. But if a commander wanted to know it all, to see whether or not he really had a shot, the only place to be was topside. Tankers fought best when exposed to the elements, and Karstil was no exception.

"Three Horatius tanks. Range one-zero-double-zero. Vehicles traversing from five-six-double-zero to four-double-zero. Velocity two-four. Lock not achieved. Target painting unavailable." The DDP had picked up the approach of the enemy tanks. They were coming down the long, sloping cut that led to the breach. They were only a kilometer away, but they were completely shielded from a weapons or painting-laser lock. Karstil's stomach clenched.

"This is Three-one-six. All Three-one units, here they come. All shots on the first vehicle, then engage targets of opportunity." Karstil already had given those orders, but he felt the need to be in contact with his units as the enemy approached; it was better than doing nothing. He wondered if the fear that always seemed to clutch at him right before battle would ever grow less or go away completely. The other Liberator and the Viper acknowledged his transmission.

The first Horatius tank exploded from the breach in a shower of ice and blinding smoke; the tank must have fired smoke as it hit the wall. Though expecting the tank, the defending Liberators were surprised, but only for a moment.

The Horatius didn't show the finesse of the earlier Aeneas attack. Instead of hiding behind the ice crater and taking snap shots at the defenders, it burst from the opening and continued straight into the city. Either the driver didn't realize that he was still some fifteen meters above the floor of the city, or he thought that the violence of his attack and the strength of his bottom armor would save him.

As the hull cleared the rim, the waiting Liberators fired their 150- and 50mm cannon. All weapons were loaded with HEAP, in order to blast the largest possible initial craters into the armor. The lighter stuff would penetrate through the holes blasted by the heavier guns. As the enemy tank cleared its smoke screen, every painting laser within range opened up on it; three different lasers deciphered its shields. The heavy lasers on the defending Liberators fired first.

Karstil, his Liberator centered in the street the Horatius was charging down, fired at the tank's front. The 150mm-cannon shot gouged the hull below the mantlet of the main gun, the 50mm shot burrowing in after. The laser hit the bottom armor next, the aligned light burning through it easily. The Horatius driver's helm controls went slack, steering and thrust control shot completely away. The other Liberators savaged the sides of the enemy tank, shields and vane control disintegrating under the combined firepower.

The penal infantry were riding the turret and the top armor, protected from direct Renegade fire but covered by a cloud of searing armor fragments that burned through their light battle armor. Still fighting to revive their oxygen-starved brains, they hung on, useless appendages on a dying vehicle. The tank roared down the street over Karstil's Liberator. Spentling Crowder tracked it and waited for another chance to shoot. That chance never came.

The Horatius, completely out of control, smashed into the side of a building, its sharp forward-hull sponsons crumpling against the massive masonry of the ancient structure. A stream of sparks and smoldering cables poured down the face of the building. The tank swerved away from the building, shattered systems spilling from the ruptured hull. It careened across the street, rolling over as it went, and the penal infantry lost their desperate grip on the turret, falling into the street. They struck the solid pavement with the sound of overripe melons dropping from a cart.

The tank struck a building on the opposite side of the avenue. The bow sponson rode up on the structure's parapet, angling the Horatius further and further skyward. The hull hit the side of the building and smoke and flame flooded from the shattered underside. The tank hung for an instant upon the parapet and then overbalanced, crashing forward, down through the building, to smash onto the street. The hull burst open with a shattering explosion as the ammunition cooked off in the heat of the grav drive. The building stood out in sharp relief against the brilliant glare of the burning vehicle.

Other tanks had followed the first. The Liberators, hidden in the streets reaching out from the breach and disguised by holotarps as long as they remained stationary, always got in the first shot. TOG vehicle after TOG vehicle ran the gauntlet of fire, none destroyed but none undamaged. The slope at the breach was littered with external equipment and the bodies of the penal infantry blasted from their precarious positions atop the tanks.

To the right of the platoon's position, Sergeant Honor Ross and her squad fired over the parapet of their building. The tanks were passing less than ten meters away and the Renegades raked the infantry clinging to the tank's sides and tops with spike rifle fire. The peds plunged to the street below in gory streams, but the tanks kept going.

Behind the Horatius tanks came the Romulus carriers. Camus had committed his last four heavy infantry transports to the assault. Armored more heavily than the Horatius tanks they followed, the carriers were instantly targeted as they broke through the breach.

"Three-six. This is Three-one-six. The line has broken. Horatius tanks and Romulus carriers are through." Karstil sent a quick sitrep to Rinter. She probably already knew and was doing something about it, but Karstil had to report.

"Three-six. Roger."

Karstil was up in the turret, watching the fight from the command hatch. There was nothing for him to do but keep an eye on the battle flowing around him. Crowder was engaging everything he could see; too many targets were presented too quickly for him to pick and choose. The front of the Liberator was continually illuminated by the flash of the turret-mounted weapons. Occasionally a missile would arc high over the fight, aiming for a target that was usually gone before the shot reached its destination. When an enemy vehicle passed overhead, the TVLGs were used to devastating effect. The armor on the bottom of both the Horatius and Romulus was too thin to survive a missile hit, and strikes near the tanks' center-line destroyed the helm controls. The street behind Karstil began to fill with burning TOG equipment.

When Karstil saw the infantry was riding on the outside of the tanks and carriers, he knew that the TOGs had somehow reinforced their troops with a penal unit. He also realized that not all the penal infantry were dying in the inferno. No matter how concentrated and devastating the enemy fire, the odds favored the survival of at least some of the tank-riding infantry. They clustered along the faces of the buildings, taking cover in doorways and window openings. It was only a matter of time before a sergeant or officer survived the initial assault and took command of the situation, and when that happened, Karstil and his tanks would be in deep trouble. Karstil sensed that that time had arrived.

Karstil saw a shape dart across the front of his tank, then vanish in the deep shadows. Another followed. He dropped down inside the fighting compartment to snatch a Tektara spike carbine from the rack beside Crowder. Clearing the edge of the command hatch, he sent a quick burst into the darkness, ducking back down. No response. "Three-one. This is Three-one-six. Enemy infantry in my position. Be on the lookout. Fight your tanks up." He rose above the coaming and fired again. This time a streak of spikes erupted from his target area, striking off the glacis and Vulcan housing. Karstil ducked again. Tankers were trained to fight as infantry when necessary, but this was not his ideal of the way to go to war. Much too personal.

"Boots. Prepare to back up."

"Ready when you are, chief."

So, "sir" had become "chief." Right. Not the time to discuss it. "Now." He fired another burst into the darkness. "Spent. I have control of the turret."

"Yours."

Karstil swung the main gun toward the spot from which the spikes had come. Shooting infantry with a 150mm cannon was a big waste of ammunition, but the peds would still end up dead. "Load HEAP." He wasn't looking for penetration, he wanted blast effect.

"Ready."

Karstil hit the firing button and the main gun blazed against the darkness of the building. The round struck high, as Karstil had intended. The detonation brought huge slabs of masonry crashing into the street. If there had been any infantry near the spot, they would at the very least be discouraged.

"Gunner. You have turret control."

A TVLG exploded against the rear of the Liberator, and Karstil turned in time to see someone duck into the doorway fifty meters to the rear. "Stop!" The Liberator shuddered as Boutselis applied full forward thrust to counteract the backing action.

Karstil stood in the command hatch and leveled the spike carbine at the doorway. The next time the TOG appeared, he would have a little surprise for him.

Another TVLG arced toward the Liberator, but this time from the other side of the street. Karstil switched targets, but by the time he located the launch site, the man was gone. The Vulcan antimissile system whirred, and the TVLG was blasted into fragments before it struck. Karstil knew he was fighting a losing battle. As long as there was more than one launcher in the street, he would never be able to guess which one would fire next. He would eventually cut down one or more, but unless the peds ran out of missiles, they would probably get him first. He was trapped between the enemy tanks that now held the breach, and the infantry in the street behind.

Another TVLG arced toward the Liberator from out of nowhere and crashed into the street beside the tank. The penal infantry was firing without painting, but even without targeting assistance they would eventually be successful. If they coordinated a volley, his shields and the Vulcan would be swamped. He fired steady bursts at anything that moved.

A lumbering vehicle appeared out of the darkness down the street ahead of them. Its driving lamps were full on, illuminating the buildings with a blinding light. The AP laser on the bow poured fire into the TOG infantry positions. Each side of the vehicle was covered by Renegade infantry firing steady streams of spikes into the window openings. More fire poured down on the enemy positions from the parapets. Penal troops, flushed from their secure positions by light, fire, and grenades, began to emerge, their hands aloft. A few tried to fight the combined Renegade assault, but it was hopeless. Moldine Rinter had committed the Century headquarters to salvage the situation.

39

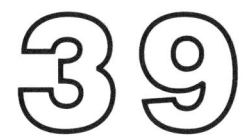

0415, 13 Martius 6831—Rinter's counterattack at the main breach had turned the tide. The Century headquarters, reinforced by the two infantry squads already in place, flushed out the last of the penal infantry. The Horatius tanks and Romulus carriers that were still mobile beat a hasty retreat as their infantry support dissolved. The last Horatius, dragging grav coils from its wounded underside, never made it up the slope to safety. The Liberators, no longer engaging too many targets, concentrated on the wounded tank. Armor was hammered to slag, and the vehicle subsided into glowing rubble that melted the ice upon which it rested.

The Renegades cheered their victory, but their voices were suddenly muffled by rumbling explosions from elsewhere on the perimeter. The second phase of the attack had begun. The crash of 150mm cannon and the high-pitched crack of their 50mm cousins reverberated through the city.

Karstil listened to the reports being sent back to Cohort headquarters over the command net. Lighter vehicles were attacking away from the main breach, mostly Aeneas tanks and Lupis carriers. Those TOG vehicles were easier to destroy, but their commanders were being more cautious. The penal infantry was entering on foot, swamping the defending tanks with missile fire and smoke. The supporting vehicles slipped in behind this screen to take up positions within the city itself.

The normally soft burr of Jamie MacDougall's voice was becoming more and more pronounced as he reported positions overrun and vehicles lost. Two of his Liberators were not reporting, and Karstil could see an eerie glow in the direction of MacDougall's front. It could only mean burning tanks. "Boots. Be prepared to move on my command. Turn this thing around while we're waiting."

"Roger." There was a long pause on the comm. Then, "It's not a thing, sir. You have to treat the vehicle with respect."

Chastised by a triarii, thought Karstil. He opened his mouth to speak, and then thought better of it. Boutselis and Crowder would need all the luck at their command to survive this battle. Far be it from him to discount one of their superstitions. He looked down at Triarii Spentling Crowder, crouched behind the controls of his weapons array. He was looking up at his tank commander expectantly. "Sorry, guys. It's not a thing. It's a tank. I'll call it a tank from now on." Crowder smiled and went back to his sight; the Liberator pivoted in the street.

MacDougall's reports became increasingly frantic. The penal infantry was pushing him back. He called for help, and Harras led his Liberator and two Peddens into the melee. The

Cohort headquarters stemmed the tide but could not turn it.

Moldine Rinter climbed onto the front glacis of Karstil's Liberator. He looked up as she approached. "MacDougall needs help," she said. Karstil nodded. "You're the only one I can break free. Take an infantry squad and go to his area. Can you handle it?"

Karstil looked at his tank. Great chunks of the rear armor hung from the frame. The ballistic protection showed through in two places, even though the ceramic protection was not burned. He gestured toward the damage. "I'm all right as long as no one comes up behind me."

Rinter smiled. "We'll give you an infantry squad to see that that doesn't happen. They'll ride on you."

"They don't have a vehicle?"

"Not any more," replied Rinter. "It's been cannibalized for spare parts."

Karstil heard the exhilaration of active command in her voice. "You gonna command the squad?"

"No," she said, "but I'll give you someone just as good." She signalled sharply, and a squad broke cover from a nearby building. The squad clambered up the front and side rails of the Liberator, finding handholds with no regard for the amount of space the gunner needed to use the weapons systems. Troopers draped themselves over every external bulge, blocking the main gun sight, the Vulcan antimissile system, the 5/6 laser, and the turret traverse.

Karstil was repelled by one of the squad members. A huge spider-type creature scampered up the glacis and stood in front of the turret. "Archon Divxas, at your service," rattled the alien. "I hope you will not think it presumptuous of me to comment on the state of your vehicle."

Karstil stared at the spider, his mouth open. It was not that the creature had spoken to him so well, it was that he had spoken at all. "What?"

The spider had just opened his mouth to explain, when the squad leader interrupted. "Archon!" came a voice. "Be quiet and hang on."

Karstil whipped around to face the squad leader as she climbed toward the turret. His mouth opened, then shut. It opened again. "You!"

"Sir?" The sergeant looked up at him. The squad leader and the tank commander stared at each other for a moment in surprise. Honor Ross felt her heart jump. Even with his face altered by several day's growth of beard, she immediately recognized Optio Roglund Karstil. She felt the blood rush to her face. "Roglund! I mean Karstil. I mean Sir." Suddenly aware that she was babbling, she snapped her mouth shut.

"Ross?"

"I didn't know you were here. I'd hoped—"

"Hoped?"

"I meant to say—"

Karstil cut her off. He was suddenly awash in emotion. He struggled to regain control, and, unable to understand what he was feeling, retreated to professionalism. "We have a job to do, Sergeant. Get your people ready."

Ross felt like a child unfairly slapped as punishment for something she hadn't done. She could see no trace in his face that he even remembered their shared adventure during the last push on Alsatia. The color drained from her face, and she replied with as much dignity as she could muster. "Yes, sir!"

Karstil watched Ross clear her troops from the operating portions of the turret and assign riding positions. She was a professional, and he wanted to tell her that he respected her. He wanted to tell her a great deal more, but he had a feeling he had already said something wrong, and he didn't want to compound his error. "Driver. Move out."

The Liberator, bearing its load of infantry, trundled off down the street. They approached the Cohort headquarters and then turned left toward the constant flash and fire of MacDougall's position. Honor Ross rode behind the turret, less than an arm's-reach away from the tank commander. She was tempted to stretch out her hand and touch Karstil, but she stopped herself. He had cut off their reunion so abruptly that she decided to let him make the next move. She was ready to meet him halfway, but only halfway.

The street was brightly lit by burning vehicles. A Liberator with its turret split open blocked the passage. Beyond it, crumpled on one side, was an equally dead Lupis infantry carrier. Bodies were scattered across the passage; broken toys discarded by a giant. Karstil directed his driver to move slowly enough that the grav drive would act like an immense plow. Bodies were gently shoved aside by pressure as the tank approached. Karstil didn't know if the dead were from his side or theirs, but they had been men. They deserved respect. He saw the infantry on the tank look away. Those broken toys could have been them.

More than one tank commander has considered the thought that infantry are a strange breed. They willingly face terrible privation and endure horrible conditions, requiring in return only a hot meal, a dry bed, and dignity in death. They were willing to march against any odds because their officers shared their hardship. The first and best infantry officer had been Julius Caesar, the symbol of old Rome. According to legend, he had never eaten or slept better than the men in his command. Karstil knew that that tradition had not changed.

"Let us off here," Ross requested through the commlink. "I'd rather not ride this thing too close to the fighting."

"It's not a thing, Sergeant. It's a tank," Karstil chided her.

"All right. This tank. But I'd still like to dismount here."

The Liberator slowed to a stationary, one-meter hover. The infantry slid down the sloping sides and staggered into the street, moving stiffly, as if unable to completely control their own movements. The spider (Karstil knew the creature was called a Baufrin, but his mind couldn't get past its spider-like appearance) stopped in front of the turret. "A most appreciated conveyance, my good friend. Thank you for the transportation."

Karstil's response was again an open-mouthed stare. Then the spider was gone, quickly joining the knot of infantry gathering at the side of the tank. Karstil looked for Ross, but she had already slipped over the stern.

"Boots, move out slowly. Keep the peds with us." The tank drifted forward and the infantry fanned out across the rear, weapons at the ready.

"Two-six. This is Three-one-six." Karstil called MacDougall to let him know help was on the way. "I am entering your position from the rear. I have just passed a burning Liberator and a dead Lupis carrier."

"Roger, Three-one-six. That's as far as any of them got. The Liberator belonged to big Six." MacDougall's burr was not as thick as it had been the last time Karstil heard it; the fight must be going better. "You're approaching a small temple, Three-one-six. There're a bunch of penals in it with a Lupis carrier. If you could deal with them, I'd appreciate it. They've got my headquarters pinned down across the courtyard to your right front."

"This is Three-one-six. Wilco." Karstil acknowledged the order and switched to local commlink. He repeated the information about the enemy strong-point to Ross, and she immediately led her squad off through a warren of buildings to the right. As he watched her go, the spider right behind her, he thought about the information MacDougall had given him: the penals had penetrated well into his position, and the Liberator dead in the street had belonged to Milton Harras. He was too tired and cold and hungry to feel rage or grief; he just felt an overwhelming sadness.

"Three-one-six. This is Three-one-one." Ross had taken the call sign of Karstil's platoon, designating herself with the suffix "One." "The temple is real solid. The Lupis is well off to the right. You won't be able to get a shot at it. I'm out of TVLGs, but if you could take a couple of shots at the stonework, I think that'll get them moving. I'll hold my fire until they break."

Sure, thought Karstil. I'll stick my butt out in the street and take a couple of shots to "get them moving" while you hide in the buildings. Great. "Spent. Load APDS. We're going into the business of urban renewal."

"You got it, sir. APDS up." Spentling Crowder touched the screen of the fire-control computer and indexed the new ammunition. "Ready when you are."

"All right, Boots. Let her slide out far enough that we can get a shot at that temple, but let's not get too brave. I'd rather ride her home than walk." The Liberator crept forward, swinging its stern to the left to face the temple with the front armor. Karstil momentarily regretted that the tank's configuration placed the main gun on the right side of the turret. If the gun had been on the left, he would have been able to fire it without exposing the whole tank.

"Identified," the gunner called as the cross hairs of his sight touched the building.

"Fire!"

"On the way."

The 150mm cannon crashed, followed immediately by the 50mm cannon and the 5/6 laser. At pointblank range, the report of the cannon was almost overlapped by the explosion of the hit. Masonry rained down into the tiny plaza that surrounded the building. Even before the debris had settled, the cannons and laser fired again. The walls of the surrounding houses reverberated with the concussion. There was no replying fire. I'll bet there's no one in there, thought Karstil. They've probably moved off somewhere else.

"Do you want me to keep shooting?" asked Crowder, eyeing the cloud of dust that rose from the flank of the temple. "I can't tell if we've even gotten a shot into the place yet."

"Take a couple more. We're not paying for this ammunition, but we should probably try to keep some of it around for future use." Karstil almost added, "If there is a future," but he decided that the crew didn't need to hear his negative thoughts. The 150mm roared again, and more chunks flew off the building.

"They're moving out!" Ross' report was followed by the sharp staccato of spike rifles firing. Streams of tracers poured from the walls surrounding the plaza. A long line of tiny ice fountains traced a path across the shattered rubble. Karstil caught a glimpse of movement within the building. "Lupis carrier moving away," Ross updated him.

"Driver, let's move." The Liberator surged toward the temple. "Go left. Don't block the infantry fire." The tank turned to pass on the far side of the temple. "Gunner. Load HEAP. Local control."

"Lupis carrier. Range two-double-zero. Bearing six-five-zero. Moving left at six-zero. Target identified. Lock not achieved; target blocked by terrain." Karstil didn't need the DDP to tell him that the Lupis was about to break cover directly in front of him. At that range the painting laser was almost redundant.

"Gunner. No missiles. Cannon and laser only."

"Roger. Cannon and laser only. I have control of the weapons."

The Lupis carrier roared into sight, penal infantry clinging to the rear deck. The Liberator's two cannon and the laser fired together. Crowder was learning his trade. Karstil felt the turret jink slightly in the heartbeat's space between the firing of the 150mm, and the detonation of the 50mm and the whine of the lasers. With the weapons set on opposite sides of the turret, the three weapons' strikes would be separated by a fraction of a second. Crowder was firing the main gun, then shifting the turret slightly to the right so that the 50mm and the laser would strike the same place. He was getting good at it.

The carrier seemed to stop, suspended in the street two hundred meters away. Then it was engulfed in fire. Out of control, the ammunition and power plant burning, it struck a building across the plaza. The violent impact threw the turret, dismounted by the blast, against the wall. Then the hull came apart, infantry access doors and grav coils flying away from the glowing mass. One of the doors ricocheted off the glacis of the Liberator and disappeared into the surrounding dark.

Ross' squad appeared, herding three surrendered penals. The sullen bunch walked awkwardly with their fingers locked behind their necks. They were keeping well clear of the spider, who carried several weapons in his lower pair of arms. The four survivors of the Renegade infantry squad also carried their own dead and wounded.

40

0700, 13 Martius 6831—The TOG officers who gathered around the plotting table in the Pompey command vehicle were a sad lot. Legatus Cariolanus Camus, commander of the Cohort originally sent to destroy the Renegade strike force at the south pole, had seen his unit decimated. He had only enough vehicles remaining in his command to organize a full-strength Century; three medium Horatius tanks, three Romulus carriers, four Aeneas light tanks, and three Lupis light infantry carriers. The infantry complement was slightly better, mainly because he had sent the 356th Penal Auxilia troops to fight the most recent offensive.

The Auxilia commander was in better spirits. Legatus Maximus Rocipian Olioarchus had entered orbit around Caralis with twenty-five hundred combat troops. Some five hundred were sacrificed in the launch sequence, used as a decoy and burned up upon re-entry into the atmosphere. Additional troops died during the orbit of Rock Wall, but these losses were part of the plan. Approximately sixteen hundred troops had been deployed at the pole. The first attack, particularly the underplanned charge at the first breach, had been costly. More than five hundred troops were dead, wounded, or missing. Bad numbers, but certainly not crippling. The Ssoran guards had rounded up the stragglers, and all Cohorts reported battle readiness. Now they just needed a good plan.

Centurion Marmoreus Patrius was glad to see Centurion Miles Stratton, operations officer for the Penal Auxilia. Unlike the officers in the penal Cohorts and Centuries, Auxilia commanders Stratton and Olioarchus were not criminals. Their assignment to the 356th was a reward for excellent service and a steppingstone to higher command. More penal veterans served in the upper echelons of TOG command than in any other part of the service. Success as a penal commander or staff officer was a sure pathway to higher command, and penal commanders were almost universally successful. Patrius considered his association with Stratton and Olioarchus an excellent opportunity to advance his own career.

Prefect Claudius Sulla was also in the headquarters Pedden. His watching brief of Camus' command was obviously nearing its end. The Cohort had been so badly used that it now existed in name only. But as the representative of Brigadier General Drusus Arcadius, the planetary commander, his position had actually become more important with the arrival of the Penal Auxilia. Any victory the combined Auxilia and Cohort achieved would reflect to his honor. "My friends, we must treat the Renegade force like an egg. We have tried to crush them, but it is impossible to crush an egg in your hand. We need to strike a sharp blow to fracture their shell."

Camus and Olioarchus looked at each other across the table. Sulla's oddly stated idea was interesting, but they had delivered several sharp blows already, and all they had to show for it was too many destroyed vehicles and a long casualty list.

"The idea of an egg," said Patrius, "is well taken. Certainly the dome over the city encourages the simile. But perhaps what we need to do is to make it a blown egg."

The other officers stared at Patrius. "What, pray tell," sneered Camus, "is a blown egg?"

"In my youth," explained Patrius, ignoring his commanding officer, "we used to color eggs as gifts on certain holidays. Permanent decorations were made by emptying the inside of the egg so that it would not spoil. Two small holes were broken in the shell at either end. We would pierce the inner membrane and break the yolk, then blow into one of the holes. The meat of the egg would pour out the other hole. This process gave us a perfect shell for the ornament, and we were able to eat the rest of the egg. I think we could apply the same principle to our Renegade friends."

"Go on," said Sulla. He was a little upset that his idea of the sharp stroke had been discarded so quickly, but he was pleased that his egg analogy was being used.

"The Renegades are like the meat of an egg. We have been trying to get at it while it was still inside the shell." Patrius was warming to his theme. "What we need to do is get the Renegades out of their shell and onto our fire. We must allow, persuade, or trick the Renegades to the surface." He had run out of ideas. He had no idea how this would shape up as a plan of action, but he had presented a sound idea. While the Renegades stayed under the ice, they had all the advantages. The TOG forces needed to get them up on the surface in order to finish them off.

Olioarchus struck the table with his fist. "A perfect idea. Absolutely brilliant!" He pointed to the map on the plotting table. "We leave the Renegades a way to the surface. This breach is excellent. It's wide enough to take all their vehicles and they know it intimately. We back away as though we need to consolidate our troops, leaving a few light troops behind for them to see. The heavy equipment we can back off a full kilometer. They won't be able to detect our lines until they reach the surface, and by then it will be too late. That takes care of Camus' Cohort. My infantry will enter through the breaches we used before as well as the smaller ones we haven't tried. We will begin to push the enemy toward the main breach. They will have no choice but to make a run for it. And as soon as they appear," he finished, rubbing his hands together, "we cook them on our fire."

Milton Harras swung his throbbing feet off the surgical table. Plasto-skin covered his burns and enabled him to walk. Stagger was actually a better word. Kelton Hess had shot his legs full of local tranquilizers to kill the pain, but the drugs also kept Harras from feeling the floor. He had to watch his feet in order to make them do what he wanted. But even the painkillers could not ease all his discomfort. His head was filled with a constant pounding that reminded Harras of the destruction of his tank.

His Liberator had been deluged with TVLG and SMLM hits. Too many missiles were in the air at once, from both the Lupis carriers and the dismounted infantry, for the Vulcan system to deal with. The tank had been hammered into a marble. The main gun had been destroyed, the driver killed, the outer hull perforated so many times that the undamaged armor sloughed right off the ceramic shielding. Then the tank had burned. Harras could have made it out of the vehicle unharmed, but he had stopped to help the wounded gunner from the turret. The man had gone over the side just as the turret filled with flame, and even Harras' battledress uniform, resistant to fire, could not protect him against the searing heat.

"Well," said Harras, his numb feet dangling from the table. "What's the situation?"

His remaining officers stood around him in the hospital ward. Rinter still commanded what was left of her Reserve Century, but with only one Liberator and two Peddens, it wasn't much of a force. Jamie MacDougall still had two tanks, an infantry carrier, and his apparently charmed Wolverine. Matruh, his face and arms also bandaged in plasto-skin, commanded only a Liberator and two Vipers. Karstil and Stone were also present. Braxton Sloan, the engineer, and Rand, the former comm chief and now acting headquarters commander, completed the staff.

Moldine Rinter spoke first. "Not good, I'm afraid, Milt. We lost more equipment, but you already know that. We have more critical problems. Hess can speak in more technical terms about the condition of the men, but it's not good. Operationally, we held our own in that we didn't give any ground in the last attack. But we won't be able to hold them again. We need to get some help, or there will be only one more fight. The TOGs got big reinforcements. Those infantry we drove off were penal troops. They'll use them as cannon fodder, but they have enough to eventually crush us. They probably sent a regiment, so there're several thousand of them."

"The men are about spent," Hess took up the report, "and the cold is getting to every soldier down here. You know, the Human body is a marvelous thing. You can force it to do all sorts of things, and it will keep going. You can abuse it, chill it, work it, scare it. But it can only take so much adversity. And you must feed it. Food is specially important when it's cold, and it's critical in temperatures like this. We no longer have to contend with the wind, but at minus seventy degrees Celsius, a body loses a great deal of heat. To compensate, you have to put fuel in the furnace. The average, active, adult male burns between twenty-five hundred and three thousand calories every day. At minus seventy, that caloric requirement is almost doubled. The troops are currently consuming less than two thousand. They are literally starving to death."

"What can we do?" Concern for his men was reflected in Harras' voice. He knew exactly how the troops felt, because he was also on reduced rations.

Hess pursed his lips in thought. "Milt, this city was not abandoned. The bodies we have found here were healthy enough, but they seem to have given up. They were all dressed in their best, just waiting for death. They must have been pretty stoic to go like that. My guess is that they froze after they died. If that's the case, they may have left food around. All we have to do is find it. The intense cold will have preserved most of it."

"What about it, Braxton?" asked Rinter, obviously intrigued by the possibility. "Have you seen anything that looks like food-storage areas?"

"Not a one," said the engineer. "The place has been swept clean."

"There is another possibility," interjected the doctor. "I spent some time with the Naram, and this is obviously a Naram city. They used to place food under their temples. Of course, what I saw was only a gesture, to remind them of the bad times in their past. In a place as old as this, they might have done it for real. It's worth a look."

"Right." said Harras. "Braxton, unless you have something specific for us, why don't you get on that right away."

Braxton Sloan nodded. He had nothing to add to the conference and departed at once. In fact, no one had anything to add. The discussion degenerated into idle talk about what to do if and when the TOGs attacked again, and what kind of food would be discovered under the temples.

"This is getting us nowhere, people," said Harras. "Let's get back to our commands and try to prepare for what the TOGs throw at us next. Doctor, how about a tour of your hospital?"

I'm afraid I was in no condition to really look at the place when I was brought in."

"You won't like what you see, Milt."

"That's all right, Kelton. I've been in the service long enough to have seen most of it."

But even Harras' field experience didn't prepare him for what he saw next. The hospital was unlike any he had seen before. The extreme cold kept them from using anesthetics. A drugged man would be able to relax, but at these extreme temperatures, a relaxed man was a dead man. And there was plenty of evidence of what death looked like.

Portions of the hutch had been set aside as a morgue, and the stiff bodies of both Renegade and TOG troops lay there. They lay as they had died, in frozen contortions of agony. The wounded, still clinging to life, lined the walls. Their breath was visible in puffs that hung before their cracked lips and moistened the walls with condensation that froze in sheets, giving the interior of the hutch a silver sheen.

On the operating table, surgical assistants bent over the wounded, trying to close lacerations before the cold claimed another life. The breath of the surgeons created a mist that at times obscured the patient. As soon as the wounds were closed, the patients were wrapped in thermal blankets in an attempt to save as much body heat as possible. Men were wrapped together in blankets to share their body heat.

In the gloom of one den, a sergeant knelt beside five figures lying slightly separated from the others. Harras stood behind the sergeant. "There's nothing you can do for them now, Sergeant," he said in a soft voice. "You should be with your squad."

Honor Ross lifted her head to meet the eyes of her Cohort commander. "This is my squad, sir."

41

0930, 13 Martius 6831—"There's something weird going on topside, sir." Aktol Graviston, senior sergeant of Cohort Harras, beckoned his commander to the plotting table. "We have a sensor placed just at the breach, and it picks up any TOG activity within five hundred meters of the opening. They've kept several vehicles in the area up until now, including a Pompey that I think is their command vehicle. They also usually leave a tank or two around it. Now they're all gone."

Milton Harras studied the electronic display. The locations of various TOG vehicles were shown on a time plot. Graviston ran the plot to show the past few hours. Red indicators moved across the display. The TOG attacks stood out as sharp explosions of color, vanishing as quickly as they appeared. "Notice the indications here."

Harras was not paying attention. He had been entranced by the computer display of TOG attacks. "Sorry, Aktol. Run that again." Graviston reversed the display and then brought time forward again more slowly. He was right. The TOGs had stationed vehicles near the entry to the passage from the time they arrived at the pole. Now they were gone, disappearing one at a time until there were none left.

"Conclusion?" asked Harras.

"None, sir. Not yet."

"Have you notified Centurion Rinter?"

"No, sir. I just noticed it myself, and you were close at hand." The senior sergeant pressed the call button to signal the operations officer.

When Rinter arrived at the headquarters Pedden, Graviston ran through the display again. She, too, was puzzled as to what it meant. The possibility of the TOGs pulling back was too much to hope for. Perhaps they had taken such a beating that they were pulling back to lick their wounds.

"Can we fight it out on the surface?" Harras asked the question already knowing what the answer would be.

Rinter thought for a moment. "We have four fully operational medium tanks and another two or three we could nurse along. Besides that, we have a Wolverine and a couple of Vipers. Not enough to win. And even if we did, what then?"

"Yeah." Harras sounded tired. He leaned over the display of the current positions, his hands braced on the sides of the table. "I know. It was just a thought. I wonder what they think of all this back on Rolandrin." His head hung forward, his face slack with fatigue.

Rinter looked at her commander. She could not remember ever having seen him so tired and so depressed. He certainly looked his age; more than his age. Of all the officers she had served with, Harras had touched her most. Others had been more brilliant tactical commanders, and some were better administrators, but she had never been close to them. Harras, on the other hand, kept no one at arms length. He was completely open with everyone with whom he came in contact, treating each soldier as an equal. She had never heard him put down any suggestion, no matter how absurd. He was never hurtful in his comments. He loved his men, and they returned that emotion. And now he was watching his command disintegrate, ground down by the inexorable pressure of the TOG attacks. She wanted to put her arms around him and comfort him. "Milt—we'll make it out."

He turned his head to face her, sunken eyes dulled with strain, white patches of frostbite on his cheekbones. Their eyes met and held for a long moment. Then he straightened. "Right. Right, we'll make it."

"Sir?" Graviston was still surveying the display. Now he turned toward Harras. "You wondered what they would think of this on Rolandrin. They probably don't think anything. They may not even know we're alive. We haven't been able to send a signal since we left, and we haven't even been above the ice for days. We should try to signal them."

"How do we do that?"

"I haven't a clue, sir," replied Graviston. "I'm an idea man, not a detail man. You should ask the comm guy, Sam Rand."

"You didn't get where you are today by just being a detail man, Aktol." Harras clapped his friend on the shoulder.

"But I really don't have a clue, sir."

"Moldine, see if you can get Rand in here."

The communications optio came at once. His technical training had been less than complete, but he had a good grasp of the theory.

"On Caralis," he explained, "the main obstacle to communications is the lack of a stable ionosphere. We have three basic types of communications available: the P-comm, either amplitude- or frequency-modulated, and laser telemetry. Frequency-modulated and laser communications depend on the output of the signal for range and fidelity, which, for P-comm signals, depend on the antenna. Our problem is that when we rolled the comm Pedden on the way in, we destroyed the antenna/set interface. In order to restore a commlink with Rolandrin, we need to replace that damaged module. Unfortunately, Sergeant Arsen has been unable to fabricate the necessary replacement parts, and with the Cohort maintenance vehicle also lost on the run in, we have no immediate spare. Now, if we had the antenna and the power, we could direct a frequency-modulated signal to any COMSAT in this sector. Without the antenna, we can't. We have the same problem with the laser signal. If we could hit the COMSAT with a laser pulse, we could bounce the light back to Rolandrin. But without the frequency set, we can't find the communications satellite. The advantage of the laser for communications is that it operates on a very narrow arc, making it almost impossible to jam or compromise. The disadvantage of the laser is also that it operates on a very narrow arc, actually about the diameter of a stylus, so you have to know exactly where the receptor is at the time you send. Is this clear so far?"

"We understand the problem, Optio," said Rinter. "What we want is a solution. Get to the point."

"That's all right, Sam," interrupted Harras. "The better we understand the problem, the easier it will be to find the solution. Go on."

"The easiest answer to our predicament is a P-comm amplitude-modulated signal. All transmissions are straight-line, but only AM signals bounce off the ionosphere. Essentially, they can go around in circles. That's why an amplitude-modulated signal is not a *good* answer to our problem. The Caralis ionosphere is a ragged belt and tends to trap signals rather than reflect them."

Graviston had a fleeting mental image of thousands of messages rattling around in the ionosphere, waiting to be set free.

"But if we could get an antenna high enough, we could easily reach Rolandrin with either P-comm frequency-modulation or laser telemetry," Rand continued. "The problem is, we can't."

"What about an airborne station?" asked Rinter. "If we could get a vehicle high enough, we could reach over the planet's arc."

"That's technically possible," mused Rand, "but the operational ceiling for a grav vehicle operating from the ground is ten kilometers. Taking off from the surface allows it to reach an altitude of fifteen kilometers on a straight power climb, but it can't maintain that height for long, and would have to cruise at ten. At that altitude, based on the knowledge that Caralis has a radius of slightly more than sixty-five hundred kilometers, the tank would have a visual horizon of about two hundred kilometers. We can assume a signal horizon of twice that, but because the distance from the pole to Rolandrin is about ten thousand kilometers, the four or five hundred we would gain from achieving altitude would not be significant unless we could move the airborne station at least seven hundred kilometers closer to Rolandrin."

"We could get someone that close." Harras' statement sounded a lot like a question.

"Probably," responded Rinter.

Honor Ross looked over her squad's position. The unit was different from the one she had brought across the polar cap. Grain, Brace, and Alcyone from the first section were gone; Grain wounded, the others dead. The second section had lost its section leader, Massai Boost, at the ambush; Barstow Drinn, his replacement, and Dorothea Calvert had died at the main breach.

Of the original eleven in the squad, only four remained. Hull and Archon as replacements made it six. Not enough to cover the three buildings assigned as their fighting positions. She had lost a lot of people, too many friends. She especially missed Dorothea. It was nice to have Millicent Connor with the squad as a ped, but Dorothea had been someone she could talk to. She came to a sudden decision, and stood up so quickly that Archon Divxas, nestled in a corner of the den, gathered his legs under his torso in anticipation of an attack.

"It's all right, Archon," she said. "There's something I must do."

"And it is so important that you must do it immediately?"

"Too many of my friends are already gone. I don't want to miss telling one of them how I feel before it is too late."

"So you have made up your mind to speak to the young officer upon whose tank we rode to the conflict?"

Ross blushed. "Something like that."

"I am continually amused by the courting ritual of Humans," said the Baufrin. "Two people who are mutually attracted pace around, watching each other for a sign of vulnerability. If one of them looks away, the other moves in. But if neither of them will give even the appearance of being subordinate, then the contact will not take place. The two parties will eventually tire of the game and go off in search of a different, possibly less satisfactory, partner. This is regrettable, because it does not encourage the union of the strong. We Baufrins are quite different. We search for strength rather than feigned weakness. Thus the Baufrins grow more superior as we commingle."

"We don't need to pretend to be weak! We don't play those games!"

"In your last encounter with the young man, neither of you was willing to say what you meant, so you retreated into your professional relationship. Why did you not say that you were glad to see him? Why did you not say that you cared?"

"It wasn't my place."

"Your place? Your place? Was it his place?"

"I don't know."

"That is precisely what I mean. Neither of you was willing to show that vulnerability. You Humans are a strange race. It is a wonder that you have survived this long. Go. Tell him now."

"I was thinking about it."

"A Baufrin would never spend so much energy thinking about something that would be easier to solve by acting." Divxas scrambled to his feet. "Would you feel terribly self-conscious if I accompanied you? I would like to see a closure to the ceremony."

"Do what you like." Ross left the den. Archon Divxas followed her into the street and toward the Liberator concealed under its holotarp. The only sign of life was a light that reflected a soft glow from the hatch on the underside of the covering. Divxas walked a respectful distance behind the sergeant and waited in the street as she climbed the front glacis of the tank.

As she reached the turret, a figure emerged from the tank, rising above the coaming. Ross stopped. She recognized Centurion Moldine Rinter of the Cohort staff. Ross had seen her once or twice before and knew that she now commanded the Reserve Century.

"Can I help you, Sergeant?" asked Rinter.

Karstil exited the tank behind the centurion. "Hello, Ross. Here to say goodbye?"

"Goodbye?"

"The centurion is sending me on a mission. I'm going to break out with a message for Rolandrin."

"Message?" Ross' resolve to speak her feelings seemed to have vanished from her thoughts.

"The problem, Optio," continued Rinter, disregarding the presence of the sergeant, "is that you will not be able to take both your crewmembers. Based on the engineers' assessment, that would add too much mass to the equation. You will have to take one or the other. Your choice."

"I choose Boots. He weighs more than Spent, but he's a damn good driver. I can shoot from the command seat if need be."

"With all due respect, sirs," said Divxas, speaking from the street below the conclave. "I am a qualified driver, and my physiology allows me to drive and shoot at the same time. I am also of significantly less mass than the average Human. There are other reasons why I am the best choice for the assignment, but I will not elucidate them at this time."

"Nonsense," said Rinter. "You could hardly be qualified."

Archon drew himself up to his full height. "I beg your pardon, madam. I am a fully qualified pilot of grav vehicles. I have a license to operate both within and without planetary atmosphere, and I am an expert in interstellar navigation. In addition, I am expert with every Commonwealth weapon from a laser stiletto to a 200mm Gauss cannon."

The three Renegade soldiers stood in open-mouthed amazement at this outburst. Archon continued in full cry. "It may not have occurred to you that I am technically a civilian. Even though I have been in combat with the Renegade forces, and the qualifications for being considered a Renegade are quite broad, I am not a true combatant. If I were taken alive by the TOG forces, my fate would be in doubt. If, on the other hand, I were to be lost while accomplishing a mission, it would be of small consequence to the forces gathered here."

Rinter looked at the Baufrin who had challenged her decision. She opened her mouth to reprimand the spider, and then she remembered Harras' haggard face and his unfailing diplomacy, and changed her mind, humbled by the memory. "I'm sorry. I spoke before I thought. I can excuse my poor judgment as a result of my own fatigue, but it was not justifiable. I am sorry. What you've said makes good sense. Go with the optio."

Ross was left standing on the upper deck of the Liberator as the three moved off down the street. The Baufrin tailed behind the two officers discussing plans for the escape. Before the trio disappeared into the darkness, Divxas turned to Ross, raising his upper arms in a sign of resignation. Ross returned to her post, her sense of frustration and loss more intense than before.

42

1145, 13 Martius 6831—The TOG Scipio antiaircraft vehicle slowed to a hover and sank gently to the ice. The turret traversed slightly to the assigned azimuth, bringing the 25mm cannon on line with the Renegade escape hole cut into the ice cap at the south pole. The commander wanted to be able to engage ground targets with his forward-firing gun. The Scipio's main weapons, however, were the Scanner Silhouette-Seeking antiaircraft missiles mounted behind the turret.

The Scipio was as adaptable a machine as appeared in the TOG inventory. Significant design problems with the original craft had required compromises to allow the weapons systems to be used against different targets, including high-flying interceptors, medium-altitude grav vehicles, and ground targets. The final version of the vehicle successfully integrated three different fire-control systems within the hull, but at great cost in terms of space and weight. The vehicle's commander, following orders received from the commander of the TOG forces at the pole, reprogrammed the target-acquisition and fire-control systems to establish an uncommon priority of targets: the Scipio would engage high-altitude grav vehicles as its first priority, then interceptors, then ground targets. That reconfiguration accomplished, the Scipio shut down to await the arrival of its ammunition carrier.

The Scipio's multiple targeting systems required a massive array of satellite communications and datalink equipment. In order to keep the vehicle at a reasonable size, the tank's main weapons were restricted to only three hardpoints of missiles. Adequate coverage of controlled space was accomplished by assigning the tank an ammunition vehicle to ensure that the Scipio would provide sustained fire. The Lorica armored ammunition tractor (actually a grav vehicle rather than a tractor) provided the Scipio's missile-reload capability. The vehicle's enclosed cab was proof against the launch signature of the SSS missiles, and so the tractor could park directly alongside the Scipio, reloading ammunition with a robotic arm designed to lift a prepackaged rack of three SSS missiles from inside the Lorica's armored carapace and snap them onto the Scipio's launch hardpoints. The Scipio reloaded in less than a minute.

Archon Divxas struggled into the driver's station of the repaired Liberator. He grunted and clacked as he worked his body in behind the console, wondering why Humans designed their equipment as if they were the only sentient beings in the universe. The Liberator's designers had obviously never considered that anyone but a Human would need access to these controls. He eventually squeezed his torso and multiple limbs into the seat, and realized it would take him just as long to get out. There would be no emergency exit for the Baufrin.

Archon ran his arms and legs over the controls. He moved the telelink vision system to the right, where his two right-most eyes would be able to see it, allowing him to concentrate the other four on the sight display that controlled the weapons. His upper arms controlled the turret mechanisms and the lower arms the drive controls, proving true his claim that he could drive and shoot simultaneously. The Baufrin would experience difficulty with his multiple tasks only if he were required to traverse the turret more than 1600 mils right or left.

The Baufrin was a qualified Liberator driver, but he had not driven one of the medium tanks in over a year, and so wanted some time to reacquaint himself with all the systems. The main plaza of the city provided plenty of practice space, which he used to drive the Liberator slowly around. His audience, including both Rinter and Karstil, ducked behind outlying buildings after Divxas bounced the Liberator off a couple of the structures. After a few minutes he stopped hitting things, and the spectators returned.

Karstil stood with the small group of officers and enlisted men on one of the broad avenues that led away from the plaza and received his final briefing from Moldine Rinter. Shawn Arsen and Braxton Sloan also gave him last-minute instructions. Arsen, the senior comm sergeant, had rigged a special antenna between the forward arms of the Liberator's hull. It was a fragile system, but it would allow the vehicle commander to send and perhaps even receive messages from a station over a thousand kilometers away. He had also created, with the help of Rinter and her staff, a preset transmission giving the trapped Cohort's pertinent data to planet headquarters.

Arsen was very proud of the apparatus. Setting the restraining bolts in the glacis had been his only real problem. It was all well and good to have titanium armor on a vehicle, but when it came to making structural modifications to the exterior, the titanium was a real pain. It had taken all of his carballoy drill bits to set the anchor Mollies in the surface. If not for that, he could have made the lead wires more secure by drilling through the hull to fasten them down. The wires ran up the glacis and over the turret top, connecting to the commlink system through the command hatch. "Closing the hatch will cut the wires," he reminded Karstil. "Don't close the hatch until after you send."

"Look, son," Centurion Braxton Sloan said, resting his hand on Karstil's shoulder. "This Liberator is a piece of junk. We've been cobbling it together from parts of other tanks, just to keep it going. Starting with the weapons, the 150 is warped, as your Baufrin friend is going to find out pretty soon. It shoots low and to the right, and the ammunition has a tendency to jam. If you have to index HEAP from APDS, let the ammunition tray cycle through once before you fire; otherwise, the rounds may jam the breach. The 50mm and the laser are all right, though."

The Liberator stopped and hovered near the group. Divxas, deep in the hull, didn't bother to exit. "Now about the hull and drive system: they're junk. Of the six grav coils under the thing, four came from other tanks. As a matter of fact, one of them isn't even from a Liberator, it's from a destroyed Wolverine. The controls have been rigged to compensate for the differences, but driving may be a little tricky. I think the spider may have found that out already. The hull has been patched up so that it should hold together, but there's no ballistic protection on most of the left side. It's airtight, but it's hollow."

Karstil listened to all of this information with only half an ear, knowing he couldn't do anything about the condition of the tank. "Don't close the hatch and don't turn your left side to the enemy" would have sufficed. That would have said it all. Karstil climbed into the command hatch.

Divxas watched Karstil carefully avoid the wires that led to the antenna as he entered the tank. The Baufrin fixed all six eyes on his new commander. "This vehicle," he said, "has some unique drive characteristics."

"So I've been told."

"I have managed to become accustomed to the idiosyncrasies of the system and will not have any undue difficulty with it in the future. I regret striking those buildings; I am a better operator than that."

"You're forgiven. Let's get on with the program."

"As you wish." Archon Divxas turned back toward the driver's station. "Centurion Braxton Sloan has briefed me on the passage through which we will access the surface. I believe we can reach a significant velocity with this conveyance by accelerating over the city prior to entering the exit passage."

"Ready when you are."

Archon depressed the accelerator and set the left vane. "We are in motion." The Liberator lifted off from the plaza and began to gain speed. Archon kept the thrust low as the vehicle climbed above the parapets of the surrounding structures. Once clear of the obstructions, having gained greater maneuver space, he applied more power. The Liberator picked up speed in preparation for its break to the surface.

A red blip appeared on the plotting table in the Pompey command vehicle. "Activity below, sir," said the TOG intelligence sergeant. "They're getting something up to speed. Could be a reconnaissance shot."

Camus looked over the sergeant's shoulder at the red streak orbiting above the underground city. The digital readout, appearing as an overprint on the screen, identified the vehicle as a Liberator, clocked its speed at 120 kph, and showed it still accelerating. "They're coming out," said Camus. "Notify the command. Let the first one out go. We'll engage the second and third as they appear."

"There's only one." Olioarchus was watching as well.

"That's what we see now. The Renegades would not be stupid enough to send only one vehicle on a mission. Tell your men to hold their fire on the first tank. That's an order."

"As you wish, Legatus. But please remember that, though you are still technically in command here, I outrank you."

"We have achieved optimum speed," Archon spoke into the internal commlink. "We will be aligned on the next pass."

"As you set up, hit the hole."

The Liberator made one more sweeping pass over the city. Archon triggered the driving lights to illuminate his way, and then hit the exit hole. The Baufrin was a good driver, but the opening was only barely wide enough for the tank. The right sponson scraped the side of the dome, showering sparks over the wreckage scattered on the slope. Then it vanished into the gallery.

The Liberator blazed into the passage. The driving lights reflected off the sides of the gallery, casting a brilliant glare ahead of the charging tank. Archon, with all six eyes fixed on the driving screen, struggled to control the bucking tank. The passage was steep enough that lifting thrust had to be applied at full strength, and the surging power broke chunks of ice from the floor and sides of the passage, scattering them behind the tank. A final tight turn, the tank bounced off the wall, and the surface loomed ahead. The darkness of the opening was a sharp contrast to the glaring whiteness of the tunnel. The Liberator erupted from the cleft in a shower of fragmented ice. Karstil hit the smoke discharger as the vehicle cleared the edge.

The DDP in the Liberator flashed solid red for a moment as the tank gained the surface of the ice. There were so many targets in so many directions that Karstil couldn't choose one. Even the DDP couldn't evaluate the greatest danger. The paint warning klaxon screamed in Karstil's ear, and the DDP chose one threat. "Scipio antiaircraft vehicle. Range five-double-zero and increasing. Bearing two-eight-double-zero. Stationary. Vehicle tracking." The Liberator climbed on full power. Karstil was looking straight into the dark sky, the polar cap receding to a dim, white shadow. He could feel the wind against his face, even with the face plate on his helmet lowered.

"Don't let that anti-air hit us in the bottom. Roll the tank."

"I will do it," Archon responded, and sent the Liberator into a slow roll that would bring the right side and rear toward the Scipio.

Karstil only knew they were rolling because the horizon of the ice cap crossed the forward sponsons. He was hanging half-inverted in the hatch, the pressure of acceleration holding him in the chair. "Scipio antiaircraft vehicle. Range one-five-double-zero and increasing. Bearing two-two-double-zero. Stationary. Vehicle tracking. Vehicle weapon system has locked on target." The DDP paused. "Missile fired." The voice sounded excited. "Second missile away. Third missile away."

Karstil felt his stomach tense. The stern armor of the Liberator was thick, but three missile hits was probably more than it could stand, and these hits were almost guaranteed. At less than two thousand meters, missiles locked onto a painted target would be dead-on. The Vulcan antimissile turret spun to the rear and opened fire. Karstil, his eyes level with the hatch coaming, saw the flash of two destroyed missiles. The third one got through to strike their right rear skirt, but the explosion seemed muffled.

The SSS missiles were designed to operate under the most hostile of conditions, and the polar cap certainly fulfilled those parameters. The designers had, however, issued one operational warning with the missiles. This warning cautioned the operators that the missiles should not be exposed to rapid changes of temperature. Under those conditions, condensation could occur, which would freeze, cracking the explosive housing or the firing-circuit systems, which would degrade the blast effect. The Scipio commander did not disregard this warning, he merely forgot completely about it. He chose to remain in the warmth of the fighting compartment rather than emerge into the frigid arctic air and struggle to test his missiles. His choice was to the Renegades' advantage.

When the SSS struck the right rear shroud of the climbing Liberator, the fuse initiated the firing sequence. But when the booster detonated, the booster/explosive synapse failed to respond. The missile was a dud, and the Liberator climbed away.

"Scipio antiaircraft vehicle. Range five-five-double-zero and increasing. Bearing two-two-double-zero. Stationary. Vehicle tracking. Vehicle weapon system has locked on target." The warning klaxon had dropped several decibels to indicate only one painting laser still active. The Liberator continued to corkscrew upward into the darkness.

On the surface, the carapace of the Lorica armored resupply vehicle snapped open. The robotic arm lifted out a rack of three missiles and reached toward the rear of the Scipio turret. It hesitated for a moment to allow the load to stabilize and then lowered the missiles to the hardpoints. The three SSS missiles clicked into position, the electronic joints mating as the weapons settled. The robotic arm moved clear, and the Scipio's firing system board showed green.

"Scipio antiaircraft vehicle. Range eight-five-double-zero and increasing. Bearing two-one-double-zero. Stationary. Vehicle tracking. Vehicle weapon system has locked on target." The DDP paused again. "Three missiles away. Vehicle is the target." The Vulcan system spun, fired, and missed. Perhaps the Liberator had rolled so far that the bulk of the hull blocked the antimissile system's line-of-sight. Whatever the reason, all three missiles survived. Two struck the damaged stern, and the third, slightly behind the others, found the bottom of the tank.

The explosions on the rear of the tank tore the remainder of the right shroud away, smashing through the ballistic protection and into the thrust control. Archon felt the thruster bar go slack under his hand. The third missile disintegrated the Liberator's bottom armor. The tank was not equipped with ballistic protection on the underside, making the power systems vulnerable. The grav drive system somehow escaped damage, but it was now almost completely unprotected.

The first missile struck the stern, and the shock of the explosion threw the tank forward, snapping Karstil's head, neck, and shoulder against the rear edge of the coaming. His damaged shoulder, repaired but not healed, cracked again under the impact. His helmet absorbed most of the concussion, but the force of the blow was too great for the helmet to absorb it all. Karstil felt like he was falling. He grabbed for a handhold but came up empty. His world went quickly gray, then black.

Down inside the fighting compartment, Archon saw Karstil snap back against the titanium hull. The optio stood for a moment groping for the edge of the hatch, then the force of the climbing turn pressed him down into his chair. The Baufrin saw the Human lurch to one side, and used his upper appendages to steady the falling officer. He laid the unconscious man beside his own seat, pinning him in place with one of his several lower legs. The Liberator continued to climb toward the ten-kilometer operational ceiling.

43

1215, 13 Martius 6831—The remaining staff of Cohort Harras watched the escaping tank until it passed out of range of the command plot. They saw missiles streak across the surface of the display and merge with the Liberator location indicator, but the action was too far away for the plot to indicate damage. A second salvo streaked out to reach the target. Then the Liberator vanished from view.

"That's an interesting piece of equipment for people who are supposedly pulling back," commented Larry Stone. "They don't seem to have gone too far."

Milton Harras considered the situation. "We have reports of activity at the other breaches. Their penal infantry is moving in force." He stood looking at the plot. "We're getting close to the end, and when it comes, I want to know where the regulars are. I'd hate to have to negotiate with the penals. Those Ssoran guards don't know the meaning of mercy, and they have a tendency to retaliate against their adversaries."

"We should find out where everyone is." Stone rubbed the sling on his arm. "A small patrol could slip to the surface and have a look-see."

"Are you suggesting that you go?" asked Rinter. She was hunkered down against the side of the Pedden, her eyes closed, almost asleep. She remained seated, too tired to stand. "You're hardly in any condition to make that trip without help."

"The arm is all right. Hess gave me some stuff for it, and it hardly bothers me now."

"What if you run into trouble?" Rinter forced herself to stand so that she could look into his eyes.

"I don't plan to, and if I do, two good arms won't help."

"You should take someone with you."

"Like you, maybe?"

"Not her," said Harras, a bit too quickly. The others turned toward him in mild surprise. Harras looked away. "I need at least one staff member, and she still commands a Century."

"He's right," said Stone. "No use sending all the officers. What I really need is a good infantry sergeant."

"I've got one for you. She's got a squad at the breach now, so she should be aware of what's going on. You can pick her up on the way out."

"Let's do it."

Rinter found Ross huddled behind a firing port in one of the hutches. She protested when her new mission was explained, pointing out that, with the Baufrin pulled out, her squad was already down to five. She felt a pang of fear and sadness at the thought of the reason for Archon's defection. But the centurion was not to be denied. Ross left Grold in command of the squad's remnants while Ross went on patrol. Rinter also promised the squad would be reinforced by the time the sergeant returned. Ross left her carbine behind, taking Rinter's spike pistol and two hand grenades as her only armament. Stone was similarly armed, and both wore bounce-infantry armored suits and helmets equipped with Basic Lifeform Sensor systems. Stone argued against the suits, saying they would restrict movement, but the suits had internal heating systems, and at negative seventy degrees, that was essential.

Ross and Stone made a quick personal inspection before they left the Renegade-held area. The infantry suits were in working order, the pistols had two extra power/ammunition packs, and each carried a fragmentation and a flash grenade. A commlink check showed good communication between the suits, but not enough power to send a signal back to headquarters through the mass of the dome. The only additional equipment each carried was a holotarp. With Ross leading, they climbed the wreckage-strewn slope that led to the main breach.

Just inside the tunnel, they paused to sweep the area with their BLS systems; there were no signs of activity. They crept forward, pistols drawn, into the dark gallery. Neither carried a hand torch, not because they didn't need them, but because they didn't want to use them and chance giving themselves away to the enemy. The BLS system would allow them to keep track of each other.

It took several minutes for the pair to reach the surface. The tunnel was completely black, but the opening to the surface was blacker still. They paused at the lip of the crater, now worn smooth and enlarged since both had traversed it days before. There had been so many vehicles across the rim that the original cut had been eroded and polished to a glaze. Ross and Stone were forced to wriggle forward on their stomachs across the glassy surface, kicking their toes into the ice to gain even minimal traction. They rolled out onto the ice cap and lay panting to catch their breath.

Ross could feel her perspiration, even in the cold. The thermal system within the armor provided heat, but the controls were based on environmental temperature rather than the activity of the wearer. With the exertion of crawling the last twenty-five meters, the suits were overheated. She lay on the ice waiting for her internal temperature to adjust to the suit's temperature, and her stomach growled.

She was full enough, it was just that recently she had been eating a strange mixture of emergency rations and the food found under a Naram temple by search teams. The Naram food was unlike anything she had eaten before, a combination of dry vegetables and some strange grains. Doctor Hess claimed that the grain was actually a flower seed that the ancients had used in religious ceremonies, not to be consumed by the populace. The legionnaires didn't care. Crushed and mixed with oil from the emergency ration packs, then heated, it had become an edible, if not palatable, paste. At least it filled the void in their bellies.

Stone wriggled into position beside her. He had had an even more difficult time crossing the ice to the surface. With his left arm in a sling, he had not been able to pull himself along very easily, and now he was breathing hard. Ross could see his breath steaming the face plate of the BLS. Using hand signals, he indicated the area she should sweep, and for the next minute, each concentrated on an assigned sector. Nothing.

Stone made another hand signal, and they rose to a crouch and moved out. Stone led now, and Ross stayed close behind.

They hadn't gone more than a dozen steps when Stone suddenly stopped. He flipped up his face plate and indicated for Ross to do the same. They crouched in the snow and visually scanned the horizon; it was dimly illuminated all around them. The soft glow outlined towers of ice that rose like jagged teeth and reflected from the lowering clouds above. Certain points were so intense that halos of light rose against the sky. What should have been complete darkness was filled with a soft, blue glow. They left their face plates open and made for the nearest strong light.

Wearing the holotarps over their armor, the pair moved slowly toward the cover of an ice pinnacle. Crouched behind it, they dropped their face plates and scanned again with the BLS system. Within the three hundred meters of the system's operational range, they detected movement; significant movement. The activity was centered around the apparent light source, and it was toward that light that the pair now moved. Ross led, crawling on all fours, with Stone in a crouch behind her. There didn't appear to be any outpost guards, at least none that appeared on the sensor screen, but they moved cautiously nonetheless. At the last ridge before the light, they began to creep forward, a mere centimeter at a time, until they were able to see past the rim of ice.

Spread before them was a TOG encampment. Tall stanchions supported arc lights that cast a blue-white light that glared off the ice cap. Vehicles surrounded by TOG legionnaires in battle armor were scattered under the lights. A row of vehicles stood facing them, and they were able to count three Horatius tanks and a pair of Romulus carriers. A second row of as many more tanks stood beyond those, their access doors open and surrounded by scurrying legionnaires. The sharp ring of hammers and the hum of power torches echoed across the frozen waste. Farther back were administrative vehicles parked in a loose circle. Within that circle were stacks of ammunition and crates of unknown stores. The outer perimeter of the encampment was marked by several of the temporary huts that the TOG research team had abandoned in the face of the initial Renegade presence on the south pole.

Stone touched Ross on the left shoulder and signaled her to slip back down the ridge. In the lee of the ice, he bent forward to whisper in her face, unwilling to use the commlink for fear that the transmission might be heard. "Get back to Harras as quick as you can." His voice was a mere thread of sound, and Ross strained to hear his words. "Tell him the TOGs are still here." Ross shook her head and indicated they should both go. Stone nodded. "Don't worry," he whispered. "I'll be right behind you, but you can move faster than I can." When she hesitated, he pushed her down the slope. With his right arm he pointed back the way they had come and then double-pumped it to indicate she was to move as quickly as possible. She hesitated for a moment longer and then moved away in a crouching run. Stone took one last look at the TOG activity and then followed her back toward the breach.

The crippled Liberator wobbled slightly, its nose dipping toward the planet's surface. Inside, Archon Divxas twisted the thrust controls once again to try to stabilize the tank. Most of the thrust control had been shot away, and he wasn't quite sure how much longer he would be able to direct the damaged vehicle. The helm and drive worked most of the time, but there were sudden pauses in both systems that sent the Liberator plunging out of control toward the surface.

He had been able to maintain the ten-kilometer altitude for some time, but the height was beginning to have an effect on both him and his commander, who still lay unconscious and pinioned to the deck of the fighting compartment. At ten kilometers, there was too little oxygen for either the Human or the Baufrin to survive. Under normal operating conditions, the Liberator's internal life-support system allowed the crew to operate efficiently at extreme altitude, but use of this system required that the hatches be closed and sealed. The command hatch of the Liberator was still open, and Archon, even if he had been able to reach it from his driving station, would not have closed and secured it. The commlink signal wires ran through the opening, and to close the hatch would have been to admit that they would never send the vital message to planetary headquarters on Rolandrin.

Both of the crew members had been issued emergency oxygen tanks for this eventuality, but they were designed for one hour of use. Because the tank was out of control, Archon had already maintained this height for longer than that. He was afraid to give up the height he had gained. He could make a drop to lower altitude, but feared not being able to stop the tank once it began its descent. The Liberator would plunge into the ocean and vanish forever.

The Liberator's flight control computer steadied the drifting tank as it dropped toward the planet. The long slant toward the surface had begun. Archon checked the drive computer: in three hours they would re-enter breathable atmosphere. By then it wouldn't matter. He set the autopilot, punching in the coordinates of the command base at Alabaster on Rolandrin. The Liberator would fly itself for as long as the power lasted. That accomplished, the Baufrin unsnapped the oxygen supply tube from his individual life-support system. Carefully inserting the hose into the external port on Karstil's life-support system, he closed the controls to their minimum setting. He pushed the body under the stanchion of the command chair, bracing it in place with one of his own legs. Then he settled back in the driver's station to await the inevitable.

The Commonwealth *Cheetah* space fighter rolled over for one last look at the ocean. The pilot, making a scheduled run toward the pole, had seen the TOG activity, but he had not considered their presence unusual. Giving his DDP only the most cursory glance, he began to streak for home. A soft tone sounded in his helmet, and his eyes snapped back to the display.

The lower corner showed the blinking green symbol of an unidentified friendly craft. The pilot pushed the control wand forward and to the right, and the *Cheetah* banked into a sharp split-S dive. The planet filled the cockpit screen as the fighter careened toward the surface. At fifteen kilometers from the surface the pilot pulled back on the control wand and the fighter arced upward. The blinking square on the DDP became solid, and the data scrolled across the display: a Liberator tank with no detectable life forms inside. Keying his commlink, the Commonwealth pilot downloaded the information to fighter command.

44

1830, 13 Martius 6831—The howl of sirens echoed through the ferrosteel caverns of Renegade fighter command. Titanium blast-doors rolled silently into custom-made crevices, chased by swirls of dust stirred up by the sudden surge of grav drives. Crew chiefs and maintenance troops slammed shut access panels and disconnected a serpent's nest of hoses as pilots sprinted across the floor from the ready room, cables and varicolored tubes dangling from their blue-and-white flight suits.

Two techs held the boarding ladder against the narrow hull of a *Cheetah* while the crew chief balanced himself on the fuselage above. The running pilot leaped to the third rung of the ladder and vaulted into the cockpit. The crew chief lifted the helmet from the rear of the seat and settled it onto the pilot's head, but the pilot never stopped moving. His hands made a rapid check of the control bars and working surfaces. The pilot sounded off the checklist to the techs standing behind the craft monitoring the control surfaces and vector-thrust apertures. The crew chief connected the life-support and commlink systems to the onboard sensor and select systems.

The checklist complete, all systems showed green, and so the crew chief swung clear of the cockpit as the canopy began to close. His feet hit the top of the ladder, and the two techs below pulled it away. Chocks came clear of the undercarriage, and the *Cheetah* rolled through the open doors. Three other space fighters were headed for the same opening, falling obediently in behind the leader. A light above the blast doors flashed from red to green, indicating that the doors were locked open, as the ogive of the first fighter crossed the door channels. Crewmembers scattered away from the howling fighters. Canopies snapped shut and life-support systems activated as the cruciform wings cleared the doors.

The first fighter crossed the marked taxiway and locked his right hand-brakes, forcing the *Cheetah* into a tight right-hand pivot. The fighter immediately behind executed the same maneuver simultaneously. The fighters sat side-by-side for an instant, then the leader spoke a single word, and the craft began to roll. As the fighters reached maneuver threshold, the twin wing-engines blossomed fire. The thrust concussion swept over the field. In an instant, the *Cheetah*s were a blur, twin gashes of silver against the green of the runway shoulders. Then they were airborne, noses pointed skyward. The wheels snapped into their recessed housings.

From siren to "wheels up," three minutes, seventeen seconds had elapsed. The second pair of *Cheetah*s followed two seconds later. The squadron leader was satisfied. Not the best his pilots had ever done, but well within the four-minute standard set by Commonwealth command.

Three hours later the flight rolled back toward Rolandrin. Their mission had been to patrol above the battered, drifting Renegade Liberator and await the arrival of the rescue unit. A pair of TOG *Lancea* fighters had appeared at the outer limit of sensor range, snooped for a while, and then fled, presumably for Malthus. Flying Officer Gorgas Star knew that it was only a matter of time before they returned, and in greater strength. He watched his look-down display board for signs that the recovery had been completed.

Recovery Chief Officer Llewellyn calculated the Liberator's fall. Gravity was drawing the damaged tank down too quickly for his Crawler to snap it out of the sky, so he would have to settle for a water snatch. He would let the Liberator hit the southern ocean's surface and descend on it before it sank. His data display showed that the structural integrity of the tank was intact, but he would have been happier if all the hatches had been closed. High waves in the retrieval area could swamp the vehicle before he could grasp the lifting shackles, which meant he might have to put his people over the side. "All right, you cruds, get ready for a bath." In reply, the recovery-team chief snapped a friendly obscene gesture at his commander.

The Liberator struck the surface of the water with an explosion of spray. The tank bounced once, immediately spinning out of control, and struck the surface again. The right sponson slipped under the choppy water, and a solid gray wave rushed over the turret. "Damn," cursed Llewellyn, maneuvering the Crawler above the sinking tank. "She's going under. Prepare to jump."

The standard four-man recovery team opened the side ports on the Crawler and stood on the sills as the craft steadied in a hover three meters above the tops of the highest waves. The sinking tank was a good eight meters below the Crawler, and the recovery team watched the frigid water pouring into the Liberator through the open turret.

"At my command." Llewellyn jockeyed the 900-ton recovery vehicle over his prize, watching his down-looking sight on the DDP. The cross hairs steadied over the target.

"Go! Go! Go!" Llewellyn shouted, and the recovery team dropped clear of the sides, each man carrying a snap hook attached to a monofilament carballoy cable.

Two members of the team landed on the exposed left side of the Liberator and made directly for the D-rings welded to the upper glacis. They knelt over the hardpoints, waiting for the word that the others had reached their goal. The two recovery personnel on the right side plunged straight into the water, sinking fast as the weight of the cable and hooks pulled them down. They knew what they were looking for, and they could perform their task blindfolded and upside down. Llewellyn saw his control console go green, showing that all members were in place. "Hook!" he commanded, counted to three, then engaged the recovery motors. He felt the Crawler vibrate with the strain. The Liberator began to rise from its would-be watery grave.

As the Liberator righted itself and came clear of the water, the recovery team crawled into the fighting compartment. "Hey, Lew," the first man said into the commlink. "You ought to see what we got here. There's a guy pinned under the seat who's barely alive, and some other thing all crumpled up in the back that must be dead."

"Bandits! Three o'clock. Angles two-five."

"Roger," replied Star. "I've got them. Flight, break right." The DDP identified the incoming TOGs as four *Lancea* light fighters. The Commonwealth formation spread out in a loose line as the enemy's tight box formation swooped down. "Wait for the missile launch," said Star.

The same litany ran through the minds of each *Cheetah* pilot at this moment. They knew that the *Lancea* fighters in an anti-recon squadron were typically armed with five missiles each. TOG standard operating procedure called for the *Lancea* to fire at long range, then break for home to reload before returning to the battle. The best tactic for avoiding the missiles was to fly directly at the approaching enemy and wait for the missile launch. Just before impact, the fighters would break right or left, leaving the missile sensor systems targetless. The tactic required incredible courage. Every instinct screamed at the pilot to turn away, but a fighter would have a hard time outrunning a missile. Turning too soon would allow the missile to strike the fighter in the side, smashing its way through the armor into the internal systems. Turning too late would allow the missiles to strike on the bow armor, and the *Cheetah* would crumple up like foil.

The only advantage of the tactic was that when and if the fighters evaded the missiles, the *Cheetah*s would be within close range of the enemy. The *Lancea*s, their missiles expended, would be helpless under the hammering of the *Cheetah*'s wing-mounted lasers and electron particle cannon. The DDP in the leading *Cheetah* flashed a warning. "Birds in the air," said Star. "Wait for my order." The Commonwealth fighters and the launched missiles rushed toward each other at fifty kilometers per second. When the range closed to less than fifteen kilometers, Star spoke again. "Break!"

The four fighters turned sharply away from the missiles. The incoming missiles' silhouette scanners lost their targets and screamed past the looping *Cheetah*s, which were targeting the fleeing enemy. The *Lancea*s had not waited to see the effect of their fire. As soon as their missiles were well away, they had turned for home.

The *Cheetah*s' sensor systems acquired the fleeing *Lancea*s. Three of the four were already well away, but the last one was still within the one hundred and fifty-kilometer range of the Radiation Intensity Seeking missiles carried on the *Cheetah*s' nose hardpoints. Star heard the soft tone of the RIS lock-on sensor sound in his helmet. He toggled the firing switch, and the exhaust of the missile launch bloomed across the nose of the fighter. Out of the corner of his eye he saw his wing man launch as well. "Break off. Break off. They're gone." Less than a minute later a red flower bloomed against the dark sky. One of the *Lancea*s would not reach its base.

"They're alive!" exclaimed Prefect Kenderson. "I knew Harras was too good to be caught!"

Lieutenant Colonel Alban Tripp smiled at the Renegade Legion commander. He had experienced the same euphoria when the damaged Liberator's message was received at headquarters. But he knew that the elation would quickly give way to frustration if something weren't done, and done quickly. "And what now?"

"Why, we go after them, of course."

"With what? Will we be throwing good money after bad?"

"That's not the point," argued the prefect. "They're my troops, and we must do everything we can to save them."

"But that *is* the point," interrupted Brigadier Bernard Maxall, Chief of Operations for Caralis. "We're all in the same army, whether we're Commonwealth or Renegade. The force has needs, and one of them is keeping the troops alive for the real mission. And the real mission is on Alsatia, not at the pole."

"So we give them up?" Kenderson was suddenly weary. His joy at finding Cohort Harras alive was quickly overshadowed by new despair.

"In a word," replied Maxall, "yes."

"And that's the consensus of your entire staff?" asked Kenderson.

"It is."

"With your permission, sir." Major Rebecca Harn stepped forward from behind the brigadier's chair. "I believe there is an important consideration we may be overlooking." Harn was acting as Maxall's aide, and it was unusual for an aide to disagree with his or her superior officer publicly. Maxall eyed her sternly, but she didn't flinch. He nodded for her to continue.

"The TOGs have given a great deal of effort to the polar position," she began. "From Optio Karstil's description of the under-ice city, TOG probably wants it very badly. The TOGs have always sought to couch their conquests in terms of establishing enlightened exploration. If that city is Naram—and we must assume it is—its discovery would establish this planet as one of the long-lost Naram home worlds. That discovery could be used to influence public opinion among the Naram. If the TOGs were able to open the city and invite the Naram First Consul to visit under TOG's auspices, the impact could be significant, especially on those Naram currently in TOG-occupied space. The discovery might also influence the Naram currently serving with the Commonwealth."

The room was silent as each officer considered her words. "You're making sense so far, Becky," commented the brigadier. "Continue."

"I believe, sir, that we should consider the consequences of our action or inaction, based not so much on what will happen here on Caralis, but what will happen throughout TOG and Commonwealth space. Viewed from that angle, it would be worth our time and effort to contest the pole. And, of course, the troops we deal with on the pole won't trouble us on Alsatia."

Brigadier Bernard Maxall rose from his chair. "All right, Kenderson. We'll have a go at your Cohort Harras. Come up with force requirements and a plan. Brief me in twelve hours. You can't have anything that's been committed to Alsatia, but you can have anything else within reason." He stared at the prefect. "You should be a happy man, although I'm not sure why. You've tried to relieve this force before, and it failed miserably. Make this try a good one, because it's your last shot."

45

0600, 14 Martius 6831—Legatus Maximus Rocipian Olioarchus leaned back in his chair and stretched. At the same table in the command Pompey that rested near the center of the south pole sat Prefect Claudius Sulla, operations officer from TOG planetary staff, and Centurion Marmoreus Patrius, Olioarchus' adjunct in Cohort Camus. "You both have been very helpful, and I appreciate all you've done," said Olioarchus. "I am confident that we can bring this little adventure to a satisfying conclusion." He looked at Patrius. "I have suffered losses within my staff, Centurion, and I would be happy to have you fill one of the vacancies."

Patrius smiled at the legatus maximus. He knew for certain that he had made the correct decision, one that was right for the Cohort and right for his own career. "With pleasure, sir."

Olioarchus turned to Prefect Sulla. "Technically, sir, I am not under your command. Neither am I under the command of Brigadier General Drusus Arcadius. All my reports are sent to sector headquarters, and though I am under operational control of planetary staff while on Caralis, as leader of a transient unit, I report directly to Grand General Oliodinus Severus Septimus. My report will include full details of your assistance. I know he will be quite pleased." Sulla flushed with pleasure. The ruddy glow drained from his cheeks as the vehicle's entry portal hissed open to reveal Legatus Cariolanus Camus. Olioarchus waved Camus into the chamber with an expansive gesture.

"You have changed the deployment of some of my units," said Camus, the anger in his voice reflected on his face.

"Certainly not, my dear Legatus. I would not dare."

"You have. I have just come through the emplacements, and my men have been moved."

"I have not moved your men, Legatus Camus. I have, however, moved mine."

"What do you mean?"

"As of approximately half an hour ago, the entire mission at the pole passed to my command." Olioarchus curved his lips into a chilling grin and casually rested one arm on the control console.

"You have no right to do this!"

"But I do, I do." Olioarchus stretched his grin wider.

"My men won't stand for it." Camus dropped his right hand down to the holster of his Hantrus spike pistol.

"Your men have no choice. This change has been authorized at the highest level."

Camus turned on Sulla. "I should never have agreed to allow you on this mission!" he shouted.

Sulla paled further under this attack, and looked to Olioarchus for help. The legatus maximus smiled back encouragingly, reassuring the prefect that he was really in charge. Olioarchus pressed one of the buttons on the console.

Camus, his fury overtaking his judgment, fumbled for his pistol, but didn't even get the holster flap open. The three-fingered claw of a Ssoran guard closed firmly on his wrist from behind, twisting his hand away from his gun.

"I believe, Legatus Cariolanus Camus," Olioarchus whispered icily, "that the change of command is complete."

"This is impossible!" thundered NaBesta Kenderson, sweeping the papers from his desk. "Not every Renegade and Commonwealth unit on Caralis can be doing something important."

Lieutenant Colonel Alban Tripp looked at his Legion commander. He was well aware that all available units listed were committed to Alsatia. The brigadier must have known this when he approved the relief mission and charged Kenderson not to touch commands earmarked for deployment. Success for the mission at the pole seemed determined to elude the prefect. "There may still be a chance," said Tripp. "I know just the man to help you find what you need. I've got a captain on my staff who can do anything with a computer that can be done."

"Well, send him to me. Wait—don't send him to me. Just tell him what I need, and let him get to work."

Half an hour later, Captain David Pharker checked off one more line on his computer screen, laid down the stylus, and placed a call over the commlink. An officer answered the other end of the link. "Hi, Rob," said Pharker. "This is Dave. I need a favor." He paused. "Need to know if there's a semi-operational unit from the 2567th not listed on the availability chart." He listened for a moment. "Great. Send me the info, will you?"

The screen on his desk-top console blurred as the computer accepted the download. Pharker watched until the send was complete. "Got it," he said into the commlink. "Thanks." He stood, ejected the chip from the computer, and went to see Lieutenant Colonel Tripp.

"There's a lot out there, sir," he said abruptly, as he entered Tripp's office.

"I knew if anyone could find uncommitted troops, it would be you, Dave," Tripp replied with a smile. "What've you got that I can give to Kenderson?"

"There's a half-strength Cohort listed as in training, and there's another unit undergoing full maintenance. Neither is listed as available, but both could definitely be had. There's also a transport carrying men and gear due in. They're not organized yet, but we could get them started at their next breakout. It's all on here." Pharker put the chip into the desk-top access port.

"I don't know how you do it, Dave." Tripp shook his head in admiration as he scanned the information.

"It's pretty simple. I just keep in touch with most of the people I meet. For example, there's a civilian at the training center who is a friend of my brother. I met him when I was about eleven years old, and he's given me some good advice. He still has connections in the Commonwealth forces from his time in the service. The colonel at the maintenance facility was one of my instructors at the Officers' Training Center. We got to know each other better over the card table. One of the staff sergeant-majors in Personnel was my drill sergeant. He taught me a lot about people. It all comes together." He shrugged off the compliment.

"Well, we'd better send a warning order to the transport *Caelestis*, letting them know what we have in mind," said Tripp. "Put one together, will you, Dave?"

"Already done, sir. I have it here."

"Do you think of everything, Dave?"

"Probably not, sir. But I try."

As the transport RLS *Caelestis* broke out of tachyon space to make its final course change for Caralis, it opened all frequencies, not because it expected any communications, but because that was standard procedure. The captain was surprised to receive a short, coded message burst from a distant P-COMSAT. He sent it to the deciphering station for immediate transcription, and frowned when he read it.

The order was directed to both him and the senior Renegade officer on board. Instead of making a normal, administrative debarkation, the *Caelestis* would make an assault drop over Caralis. The changed orders required a much closer, and therefore dangerous, approach, as well as increased their chances of facing opposition, and the skipper didn't like the sound of that. He passed the message on to the centurion assigned to ride herd on the troops and equipment in the cargo bay. *Caelestis* made a sharp turn and refired the faster-than-light drive.

Milton Harras studied the personnel roster for his Cohort displayed on the screen in the command Pedden. The fierce fighting at the breaches in the dome under the ice had taken its toll, but the Cohort was in better shape than he had thought. Discovering food under the Naram temples had lifted the trapped legionnaires' morale, and had had a surprising effect on the hospitalized troops. Whether it was because of increased rations or just a variety in the troops' diet, the atmosphere under the south pole had definitely changed.

A number of things had come together at the same time. The cessation of TOG aggression was allowing the men to get some badly needed sleep. The Century maintenance people had used the lull to cobble together a few additional vehicles. They lacked the equipment to do the heavy lifting needed to reassemble the big tanks, but they managed to cannibalize enough of the irreparably damaged vehicles to get a few more pieces operational. The three Centuries of the Cohort now boasted five vehicles each, and fifteen fighting machines was a significant increase from the eight they had ended up with in their last battle. Finding people to put in the machines was the problem now.

With the salvaged equipment up and running, the qualified crewmen that had been temporarily assigned to the infantry went back to the positions for which they had been trained. That left the infantry squads short on rifle strength, but the situation couldn't be helped. If the TOGs began another push, Harras would call the crews off the tanks to fight as infantry. A city was no place for armored vehicles; the narrow streets made perfect ambush sites for peds, and with a little imaginative planning, a platoon of infantry would more than match a Century of armor.

Harras swung his chair around to face his companions in the command center. "You did a good job of recon for us on the surface when we needed it, and I'm going to ask you to do it again." Ross and Stone looked at each other.

Honor Ross' face showed her frustration and anxiety. She wanted to get back to her squad. She had run the recon mission with Larry Stone under protest, and had agreed only after she was promised more legionnaires for her infantry section when she returned. In fact, the opposite had been true. Grain had returned to the squad classified as walking wounded, but she had lost both Hull and Blackstone to resurrected vehicles. Three infantry was not much of a squad. She was beginning to hate tanks. "I'd like to get back to my squad, sir. There're only three of them in the position now, and they could use me."

"I appreciate the situation, Sergeant, but you're more use to me on the surface at the moment. You and Stone are familiar with what's happening topside. We don't have time to train someone new."

Ross' heart sank. She knew her commander's arguments were valid, and that didn't change the way she felt, but she resigned herself to her fate.

"Don't worry, Sergeant," said Harras. "Just this one last time, I promise, and I'll let you go back to your squad." He pointed at the screen, which had cleared the personnel roster to show what they knew of the TOG positions. "Things are changing up there, and I need to have a better idea of what's going on. Sam Rand, the comm officer, says that if we can get a passive sensor up there and hardwire it to a vehicle down here, we can find out exactly where they are. That's what I want the two of you to do."

"Dragging a wire up that slope is going to be interesting," Stone said drily. He jerked his thumb at his recon partner. "Ross here is fine, but I've still only got one wing. We could use a third person."

"I know you could, but I haven't got one to give you. The size of Ross' squad is typical, unfortunately. I'm afraid you're it."

Ross and Stone crept up the deserted gallery once more toward the surface. Ross led with her pistol drawn, followed by Stone, who carried an M-364 dispenser on his back. The center-wound coil of optical communications cable paid out as he moved. The hair-thin filament was strong enough to support twelve kilos dead weight, so there was almost no danger of it snapping from any move he made. The cable was also fully insulated, and so even though it was lying on ice, the signal from the sensor unit would not be degraded or bleed off enough energy to be detected.

The opening to the surface was still deserted. Ross edged her way to the lip of the crater first and cleared the area. Then she signaled Stone to make the climb. With one useless arm, it was a long, painful crawl. Ross could see the steam of his breath pouring from under the face plate. By the time Stone reached the surface, he was sweating from exertion and pain.

"Remind me to turn down this honor next time," he whispered to Ross. "I'll let someone else get the credit and the medal. It's just not worth it."

The pair waited at the edge of the crater until Stone's breathing evened out. The first time he signaled that he was ready to go, Ross demurred. She could tell he was still breathing hard, and Ross didn't want to move until she was sure he was ready. The next time Stone signaled he was ready, Ross agreed, and the pair moved off.

The sky, illuminated by arc lights on their last trip topside, was dark. Stone crawled over to Ross and whispered that this was either a good sign or a bad sign. Either the TOGs had gone, or they were ready to launch another attack. Ross shrugged her shoulders. All she wanted was to get the job done and get back to her squad.

They scouted out a likely-looking place and implanted the passive sensor. Ross felt a sense of accomplishment; the task was completed. Stone unplugged the commlink from his helmet and inserted the sensitive probe into the access port on the sensor. He ran a manual, spoken testing sequence checking the communications link and the readout shown on the sensor. He shook his head several times and then removed the commlink coupling. "No good," he hissed. "The readings aren't strong enough. We'll have to get closer."

Frustration boiled up in Ross. *Just because I was the one nearest the breach the first time is no reason I have to keep on doing this,* she raged at the sky. She yanked the sensor from the ice and gestured sharply to Stone. The best way to solve her problem, she decided, was to get the damn thing planted somewhere. Then they could get back where they belonged.

46

1200, 14 Martius 6831—Legatus Maximus Olioarchus studied the plot showing the deployment of the forces he commanded at the south pole. Legatus Cariolanus Camus had done a good job; or, rather, Centurion Patrius had developed a good plan. The remnants of Cohort Camus had pulled back, well clear of the access to the Renegade position under the ice, to prepare an ambush for when the enemy was forced to the surface. The 356th Penal Auxilia had deployed one Cohort in support of the armored vehicles and the rest at the known breaches in the dome over the hidden city. Olioarchus pressed a button on the command console and the door to the outer cubicle slid open. Centurion Miles Stratton appeared at once.

"Sir?"

"Stratton, we are ready to proceed. What is the status of the command?"

"All troops are in position, sir. They await only your orders."

"Very good, Stratton," smiled the Auxilia commander. "But your enthusiasm is misplaced."

"They are willing to die for the emperor, sir."

"And so they shall, Stratton, so they shall. But even penal troops should not be foolishly wasted. Although they are well trained, and you saw to that, I'm sure, they need combat experience. Only experience under fire will weld them into a fighting unit, and a few losses will promote their blood lust. It will make them fiercer still."

"What size assault then, sir?"

Olioarchus pretended to consider his answer. "I think no more than a platoon at a time."

"A platoon, sir? They can't win with just platoon assaults."

Olioarchus smiled unpleasantly. "But, Centurion Stratton, is that not the desired result? That they will fail and take losses?"

Stratton looked at his commander with new respect for his calculating nature. "Wonderful, sir," he said with marked enthusiasm. "Wonderful. I will issue the orders at once."

Sergeant Lucifer K. Mullins squirmed deeper into his seat. The mission had all the earmarks of a classic screw-up. The transport RLS *Caelestis* had been loaded on Rilus V for an administrative approach and drop. The cargo deck was a shambles, vehicles stuck in where they would fit rather than arranged for a deployment. Now some fool had decided to commit this rabble to battle as soon as they arrived over Caralis. He chewed on the stub of his unlit cigar and growled softly to himself.

The briefing officer was a very young Commonwealth lieutenant. "Because we can't very well move the equipment, we'll assign crews to the vehicles as they are spotted on the decks. The Renegade replacements will take the tanks and carriers in the forward portion of the hold on all decks. The Commonwealth troops will be assigned to the rear vehicles. I realize that this means some of you will not be in the vehicles to which you were assigned when we loaded, but it can't be helped. Just go with the flow and we'll do the best we can."

Mullins bit deeper into his cigar. His assignment had been to an old Crusader, the heaviest Commonwealth tank ever developed. It was an old design, but it was heavily armed and armored. He had been looking forward to sitting in the turret of a 400-ton tank, leaving the lighter Liberator he was used to behind. Now he was losing his more secure ride to a Commonwealth sergeant.

"As you know," continued the lieutenant, "the operation at the south pole that we are dropping to support is a purely Renegade operation. The Commonwealth troops will make their entry to Rolandrin as scheduled."

Typical, thought Mullins, cynically. The Renegades do the fighting and the Commonwealth forms the reserve. But he had to admit that he liked it that way; better to be out front than stuck in the rear listening to the battle over the commlink. The popular notion that Commonwealth forces just sat around was not true, and Mullins knew it. He just liked to think that he was in the better of the two forces.

"After you have been assigned to your vehicles, we will organize you into ad hoc platoons and Centuries. Report to the assignment officers as you depart. That's all." The briefing officer turned smartly on his heel and walked away, followed by the rest of the briefing party.

The Renegade troops rose to their feet and a buzz of conversation echoed through the vast hall. None of it expressed approval for the Commonwealth or the new plan.

The Renegade maintenance park on Rolandrin was a hive of activity. Maintenance personnel put the finishing touches on weapon systems, sensors, and armor, readying the tanks and infantry carriers of the Century scattered through the area for combat. Incoming replacement officers and soldiers checked in at long tables manned by harassed clerks. Assigned troops wandered through the maze of vehicles seeking their new homes.

Optio Roglund Karstil tested the brace on his left shoulder. The medical officer had returned him to light duty: no heavy lifting, no strenuous activity. Commanding a tank platoon didn't require heavy lifting, he decided, so he reported for duty. He hadn't mentioned his recent hospital stay to the personnel officer when he reported in for the second relief force forming in the maintenance area, and had been assigned a Liberator and a platoon with no questions asked. There wouldn't be much time for a briefing before he was headed back to the pole, he knew, and he hoped that the Century commander was a good one.

The other officers and senior sergeants stood in a loose circle almost in the center of the yard, introducing themselves to each other and making nervous conversation. They were unsure of themselves and their situation. Their Century had just been through a major refit at the Alabaster Maintenance Center, and most of the officers and men were newly assigned. Raw troops never reported as combat-ready, but somehow this group's status had been changed. Even the centurion was new. The group stiffened to attention as the command party approached.

The Century's senior sergeant called the officers to attention as the centurion entered the area. The commander practically bounced into the opening the officers created. He was the most energetic man Karstil had ever seen; the man seemed to spring off his toes as he walked. The centurion stopped in the center of the circle and removed his combat helmet, revealing a boyish face and an unruly shock of golden hair. The officer ran his hand through his hair and the tousled locks immediately fell into place.

"Good afternoon, gentlemen," the centurion began. "It's nice to have you here. I am Centurion Greerson Kane, newly appointed to this exalted rank from among the swamp of optios. Please take note; if you persevere and survive, you will become a senior optio, and then, before you know it, they will make you a centurion. It's all really quite wonderful."

Karstil stared at the centurion. There was something familiar about the man. The golden hair, the voice, the irreverent, mocking attitude were there in the back of his mind.

"What we have here," continued the centurion, "is a wonderful chance for all of us to die a most glorious death. Some of our friends have gotten themselves into a bit of a muddle down on the south pole." He shivered. "Brrr. Frigid place, I hear. Our job is to go down there and rescue them." He surveyed his officers' faces, his eyes bright with excitement.

"Now, lest you think that you are in this alone, let me remind you that others are going on this delightful excursion as well. NaBesta Kenderson, the prefect of our glorious provisional Legion, is leading this Manus-sized force himself. At least, it will be Manus-sized after we link with our reinforcements. Until that happens we'll just be a bloated Cohort."

Karstil was barely listening. He was already familiar with the broad scheme of this mission. He was concentrating on remembering where he had met Greerson Kane. It could have been on the *Tacitus* or the *Maiestas*, but that didn't seem right. For some reason, he associated Kane with a hot breakfast of eggs, sausage, fried potatoes, and gravy. He frowned with the effort of remembering.

"What we are going to do," said the centurion, using his hands to help explain, "is come swooping up from Rolandrin. We'll make a long, low transit across the ocean until we get about halfway to the pole. Then we'll make a sharp climb to ten kays. As we begin to nose over for the descent to the pole, a transport will appear out of the void. *Voila!* The transport will open its doors, and out will pour a virtual torrent of tanks and infantry carriers to join us as we dive toward the bad guys. It will all be too beautiful for words. We will all be very excited and happy. The unfortunate TOGs will see this marvel of military coordination, and they will throw down their weapons and surrender en masse."

Alsatia! thought Karstil. It was "Senior Optio Greerson Kane" from the last push on Alsatia! Karstil smiled as he remembered the desperate night battle, his platoon overrun by TOGs, and the timely arrival of the Deliverer tanks commanded by Senior Optio Kane. He also remembered the cavalier treatment Kane had given Centurion Alanton Freund, Karstil's commander. His smile widened at the memory. One of Kane's men had made breakfast for Karstil's unit. That's how it all fit together.

"We do not have much time left before we depart." The centurion spoke seriously. "This operation is being thrown together from what's available, and we'll have to make adjustments as we fly. Stay together, stay loose, and stay awake. Normal comm will apply. Nothing fancy about the attack, so we'll fight with the platoons on line, from left to right: Two, One, and Three. Any questions?"

The platoon leaders wanted to know about rations, equipment, and some administrative details. Kane answered the questions he had to, and directed the rest to his senior sergeant. When the last officer left, Karstil stepped forward. "I'm Karstil. We've met before."

"Really? Where?"

"On Alsatia a month or so ago. You pulled my butt out of a bad situation."

"Karstil? Karstil. Ah yes. You had a rather battered Liberator platoon, and, if I remember correctly, a complete idiot as a Century commander." Kane laughed, his head tilted back, eyes crinkled shut. The sound of his voice rattled off the sides of the surrounding tanks. "I hope I didn't get you into too much trouble with my little contribution."

"Some. But it turned out all right."

"Well, I'm glad to have you with me. You seemed pretty steady back then for a man who'd been through that kind of fight, and I like to work with people I can count on."

The two officers shook hands and returned to their separate commands. Karstil felt better about the operation. The way Kane had described it, there was a chance of success. He wondered, idly, where Freund fit into all of this. He hoped that wherever the man was, it was far, far away.

Sergeant Lisectus Barcus looked down the column of advancing men. The lead figure was crouched beside a jagged slash that creased the surface of the dome and revealed the city below. The ice walls of the gallery just below the surface of the ice reflected dull light from beyond the opening, casting an eerie glow over the troops. The soft sound of open-mouthed chewing behind him told the sergeant that his platoon leader, Optio Strovasi, was close at hand.

"They're moving too slowly, Sergeant," the optio whined. "Make them move faster. I'm cold."

Barcus trotted away from the optio to find out why the column had stopped. The lead man was peering through the break at the crater-shaped ice fall that lay between the TOGs and their enemies' hiding place. Tops of buildings appeared through the gloom, and the soldier was using his sensor system to scan for heat sources in the structures. Barcus dropped to the ice behind the scout. "What's up?" he asked.

"I'm checking for people in those buildings. They must be out there, and we'll be right out in the open when we move across the ice."

"Strovasi wants you to move out." Barcus didn't mention the reason. He figured the ped didn't really need to know.

The soldier gave his platoon sergeant a long look. It was foolish to move across open ice without checking it first, but you didn't complain in a penal unit. Complaining had brought many of the troops here as it was, and they were given only one second chance. He tensed his muscles, then sprinted the five meters to the edge of the crater. He survived, and Barcus signaled the next man to follow. The column began to move again.

The sensors in Herman Grold's helmet alerted him to the first TOG trooper's movement across the ice above. He signaled the other two members of his squad, and all three moved cautiously up the stairs to the parapet fighting positions. As they settled behind the firing ports, Grold called in the presence of the TOG platoon to his Century commander.

The three Renegade infantry, set up in positions at least twenty meters apart, watched the TOG platoon assemble behind the lip of the crater. Two men were visible above the edge of the crater, but most of the force was protected from direct attack. Grold lifted the Douglas grenade launcher from the roof and aimed it over the parapet. He didn't have line-of-sight, but the crater was well within the two-hundred-meter range of the launcher. He eyeballed the slant of the tube, raised the muzzle a hair, and fired all four rounds.

The four Yosaki 515 grenades arced through the gloom, cleared the rim of the crater, and landed dead-center of the TOG platoon. The explosions were too close together to be distinguished as separate detonations. Grold watched with approval as his sensor showed the heat-signatures of men scattering away from the blast. One of the TOGs raced back toward the crevice through which they had come.

Barcus saw the grenades out the corner of his eye, but too late to shout a warning. He rolled away from the concussion, shielding his face with his arms. His helmet sensors showed him that most of the troops had escaped the blast, but for some reason, one was heading back toward the entrance. He made a quick mental note to figure out later who was the coward. He felt the shards of plastic, mixed with fragments of ice, rattle against his light battle armor. Before the smoke cleared he was on his feet. "Let's go!" he shouted, and leaped over the rim of the crater. The rest of the platoon followed.

Grold saw the TOG infantry burst over the rim. He dropped the grenade launcher and grabbed his spike rifle. Grain and Tscholmankia were already firing sustained bursts at the penal infantry as they careened down the slope. Many stopped and huddled behind the detritus that covered the ice. Others kept coming, closing until they were protected by the walls of the building. Grold leaned over the parapet to fire down into the street below. He saw a shadow merge with the wall and gave it a full burst.

Barcus huddled against the wall as the spray of plastic spikes dug into the street beside him. He could see the head and shoulders of his adversary leaning over the protective masonry above. He raised his weapon, but the target vanished before he could fire. He lowered his rifle and checked for the rest of his platoon. Seeing three shapes in a group, he signaled them to follow as he turned down a side street. Having broken through the outer edge of the Renegade defenses, his unit now had to exploit its success.

On the parapet above, the three Renegade soldiers paused to reload. There were still more TOG targets than the squad had weapons in front, and several TOGs had escaped past their position down the street. The enemy on the slope was firing back, and it would be foolhardy to expose the members of his squad to the counterfire. Grold decided to fall back to their next positions. He bolted for the stairs and the other two followed.

They raced down to the ground floor. They heard grenades exploding in their vacated positions; they had moved just in time. Staying well clear of the firing ports and windows on the first floor, knowing that any movement there would trigger a torrent of fire from the TOG infantry, they exited the building to a street that slanted away from the fight. Grold wanted a new firing position, but he had to reach it before the TOG infantry took advantage of his departure.

Barcus froze in mid-stride. Strovasi was calling the platoon back, ordering a withdrawal. He couldn't believe his ears. The optio was ordering a retreat just as they had succeeded in breaching the Renegade lines. He opened his mouth to protest, but closed it without speaking. It was no use arguing with Optio Strovasi, but Barcus knew his commander was taking the plan to press the Renegades without bringing on a general action too literally. Barcus raised his hand to signal the others to fall back. They darted back up the street to the edge of the slope. Fire no longer came from the building, and the attackers' fire was sporadic. Most of the troops had already fallen back; Barcus could see their shapes moving up the scarp.

He gave the signal to head for the crater. As they made their break, the sergeant turned back for one last look. Three shapes emerged from a building down the street he had just left, and sprinted across the alley. He didn't even bother to raise his rifle, shooting a burst from waist level. The three Renegades went down in a clump. He knew his shot wouldn't kill the enemy peds, but he didn't have the time to give them another burst. His own troops safely up the slope, he turned and followed them.

At the breach in the dome he joined the rest of the platoon. The original thirty-three men had been reduced to twenty-five, and three of those were wounded. Signs of the fight, scorched armor, smoking weapons, and empty ammunition carriers, marked every soldier. Only Optio Strovasi was clean. Barcus realized that the optio was the figure who had bolted for the rear when the first grenades exploded.

47

1500, 14 Martius 6831—"I don't understand it," Centurion Moldine Rinter said. "I thought I did, but now I don't. The TOG probes were such weak attacks that we drove them off easily. But their probe at the main breach in the ice pulled back before we could even organize a counterattack."

"You're right," said Centurion Maximus Harras. "They attacked six hours ago in small actions all around the perimeter of the dome, using their standard combat style of hit, wait for the counterattack, then fall back. They were most successful at the main breach we cut, but they pulled out before we got there. The strangest part of the whole situation is that they pulled back penal troops. Penals usually keep coming until they're all dead. I don't know, maybe their commanders don't have the stomach for it anymore."

"That's too much to hope for, Milt. Penals who have no stomach for a fight? I don't believe a word of it."

Milton Harras hobbled away from the situation plot and sank heavily into a chair placed against the inside wall of the command Pedden. He was still having trouble with his feet, burned several days earlier in the ambush that had left his command Liberator destroyed. He lifted his legs and swung his feet onto a second chair. "At the rate they're taking casualties, we might be winning the fight. It's supplies I'm worried about now."

"Reports from the units in contact indicate that at the current rate of expenditure, the peds have enough ammunition for two more days," said Rinter, leafing through a short printout. "Missiles are in very short supply, and so I passed word not to fire unless they're aiming at a painted target at close range, and to try to hit bottom armor. That gives the Vulcan system fewer chances to knock the missiles down before they hit. Our tanks are in reasonable shape."

"Two days? In two days we'll all be gone. At some point the TOGs will refuse to retreat, and we won't be able to make them. We'll have to be prepared for that eventuality." Harras leaned forward to massage his legs. "Tell me about the vehicles again."

"MacDougall has his Wolverine, three Liberators, and a Viper, plus an operational Viper without a turret. We're trying to find a working turret, but even if we do, it'll probably require some heavy lifting equipment to set it in place. Sedden Matruh has two Liberators and three Vipers. He's also got a damaged Liberator with a thrust problem. It moves, but slowly. I've got two Liberators, a Viper, and two Peddens to carry troops. Optio Rand has the headquarters with four Peddens including this one, the comm vehicle, and two for Hess and the medical people." She stared at the deck for a moment, then looked at Harras, as if she were preparing to broach an unpleasant subject.

"Speaking of Hess," she said finally, "I think he'd better move the wounded back into his Peddens. The hospital equipment he can leave in the dens. When we move him, we won't have time to load, so we'll leave the equipment. Given the choice between moving people or stuff, we have to take the people."

"I don't like to think it will come to that."

"Sooner or later, it has to."

Harras sighed. "What is our engineer up to?" he asked. "He's coming and going every time I look up."

"Braxton Sloan is in his element," said Rinter with a smile. "I don't know where he gets the energy. He's got HEAP rounds buried at each breach, and by now he's probably got half the buildings in the city wired for demolition. I'm careful every time I open a door for fear he's trapped it. He's got the heart of an infantryman."

"High praise, coming from you, Moldine."

Rinter blushed. "It's true."

"What? The heart or the praise?"

"Both, I guess."

"Well," mused Harras,"you deserve some praise yourself. You've changed a lot since we got here, and all of it for the better."

"Thank you, sir." Rinter stared at the deck again, unwilling to look her commander in the eye. She wanted to say, "I just try to be like you, Milt," but instead she only said, "I'll pass the word to Hess."

In the TOG command Pompey, Legatus Maximus Olioarchus glanced over the casualty returns, then threw the report in the general direction of the burn basket. Centurion Miles Stratton, the operations officer, stood at rigid attention in front of his commander. "Do you think I'm interested?" sneered Olioarchus. "You have mistaken me for someone who cares about these stinking penals, Centurion. Their only job is to die when I tell them to. The platoons have done exactly as I wanted. Each one has attacked and suffered casualties. When I tell them to attack again, there will be no holding them back."

"Some of them were pretty badly handled, sir," mumbled Stratton.

"I don't care!" shouted Olioarchus. "It doesn't matter what happens to this trash. The only casualty report I want is when a Century has ceased to exist. Until that time, each unit will be assigned a Century's mission. If they can't accomplish the mission, then let them all die! The sooner they get killed, the better for all of us. They're not supposed to make it through a campaign."

Olioarchus watched his operations officer wince under the attack. He smiled to himself; he had achieved the desired effect. Now he would soften his words. "You have not been with the penals long enough, Stratton. You have yet to understand the philosophy behind their existence. These men are scum. They have screwed up, and this is their chance to redeem themselves. You see, New Rome believes that incarcerating trained troops and assigning more trained troops to watch them is a horrible waste of valuable assets. Instead, they organize these criminals into penal units and let them fight their way out of their own pasts. But we don't care if they die. And they know that."

The legatus maximus leaned back in his chair. "We want a small percentage of the penals to survive. It would be very bad for morale if none survived. Otherwise, a penal unit would become nothing but a death sentence, and the troops wouldn't fight at all. We release the few survivors back to the regular units, where they tell stories about the penal Cohorts, and that works as a deterrent to keep others in line. The fact that some survive means that those assigned to a penal unit will fight to live. That's what we want. Now do you understand why I don't care about the casualty reports? They actually have no meaning for me—or for you."

"What are acceptable losses, sir?" asked Stratton.

"A casualty rate around 70 percent is usual, but 80 is still acceptable. Beyond 90 percent, the return on the investment is too small to be worthwhile. So far, our losses here at the pole are close to 50 percent, even including the total loss of Cohort Quintus, which alone accounts for 20 percent."

"What is our policy for losses among the Ssora?"

"We're supposed to keep their losses as low as possible, but personally, I don't care if they all die. I hate those lizards, no matter what headquarters says. They're useful in their own way, but they make my flesh crawl. The penals usually take care of quite a few, especially when the casualty rates get higher. The peds tend to turn on their guards when the fighting gets really fierce. I don't worry about it."

Stratton considered the philosophy of penal combat as explained by his commander. He recognized the value of such a philosophy, and it was common knowledge that serving on command or staff in a Penal Auxilia was a sure path to higher rank. Those officers who could view the troops as mere meat were an asset to the Terran Overlord Government. "When do we schedule the next series of attacks, sir?"

"We'll give the troops another couple of hours to rest and reorganize. We'll attack in force in three hours. What's the status of Cohort Patrius?"

"Better than expected, sir," said Stratton, switching mental gears with the lightning speed of an experienced staff officer. "They have responded quite well to the new command. They have been reorganized into four Centuries plus a platoon, made up of twelve Horatius tanks, seven Romulus carriers, four Aeneas light tanks, two Lupis light carriers, and the antiaircraft Scipio. A little prodding and the example of the penals seems to have inspired their maintenance effort."

Olioarchus smiled at his operations officer. "You see. The penals serve New Rome in many ways before they die."

"We've got to send them out again." Moldine Rinter looked over at Harras, who, like all experienced soldiers, had fallen into a light doze where he sat at the first moment he wasn't needed.

Now he opened his eyes and looked at his operations officer. "I know." He lifted his legs gingerly from the chair to the floor. The pain in his feet showed briefly in his eyes. "Better send them to me so that I can tell them."

Fifteen minutes later, Stone and Ross stood once again before the Cohort Commander. Ross had known as soon as the message to report to the command Pedden arrived that she was going topside again. Her squad was a force of four with her there, barely enough to cover the breadth of the position as long as she deployed in one-man strong points. Not that one man could be considered a strong point. Even the manual said that it took at least two, and was better with three, to make a secure fighting position. With Ross pulled out of the squad, they would be too short-handed to handle the position.

Duty was tearing her apart. She knew that her first responsibility was to the Renegade force as a whole, and that she should willingly accept any assignment her commanding officer chose for her. But she also felt personally responsible for the men in her squad. That sense of responsibility was what made her an effective leader, but now it was making her desperate. She had lost nearly an entire squad on this mission, and she almost couldn't bear to leave her remaining peds to defend a position too large for their numbers, knowing that if she were there, the squad's chances for survival increased dramatically.

She silently cursed Stone, Rinter, and Harras, and reported to the command vehicle.

"The TOGs have been quiet for more than two hours," explained Harras. "We need to know what they're up to. The sensor you placed on your last trip is doing a good job, but we've got to have visual confirmation to make sure they're not sneaking anything past us." The commander looked at his two scouts. Stone was showing some movement in his left arm; the healing was not yet complete, but he had mobility in his fingers and lower arm. Ross looked tired and angry. She obviously wanted to be with her squad, and Harras didn't blame her. "It will be a short look-see, Sergeant," he said to Ross, trying to soften the blow. "Try to understand how valuable you are to us. There's just no one else."

Ross smiled grimly, looking her commander full in the face and letting her frustration show. She nodded.

Rinter addressed the pair. "You'll go up one of the other breaches, not the main one. Go as soon as you're ready."

Stone and Ross knew what they needed, and it took very little preparation. They had been topside so often now that they didn't even make a plan. Ross was in the lead on the way up the gallery. They moved slowly, the TIS in Ross' helmet on full power. When they reached the surface, she reduced the sensor scan to avoid detection by any TOG sentries or instruments focused on the breach. The TIS thermographic sensors reached out three hundred meters and found no sign of activity.

Ross and Stone moved away from the breach. Their mission this time was to see what the TOGs were up to. The terrain offered plenty of avenues through which they could move while still avoiding the enemy, and the rugged ice crags blocked line-of-sight, but the intense cold made the heat of Human movement produce a strong signal. Ross and Stone wrapped themselves in holotarps to reduce their own emissions.

They moved more than five hundred meters away from the breach before they encountered the first TOG emission. To their surprise, it was a vehicle, moving toward them faster than a man could walk. They dropped into a crevice and waited for it to pass. Stone recognized the vehicle as it came abreast of their position; a converted Nisus light recon tank. The Ssoran commander was fully exposed in the command hatch, relaxed and unobservant. Stone had to control his immediate instinct to shoot him with his pistol. The Nisus drifted past.

They were about to move on when the sensors detected more activity. Two more Nisus-S tanks were approaching, and between them was a mass of TOG infantry. The column extended well beyond the range of the sensors. The two scouts crouched lower in the crevice, pulling the holotarps over their heads. Their helmets' sensor plates showed so many images that they lost count, and flipped the plates away from their faces. The first Nisus-S drifted back toward their position, coming to a hover a mere fifty meters away. The Ssoran commander swung one of the antipersonnel lasers toward the column of marching infantry. The men in the column ignored the threat, continuing past the crevice hiding the Renegade legionnaires.

The advancing penal troops came to a halt. Their leaders huddled beside the hovering Nisus-S, then separated again to issue orders. The column broke up and re-formed into its component parts to move toward the breach.

Stone leaned close to Ross, his lips almost touching the side of her helmet. "We're surrounded," he whispered. "We'll have to lie low for a while and wait to move."

Ross nodded. She was thinking about her squad and the other troops they had passed as they left the breach. This TOG force was going to make a big push, and there wasn't enough Renegade infantry to stop them. It would be futile to attempt a commlink message. The dome blocked all but the most powerful transmissions, and attempting to send a warning would only bring the TOG infantry and their Ssoran guards down on an already precarious position. She wriggled further into the crevice, wedging her body tighter against Stone's.

48

1800, 14 Martius 6831—Optio Asinus Strovasi stumbled down the ice gallery below the surface of the south pole toward the breach in the dome. His stomach growled again, protesting the recent lack of the bulk to which it had become accustomed. The Human body required more food in intense cold, and it was becoming more and more difficult to supplement his rations with those of the platoon. The men had begun to hide when they opened the food pouches, and they even consumed them cold rather than risk a heat source that would attract his attention.

Trudging along behind the optio, Platoon Sergeant Lisectus Barcus let the muzzle of his spike rifle center on his leader's back. Sooner or later, he thought, the opportunity would be too good to pass up. Even before assignment to the penal infantry he had considered killing an officer, but his training and experience had stopped him. Strovasi made him consider the option more seriously. But not just yet. The muzzle drifted away again. Not yet.

The leading element of the platoon reached the breach and halted. Barcus moved forward, brushing past the optio, who staggered under the thrust of the platoon sergeant's shoulder. The sergeant hunkered down beside the opening as the ped in front scanned the area. "We've got three targets," he said, continuing to sight his rifle slowly across the structures. "That's all I can find." He turned slightly toward the sergeant. "I'll download to you."

"Hang on. Let's do this manually. That way we won't leak any emissions for the Renegades to pick up." Barcus inserted his helmet's cable into the rear access port on the soldier's combat helmet. A moment later his face plate displayed the acquired information. He watched the images as the ped moved his rifle across the targets. At least one of the targets was probably asleep, judging by the low amount of heat being generated. The others were awake. Another soldier wedged himself in next to the crack in the dome. He connected his combat helmet with the sergeant's. Using the HUD eyeball-parallax capacity in his battle helmet, Barcus designated targets for both men. They would neutralize the two alert targets as the platoon rushed the buildings. Barcus waited until sight designators marked both heat sources and then unhooked from the peds. He raised his arm and signaled the squad leaders behind him to prepare to move.

Optio Strovasi wandered down the corridor toward the platoon sergeant. "Hey, wait for me. I'm in charge." The optio blocked Barcus' view of the squad leaders. "What's going on here?" he demanded, as he reached the three men at the breach. "Who are you shooting at?"

An old joke immediately leaped to Barcus' mind: An off-worlder is walking through

New Rome. The man is dressed in the most outlandish of costumes, colorful, thigh-high boots, wide hat, flowing sleeves, tight pants. Coming toward the man is a senator in a purple-trimmed white toga.

The off-worlder hails the senator and says, "Can y'all tell me whar the forum's at?"

The senator stops dead in his tracks and stares haughtily at this stranger. "Now that you are in New Rome," says the senator in his most pontifical manner, "you must learn not to end a sentence with a preposition. Try it again."

The off-worlder ponders the request for a moment. "Can y'all tell me whar the forum's at, butthole?"

Barcus composed a similar answer to the optio's question in his mind. It made him feel better. "We've got a couple of targets in the Renegade positions," he explained to Strovasi. "I'm going to eliminate two of them and move the platoon forward."

Strovasi peered toward the dark Renegade positions. "I don't see them. Where are they?" The officer stood in the breach, swaying slightly. He reached out to steady himself, pointing his spike pistol into the darkness with his free hand. "Where are they? I'll make the decision about when we fire and who we shoot at."

There it was again, thought Barcus. Butthole.

Strovasi stepped through the breach, positioning himself in front of the three soldiers. He turned to face his men hunkered in the breach. He leaned back through, bracing himself with his hands on either side of the opening. "All right, you people," he bawled at the column crouched against the sides of the passage. "Let's move out!" Strovasi turned back to the city and slipped on the ice. He staggered, arms flailing wildly as he struggled to keep his footing. His bulk carrying him down the slope, his right foot struck a chunk of ice, clipping his leg out from under him. The optio balanced on one foot for an instant, then toppled forward onto his belly. On his second bounce his spike pistol fired, emptying the entire ammunition block into the empty sky above the city.

By the time the optio had bounced clear of the line of fire, the Renegade targets had disappeared. Barcus rose to his feet, signaling the charge by pumping his arm twice over his head. He sprinted through the breach, followed closely by the first two infantrymen and then the squad leaders. Strovasi was cursing wildly and scrabbling to regain his feet. Barcus could hear the trigger on the spike pistol clicking as the officer pulled it back repeatedly. As he passed Strovasi he gave him a vicious kick behind the right knee just above the armored greave. The officer howled in pain. Then Barcus was past him and running down the slope.

A stream of spikes tore at the ice as he ran. Behind him he heard the vicious crack of a grenade exploding against the ice, then he was against the solid masonry wall of a building. He turned to the left to make for the alley that led away from the breach. A body thudded against the wall in front of him, and he pushed the man toward the passage. Together they stumbled forward over the scattered ice and stonework toward the street opening. More troops reached the cover of the wall and moved to join Barcus.

At the mouth of the alley they paused, sweeping the area for heat sources. Nothing. The first man sprinted the six meters across the road to the cover of the adjacent building. At a signal from Barcus, the man across the street stepped out and began to move cautiously along the face of the buildings, mirroring Barcus' movement on the other side. A Liberator tank glowed on the sergeant's HUD, out of range of the spike rifles. The tank fired its main gun, the HEAP round striking the wall just above the other soldier's head. The wall exploded in a shower of fragments that scythed the frigid air and rattled against the building above Barcus as he crouched, seeking cover. When the air cleared the other soldier had vanished.

* * *

Hamilton Hull was glad to be back in a tank. His brief stint as infantry after his tank was destroyed in the first TOG attack after the ambush had not been to his liking. He squinted at the Liberator's DDP and watched images flit like ghosts across the display. He twisted the power knob to bring the diminutive heat sources into better focus. The data display of the Liberator was designed to detect significant ion and heat emissions; the designers had never intended it to detect infantry. The bitter cold of the atmosphere, however, made even the small heat source of a Human stand out, and the DDP had shown the first peds breaking from the protection of the dome. Hull swung the turret slightly to target a large chunk of men, but he knew from a visual recon that they were behind a wall, immune even to the blast of the 150mm cannon. He would wait.

Aktol Graviston, senior sergeant of Cohort Harras, commanded the repaired Liberator. "Blackstone," he murmured into the commlink, "drift a bit to the right. There's an opening directly across the street. Slide into it and hold her there." A grunt came from the rear of the fighting compartment, and the Liberator floated across the street and into the cul-de-sac on the opposite side. The new position opened a wider field of fire for the turret weapons, although the 150mm cannon mounted on the right side of the turret couldn't traverse right any further. The blob of heat began to disperse as the soldiers broke apart and made for new positions. "Hammy," Graviston said to the gunner. "Hit that building with the laser. That'll warm it up so we can see it."

The 5/6 laser on the left side of the turret whined, and the masonry blocks of the building came into sharp focus on the DDP. Behind the thin wedge of light, Hamilton could see three targets huddled together. He slid the cross hairs of the sight onto the corner and waited. The first figure began to move as though pushed forward by the others. It stepped into the street. Hull's fingers closed on the trigger, but he released the pressure and waited for the others.

"You've got a target, Ham." Graviston's statement sounded more like a question.

"I'm waiting for the rest to join him."

"Right. Get the whole bunch," came the reply.

The others peered around the corner as the first target staggered across the street and into the shelter of the building opposite. "Load HEAP," came the order from Graviston. "Shoot for the center of the mass."

Hull flicked the ammunition index from APDS to HEAP, heard the autoloader whir in the breech of the 150mm cannon. The green light came on above the correct ammunition indicator. "Loaded."

"At my command," said Graviston. The targets began to move into the open. "Fire!"

The muzzle flash of the cannon filled the street with brilliant light, showing the shattered sides of the buildings in sharp relief, and then the HEAP round struck in the center of the street a block away. The two figures were caught for a moment in a glowing sphere, then the street went dark again and the DDP showed one figure running away.

"Friendly infantry withdrawing on our left," said Graviston. The paint warning klaxon howled through the Liberator's turret. "Blackie, prepare to back up."

"Roger, chief. At your command."

There was a moment's pause as Aktol Graviston watched the friendly peds scurry across an alley to his left rear, gaining their fallback position. He watched the DDP fill with enemy targets as infantry filtered down into the city from the breach in the dome. This was no probing attack. The TOGs were coming in Century-force at least, and it looked more like a full Cohort had been committed. The DDP was also showing vehicles moving beyond the opening in the dome, but they were still out of targeting range. He couldn't wait much longer. A TVLG arced across the blackness toward the tank, and the Vulcan antimissile system swatted it from the sky.

"You got the demo harmonics on your sight?" Graviston asked Hull.

"All ready to blow," replied the gunner.

"When I give the word, it all goes together. Blackie, you back up as fast as you can. Ham, you hit the demo. I'll fire smoke. Ready?" The two crewmen acknowledged. Another TVLG flamed across the sky to impact with a shattering crash on the street beside the tank. "Now!"

The tank lurched clear of the alley, tearing away part of the building behind it. Graviston waited for Hull to activate the harmonic detonators that would fuse the demolition charges at the end of the street before he fired his smoke charge. The buildings that sheltered the entrance to the avenue shook at the force of the explosions. Graviston felt a brief flash of regret at the destruction of so much history, but as Harras had pointed out when they first retreated under the ice, either the city or the men would survive. There was no room for sentimentality in war. The ancient structures shattered into chunks of masonry outlined against the brilliant whiteness of the ice beyond. Then the smoke obscured the road and the tank was backing away.

"They've broken in at Breach Three." Rinter was intent on the plot. "Reports say it looks like a Century-plus push." She pointed to the widening red circle at the breach. "They're coming in at Five as well, in about the same strength."

Milton Harras looked over her shoulder at the plot. "Better send one of the Peddens to Three. Tell them to deploy in the supplementary positions along phase-line NAVIS. We'll try to hold them there. Alert the other Pedden for possible use at Five."

"What if we can't hold them?" asked Rinter.

"Let's not worry about 'what if' right now. If they get across NAVIS we'll have to commit Rand's people."

Moldine spoke into the commlink, then reported to her commander. "Pedden One on the way. Sergeant Gareth Tavell, my operations sergeant, has the command."

"He's a good man," said Harras, patting Rinter's shoulder. "He's done this before." The concussion of a demolition charge shook the command Pedden. The plot went blank momentarily and then appeared again. "There goes one of Braxton's little surprises. Too bad we have nothing for an encore."

Stone and Ross wriggled deeper and deeper into the crevice that hid them from the TOGs. At last, their slow, painful movement into the icy grip of the fissure brought them clear. They were separated from the deploying penal infantry by a narrow ridge of ice. Stone pointed toward another outcropping, and the two figures crawled toward it. Once in the shelter of the ice, Stone leaned toward Ross. "I've got an intruder on my display," he whispered. "He might see us, so get ready to run." He indicated a more distant ridge. "You go left. I'll go right. We'll meet behind that one." Ross nodded.

She looked at Stone, but the officer was concentrating on the approaching enemy soldier. Fear twisted in her stomach. It was bad enough being on the surface with only one other friendly, but to strike out alone...she suddenly longed for the claustrophobic cocoons of an infantry carrier.

"They've seen us!" shouted Stone. "Run! Run!"

Ross didn't look back. In one motion she was up and tearing through the dark toward the sanctuary of the next ridge. The flash of rifle fire lit the ice. Spikes cracked past her shoulder. There was the shattering explosion of multiple grenades. Then she was over the ridge in the blackness, her breath rasping from her lungs. She waited, her rifle sighted on the top of the ridge. Nothing happened.

She crawled cautiously back to the lip of the ice. The terrain swept down and away, empty of light and movement. She lowered the face plate on her helmet and activated the BLS. There were no living targets within three hundred meters. Stone and the penals had ceased to exist.

49

0010, 15 Martius 6831—Optio Karstil watched the indicators on his display panel. The almost-Manus of tanks had screamed toward the south pole at 900 kph for hours at the ten-kilometer maximum altitude. Now he waited for the "boost" command to fire the specially designed acceleration pods that would lift the vehicles of the 2567th Renegade relief force past the tanks' design envelope. The accelerators would throw the formation through the tanks' theoretical barrier of altitude and speed to a height of twelve kilometers above the planet. They wouldn't be able to maintain that height, but their trajectory would push the formation to the rendezvous with the additional reinforcements the *Caelestis* was dropping to meet them. Having gathered all the vehicles assigned to his command, Prefect Kenderson would nose over and head for the pole.

"Firing sequence initiated," came the words over the commlink. Karstil sealed the fighting compartment. His DDP accepted the downloaded commands from the control vehicle, the numbers scrolling backward as the time for firing grew closer. Though he'd braced himself against the thrust, the blast from the additional pods still came as a surprise, pressing him back against the command chair. The Liberator's DDP flashed through the ten, eleven, and twelve-kilometer altitude readings. The rate-of-climb and velocity indicators pegged.

Karstil looked up through the carplexy bubble. He knew that the transport, at ninety kilometers, would be well beyond visual range. Even a vessel as large as an intergalactic transport would be only an infinitesimally small dot in the vastness of space. Looking out was pure reflex. He felt the top of the acceleration arc as his butt came free of the chair. The shoulder and lap straps restrained him, and he opened the command frequency to listen to the link-up.

"Mambo Distaff Four. This is Mambo Distaff Six. Commlink check." Kenderson called the reinforcements and waited for a reply. The commlink remained silent. "Mambo Distaff Four. This is Mambo Distaff Six. Commlink check." Kenderson repeated the call, and again there was no reply. "Mambo Distaff Four. This is Mambo Distaff Six. Commlink check." Karstil could hear the frustration in Kenderson's voice.

Karstil glanced at the instruments. The rate of climb was at zero. The command was drifting at fifteen kilometers, but they wouldn't be able to hold this altitude for long. "Mambo Distaff Four. This is Mambo Distaff Six. Commlink check." The commlink channel crackled softly. Someone was trying to reach them, but either the range was too great or the power of the other station was too low. He couldn't hear the message. Rate of climb became a negative number. The command began falling toward the planet.

*　*　*

The Commonwealth transport *Caelestis* drifted through rational space. The skipper of the transport was satisfied with his navigation of what had turned out to be a complicated set of orders. The transport was headed directly toward the center of Rolandrin, just as the NAVCOM had been programmed. He was well above the ninety-kilometer altitude required for a successful drop, which would give him plenty of time to jockey the ship into the correct position for the rendezvous. The sensor display showed a flock of protective fighters rising to meet the ship. He settled into the command chair to watch the drop. Warning sirens suddenly screamed.

"*Lancea* light fighters approaching, sir," the weapons officer reported in a steady voice.

"*Lancea*s? Those are TOG fighters! What are *Lancea*s doing over Rolandrin?" The skipper spun to face his navigator. "Confirm our location, Nav."

"Message from Mambo Distaff, sir," interrupted the commlink operator. "They're trying to contact us."

"We're in the wrong place, sir," said the navigator. "That pause at the last turn threw off the calculations. That's not Rolandrin, sir. That's Malthus."

"*Lancea* fighters closing. In range in three-zero seconds."

"What shall I tell Mambo Distaff, sir?"

"Shall I reset the NAVCOM with the correct coordinates, sir?"

"What in the name of all that's holy are we doing over the TOG base, Nav?" the skipper shouted.

"As I said, sir, the computer was off by fifteen thousand kilometers."

"Well, Nav, get us out of here. Comm, tell Mambo Distaff we'll be late. Tell him to wait for us."

"*Lancea* fighters closing. In range in one-five seconds."

"Message sent on short-range commlink."

"Coordinates reset, sir."

"Short-range won't reach them, Comm. We're too far away. Use long range, high power."

"Resetting commlink, sir."

"Exiting rational space." The blackness of space went milky white as the transport shifted to faster-than-light drive.

"Message sent, sir."

"I'm afraid you're too late, Comm. We were already in tachyon space when you sent." The skipper turned to the navigator. "How soon will we make the rendezvous?"

"We have to make a turn to avoid going straight through TOG-occupied space, so it will take a couple of hours."

"I hope Kenderson's force waits for us." The *Caelestis* slipped back into rational space to make the course adjustment.

"Mambo Distaff, Mambo Distaff. This is Mambo Distaff Six. Pushing over now. Follow your leaders. We're going down."

The horizon of Caralis appeared between the forward arms of the Liberator as the tank nosed over toward the surface. The velocity indicator was still pegged, and so Karstil knew they were going fast, just not how fast. The polar ice cap was just visible along the edge of the planet. "Keep the angle-of-attack indicator as low as possible," he reminded his driver. "You ever made a drop before?"

"In practice, sir," came the reply from the driver's station. "Actually, sir," he added, "it was only on the simulator." The voice sounded nervous.

"No sweat. Just follow Centurion Kane. Do everything he does. Let yourself feel the tank. This Liberator is pretty smart and it won't screw you over. I've done this before."

"You bet." There was a pause. "I'll be fine. Thanks, sir."

The Renegade formation, a giant sheet of scattered vehicles, curled away from space and pointed toward the surface. Karstil could see the many vehicles spread around him, reflecting sunlight from their polished hulls that sparkled against the blackness of the void beyond. He looked back over his shoulder, searching again for the missing transport and the reinforcements they had been promised. Remembering his last dive for the south pole, he felt a deep dread clutch at his stomach. Like the mission Freund had aborted at the last moment, this one too had all the earmarks of a disaster. At least this time, he thought, there would be no turning back. Kenderson would take them all in, no matter what.

Karstil watched the edge of the polar cap steady just below the forward hull. At this angle of approach, the formation would skim the edge of the ice at tree-top level. The velocity indicator was still pegged at maximum; the formation was moving at something over 900 kph. He wondered if the command tank's instrumentation showed just how fast they were really going. Karstil figured as long as someone knew, they would be all right.

Sergeant Barcus glanced around the inside of the hutch. The small dens that honeycombed the walls were superb fighting positions. He didn't understand why the Renegades had abandoned them so quickly. The demolition of the buildings on the edge of the city had been a nasty surprise, but nothing he wasn't expecting. Now they waited while Century command planned the next stage of the assault. The three platoons of the Century were roughly on line, and the other Centuries of the Cohort were deploying in the cleared zone.

Barcus listened as Centurion Frankreich Setuon, commander of the Third Century, sketched out the plan. The platoons were to attack straight through their own sectors, eliminating Renegade positions as they encountered them. Vehicles were to be destroyed by TVLGs and light weapons would take care of the infantry. Each squad was issued a breaching charge to break into buildings, but the charges were not to be used unless it was absolutely necessary. Platoons were free to maneuver across their own one-hundred-meter zones, but they were not to cross into adjacent sectors. In Strovasi's absence, Barcus would lead the Second Platoon. The sergeant hadn't seen his commanding officer since the opening moments of the assault.

The platoon he returned to was smaller than the one he had led through the breach in the dome. Fifteen men huddled together in a den, munching on combat rations. A thermotablet in the center of the room gave off limited warmth that only several men at a time could enjoy. The soldiers rotated from the edges of the room to the center, each man soaking up as much heat as he could in the time allotted. The Ssoran guard was not invited to participate. The men looked up expectantly as the sergeant entered.

Barcus described the sketchy attack plan. It was nothing special, and all the peds had been well trained in the execution of urban combat. Penal Auxilia were used almost exclusively for fighting in built-up areas, and their training reflected that mission. Urban fighting was different from battles on open land. The theories of observation and fields of fire remained the same, but the troops also had to deal with elevated positions and limited ranges. Urban combat was a war of full-automatic fire and hand grenades, of peds operating in two- and three-man teams, cleaning out enemy strong points one at a time. It was a slow, deadly process.

Parallel streets marked the platoon boundaries as they moved from building to building. Each squad moved down its own avenue, on line with the other squads. Thermal imaging in the combat helmets kept them in contact, and the TIS in Barcus' helmet showed him enemy positions. The thermal sensors in the regular infantry helmets could be confused by non-Human heat sources, fooling the peds into engaging the wrong targets. It was Barcus' job to control their fire.

The three streets ended in an open plaza that stretched further than they could see. The plaza could be traversed, but they needed covering fire on the Renegade positions beyond. He began to give the orders to deploy two squads to provide cover while the other squad crossed. He was aware of someone coming up on him from behind. He turned to see Optio Asinus Strovasi lumber up to the platoon command.

"What's the holdup, Sergeant?" puffed the optio. "You should be proceeding as quickly as possible."

"I'm deploying First and Third squads to give covering fire, sir. As soon as they're in place, we'll cross."

"Nonsense, Sergeant," said the optio, pushing forward to the opening in the building. "Tell the men to cross at once."

"Sir, they'll need covering fire."

"Are you questioning my orders? My authority?" He glanced pointedly toward the Ssoran who had followed the optio. "We'll see about that, Sergeant. You take this squad across. Now."

Barcus looked at Strovasi and the Ssoran. The lizard-man's long, narrow tongue flickered in and out in anticipation of the pleasure of disciplining one of his prisoners. Barcus knew he could kill one or the other of them, but he wouldn't be able to get both. And then someone else would lead the squad. He turned to the opening in the wall. "Follow me!" he shouted, and dashed through the hole. The rest of his squad followed.

Barcus was running for his life. He was halfway across the plaza, beginning to hope he might make it. Then the defending Renegades opened fire with a crash of spike rifles, concentrated streams of plastic death raining down from four different directions onto the scurrying men. Spikes ricocheted off the frozen ground, kicking up shards of ice and pavement. A stone monument loomed out of the darkness in front of him, and Barcus dove behind it. He looked back for the others to direct them to the temporary cover.

The rest of the assault force was down, some of them writhing in pain, the others lying still. The TIS in his helmet told him the story. Of the six men who had followed, four were dead, and the others were dying. This group would not make the assault. Spikes began to chip at the stonework around him.

The commlink in the helmet spoke into his ear. "Return to my position," said the voice of the optio. "Your attack has not succeeded. I want you back here." Barcus cursed silently, his jaw clenched in hatred. "Sergeant," came the insistent voice, "return to my location."

Barcus gathered himself to make the dash. He sprang from his sanctuary with his back to the Renegade positions and ran for all he was worth. He leaped over the bodies of the dead squad members. One man reached for him as if to ask for help, but the sergeant evaded the outstretched arm and kept going. His movement caught the Renegades by surprise. They belatedly fired at Barcus, but none of the deadly spikes hit, instead striking the ice behind him as he ran. He crashed, breathless, through the opening and fell at the optio's feet.

"Squad Two, move to the right, beyond the edge of the plaza," said the optio. He was speaking into the commlink, and Barcus could barely make out his own words through the buzz in his ears.

"Sir. That's out of our area. We're not allowed to operate out of our area."

"Nonsense. They'll do like I say. Anyway, we know where the enemy's at."

The other squad paused, then Barcus heard them acknowledge the order. He crawled to the opening in the wall to watch the darkness to his right. The BLS showed the moving squad. He saw them cross the platoon's boundary limit. He held his breath. This might just work. The squad was well beyond the arc of fire of the defending Renegades. Then three AP lasers opened on the squad from behind. The first casualties burst into steam under the impact of the aligned light. The others stood, too surprised to advance or retreat, transfixed by this unexpected attack from the rear. The AP lasers cut them down where they stood. The BLS showed no life in that area.

The platoon sergeant turned toward his commanding officer. Strovasi shrugged. "Well, bad luck," said the optio. "I'll return to Century to get reinforcements." He turned his broad back on the prone sergeant. Barcus lifted his spike rifle, but he saw the Ssoran guard still standing in the shadows, his great eyes mere slits. The platoon sergeant stood and joined the remains of his platoon.

50

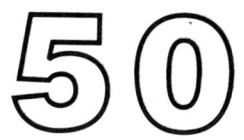

6066, 15 Martius 6831—Task Force Kenderson swept downward toward the south pole of Caralis. Having failed to make contact with the reinforcements from the transport, they still lacked Manus strength. The DDPs of the lead tanks blossomed with indicators of TOG equipment fifty kilometers below. The force had slowed to 600 kph, and it would be a good five minutes before they could engage. The lead vehicles applied negative thrust, trying to slow themselves to a more reasonable 240 kph before they got too close to the surface. The force began to spread out into combat formation, Kane's Century fanning to the right as it approached the enemy. Karstil kept his Second Platoon well to the left, according to the original plan. His platoon was in a loose wedge with Karstil in the center, the platoon sergeant flying his left wing, and Tank Three on the right. He tried to remember the names of the other two tank commanders, but only the image of Lucifer K. Mullins, his first platoon sergeant, appeared in his mind. He wondered where the old guy was today.

"Scipio antiaircraft vehicle. Range four-nine-zero-double-zero. Bearing two-zero-zero. Scipio is stationary and scanning this formation. Scipio has not locked." The familiar, disembodied voice of the computer sounded in his ear. The same female voice always spoke as the computer, and Karstil sometimes fantasized about the designer's wonderful friend who had given her voice patterns for the system. Karstil always thought that someday he'd like to meet that woman, but also wondered whether he'd be disappointed.

"Multiple Horatius tanks, Romulus carriers. Range four-nine-zero-double-zero. Bearing two-zero-zero. Vehicles are stationary and scanning. All vehicles beyond range of sensor lock." The voice in the DDP spoke again.

"Scipio has locked onto Liberator seven-three-two. Scipio has launched two Scanner Silhouette-Seeking missiles." The target wasn't in Karstil's Century. He glanced to his left. Somewhere out there, a Liberator was about to take a pair of hits from two heavy missiles. The SSS missiles blew huge holes in whatever they hit, and Karstil was glad that he wasn't the target. A brilliant flash lit the dark sky to the left.

"Multiple Horatius tanks, Romulus carriers. Range three-five-zero-double-zero. Bearing two-zero-zero. Vehicles are stationary and scanning. All vehicles beyond range of sensor lock."

The attack force was still moving at a speed too great to drop down to the surface. Their first pass over the enemy location would be at tree-top flight or higher, or Kenderson would have to turn the formation away to lose speed. Karstil was well aware, however, that turning a formation better than six kilometers wide was out of the question. A well-trained force, operating under parade-ground conditions and moving at low speed might consider it, but Kenderson would not. Task Force Kenderson would enter the battle with its fragile bottom armor exposed. Their only advantage was that they outnumbered the TOGs by at least three to one.

The underside of the dome was constantly illuminated by the explosions around the perimeter of the fighting. Even in the command Pedden the flashes of light provided more visibility than the battle lanterns. "Tell Hess to move the wounded," Harras said aloud. When no one responded, he realized that he was alone in the Pedden. Rinter had gone to command her dwindling Century, and all the loose headquarters troops had been deployed under Rand and Sloan. He picked up the commlink and gave the doctor his orders. There was no argument. Hess had anticipated the command and loaded the casualties. The hospital vehicles moved toward the currently unengaged breach the Renegade forces had cut for an entrance to the buried city what seemed like ages ago.

Harras watched the plot. The TOG penal infantry was making progress at both assault points. They had committed at least a Cohort at each breach, and the depleted Renegade Centuries could not hold them back. Slow them, yes; inflict casualties, yes; but the numbers favored the TOGs. The Ssoran police Nisus-S vehicles were coming closer, some of them driving their own infantry ahead with antipersonnel lasers. Harras moved to the door in time to see a glowing Liberator limp past the command post. The turret had been pounded down to nothing and the cannon on the right and left side dangled from shattered mounts. Grav coils scraped on the roadway, sending up showers of sparks from the frozen surface. Spikes struck the wall behind Harras. It was almost time to go.

Moldine Rinter staggered to the door of the command vehicle. Her light combat helmet had been shattered by multiple spike hits and hung down her back, connected only by the chin strap. Her hair was matted with blood, and great streaks of it covered her face. "They're close, Milt," she gasped. "They've broken through all around. We'll have to pull back to another position."

Harras helped the wounded officer into the command post, pressed her into a chair, and tried to wipe her face with his handkerchief. "I'm moving the command post now." He spoke into the internal commlink, ordering the driver to move the Pedden. There was no response. He repeated his order. When nothing happened, he realized there was no driver. He too had been sent into the fight. Harras opened the doors to the driving station and climbed into the chair. It had been a long time since he had driven a bus like this, but it was a skill once learned, never forgotten. He activated the grav drive and felt the Pedden rise to a one-meter hover. He let the vehicle drift toward the breach.

Tachyon space dissolved into rational space as the Commonwealth transport *Caelestis* reappeared above Caralis. The skipper turned to his navigator. "We got it right this time, Nav?"

"On target, sir. Right on target. That's Rolandrin below and behind. The polar cap is ahead."

"Right. Where's this Kenderson guy who's supposed to meet us?"

"No contact, sir. He should be right below us."

"Another screw-up. Scan to the limits of the horizon. Use full power."

"Scanning now, sir." There was a pause while the sensors searched for the Renegade vehicles. "Nothing, sir. A momentary reading at the edge of the southern horizon, but it vanished immediately. No time to lock onto it for recognition or communication."

"Comm. Notify Alabaster of the situation. Request instructions."

Far below the command bridge in the depths of the hold, Mullins felt the transport make another transition to rational space. He never quite got used to the stomach-flutter that always came with the change. He knew what the change meant, and he was ready and raring to go. The outer and inner doors would open to reveal black space. Then the transport would tip down to allow the tanks to slip away. He had felt three re-entry lurches that the ship shouldn't have made, but the skipper had come on the horn and explained them away as quick maneuvers to avoid TOG interceptors. The announcement that they were on target over the correct coordinates had been greeted with a derisive howl from the crammed cargo deck.

"Driver," said Mullins into the internal commlink, "fire up this beast and get ready to move."

"Roger. Have we gotten the word to drop?"

"No. But I want to be ready when the time comes." Mullins checked the DDP and saw the other two tanks in his provisional platoon fire their grav drives. His tanks were ready to move. His own Liberator was almost up against the inner doors of the cargo bay. As soon as the doors opened, he would be on his way.

"Bashful Laundry Two-two-six. This is Bashful Laundry Two-six. Have you received notification of launch?"

"Laundry Two-two-six. Negative. Just getting ready." Mullins wondered if the commanding centurion accepted his explanation. He decided he didn't care. The frustration of waiting and the almost-certainty that this mission was a screw-up were gone. Now Mullins felt the familiar, welcome anticipation of combat. He was ready to get on with it.

"Bashful Laundry cleared for departure. Open outer doors."

Mullins felt the pressure in the cargo bay drop slightly. The seals on the Liberator popped as they inflated against the turret. He dropped the carplexy dome over the command hatch. Because they were in the upper atmosphere he'd have to control the tank from the DDP, but, like all tank commanders, he preferred to be able to look out if he wanted. Closed tanks seemed claustrophobic.

On the bridge the skipper looked up in surprise. "Say again, Comm."

"Alabaster says that Kenderson couldn't hold orbit to wait for us and went ahead to the pole. They said to use your own judgment about the drop."

"Well, fine. How am I supposed to know what's going on? I don't even know if this Kenderson force is still alive." He struck the console in front of him with his fist. "I refuse to launch people into an unknown situation." He turned to his navigator. "Lay a course for Alabaster. We'll push them out there. Comm, notify the Renegades below that we've canceled the launch, and let Alabaster know we're on our way."

Those on the cargo deck noticed the slight turn of the transport. Mullins watched the doors, waiting for them to open. "Bashful Laundry. This is Mother Hen. There's been a change in plans—again. It seems that the other force is not at the rendezvous. They've been and gone. We've decided to cancel the drop and put you down over Alabaster."

Mullins stared at the doors; they were not going to open. He made a snap decision. *He wasn't going to abort the drop and leave those other Renegades stranded.* "In a pig's eye we will," he muttered into the commlink. "In a pig's eye."

"What was that you said, Sarge?" inquired the driver.

"Never mind. Gunner, load HEAP."

"Say again, Sarge?"

"Gunner. Load HEAP. Releasing hold-downs now." From inside the turret Mullins could hear the gunner index HEAP on the ballistic computer. The ammunition-selection drum whirred and stopped. The Liberator began to drift slightly as the hold-down clamps released it from the deck.

"Gunner. Target cargo door. Range five-zero. Fire HEAP."

The turret swung slightly to the left as the 150mm cannon lined up on the center of the port-side cargo door. "Identified," said the gunner. Mullins heard the excitement in his voice.

"Fire!"

"On the way." The roar of the main gun was deafening in the enclosed cargo bay. The shot and the impact of the 150mm shell against the titanium door were virtually simultaneous. "Target," announced the gunner, notifying Mullins that he had hit the intended target.

"Shift ten mils left," responded Mullins. "Target door. Range five-zero. Fire HEAP." The turret moved again. "Identified."

"Fire."

"On the way." Again the cargo bay filled with the roar of the twin explosions.

"Laundry Two-two-six! This is Two-six. Have you gone completely out of your mind?"

"Negative, Two-six. I know exactly what I'm doing. Break. Laundry Two-two. This is Laundry Two-two-six. We're heading out. Release and follow me." Mullins waited several seconds for the smoke to thin and the debris to drift clear of the shattered door. "Driver. Take us outta here."

"With you all the way, Sarge." The 273-ton Liberator surged forward as the driver applied maximum thrust. The HEAP rounds had created a gaping hole in the doors, and the tank crashed through the opening, widening the gap. Glowing bits of titanium crumbled away as the tank's wedge profile sliced through. Mullins felt the upper edge of the broken door crack against the carplexy dome. The dome crazed into a tiny spider-web of cracks that hissed slightly as the tank lost pressure to the near-void of space.

Then the Liberator was over the brow of the loading ramp and into blackness. Mullins felt the tank tip forward as it began its fall to the surface. He looked back over his shoulder for the rest of his platoon, but the shattered carplexy dome made it hard to distinguish objects. He was tempted to blow the dome free, but the certainty of rapid depressurization at an altitude of ninety kilometers stopped him. He glanced at the DDP. He was making the journey alone.

The Liberator accelerated as it fell. Mullins alternated between watching the artificial horizon and the angle-of-attack indicator. Without a visual fix he would have to take the vehicle in on instruments alone. That wasn't an impossible task, just a more difficult one. The velocity meter slipped past 240 kph, and still the driver was applying thrust. "Take it easy," said Mullins over the intercom. "We'll get there fast enough."

"Bashful Laundry Two-two-six. This is Bashful Laundry Two-two-one. Have cleared the cargo doors. Am following you down. Boy, did you leave a mess back there."

Mullins checked the DDP. A kilometer behind him was the blue square of another Liberator, and behind that, another, and another, and another. He wasn't going to make the drop alone after all. Disorganized, yes, but not alone.

51

0700, 15 Martius 6831—Honor Ross crouched against the icy outcropping hiding her from the TOG tanks on the surface of the pole. The grav-drive screams of the incoming Renegade tanks filled the atmosphere with almost-tangible noise that even the systems in her helmet could not blot out. The formation swept overhead, spread out from horizon to horizon. They were flying too high and moving too fast to make the surface, but there were a lot of them. The TOG vehicles began to fire.

An antiaircraft mount took the first shots, missiles whooshing away into the dark sky with tails of fire. The missiles blossomed in fiery flowers of red and gold. Many vehicles survived the attack, others responded with giant flowers of their own, spewing glowing bits of armor and internal systems that twinkled and went out. As the Renegade tanks got closer and range decreased, the TOG grav tanks joined the battle. The ground around Ross quivered under the recoil of heavy guns. More Renegade tanks were hit, their path across the void marked by trails of flame.

She was surprised by how close she was to the TOG vehicles. Her thermal sensors had not detected them, but they marked their positions as they fired. She rose from the snow, trying to think what she should do. She moved toward the TOG vehicles, not sure what to do when she reached them, but wanting desperately to do something, anything to help her own troops.

The TOG vehicles described a rough half-circle, their bows pointed inward as if expecting an attack from the center. Ross crept easily and swiftly through the cordon; the enemy was too busy with the threat from above to deal with a single figure on the surface. Still without a plan, she reached the middle of the formation and saw a gaping hole in the ice. Debris littered its rim, and it was lit by the continuous flashes of the weapons on the tanks that surrounded it. The sky and surface seemed to glow a terrifying red as gunfire and burning vehicles mixed their light. She stared uncomprehending at the opening for an instant before she recognized it as the bolt-hole through which the original Renegade force had escaped. The aspect of the terrain was changed almost beyond recognition, but she saw the wreck of their Spartius carrier frozen into the ice. She darted toward it and crouched beside its shattered turret. The TOGs right beside her continued to fire at the sky.

Harras watched the plot on the table change moment by moment. The red lines indicating TOG activity crept across the grid of the city. The commlink chattered constantly as reports of ground lost and requests for reinforcements flashed across the ether. The access doors on the side of the Pedden stood open, and the rising cacophony of combat reverberated through the interior.

The TOG penal infantry advanced, compressing the defending lines. Harras pulled MacDougall's command from the lines to establish yet another fallback position. The tank Centuries were in remarkably good shape, considering the intensity of combat. The Renegades were giving up territory in order to maintain enough troops to continue fighting, inflicting casualties on the attackers without taking significant losses. Once the penal infantry had driven into Renegade lines, but a short, fierce counterattack had re-established the position. But the Renegades were losing ground and the battle because there weren't enough people on the firing line to prevent infiltration. Each time the TOGs found a break or soft spot, they poured their infantry through the hole. Their line compromised, the Renegades had to counterattack or fall back, and thus far, they had opted to fall back.

A shadow fell over the plotting table, and Harras glanced up to see Jamie MacDougall filling the entrance to the Pedden. "Come in and sit a spell, Jamie," said Harras. "You look as though you could do with a sit-down."

MacDougall smiled at his commander. He marveled once again at the way Harras was able to make a person feel as if he were the most important thing in the commander's life at the moment. This ability couldn't be quantified as a leadership trait. It probably stemmed from the simple fact that Harras really did like and care about his subordinates. The centurion stepped into the Pedden and flopped down in the proffered chair. "I can use your sit-down, Milt. You probably need one too."

Harras flashed a tired grin. "Don't we all. What's the story on the new line?"

MacDougall leaned on the plotting board. "I've got tanks here and here," he said, pointing to the map. "My reserve, a single Lib, is back here. The infantry are deployed around the tanks for protection. We really need more ground troops. This killing peds with HEAP rounds is for the birds."

"Not efficient, I know. But it's all we've got." Harras considered the locations MacDougall had shown him. They were good positions, but woefully inadequate for covering all the ground in between. Retreating Centuries would fill some of the spaces as they dropped back, but there was just too much area to cover with the troops available. "If they bring any heavy stuff down here, we're in deep trouble."

MacDougall pointed to the main breach. "There's no activity here, Milt. Could it be that they've pulled away to apply pressure at the other openings? They could be really thin up there."

"I've been thinking about that, too. If they've sent all their strength down here, we might be able to reach the surface with very little opposition. Some of the vehicles might be able to break out."

MacDougall rubbed his shoulder in a spot where a spike had glanced off his body armor. From the way the muscle hurt, he figured he must have a huge bruise there, but he hadn't bothered to report it to Hess or anyone else. "What do we know about the conditions topside?"

"I sent a patrol up a few hours ago to spot a passive sensor. It was showing limited activity, but it's gone dead. The patrol went back out just before this push started, but they haven't reported back. They were good people—I hope they're all right."

Harras stared at the plot. The red indicators of the penal lines continued to crawl forward. Blue indicators pulled back toward the new lines established by MacDougall's Century. "We can't take much more, Jamie. There's just nowhere else to go down here."

"The surface, sir. I say break out."

"It's the only way." Harras pointed at several locations on the map in quick succession.

"I'll contact Matruh and tell him to take command of the lines you've set, as well as these two tanks and the infantry. You take your Wolverine and this tank, and I'll give you a Pedden from Rand's command. Get topside and set up. Keep me informed."

MacDougall rose from his chair. "No sooner said than done."

Harras turned and spoke into the commlink, ordering the plan into operation. He was relieved that the decision had finally been made. The inexorable advance of the penal infantry had pushed the Cohort about as far as it could be pushed. Something had to break. When he looked back, MacDougall was gone. Seconds later he heard the whine of grav drives as the Wolverine and Liberator headed for the exit.

Ross felt, more than heard, the high whine of a grav drive under her feet. She looked down, half-expecting to see a tank burst from the ice. Then she realized that the sound was someone coming up from the city below. A moment later a Wolverine emerged from the hole, tentatively poking its nose above the surface. For an instant it looked like its namesake, sniffing the air from the safety of its den for signs of its enemies. Ross watched as it crept over the lip, followed almost immediately by a Liberator.

The sky above her continued to flash with combat. The relief force had finally reached the altitude level of normal flight, leaving wrecked tanks scattered and burning over the entire circumference of their arrival. Now they were down, and had fully engaged the TOG defenders.

The approach and landing had been easier than expected. With the TOG Horatius tanks dug into craters for defense, they had been unable to elevate their main guns far enough to fire at the tanks overhead. That disadvantage disappeared once the attackers hit the surface and the TOGs could bring their 150mm cannon into play. The crash of the heavy guns and the ripping crack of the lasers reverberated among the ice crags like a concert of demonic timpani. The Wolverine stopped abruptly, as if stunned by the violence it saw.

Ross abandoned the cover of the Spartius and sprinted toward the Renegade recon tank. The turret swung toward her, the muzzle of the antipersonnel laser looming large as a trash can. She stopped, raising her hands above her head. The tank commander pointed at her and waved her forward. She moved to the front of the tank and climbed the scramble rails on the upper glacis. The tank commander never took the laser off her, and she was careful to keep her hands away from the holster on her hip. "Ross. Sergeant Honor Ross," she said. "I was on patrol from the city. Harras sent me."

MacDougall eyed her doubtfully. "Is this the whole patrol?"

"All that's left. Stone was with me, but we got separated. I think he's dead."

"Okay. What's going on up here? My sensors are going crazy."

"It's a relief force, I think," Ross rushed to explain, tripping over the words as she spoke. "They probably don't know where we are, or even if there are any of us left. We need to broadcast a message on a clear channel letting these guys know that we're here and what we've got planned. And tell Harras what's happening."

MacDougall switched the commlink to broad channel, high power, and began to send an identifying signal to the incoming force. Once the transmission was established, he clicked to automatic so that the signal would act as a beacon. Then he updated Harras on the surface situation, mentioning Ross in his report. When MacDougall turned to get more information from the sergeant, she had already scrambled down the front of the tank and darted away.

The news from the surface filled Harras with hope, but that feeling was offset by the disaster imminent below. The penal infantry had broken through the new defensive line easily, infiltrating the strong point manned by exhausted Renegade tankers and peds. The fighting had come too close to wait any longer. The wounded would have to move soon if they were to move at all. He picked up the commlink and gave new orders to Hess. The doctor simply acknowledged and began to move toward the breach.

Grold, Grain, and Tscholmankia huddled together for mutual support and warmth. Grain munched on the last of his rations, his knees pulled up against his chest, the tattered remnants of a thermocloak wrapped tightly around him. Tscholmankia fingered his spike rifle, carefully placing extra ammunition blocks on the sill beside his fighting position. Grold watched both men, his eyes threatening to blur from exhaustion.

"They're coming," Tscholmankia reported in a flat, even voice. The excitement he had felt in the earlier combat had passed. Now he felt nothing, his mind holding only the thought of doing it again, his emotions worn to the nub. "Are we gonna pull back again?" He still spoke with the flat edge in his voice.

Grold moved to his own firing position. The penal infantry were working their way down the street, ducking into the buildings as they advanced. He answered the question. "We'll do as we're told. I'm not going to die for a position we don't need."

Tscholmankia loaded an ammunition block into his spike rifle. "They won't take this place without a fight."

Grold looked over at Grain. The triarii was prone, sighting carefully down the barrel. The soldier looked up at his section leader, a slight smile on his lips. "I've got an easy one."

Grold nodded, and the spike rifle blazed. The commlink in the section leader's helmet buzzed with commands. He acknowledged. It was the same old story: shoot enough to hold them back, but don't engage at close quarters. Down the street, the penal infantry had ducked into cover, the Nisus-S vehicles well back and keeping the penals up front.

Grold's thermal sensors showed images moving through the buildings to the right and left. A few more moments and they would cross the line beyond his position. He primed a grenade and dropped it into the street. Smoke bloomed, and spikes spattered across the front of the building as the penal infantry opened on their position. He turned to the others. "Let's go." He sprang for the door, standing aside to let the others pass. Grain leapt past him, heading for the next position. Tscholmankia didn't move. Grold stepped forward. "Come on!"

Tscholmankia turned toward his section leader and took off his helmet. "Not this time," he said. "I'll wait here." He placed the helmet on the floor in front of the firing port, then sat down on it, facing away from the enemy. He stared unseeing at Grold.

Grold stepped back across the den, hearing the thwack of spikes along the wall behind his teammate. He grabbed Tscholmankia by the shoulder, but the soldier was a dead weight. The triarii toppled slowly forward, and Grold saw the spike centered in the back of his skull. He dropped the body and set out after Grain.

High above the ice cap, Mullins led the tanks in a wide, descending circle as he waited for the others to join up. The tanks had exited the transport one at a time until the skipper, realizing that it was foolish to try to keep them inside, swung the inner doors wide. Then the trickle of tanks became a torrent as the entire Renegade force jostled their way to the entrance. All sense of organization was lost as the Liberators and Vipers poured out.

On the command bridge, the skipper revised his report to Alabaster. Confirming that the launch was in progress, he also reported the damage; his transport was now a sitting duck for TOG fighters. Alabaster acknowledged the situation and scrambled a flight of four *Cheetah*s, thought better of it, and scrambled a whole squadron, with a squadron of *Avenger*s as support.

52

0830, 15 Martius 6831—The Renegade command Pedden rested in the lee of the row of buildings marking the perimeter of the city under the ice. Behind it rose the slope of the ice fall that led to the breach through which the Renegade force had broken into the city, and through which it would now make its escape. In front of it rose the buildings of the Naram city that Cohort Harras had defended. Strewn around the Pedden was the detritus of battle, creating shadows in the flickering light of combat.

Harras, still alone in the command center, hardly needed the plot to tell him that the perimeter was shrinking again. The relief force on the surface would only save the remains of his force if he could break contact with the penal infantry clinging to his lines. The Renegades below the surface had to counterattack to throw the penals off-balance. And that mission would require one last effort from his exhausted command.

A limited number of units would attack. The Renegades in place would provide covering fire for the troops chosen to charge the enemy. Harras chose two Liberators to make the attack: the tank commanded by Senior Sergeant Aktol Graviston, and a tank now commanded by Sam Rand, the headquarters commander. Each tank would carry an infantry squad to provide close security against the penal infantry. The Liberator wasn't equipped with an antipersonnel laser, and the ranges in this fight were going to be very short. The peds would keep the infantry off the tank.

The two Liberators hovered beside the Pedden awaiting final instructions. Harras wanted to see his troops when he gave them their orders; their mission was deadly dangerous, and he needed to look these men in the eyes before he sent them out. He climbed down the steps on the side of the Pedden and walked between the hovering tanks. Both commanders were in their command hatches, the infantry squads clinging to the hulls behind the turrets. Harras was shocked by how few infantry were left.

Graviston's tank had only two peds in its squad; Rand had three. The peds looked haggard, in worse shape than even the tankers. The peds lived with the same fear of violent death as the tankers, but they also had to endure the bitter cold. The two on Graviston's tank stared at Harras, hollow-eyed and lethargic. The Cohort commander looked at his men, wishing there was something he could do. He recognized the hopelessness in their attitude, and he prayed that it would change as they went into battle. To send men in their condition into combat was to send them to certain death.

"We're going to try to break contact with the TOG infantry," said Harras. "The plan is to mount a surprise attack along the TOG's line. If we can get them to hesitate for even a moment, our people can run for the surface. This mission is very important, but it's not a suicide mission." He made eye contact with Graviston and then Rand. "This is not a suicide mission," he repeated. "It is risky, yes. But it is not a death ride."

Harras passed both men a chip containing the most recent data on the positions along the front. "As you can see," he continued, after the commanders had downloaded the information into their DDPs, "our forces are defending a series of strong points, holding off the TOGs in the nearby buildings. What we want you to do is drive down the streets and alleys between the two forces. Shoot everything and anything on the TOG side of the line. Drop smoke behind you as you go. They could attack through the obscuring smoke, but we're betting they won't. This will give our people time to break away, mount up, and head for the surface."

Graviston and Rand looked at the proposed route laid out on their DDPs. It was several kilometers long if they counted the twists and turns they would have to make. Some of the turns were so tight that they would be forced to bring the Liberators almost to a complete stop before changing direction. The track would be difficult under the best of conditions; with enemy infantry shooting at them it would be far more dangerous.

Graviston looked over at the young optio. "Sir," he said. "I think I should lead, with you covering my wing. In the wide places, you cover to my right and I'll stay to the left. You should also be higher than me, not quite tree-top, but close. That way you'll have a clear shot past me, and if I make smoke, you won't lose visibility."

"I think I should be in the lead, Sergeant," replied Rand. He should lead, and he knew it. Because the Cohort's communications had been destroyed in the initial crossing to the pole, as communications officer he had had nothing to do since the landing. As the headquarters commandant, his only worry had been where to locate the command post when they fled from topside. This was his first real chance to fill the traditional role of a Renegade optio.

"With all due respect, sir," returned Graviston, "my tank crew has been together only a short time, but longer than yours. For that reason alone, my tank should lead. In addition, I've been a tanker longer than you've been alive. If those two arguments don't satisfy you, there's the matter of command. If you lead, you'll be involved in shooting. If you follow, you can command. And commanding, sir, is what you do." He pointed to the Cohort commander standing between the two tanks. "If your tank were commanded by Milt, here, I would make the same argument."

Rand felt the angry rush of blood to his face. He wanted to shout that he needed to feel useful, that he wanted to pound some TOGs to slag. Then his better judgment overcame his emotions. The blood drained from his face. "You're right, Sergeant. We'll do it your way."

"Bashful Laundry. Bashful Laundry. This is Mother Hen. Bandits from the west. Bandits from the west. They look like *Pilum* fighters."

Reflexively, Mullins looked through the carplexy dome of his Liberator, even though he knew there was nothing to see. He checked the DDP and saw only the loose formation of tanks and infantry carriers spiraling down toward the pole. Velocity was still at a reasonable 300 kph, and the angle of attack was nearly zero.

"Laundry Two-two-six. This is Laundry Two-six." Mullins listened to his Century commander. "You're in the lead. When the bandits arrive, keep the flock heading down."

Mullins checked the DDP again. The tactical range of the data display's sensors reached out only fifty kilometers. The incoming enemy fighters would be at close range by the time they appeared on the screen. Mullins knew that the flat-winged *Pilum* fighters carried a pair of mass-driver cannons in the nose and a 7.5/3 laser on each wing. The MDC-8s were savage weapons, but even the Liberator's weak bottom armor could survive a couple of hits. The lasers were a different matter. They would almost effortlessly punch clean holes into the bottom of a tank, and any laser hit on bottom armor would be bad; it could even be disastrous. With luck, however, the fighters would get only one pass at the tanks. They would be moving so fast that they would blow by the descending vehicles before they could get a second shot.

"Multiple *Pilum* fighters. Range one-five-zero kilometers. Bearing two-two-double-zero true. Altitude eight-four and dropping. Velocity three-double-zero per minute." The *Caelestis'* DDP was transmitting information on the incoming TOGs as her sensors picked them up. At a range of one hundred and fifty kilometers and a speed of 300 kpm, the fighters would be on the formation in thirty seconds. The *Pilum*s were already in range to use lasers and the MDCs would begin to fire in fifteen seconds. Mullins checked the DDP again. The last of the Renegade vehicles were still trickling from the bow of the transport. To break for the surface now would leave the trailing tanks to the fighters. In their current tight formation they would all have a chance. He ordered his driver to maintain the slow spiral down.

"Multiple *Pilum* fighters. Range one-double-zero kilometers. Bearing two-one-double-zero true. Altitude eight-zero and dropping. Velocity one-eight-zero per minute." The bow flicker-shields glowed briefly as the Liberator deflected a laser. Mullins felt sweat break out across his forehead and over the bald dome of his skull. His stomach muscles tightened. A ripping crash came from the left side of the hull as a pair of mass-driver cannon threw their projectiles against his tank. The 273 tons of titanium shook under the impact. The DDP flooded with yellow triangles as the enemy fighters came within sensor range.

"Gunner. Traverse left one-five mils. Take the head-on shot. Don't worry about the deflection. Fire everything together. Load HEAP. Driver, prepare for the recoil."

"*Pilum* fighter. Range nine-five-double-zero. Bearing six-two-double-zero relative. Velocity one-double-zero per minute. Target identified. Target locked." The tank's internal sensors had locked the DDP on the incoming fighters. They were still out of range, but in a few moments would be close enough to target. The flicker shields flashed again as a laser was turned aside.

Mullins wouldn't wait for the DDP to announce the fighter as within range. By the time the computer told him the fighter was close enough, it would be gone. He watched a yellow triangle streak across the DDP screen. "Fire!"

The bow of the Liberator was bathed in the muzzle flash as the 150mm and 50mm cannon fired together. Overlaying the crash of the cannon was the high-pitched scream of the 5/6 laser. Mullins felt the nose of the tank rise from the recoil of the weapons, then steady and drop back to the pre-selected angle. The DDP was a riot of yellow triangles and blue squares, then the triangles scattered away like blown leaves. One of the blue squares blinked and went out. Then another. And another. The TOG *Pilum* fighters were past the tank formation, but they had inflicted damage.

The hazy crinkle of the carplexy dome lit up with a brilliant flash. Another Liberator tumbled out of control over his tank, spewing flame from the grav coils. Huge chunks of titanium armor bent away from the hull. A stream of fragments glowed like stars against the sky. Then it winked out, and the sky was dark again. The DDP showed the TOGs reforming in the distance. They had slowed their first approach, knowing that at 300 kpm they would blow past the falling tanks too quickly to do much damage. They were gathering to strike again, this time picking on the rear-most tanks. This time they would be aiming for bottom armor, rather than the front and sides.

"*Pilum* fighter. Range nine-five-double-zero. Bearing two-seven-double-zero relative.

Velocity one-five-zero per minute. Target identified. Target not locked." The TOGs were nine and a half kilometers away and closing at 150 kpm. It was time to lead the survivors to the surface. The trailing vehicles would have to fend for themselves.

"Bashful Laundry. This is Comely Bimbo. Closing your position. Break away."

The DDP showed the yellow triangles in the rear suddenly joined by blue triangles. Identification marks showed the new craft as *Cheetah* and *Avenger* fighters. The two groups of fighters clumped together in a roiling ball stretching across a hundred kilometers of space.

"Bashful Laundry. Let's go!" he yelled into the commlink, surprised by his own excitement. "Follow me down!" He switched to the intercom. "Driver. Dive as fast as you can. Let's go by the book: 'Maximum speed commensurate with safety.'" The nose of the Liberator dropped toward the surface and the acceleration pressed him back against his seat.

Larry Stone lay quietly on the ice cliff. The cold ate into his chest, arms, and legs, but he did not dare activate the heating system embedded in the TOG armored suit for fear of being discovered. He'd figured the enemy bounce infantryman didn't need the armor any more, not with his head detached from his shoulders. But getting into the bounce suit had been nearly impossible. The enemy soldier had been frozen solid, and Stone ended up breaking much of the armor free a section at a time. The worst part had been putting it on. In order to suit up in the working armor, he had had to shed his own damaged suit, exposing his body to the subzero temperatures. He had less than a minute to perform the task, or risk freezing to death himself. The armor helped, but now he had to force his body to produce more heat. It was not an easy job. His left arm throbbed with pain from his previous injury.

The Nisus-S vehicle had passed his position before. Now it was coming back, patrolling slowly along the rear of the TOG Penal Cohort that had marched past this spot. The guards were probably looking for penal infantry trying to shirk their duty. The Ssoran commander lounged on the command hatch, his long, reptilian arms cradling an Akley laser rifle fitted with a stiletto bayonet. The Ssoran was not paying strict attention to his surroundings, confident that no penal infantry lurked in the shadows.

Stone looked down on the approaching Nisus-S from his position and formulated a plan. He rolled to his feet, rising to a low crouch. The TOG bounce soldier had been carrying a Mantichore spike rifle that still had half an ammunition block in the loading port. Stone hadn't tested the weapon, and he hoped it still worked. Steadying the rifle under his right arm, he rose from his hiding place. The Ssoran sensed the motion and turned toward him.

The distance from the command hatch of the vehicle to the edge of the cliff that sheltered Stone was no more than five meters. The edge of the hull was even closer. Stone stepped to the edge of the cliff, letting the muzzle of the weapon center on the reptile's head. The Ssoran, not quite comprehending the danger he was in, stared at the TOG soldier in the snow. When he understood his precarious position, it was an instant too late. As the Ssoran raised the Akley, Stone pulled the trigger of the spike rifle.

All TOG equipment has a reputation for being less sophisticated than its Commonwealth/Renegade counterpart. TOG machining is not as good, and one TOG rifle has more lumps and sharp places than an entire platoon of similar weapons in the Commonwealth armies. But the rifles TOG issues to its infantry are designed to work under the most adverse conditions. Even though this Mantichore spike rifle had been left unattended in the severe temperatures of the polar ice cap for hours, possibly days, it fulfilled its function. Half a dozen spikes shot from the barrel.

The Ssoran vehicle commander opened his mouth to yell a warning to the crew inside the vehicle, but the sound never left his lungs. The spikes struck high on his chest, stitching a line from where the neck wattle joined the narrow breastbone upward to the soft folds below the lower jaw. The force of the impact lifted the alien clear of the turret coaming and threw him backward across the top of the vehicle. Before the body stopped bouncing Stone leapt across the intervening distance to the top of the turret.

He stepped to the open hatch and looked in. The Ssoran gunner was crouched behind the controls of twin AP lasers. The reptile looked up, annoyed by the sudden rush of cold air occasioned by his commander vacating his position. All he saw was the flash of the spike rifle before he slumped, dead, over his firing system.

Stone dropped the now-empty Mantichore and retrieved the Akley the commander had dropped. He crawled into the fighting compartment just in time to see the Ssoran driver ground the vehicle and climb from his control position. The Ssoran came forward to investigate the disturbance and Stone dropped to the floor, Akley at the ready. Spotting Stone, the reptile stepped back, banging his head against the underside of the AP laser mount, and grabbed for his sidearm, his triple-fingered hand closing on the butt of the weapon as Stone fired the laser rifle.

The interior of the Nisus-S filled with the smell of burning flesh as the aligned light burned through the battledress and into the Ssoran's chest. The chest steamed and then blew apart under the heat of the laser. The body balanced for an instant on its long, muscular tail, then crumpled to the floor.

Stone began to feel the warmth of the interior of the Nisus, which the Ssoran kept warmer than did their Human counterparts. The heat quickly became more than Stone could handle. He felt the blood rush to his limbs and his eyes lost focus. He dropped the rifle and staggered toward the command seat, flailing his right arm to find a support, and fell.

53

0900, 15 Martius 6831—Blackstone knuckled the Liberator around the stone building, using the right side of the hull as the pivot. The two peds on the rear deck scrambled away from their positions on that side of the tank as metal ground against the structure next to them. The driver knew the titanium armor was proof against damage at low speed, but the infantry on top were not convinced. They huddled behind the turret until the screech of metal on stone died away, then went back to their positions.

The peds had received their briefing along with the tankers, and they knew that the TOG penals would be hiding to their left. The last thing they wanted was to be caught on the exposed side of the deck when the shooting started. Having regained their places, they trained their rifles across the top of the turret just in front of the blister that housed the Vulcan antimissile system. Aktol Graviston stood with his head and shoulders exposed behind the mount. From that position he could reach the nearer ped as well as direct the movements of the tank and its main gun.

The second Liberator made the turn. Graviston looked back and raised his arm. The commander of the trailing tank copied the signal. Then the leader dropped his arm, and the charge was on.

"Ham," Graviston spoke into the intercom, "you have the guns. You'll be aiming at a range between fifty-six hundred mils and straight ahead. Don't worry about targets further left than that. Rand and his crew will cover them. Concentrate on what's coming up. Shoot what's in the breach. Use only the laser. Don't fire missiles."

Hamilton Hull, crouched behind the weapons sighting system, had heard the instructions before. He acknowledged the orders, aware that his commander was just making sure he understood the plan. He would probably hear them again before the mission ended. Hull felt the tank accelerate suddenly as Blackstone fired the thrusters. They weren't trying to sneak around; they wanted the TOGs to know they were here. He hit the firing button on the 50mm laser cannon and heard the sharp crack as the secondary weapon fired. He counted to three and fired the main laser. His eyes were fixed on the sight's sensor system. He didn't need to aim, he only needed to know when the gun was ready to fire again. He would shoot targets of opportunity as they appeared, but he would keep shooting even if he saw nothing. The mission was to create confusion, not kill vehicles, and if they could generate enough of it, the Renegade infantry would be able to break free and make for the surface.

"Nisus-S tank. Range five-double-zero. Bearing five-six-double-zero. Vehicle stationary. Vehicle active. Lock not achieved. Intervening terrain." The DDP discovered a TOG light tank hidden behind the buildings to the left. He broke his shooting rhythm and waited for a clear shot. The Nisus was probably down a side street, waiting for the Liberator to appear. The TOG vehicle had nothing that could kill the Liberator on the first hit, but a combination of the vehicle's laser, 50mm cannon, and TVLG systems could do the job. The Nisus-S was said to have the best targeting computer in the TOG system, and if any vehicle could put all its shots into the same hole, the Nisus-S was the one. Hull wanted to get his shots off first.

The Liberator scraped along the right side of the street. Hull figured there was just enough room for him to swing the turret full left, which would give him the correct position for firing down the alley where the DDP showed the Nisus. He watched the illuminated representation of the Nisus-S drift across his targeting array. The outlines of the buildings they passed were pale ghosts on the screen, and he had to pay particular attention to the enemy's location. He wanted to avoid taking a premature shot and having the round explode against the intervening masonry.

Graviston guessed what was happening in the tank below him. As the turret swung to the left, he grabbed the arm of the nearer ped and pulled him toward the back of the turret. The ped scrambled across quickly, followed immediately by his companion. The two huddled behind the broad stern of the turret, waiting for the blast of the forward-firing weapons. The opening to the alley emerged out of the gloom.

"Nisus-S tank. Range four-five-zero. Bearing zero. Vehicle stationary. Vehicle active. Lock achieved." The painting laser was no use at this range, and the forward shields on the Nisus were actually quite weak, but Graviston's training took over and he treadled the bar. "Nisus-S tank. Range four-five-zero. Bearing zero. Vehicle stationary. Vehicle active. Lock achieved. Target painted."

The three turret weapons fired as one. Hull had linked them as soon as he had identified the enemy vehicle. He wanted to hit and hit hard. An instant later, one of the hull TVLGs streaked away toward the enemy in the alley.

"Gunner. Turret front. Driver, accelerate." Graviston didn't wait to examine his handiwork. The Liberator jumped forward as the turret swung back to its original bearing. A ball of fire erupted from the street as they swept past. Either the TOGs inside the vehicle had been asleep at the wheel, or they just hadn't been as quick off the mark. They wouldn't have a chance to repeat their mistake. Behind the lead Liberator, the second tank, high and to the left, hurried past the beacon produced by the flaring tank.

"Nice shooting," came the commlink message from behind. Then the rear tank bloomed with smoke that blotted out the pyre.

The Liberators broke into an open plaza and were greeted by a hail of TVLG fire. The sky above the city glowed with fiery trails that cast a livid illumination on the scene below. The fire of the rockets reflected off the underside of the dome to cast a warm light over the wreckage of the city. The Liberator's Vulcan system tracked the incoming missiles and spun to engage them. TVLGs exploded above the tanks and crashed into the street and buildings at the edge of the plaza. Some made it through to the Liberators. The Renegade infantry crouched behind the turrets, unable to affect their own survival except by ardent prayer. Their prayers must have been heard, because the missiles detonated on the Liberators' engaged sides, stitching a line of explosions away from the defending lines and the riding peds.

The tanks streaked across the plaza, discharging smoke as they went and obscuring themselves from the enemy gunners. The tanks' heavy weapons continued to fire through the smoke at all suspected enemy targets, unconcerned with whether or not they scored hits. Noise was their objective, and noise was what they got. A side street loomed ahead, and both tanks ducked in as a wild volley of TVLGs struck the roadway to their rear.

Behind the fleeing tanks, the Renegade infantry deserted their fighting positions to mount the vehicles waiting close at hand. The penals, momentarily thrown off their stride, stepped back from the firing line. By the time the smoke cleared and they regained the initiative, their Renegade targets had vanished. Not trusting completely to their sensors, yet afraid of a trap, they moved cautiously forward to regain contact. They were too late.

Karstil directed his Liberator around a gigantic ice crag. A Horatius tank sheltered on the opposite side, dug in up to its main gun. The two tanks had been stalking each other for more than a minute, the Horatius turning to face the Liberator as the moving vehicle dodged and ducked through the surrounding spires of ice. The Horatius was unwilling to leave its protected position to join the hunt, its fixed, forward-firing main weapon at a serious disadvantage in mobile, close-range action. The Liberator, on the other hand, was unwilling to close if it could not get a shot at a more vulnerable side of the Horatius than the turret exposed to his fire. Karstil had no desire to go nose-to-nose with the more heavily armored enemy. The front hulls of both tanks were equally armored, but the enemy turret, where most of Karstil's shots must necessarily strike, enjoyed a 25 percent armor-strength advantage.

The deadly dance continued. Both tanks had lost track of the fight raging around them; this was personal. "Distaff Two-two-six. This is Two-two-one. Coming up behind you." Karstil looked to the rear, expecting to see the twin booms of another Liberator swing through the ice. He gaped at the sight presenting itself. For some reason known only to the tank commander, Distaff 221 was still at tree-top flight level, well above the ice crags rising from the terrain.

"Two-two-one. This is Two-two-six. Get down! Get down! Don't fly here! Enemy tank ahead of you!"

"Two-two-one. You are broken and garbled. Say again."

Karstil watched the Liberator fly past overhead. It was moving away from his own location, exposing its stern and bottom armor to the lurking Horatius. Karstil couldn't understand it. Either the DDP in the flying Liberator had failed to detect the enemy tank, or the tank commander didn't realize what a 150mm could do to bottom armor. The Liberator was almost out of sight, almost hidden by the ice crags, almost safe from the surprised Horatius, when the enemy tank fired.

The Horatius had tracked the flying Liberator, rising out of its protective crater to bring the main hull-mounted cannon to bear on the bottom armor. The enemy commander was indulging in a little overkill, because the 3/6 laser and 50mm cannon alone were capable of bringing down the Liberator. The TOG tanker evidently just wanted to make absolutely sure of his kill, and he was. The 150mm APDS round struck just after the 3/6 laser in the same hole, making the 50mm shot redundant. The Liberator's grav drives and helm control melted away, and the ammunition storage area showed penetration as well. For a moment the Liberator hung in the air like a helpless moth pinned against the black velvet of the sky. Then the vehicle vanished in a brilliant fireball.

"Driver, let's move." Karstil spoke into the commlink as the parts of the Liberator rained down on the ice. "Gunner. Tank. Horatius. Pointblank. Shoot and keep shooting." The tank leaped clear of the blocking terrain to find the Horatius broadside-to and out of its crater.

"Horatius tank. Range five-zero. Bearing six-two-double-zero relative," Karstil treadled the painting laser. "Target locked. Target not painted."

"Fire!"

"Target not painted, sir."

"Just shoot."

The three turret weapons fired as one. Karstil saw the laser sparkle along the side of the hull as the flicker shields absorbed and displaced the aligned light. Nothing stopped the Gauss weapons, however. Those rounds also struck almost together, scouring away chunks of titanium armor from the side of the hull. The TOG commander realized too late that he had been greedy. The Horatius began to back down into its protective hole like a turtle retreating into its shell, the turret traversing toward the Liberator, its main gun swinging like a giant nose toward its target. Karstil treadled the painting laser again. "Horatius tank. Range five-zero. Bearing six-two-double-zero relative. Target locked. Target painted." The turret weapons fired again.

The laser got through this time, burning through the wounds inflicted by the first attack. As the HEAP rounds from the cannon blasted away more armor, ceramic ballistic protection, and interior control components, the laser went straight to the point. The Horatius spun out of control, huge gouts of flame pouring from the savaged side. The right hull struck the ice, throwing up a sheet of fragments that flashed to steam in the intense heat. Then the hull glowed cherry red, and the vehicle sank back into its crater. A column of flame shot skyward, and the remains of the TOG vehicle sank slowly into a pool of water created by its own death throes. The Liberator blew past the glowing wreckage and vanished into the darkness beyond.

Karstil hardly noticed the destroyed Horatius. He could see only that the terrain he crossed was covered by bits and pieces of the Liberator tank that had once been part of his platoon. Most of the wreckage was unrecognizable, but the 150mm cannon, still attached to the side of the turret, stuck up from the ice like a monument. Karstil began to search for other TOG vehicles, and he knew he would find them; the dark sky all around flashed and boomed with combat.

54

1000, 15 Martius 6831—The scene below the ice of the south pole was chaotic. Graviston and Rand had been only partially successful in breaking the penal infantry's grip on the Renegade positions. The retreating troops abandoned their fighting positions, mounting the remaining tanks, carriers, and administrative vehicles of Cohort Harras. There were no more fallback positions. They all knew that the next time they stopped they would be on the surface. The forward units broke away from the penal infantry, scrambling the remaining unit organization beyond recognition or retrieval in their desperate flight toward the breach.

It is easy for a man to be brave when he faces his enemy, but once his back is turned, he becomes the victim of all his fears. The enemy seems to be everywhere and getting closer. His own friends become an obstacle to his survival. Only strong organization and intense training can hold a retreating unit together, and Cohort Harras had had time for neither. Military history is filled with horror stories of orderly withdrawals becoming complete routs. With only a single avenue to the surface, this retreat threatened to become one of those disasters.

Harras grabbed the first soldier he saw running past his command post to drive his Pedden. He calmed the legionnaire, allowed him to regain his composure, then dismounted his tank and stood in the center of the main avenue that led to the breach. He instructed his new driver to turn the Pedden toward him and switch on its driving lamps. Thus Harras, thrown into stark relief by the tank's harsh lights, stood in the center of the roadway and directed traffic.

The vehicles rushing headlong toward the surface paused at the sight of their Cohort commander, his legs still swathed in bandages, calmly wielding glowing hand wands. Seeing their commander in control had the desired effect. Drivers, gunners, tank commanders, and peds took a second look at their fears and found them groundless. Those directed to stay behind and take up defensive positions grimly complied. Those directed toward the breach proceeded in an orderly fashion. On other streets, other officers took up the same positions. Braxton Sloan, the low-ranking staff engineer, mounted the hull of a shattered Liberator and shouted directions. Moldine Rinter, her uniform spattered with blood, stood in the middle of another road. The Renegade Cohort turned to cover its own retreat.

Rand and Graviston were the last to reach the path to the surface. They came down the main avenue side by side, spewing obscuring smoke from their last discharge points. Rand was exultant. The ride through the city had given him the most exciting moments of his life. He knew, deep in his heart, that he would never be a tank commander in the Renegade forces. He was a technician, destined to spend his career among the mysteries of communications equipment and computers, but for one unforgettable moment he had felt the wild thrill of battle. Someone said there is nothing more exciting than to be shot at with no effect; he had felt that excitement. He had had his longed-for chance to play with the big boys' toys. But as he turned to face the oncoming penal infantry, that excitement passed. The game was deadly serious now.

Graviston did not feel the adrenaline rush pass; he had hardly noticed it when the run began. As a senior sergeant with the Renegades, he had squeezed that gland too many times for it to happen again. To be sure, he had felt the excitement, but he also knew the dangers, knew that flaming death was close at hand. That he had survived so far was good enough for him. He settled the Liberator next to a shattered building and waited for targets to appear. He noticed a throbbing in his right arm, and realized it had been pierced by armor fragments.

Harras found Graviston and Rand together and issued his final instructions. The commander had decided the two tank commanders would be the last to leave. This final stage would be touch and go, because once the tanks left the shelter of the farthest buildings, there would be no stopping short of the surface, and it would be impossible for them to cover their own retreat. Tanks barely passed through the bolt-hole, and even with the sides eroded by the Renegades' initial passage through the hole and the TOG attacks, a Liberator could not hide in the opening and cover the withdrawal of another. If the first tank didn't make it through the breach, the second tank was stranded. And already the advancing penals' TVLGs were falling at the opening.

"When we move," Graviston said to Rand, "you go first. I'll cover as long as I can and move when you clear the opening."

"Negative, Sergeant. You go first this time."

"No, sir. I stand with the same reasons I gave you for the run."

"Sergeant, if I have to pull rank, I will. As you said before, you have the better driver and gunner, so you have a better chance of making it out. Harras said that if the first tank makes it, the second one has a chance. If the first doesn't, there's no hope for the second. You go first." Rand looked grimly determined, and Graviston knew the officer was coming of age. He nodded in acquiescence. They returned to their tanks to wait for the penal infantry.

They didn't wait long. The Ssoran guards, sensing that victory was near, drove the penal infantry mercilessly down the streets that led to the main breach. They didn't even allow the peds to move from cover to cover, but herded them straight down the avenues. Spike carbines and AP lasers drove out any peds who sheltered in a doorway or behind fallen masonry. The first men to protest this treatment died where they stood. The rest kept moving ahead of their hated guards.

Rand acquired the first Nisus-S as it turned a corner five hundred meters from his hull-down position. The Ssora were so intent on driving the penals forward that they did not see or else chose to ignore the Liberator amid the rubble. The infantry knew the tank was there, but they were forced to disregard it.

Rand waited until the Nisus-S slid around the corner to the center of the street. He couldn't understand why the turret kept swinging back and forth across the roadway, as if seeking targets in the buildings on either side. The enemy tank commander must have known that there were no Renegade troops left in the rubble, yet the Ssoran commander was standing in the center turret hatch, gesturing wildly at some unseen object. Penal infantry scurried ahead of the tank, barely ducking into doorways before moving out again. It was the strangest display of infantry tactics Rand had ever seen.

Graviston, watching the weird ballet from his own Liberator, understood what was happening. He was just about to open a commlink to the optio to tell him to disregard the infantry and go for the guard vehicle, when Rand's Liberator opened fire.

The 150mm HEAP round struck square on the mantlet that protected the twin antipersonnel lasers, and the 50mm round followed right behind. The combined explosive force smashed through the titanium armor and the ceramic ballistic protection. A tongue of flame licked through the communications equipment and expended itself in the weapons-control computer. The twin AP lasers went dead. That was the first thing the penal infantry noticed.

The Liberator's 5/6 laser, striking the turret next to the crater blasted by the heavy HEAP projectile, burned through the armor, the ballistic protection, and the Ssoran gunner hunched down behind the now-useless sights. His head vaporized. That was the first thing the vehicle commander noticed.

As the turret of the stricken vehicle filled with smoke from the burning equipment and steam from the laser strike, the tank commander stopped firing his spike carbine at the penal infantry to look down into the fighting compartment. The penal infantry noticed that right away, too.

The penals immediately went to ground behind rubble and into the first available doorways. One of the men, displaying more initiative than the others and perhaps stronger feelings about the Ssora, rolled to face the guards' vehicle as he dove for cover. The Ssoran sergeant was outlined clearly against the dark sky by the fire glowing inside the turret. The ped snapped his spike rifle to his shoulder and emptied a full ammunition block into the distracted alien. The impact of the spikes threw the guard from the hatch, tumbling him over the side of the tank. Their guards neutralized, the penal infantry broke for the rear.

Harras' Pedden broke clear of the surface. The driver was a little new to the controls, and so the command vehicle popped out of the opening like a cork released from a bottle. The vehicle was moving so fast, the transition from the enclosed gallery to open space was such a shock, that the driver did not see the Liberator hurtling toward him across the ice. The right front armor of the Pedden contacted the left front arm of the Liberator. Impact force is calculated from mass and the square of velocity; even though the Pedden had the greater mass, the Liberator was moving much faster, making the collision of the two tanks an even match.

The Pedden spun under the impact, its left side striking the ground as the Liberator slammed into the right side in a shower of titanium sparks. The violent grounding stopped the Pedden in its tracks, but the Liberator careened on into an ice wall, plowing the 150mm cannon deep into the frozen surface. The Liberator also came to a complete stop. No one was injured in the pileup, but both drivers needed some time to adjust to their new positions.

The Pedden wasn't going anywhere soon, so Harras opened the side doors and jumped to the snow. The jarring force reminded him that his feet were still bandaged, and the pain made him hesitate a moment before he began to move. He ran around the front of the Pedden to see if anyone in the Liberator had been injured, reaching the crumpled left side just as the tank commander crawled slowly from the turret. He immediately recognized Prefect NaBesta Kenderson, commander of the 2567th, as his victim. He began to laugh.

Kenderson, still shaken by his tank's abrupt stop, stared incredulously at the tatterdemalion figure standing laughing in the snow. The man was bandaged from his feet to above his knees. His uniform, what was left of it, was covered with grime. And this apparition had the temerity to laugh at him. Kenderson climbed down in a boiling rage, ready to give this lunatic a piece of his mind, when he realized that he was looking at Centurion Maximus Milton Harras, his reason for coming to the ice cap. He began to laugh as well.

* * *

Graviston spun the Liberator in the rubble. Too many penal infantry were still coming on. The two Liberators were not enough to stop them. With no AP lasers of their own, they had to rely on the fire of their infantry riders, and the peds chose to fight from behind the turrets, rather than deploy on the ground, which was the normal procedure for defending a stationary tank. The infantry were also shooting over the tops of the open command hatches, forcing the tank commanders to fight on instruments alone, but the inconvenience was worth keeping all but the most aggressive penal infantry at bay.

The peds stayed on the vehicles not because they were afraid to do their jobs, but because they knew that when the moment came to run, they would not have time to mount. Neither tank commander would deliberately abandon them, but they were also unwilling to wait those few precious moments it would take for the infantry to board. So all the defending Renegades hung together, waiting for the order to retreat.

Graviston pointed his tank toward the bolt-hole, the peds clinging grimly to the back of the turret. Blackstone made for the exit, the thrusters driving the Liberator up the slope in a cloud of fragmented ice and steam. Graviston held off firing his obscuring smoke for fear that it would make Rand's retreat more difficult when the time came. He spun the turret to face down-slope, the infantry scrambling to keep up. Below him, appearing to huddle next to a building, Rand's tank fired down the street. The main gun and the smaller coaxial 50mm bathed the bow of the Liberator with gouts of flame, the crash and crack alternating as the tank attempted to keep the penal infantry at bay. Graviston could see the tank's infantry firing long bursts from their spike rifles, the glowing barrels red against the black shapes of the buildings. He fired once more before he reached the safety of the opening, more as a gesture than in hope that the shot would accomplish anything. The 150mm HEAP round screamed over the heads of the combatants to strike well beyond the vicious fight around the Liberator. Then he was through the hole and headed for the surface.

Rand's DDP showed him that Graviston was clear. On his command the driver turned the Liberator and shot toward the exit. A TVLG split the darkness, followed by another, and another. The Vulcan system began to swat the missiles away, but replacements outnumbered those destroyed. The TVLGs began to strike the ice on the slope and the walls of the dome itself. Huge chunks of the plastic shroud that protected the city tore away in the explosions, the shards falling into the darkness. Rand saw a missile strike directly above the bolt-hole, rending the dome with a giant crack that seemed to echo forever. The ice around the Liberator erupted in fountains of flame and steam.

More missiles filled the air, and by their light the penal infantry rushed into the breach after the tank, firing their rifles wildly as they came. The spikes rattled on the stern of the tank like gravel thrown against a tin wall. Rand felt the shock of a TVLG striking home on the exposed stern. A second hit followed the first as the Vulcan system was overcome with the multiple launches. The Liberator shuddered, yawing as it drove for the surface. The thrusters began to fail.

The side of the breach suddenly loomed ahead. The driver fought to bring the tank back into line, centered on the opening. He failed. Moving at full speed, the right arm of the hull struck the protective dome. The Liberator came to a full stop and jolted away from the dome, swerving violently to the left. The hull struck the opposite side of the breach, throwing the infantry from the turret into the passage. TVLGs still pounded on the exposed right side of the tank, blasting titanium armor and ballistic protection from the hull. Smoke filled the fighting compartment.

Rand became aware of movement in the turret below him. He looked down to see the gunner and driver scrambling toward him. Bare wires spewed arcs of fire through the gloom.

The sighting system flared, the lights blinking on and off spasmodically. A 50mm ammunition casing flashed. Rand pulled himself to the top of the turret, reaching back to help his crew to safety. He grabbed the men by their collars as they emerged, throwing them over the side of the tank and into the protection of the gallery. Then he leaped after them.

The abandoned Liberator smoldered for a moment longer, then a column of fire rose from the vacated turret. The flames' light cast a glare against the shattered dome as chunks of the protective shell began to fall. Fragments of ice followed them down.

55

1030, 15 Martius 6831—"Gunner. Tank," cried Karstil, as another target loomed in the path he was tracking across the frozen wastes at the center of the south pole. He didn't wait for the DDP to identify the vehicle, recognizing it visually as a Romulus carrier. There was no time to go through the firing sequence. The ballistic computer was loading HEAP rounds into the two cannon as fast as it could cycle, and the laser glowed red from firing, the gennium-arsenic crystal close to overheating from near-constant use.

"Identified!" replied the gunner.

"Fire!" The 150mm cannon recoil slammed into the fighting compartment. The crater the shot blasted into the side of the enemy carrier threw splinters of glowing titanium across the bow of the Liberator. Karstil covered his face with his arms, feeling pain as the fragments burned through his armor and bit into flesh. He lowered his arms in time to see the Romulus vanish behind a pillar of ice.

The Liberator swung around a different pillar than the one the Romulus had chosen. A Renegade Spartius burned fiercely in the snow, the bodies of its crew scattered nearby across the ice. The carrier was sinking into a pool of hissing water, ice that had melted in the heat of the tank's destruction. Karstil's vehicle roared past, its passage blowing the fire into a rising halo that deepened the darkness with its momentary brilliance.

The hull scraped against yet another pillar and jostled to the left. Dislodged ice crashed down onto the tank's deck, shattered, and careened away. The DDP showed another vehicle close at hand. The Liberator spun to face it and the enemy Aeneas light tank shot past directly overhead. The pressure of the grav drives pushed Karstil into his turret, the overpressure making his ears pop. He was about to spin the turret to track the enemy when another tank appeared in front of him.

"Gunner. Tank."

"Identified."

"Fire!"

The 50mm cannon and the laser fired simultaneously, striking in the same location on the bottom of the elevated light tank. Grav coils blew away from the underside, and the tank flipped stern-over-bow-over-stern, tumbling through the dark sky beyond the Renegade tank. The painting warning klaxon was a constant, endless siren in Karstil's ear, but his brain was so overloaded with the impressions and cacophony of combat that he never heard the sound. The Liberator shook from the hit of a heavy gun and slammed sideways, throwing its occupants against the restraining straps of their combat harnesses, but the tank just kept right on going. A huge vehicle powered across the Liberator's hull, and Karstil swung the turret to track it. "Gunner. Tank."

"Identified."

Even as the large cannon roared, Karstil spun the turret away from the target. Something about the vehicle's shape and size had made him doubt that the target was an enemy vehicle. The gunner had not waited for the command to fire, and when Karstil swung the turret wide of its mark, the Liberator missed a sure shot. As the HEAP round exploded harmlessly into a wall of ice, Karstil saw that the intended target was a Renegade Pedden. The computer continued to load ammunition into the smoking breeches of the weapons mounted on either side of the turret.

Whole slabs of the dome under the ice began to break away, crashing randomly into the streets of the ancient city as Sergeant Lisectus Barcus led the remnants of his platoon toward the main breach, where the last of the Renegades had just disappeared. Shapes emerged from the surrounding buildings, running in the same direction. Others raced toward the rear. A Nisus-S tank roared past, its Ssoran crew firing at the penal infantry to force a path for the vehicle. Penals, no longer engaging the Renegades, stopped to fire back, enraging the lizards operating the tank. Vicious firefights erupted as the infantry turned on their oppressors. Barcus ignored them; ultimate safety lay in escape through the breach.

A fat officer waddled into the street in front of a platoon. He gestured wildly at the penal troops scurrying past, attempting to get anyone's attention. When Barcus saw the figure, he knew at once that it was Optio Strovasi. The optio recognized his platoon sergeant in the same instant.

"Barcus!" he shouted, barely audible above the din of crashing ice and the crack of spike rifles. "I've been wounded. Get me out of here."

Two men stopped to rescue their erstwhile leader, slinging their rifles to make a seat with their arms. Barcus let them finish the task.

"Drop him," he said in a cold voice. The peds looked at him in astonishment. "Drop him, I said."

"You can't do that," whined Strovasi. "I'll have you punished for this! Do you know what they'll do to you?"

Barcus laughed. "Yeah. They'll send me to a Penal Auxilia and make me serve under an incompetent bastard like you." He looked at the two peds. "Drop him." They released the optio, who thumped to the ground.

Strovasi grabbed the leg of one of the penal soldiers. "You can't leave me. I can't walk."

"Lose some weight," sneered Barcus. "You're too fat by half."

Strovasi grabbed for his holster, lifting the flap to reach for his pistol. The holster was empty.

"You're lucky, Strovasi," said Barcus with a grim smile. "If you had touched your pistol, I'd have shot you dead."

Strovasi paled at the thought. "Please, Sergeant. I beg you. Don't leave me here. I'll die."

"Tough. You shouldn't steal food from your platoon." He turned to the other men. "Let's go." He headed for the breach, which was still marked by the glowing Liberator.

Milton Harras and NaBesta Kenderson crouched between the damaged Pedden and

Liberator. Both vehicles were still operational, though the command tank would not use its main gun until it had been to a repair facility. Shouting to make themselves heard above the din of combat, they compared notes on the situation as explosions flashed in the sky around them.

"I don't know what happened to our reinforcements," continued Kenderson. "Most of our relief force was supposed to come from the transport in orbit. It's a pretty big screw-up, but I'm still glad we made it."

"So am I," said Harras. "Fancy running into you in a place like this."

Kenderson winced at the pun, intentional or not. "We've got to get this crazy Mashoona fire drill under control. We're going to end up shooting our own tanks."

"I've got a recall beacon set up, but I don't think anyone's paying attention. We'll just have to flag our own down as we see them. We can use the laser torches I've got in the Pedden. When we see one of our own, we just point and shoot." He stood painfully and began to hobble toward the command vehicle. Kenderson followed. "And hope they don't shoot back," he added.

For the second time within an hour, Centurion Maximus Milton Harras became a traffic-control officer. He and Kenderson stood atop the Pedden, back to back, and fired their recognition lasers at the vehicles that swirled around them. Occasionally they tapped one of the enemy, but most of the vehicles they hit were their own. "I'm getting pretty good at this," shouted Kenderson, excitement ringing in his voice.

"At least we'll have a trade to fall back on when this is over," Harras shouted back.

A Liberator tank hovered next to the Pedden, its commander astonished to see two high-ranking officers waving happily from the upper deck. The tank commander spun his vehicle to cover one of the approaches to the area, leaving the officers to their manic exercise.

Karstil's Liberator struck an ice wall, throwing him against the coaming. Fortunately, the turret had been traversed to the right, so the main gun did not bury itself in the outcropping. "Driver, back up," he shouted. The thrusters fired and the tank shuddered with its effort. A chunk of ice broke loose from the wall above the tank and shattered on the front glacis. "Careful, driver. We don't want to bury ourselves." The thrusters fired again. This time the tank didn't move.

Shadows caught at the edges of Karstil's peripheral vision. Infantry were working their way toward the trapped vehicle. He glanced at the DDP to determine whether they were friend or foe. The yellow circles of unidentified targets gradually shifted to amber and then to red. They were enemy. He reached into the turret for his spike carbine.

Something flashed in the darkness, followed by the sharp report of a spike rifle. Something ricocheted off the Vulcan housing and whined away into the darkness. He dropped behind the antimissile mount and visually searched for targets. More shadows flitted through the snow. He raised his carbine and fired a burst of spikes. The shadows scattered. A blizzard of spikes swept over him from the rear. He turned to fire a return burst. "Driver, get us out of here!" The thrusters roared as the driver fought to extract the captured vehicle. More ice caromed off the glacis. A spike struck Karstil a glancing blow on the chest plate of his armor.

A TVLG arced through the darkness, and the Vulcan spun to engage it, throwing Karstil away from the turret mount. Spikes glanced off the turret. It was becoming dangerous to remain exposed, but he had no choice. If he retreated inside the turret, the enemy infantry would surely swarm over the tank. He had to defend his position until the driver could free the tank. "Alternate right and left thrusters. Pry it out." The Liberator shuddered.

A sudden burst of rifle fire ripped through the darkness. Karstil ducked, expecting to hear the pop as the projectiles snapped overhead. Nothing. He watched for the burst. It came again; a spike rifle firing parallel to the Liberator's hull. Friendly infantry had arrived.

Karstil ignored the friendly fire, turning his attention to the enemy on the other side of the tank. He slammed another ammunition block into the breech of his carbine and fired a short burst at a shadow. It went down. A hand grenade exploded against the hull, a fiery blossom that vanished instantly. He fired again and someone fired back. The tank shuddered again.

Karstil was aware of someone climbing the back of his tank. He spun to see a Renegade ped, spike rifle at the ready, clambering up the scramble rails. "Shoot there!" he yelled, pointing at the shadows against the snow. The tank suddenly jerked backward, and a TVLG crashed into the ice where the front hull had been an instant before. The ped was thrown hard against the rear of the turret, sliding around and almost into the command hatch. As Karstil reached up to hold the soldier steady, the helmet came free to reveal a cascade of auburn hair. Karstil's heart stopped for an instant as he looked directly into the eyes of Sergeant Honor Ross.

Even through his armored suit, he could feel his heart skip a beat, then begin to pound wildly. He slipped his arm around Ross and pulled her against his chest. Recognition dawned on her face, then her eyes rolled back into her head, and she slumped against him. The tank spun free, and ice crashed down around the position.

"Driver. Turn right. Move."

The Liberator scraped the fallen ice and bumped off into the dark, followed by spike-rifle fire. Karstil bent over Ross, sheltering her body from the hostile fire. They broke into an open space filled with burning vehicles. A laser sparkled in the distance, and the driver swung the bow of the Liberator toward it.

"Gunner. Tank." The turret came left to lay on the blinking laser.

"Not seen."

Karstil treadled the painting laser. He tried to drop Ross' unconscious body through the command hatch while directing the turret toward the target. The main gun swung slightly.

"Identified," said the gunner. "Target is using a recognition laser."

"Hold fire." Karstil managed to slip Ross into the fighting compartment. "Driver, head for the lasers."

The Liberator, the scars of recent combat still glowing on its flanks, drifted to a stop beside a Pedden. On the upper deck of the command vehicle stood two officers firing recognition lasers into the darkness. Karstil recognized both men: Milton Harras and NaBesta Kenderson. On the far side of the Pedden another Liberator hovered, its main gun pointing away from the position. Karstil swung his tank to face in the opposite direction.

"If there are any medical personnel in the area," he said into the commlink, "I've got wounded in my tank."

56

1130, 15 Martius 6831—The polar cap sparkled with wreckage. Liberators, spouting flame, sank into the ice in clouds of steam. Horatius tanks and Romulus carriers dragged across the ice, dripping grav coils and slabs of armor. Slowly the combatants divided themselves into recognizable formations. Around the perimeter stood the TOG vehicles, firing into the circle occupied by the Renegades. The battle stabilized as it became clear that neither side had the strength to force the issue. Then the penal infantry, escaping the collapsing dome below the surface, emerged in the center of the combat.

Sergeant Lisectus Barcus led the eight remaining men of his platoon along the gallery to the surface. As he emerged into the flickering light and dark of the surface world, he was greeted by chaos. Near the exit hole stood a Pedden carrier, its side crumpled by a collision. Beyond it stood a Liberator with a bent main gun. Other tanks and light vehicles hovered around the Pedden, and figures in Renegade uniforms moved through the area. Barcus signaled his men into the limited cover of the entrance crater, where they waited for the remaining TVLG section to prepare its weapons. He raised his hand, waited for the response from the other leaders, and gave the signal.

The results of their fire were spectacular, the TVLG slamming through the damaged side of the Pedden to explode in the interior. Most of the force vented through the open door on the tank's opposite side to cast a sudden, lurid glow over the snow. Continuous bursts from the penal infantry spike rifles scythed through the figures clustered nearby, scattering them like chaff on the wind. The TVLG fired its last missile, this time against a Liberator tank that bolted away like a frightened animal. Hand grenades arced through the sky, exploding in deadly blossoms between the vehicles. Renegades ran in all directions.

Barcus looked back to see more penal infantry pouring from the opening. Flopping down on the lip of the crater, they began to fire. On the opposite side of the crater, a sergeant rounded up a handful of men and led them in a ragged charge against a hovering tank. They attacked it from the rear, pouring shot after shot into the crumbling armor. The tank, busy with an unseen target in the distance, disregarded the swarming peds.

A Cohort heavy-weapons team struggled up the inner slope of the crater, dragging a Terere heavy assault rifle. Gasping for breath in the frigid air, the leader of the section dropped the tripod onto the ice, digging the spiked feet into the surface. The next man placed the breech and barrel section on the tripod while the third man attached the shoulder brace. The weapon emplaced, the gunner slipped into the harness and began to fire. The heavy weapon, known affectionately to the troops as the "Kess-Crusher," began to fire with a steady *whack, whack.* At this range it was impossible to miss the swirling mass of Renegade vehicles, and the heavy slugs scoured chunks of titanium armor from the sides of its victims. Another section charged from the crater to finish the destruction of the burning Pedden.

Outside the Renegade perimeter, the TOG forces recognized that the Renegades had divided their attention between the forces attacking from without the perimeter and the mayhem caused by the attack from within. Tanks that had withdrawn were sent back into the assault. A brace of Horatius tanks attacked a lone Liberator, catching it in a deadly crossfire of 150mm cannon and heavy lasers. The sides of the Liberator crumpled under the combined fire, gaping holes torn in the titanium armor.

A Romulus infantry vehicle caught a Viper carrier as it hovered to deploy its infantry. Raking the after-section with its 5/6 laser, it incinerated most of the peds before they cleared the burning vehicle. The Romulus lumbered on, seeking other prey. A Wolverine, caught looking the wrong way, burst into flames.

Karstil moved his tank away from the fiery lump that had been the Cohort command vehicle. Spikes popped over the open hatch, and he ducked down inside the fighting compartment to escape a random hit. No one was firing directly at him, but there was enough loose metal in the air to make life interesting. He couldn't open fire in his present position for fear that he would strike friendly troops. He needed space to fight his tank. And he needed infantry to deal with the penals boiling to the surface in the middle of the formation.

The Renegades found themselves fighting inside a collapsing doughnut. The hole was occupied by an ever-growing number of penal infantry, and the outside edge was made up of the remaining combat vehicles of Cohort Patrius, supported by more penal troops. Karstil's Liberator hunkered between two giant ice mounds as it tracked an approaching Romulus. The TOG carrier had better armor than the Liberator, but the Renegade tank had the advantage in firepower. It would all come down to who took the first shot. Karstil let the Liberator ground.

"Gunner. Lay on two hundred mils. Load HEAP. We've got an enemy vehicle coming at us." Karstil felt the turret swing to the right, heard the soft whir as the ballistic computer loaded the indexed ammunition into the breeches of the side-mounted cannon. The DDP would be useless at this range. The sensors showed a clear path to the Romulus five hundred meters away, but Karstil could see that intervening terrain in the shape of pillars of ice blocked his shot. He turned down the volume on the computer voice.

Light from the battle raging around him reflected off a violent burst of steam, and the data display showed Karstil that the Romulus had fired its laser. The commander of the Romulus obviously had not been paying attention to the terrain, and had fired at the Liberator unaware that line-of-sight was blocked. He must have been ignoring his computer, too, because it would have told him that the target line was not clear. Or perhaps the targeting computer was damaged.

"Driver. Forward, full thrust." The Liberator leaped forward between the pillars. "Gunner. Traverse right." The turret swung.

As the tank cleared the obstruction, the forward hull of the Romulus came into view, a wisp of steam rising from the projecting snout of the heavy laser.

"Gunner. Romulus. Pointblank."

"Identified."

"Fire all."

"On the way!" The blast of the shots reverberated among the ice peaks. The shells and laser struck on the front of the Romulus turret, throwing it back against an ice column, and the Romulus spun away. The turret began to swing toward Karstil.

"Driver. Forward! Push him!" It was a calculated risk, Karstil knew. If he could push the Romulus around in a circle, he might be able to stay behind the deadly laser. The turret armor on the Liberator was so fragile, even when undamaged, that if the 5/6 laser got a clean shot, it would burn through the remains of the titanium and the ballistic protection, and into the circuitry. He had to get another shot off before that happened. The Liberator slammed into the side of the Romulus, the Renegade tank's left sponson crumpling under the force.

"Gunner. HEAP. Shoot!" Karstil heard the soft whir of the ammunition cylinders spinning the next round into the cannon's smoking breeches. The green light on the laser showed it was recharged. The heavy laser on the Romulus glowed, and in the frigid air Karstil could feel the heat of the aligned light as it snapped passed his head, only centimeters off target. He would fully comprehend his narrow miss only after the blood lust of combat had passed. The Liberator's turret weapons spoke again, searing Karstil's face with the heat of the exploding shells.

The turret laser of the Romulus blew away, only dangling wires and popping circuits left behind. The enemy carrier tried desperately to break free from the grip of the Liberator. With a wrenching lurch the hulls parted, the Liberator spinning away to the right, the Romulus backing hard to the left. Karstil could see an orange glow coming from the open hatches on the top of his adversary's turret. Smoke began to billow from the openings. Then a figure appeared to launch himself from the turret, riding a towering jet of flame. Higher and higher rose the dancing figure. Then the column of flame erupted in a ball, and the figure fell back into the conflagration.

Platoon Sergeant Lucifer K. Mullins led the wedge of Liberator tanks down from the sky and in over the ice. Behind him came a loose formation of Viper carriers, and then more vehicles strung out in a herringboned column. He could see the glow of combat in the center of the pole, flaming circles etched on black. He needed to know where his reinforcements would do the most good, but could get no information from the forces already on the ground. The tank wedge continued to approach the battle.

"This is Bashful Laundry Leader," he said at last into the commlink, designating his position within the formation rather than his numerical code. "Head right into the center of this thing. We're getting jammed from the surface, so I can't get a sitrep, but I'm sure we'll be useful wherever we go in. Infantry, deploy as we cross. Tanks, we'll circle the wagons." He waited for the acknowledgements. "Follow me down." He switched to internal. "Gunner. Careful of your shots. Make sure you've got a bad guy in your sights before you trigger a round."

The driver applied negative thrust, dropping the tank's speed below 200 kph, nosed the tank over into a half-roll, half-dive, and headed for the inferno below.

The center of the maelstrom boiled with smoke and flame. The approaching vehicles only added to the confusion that reigned around the bolt-hole. Neither side noticed that more equipment was piling into the fight; they were too concerned with their own survival to care about new vehicles. But both sides took notice when the Viper carriers appeared overhead and the bounce infantry blew from their pods.

The half-light cast by the flames of burning vehicles and missile blasts was filled with falling bodies, each one riding its own jet of flame to the ground. HUDs designated friend and foe, and spike rifles flashed at pointblank range. Bodies seemed to dance and stagger under the impact of spikes. The bounce armor worn by the relief force was stronger than the light battle suits worn by the penal infantry, and it absorbed much of the damage. The incoming Renegade infantry was outnumbered, but the penals were doomed. They were inundated by the falling troops, forced to rise from their positions to engage, and as they did so, the peds who had been firing into the center from the Renegade-held perimeter saw their chance and closed.

Barcus found himself in the center of a swirling melee, Renegades and penals eyeball to eyeball over the muzzles of spike rifles. Barcus began to have a hard time separating the reality of the battle from his vision of the struggle as New Rome against the forces that would resist its glory. The penal sergeant remembered all the TOG Legions with which he had served, the faces of all those he had known who had gone before. A Renegade ped appeared in front of his rifle and he fired a full burst at the man. The figure vanished as abruptly as he had come. Something hit him in the back and his left shoulder went numb. He turned to see another Renegade crouching in the ice, surrounded by steam and looking like an ancient avatar of evil. He squeezed the trigger on his spike rifle again, but the bolt snapped forward on the empty chamber. Raising the weapon like a club, he charged.

The Renegade bounce infantryman watched his TOG target turn, blood flowing from his left shoulder. The penal raised his weapon in what looked like surrender, and the Renegade stayed where he was, waiting for the man's next move. Then the penal charged. The Renegade was so surprised that he let the man cover half the intervening ground before he understood what was happening. Then he raised the muzzle of his rifle and emptied the ammunition block into the TOG's chest. The other penals saw their sergeant fall, and began to surrender.

Legatus Maximus Rocipian Olioarchus saw the blue circle marking the penals in the center of the combat gradually fade away. He cursed the inefficiency of the penal infantry; they should have sacrificed themselves more gloriously. He pressed the intercom button and Centurion Miles Stratton came through the port. "Break contact, Centurion. Pull back and reorganize." Stratton snapped a quick salute at his commander and vanished. Olioarchus began to dictate his final battle report into the transcriber. "Due to the incompetent planning of Legatus Cariolanus Camus, Operation Polar Night was compromised from the beginning. The insertion of the 356th Penal Auxilia in an attempt to salvage the situation was ill-timed, and ill-used once the infantry were on the ground. It is my considered opinion that..."

The door opened again and Stratton reappeared. "Breaking contact now, sir. How far back shall we move?"

"All the way to Malthus, Stratton. We're going all the way back."

"But sir, we can still win."

"Negative, Stratton. This operation has been a failure since the first Cohort landed here, and there's nothing we can do to redeem failure. Our losses are too high to continue. We're on our way out of here."

The operations officer did not argue. He had seen the casualty figures streaming into his logistics and personnel computer, and the magic number of 70 percent penal losses had been reached. If the penal regiment took more than 80 percent losses there would be talk. At 90 percent losses there would be an investigation and probably a sacrifice. And no one wanted a sacrifice, especially not the regimental commander. "We have no ground transport for the infantry, sir."

"Knock down the temporary shelters. Use the sides as sleds and tow them with the grav vehicles. There's plenty of Nisus tanks available for that."

Centurion Stratton left the commander to his battle report. He was determined to do the best job possible in saving the remaining penal troops. His efficiency report would probably be based on his actions in the retreat, and he remembered the old adage that said a person's first and last actions were the ones that made a lasting impression. For this mission, his impressive last action would be the retreat.

57

1300, 15 Martius 6831—The TOG tank commander wasn't quite sure what to do with his prize. The Nisus-S belonged to the Ssoran police unit, but the crew was dead when he found the vehicle. That in itself must have been quite a story, but he couldn't get any information from the sole survivor, a TOG infantryman he had found unconscious but managed to revive. He had spent the time since then getting away from the combat area, a prudent move with only AP lasers for defense. Then the second wave of Renegade tanks had swept in. Now the soldier who had come with the Nisus-S sat hunched over the gunnery sights like a stolid bear.

The other vehicles of the battered unit were assembling on the side of the pole nearest Malthus. The commander of the Nisus-S kept his vehicle well clear of its unit cluster, sure that his presence would inspire more questions than he had answers. The action in the assembly area and the commlink chatter made it clear that a retreat was in progress. The unauthorized crew of the Nisus-S suddenly began to think of the vehicle as a way home rather than a combat asset. The penal troops in the assembly area were tearing down sheds, evidently to make sledges for the trip to the edge of the ice.

The huge gunner muttered an endless stream of vile imprecations against the Ssora and the Renegades, the two enemies seeming to become one in his mind. The tank commander refrained from interrupting the man's diatribe, deciding that the survivor was probably powerful enough, even wounded as he was, to be dangerously violent when angry. Right now, the anger was just below the surface. The commander kept his distance, if not physically, at least conversationally.

In the assembly area, the penal infantry pulled the last of the temporary structures apart, needing no encouragement to demolish the buildings. They understood that there was no other transportation for them off the polar cap. Either they made their own sleds, or they would be left behind. They worked with an enthusiasm that bordered on desperation.

The thick sides of the disassembled buildings were connected to grav vehicles by emergency tow cables. Each grav vehicle came equipped with an emergency cable, and the second cable for each sled was scavenged from the dead tanks in the area. The force commander had designated the Ssoran-piloted vehicles to be used as the tows, because the Nisus-S tanks were the least useful in battle and therefore the most expendable. He also knew the Ssora would keep the penal troops in line. He had taken the time to emphasize to each of the Ssoran tank commanders that they were responsible for the safe delivery of their charges to the edge of the ice. Cutting the sled cables to make better time was not acceptable. The Ssora were familiar with

TOG's philosophy concerning penals, and sullenly agreed to the plan.

Olioarchus personally urged the troops to work faster. He didn't want the Renegade force to interfere with the retreat to Malthus, and the longer the preparations took, the greater became the danger of that happening. Their retreat formation left them open to attack, and the sledges would hamper his command's ability to fight back. The sledges would also slow the entire formation to a speed less than 100 kph; if they traveled at any greater speed, the penal infantry would be torn off the sledges by the wind and the uneven terrain. It would be dangerous enough having to deal with the ice geysers again; he didn't need the other problem as well. Some of the penal infantry would die along the way, but he wanted to keep those casualties to a minimum.

Inside the Renegade position, counterattack and pursuit ranked low on the list of priorities. The three units—Cohort Harras, the relief force led by Kenderson, and the third wave brought in by Mullins—were hopelessly entangled. Just sorting them out into coherent units would take several hours. Casualties suffered among the tank crewmen and infantry had to be made good with survivors. The second relief force, loaded into the transport completely at random and further disorganized by the launch, needed to be assigned to commands.

Prefect Kenderson decided to organize his expanded force into a three-Cohort Manus. Harras would command the first Cohort, and two senior officers would take the others. Kenderson mentioned in passing that Centurion Maximus Alanton Freund, the leader of the first aborted relief effort, was in the headquarters and available for a command, but Harras' grim look in response to the suggestion convinced him to drop the matter. Harras never badmouthed a fellow soldier if he could help it, but his attitude toward Freund continued to be one of damnation by faint praise.

Karstil brought his crumpled Liberator into the Renegade defensive circle. He had to chase infantry troops out of his path as he went because the hull-to-hull fight with the Romulus carrier had crushed the left-hull sponson housing the vane control. Now his tank would turn only to the right. He let the shattered tank ground near the medical section.

The hospital had taken most of the fire from the Terere heavy assault rifle, and the side of the medical Pedden was pockmarked from hits by the heavy slugs. They had moved the patients and laid them in short rows under a hastily constructed holotarp shelter. The wounded were completely shrouded in thermal cloaks to protect them from the biting polar cold. Karstil dismounted and walked toward the makeshift hospital.

The pungent odor of burning leaves stung his nostrils. He stopped short and stared around him. He knew that smell. Only one man exuded that aroma, even without a lit cigar in his mouth. Sergeant Lucifer K. Mullins was somewhere in the turmoil of the command post.

A hand slammed down on his shoulder. "Sir," said a gruff voice from behind, "I didn't expect to see you here." The voice carried genuine fondness, for Mullins had decided long ago that this optio was worth keeping alive, and that he would go places if he survived.

Karstil turned to face his former platoon sergeant. "Nor I you," he said. The sight of the familiar face grinning at him from under the combat helmet wrenched at his heart. He had so much he wanted to say to this man, but, as usual, the words wouldn't come. "I thought you were supposed to be in a hospital somewhere," was the best he could do.

"We all should be in a hospital somewhere," Mullins snorted. "You look a sight, sir. What happened to your arms?"

Karstil remembered that he had been hit by tank fragments that had burned through his battledress. As if mentioning the injuries finally made them real, the burns began to throb. He suddenly felt the chill of the night on his arms as well, and flexed his hands to stimulate the blood flow. He looked down at his scorched uniform. "I'd forgotten about that."

"You'd better see the doc. And get something to cover your arms. Cold as it is in this miserable place, you'll get frostbite in no time at all."

Karstil suddenly remembered why he was at the hospital in the first place and started forward again. "I've got something else to do first. There's someone here I have to find."

Mullins grabbed the optio by both shoulders and looked directly into his eyes. "Sir. She'll be the same fifteen minutes from now. Take care of yourself first. If you're out of action, it won't do her, or you, or any of us, any good. Let me tell you something about frostbite; it and diamonds have a lot in common. They're both forever. You're too good a man to lose."

"How did you know about Honor?" Karstil's face was red.

"Come on, sir. You mooned around because of her the last time we were in a hospital together. It doesn't take a rocket scientist to figure it out. I'll go look for her, you get yourself fixed up."

Karstil gave up. Mullins was obviously in charge, at least for awhile, and it was no use resisting. He turned to the medical orderly who had stood waiting patiently, and Mullins went off to search the wounded.

Finally, his arms anointed with a strange goo and bandaged from the wrist to the triceps, Karstil went in search of Mullins. The rows of wounded were laid out head-to-toe-to-head, with just enough space between them for the orderlies and doctors to administer to each of them easily. More critical cases were elevated on grav-stretchers so that the doctors could reach them without bending. Karstil entered through a panel in the end of the tent and began to work his way down the rows of patients. The low roof of the holotarp thumped against his head as he moved, and he had to step around the orderlies as they tended to their patients. Mullins stood at the far end of the row. He looked grim.

"She's not here," he growled as the optio approached.

Karstil looked at him in silent inquiry, waiting for the other shoe to drop. When it didn't come, he finally asked, "Are there any other wounded?"

"No, sir."

Karstil felt his heart go cold. She had only been with him a moment. She had gone unconscious, but he hadn't been able to find a serious wound when he looked for one. He had been so busy doing other things. If only he had checked more closely. If only the medical orderly had reached his Liberator sooner. He felt his emotions tugging at his face.

"You guys have to get out of here." An orderly, his arms filled with various vials and bags, stood beside the silent pair. "We've got work to do, and you guys are in the way."

"We're looking for someone," snapped Karstil. Mullins put his hand on Karstil's arm and squeezed gently. "Sorry," said Karstil. "We'll get out of your way."

"That's all right, sir," said the orderly. He had seen a lot of people in here searching for a friend. "Who is it?"

"Ross," said Mullins. "Sergeant Honor Ross. She would have been brought in less than an hour ago."

"Ross," repeated the orderly, frowning over the name. "Yeah. I remember. Lots of red hair."

"Auburn," corrected Karstil.

"All right, auburn. She's in there." The orderly gestured toward a door in the far wall as best he could with his arms encumbered by the medical paraphernalia.

Karstil turned to look at where the orderly was pointing. It was the door to the morgue. Karstil felt his heart stop again. He turned away to leave.

"Not that door," said the orderly, "that's the morgue." He tried again, pointing with a single finger to an opening further along the canvas wall. "I mean the warming tent."

Karstil felt his heart leap.

"She came in unconscious," said the attendant. "She was pretty banged up and cold. That's what took her out. We gave her a couple of shots and stuck her in there. She's probably fine by now." The orderly looked at Karstil. The joy on his face was too obvious to miss. "She important to you, sir?" he asked wryly.

"She's important to both of us," said Mullins, turning Karstil away from the smiling orderly. "We'll find her. Thanks for your trouble."

"No trouble, Sarge. Just doing my job."

The TOG force began its trek back across the ice cap toward Malthus. The Ssoran Nisus-S tanks, pulling sledges filled with penal troops, moved first, their retreat covered by the remnants of Cohort Patrius. Neither the lizards nor their charges much cared for the setup, but they weren't in a position to complain or change it. The Ssora felt their mission had been accomplished while the troops were under the ice and did not like playing nursemaid to their prisoners. Legatus Maximus Olioarchus, however, had impressed upon them that their own survival depended on their bringing the Penal Auxilia safely to the edge of the ice, so they refrained from cutting the cables to speed their retreat.

The miserable penals huddled on the jouncing sledges, whipped by the icy wind created by the 100-kph speed. The open transport offered no cover, and the wind whipped over them with a terrible force. Nor was there any cushioning between the slabs of metal on which they rode and the rough ice beneath. The Ssoran driving the Nisus-S vehicles were not about to slow down over the rough portions, and the penals had to cling to the ribbed walls on which they rode and each other to keep from being flung clear.

Leading the formation, Legatus Maximus Rocipian Olioarchus rode in the command Pompey so recently surrendered by Camus, former commander of the Strike Cohort. His vehicle was warm, well-appointed, and flying at an altitude sufficient to keep him comfortably above the eruptions of the ice geysers. He had called planetary headquarters to arrange for transportation for the penals to meet him at the pole's edge, and that request transferred the responsibility for the survival of the 356th Penal Auxilia to the shoulders of planetary staff. He could not be held accountable for their loss if planetary headquarters did not respond to his request. It felt good to be rid of that burden. The penal force had taken a total 72.5 percent casualties, which was an eminently acceptable number. His report on the operation, sent along with the transportation request, had placed the blame for the disaster squarely on the shoulders of Cariolanus Camus, and, to a much lesser degree, on those of Prefect Claudius Sulla. The comment about Sulla had been an afterthought, but he was glad he had inserted it. It was not even a criticism, merely a less-than-glowing judgment of the man's actions. If Sulla had powerful enemies at planetary headquarters, they would understand what was being said. If he had powerful friends, they would delete the references before passing the report on to sector. It was a stroke of genius.

58

0400, 16 Martius 6831—"I'd still like to take a crack at them," Centurion Maximus Harras argued. "I'd like to get my licks in now that we finally seem to have the upper hand. At least we could chase the TOGs off the south pole."

"You always were aggressive, Milt," replied Prefect Kenderson. "Too aggressive by half. But that's why I requested you for this mission in the first place. The Renegade Legion needs people who'll fight. That's always been at least half their trouble. They seem to court defeat and disaster. We almost had victory in our grasp on Alsatia, and then we let it slip away." Kenderson leaned back in his chair and studied the situation plot. The screen showed clear for five hundred kilometers all around their position. The only enemy forces within a thousand kilometers were those retreating off the ice. In another hour, given the 100-kph speed they were maintaining, even those would be gone. He switched the plot to high resolution. The rim of the ice cap showed as a faint blur at two thousand kilometers. He ran a quick mental calculation.

The TOG forces were slightly less than one thousand kilometers away, moving toward the ice edge at 100 kph. Assuming they maintained that speed, they would reach the edge of the ice in just over ten hours. The pursuing Renegade forces could maintain a speed of 200 kph, give or take a bit, so they should be able to cover the full two thousand kilometers to the ice edge before the end of those same ten hours. Even allowing enough time to finish the reorganization, the pursuit force would catch the TOGs just as they reached the edge of the ice. It was worth the gamble.

"How soon can you be ready to go, Milt?" Kenderson had made his decision. "I'll send you first. Cohort Martil will follow as soon as possible. She's junior to you, so if the two of you end up in the same place, you'll be in command, but she's a fighter, too. I'll have to wait here with Cohort Forblen. He's got a lot of new people around him at staff, and he had problems controlling his people on Alsatia, so I think I'll sit on him for a while. We'll join you as soon as we're ready." Kenderson shook his index finger at his favorite Cohort commander. "Look here, Milt. Just deal with whatever you find at the edge of the ice cap. Don't pick a fight you can't win."

Milton Harras smiled. "Don't worry, NaBesta. I don't plan to. I just want to harass them." He stood. "I can get off the ice in half an hour. The reorganization is almost complete; I just need to make a few final changes in my force, put some people into tanks, and I'll be ready."

"Good luck, Milt."

"Thanks, sir."

* * *

People and vehicles swirled in intricate patterns around the Cohort command Pedden. Centurion Moldine Rinter stood by the door, her combat helmet pushed to the back of her head, an organization panel in her hand. She made quick strokes on its surface with an electronic stylus, assigning crew to tanks, filling vacancies with extra people, pulling the Cohort together. Centurion Sedden Matruh leaned against the edge of the door, watching his Century fill to strength. He wanted as many old hands as possible in his command, people he knew and had fought with under the ice.

Sam Rand was not going on this trip, even though he was healthy and willing. Rinter had taken a good look at the inexperienced optio when he reported back to Cohort after the retreat from the city, and she could tell by the look in his eyes that he had had enough. He had performed his assignment in conjunction with Graviston faultlessly, but he was through with tanks, at least for a while. Graviston was in the same condition, but his tiredness was mostly physical. He had been wounded twice, and while both he and his tank were combat ready, his tank would get a new commander.

Rinter turned to the clump of tank commanders waiting at her side. "Karstil! You just keep turning up! Well, there's a tank I think you'll enjoy." She pointed to a Liberator grounded just beyond the Pedden. The driver and gunner lounged on the deck, dining contentedly on emergency rations. Steam rose from the cello-packs of fortified food. (It was not really food in the traditional sense, more like a specially designed, nutrient-rich substance guaranteed to satisfy all the body's requirements. Except for taste and texture, that is.) A person had to be very, very hungry to actually enjoy emergency rations, and the tank crew was obviously relishing theirs.

As Karstil moved toward the tank, the crewmen jumped to their feet to greet their commander. Karstil smiled; he had his old tank back. Boutselis and Crowder were as glad to see him as he was to see them. All three men interrupted each other for a few minutes, trying to tell their stories, then they were in the tank, powering up and checking the systems. Karstil picked up the commlink and checked in with the Century. He was assigned as Second Platoon leader in the Fourth Century and would be Cunning Contest Four-two-six to Matruh's Four-six. He called the other tanks in his platoon and was surprised and pleased to hear Honor Ross' soft voice respond from Four-two-one.

"Cunning Contest Four. This is Cunning Contest Four-six. Vector three-five-six-zero true. Velocity one-double-zero. Form on me." Matruh's course was set for Frotik, the planetary headquarters of the TOG forces on Caralis, and followed the same path the TOG Strike Cohort had taken toward the edge of the ice. The Century would move away from the center of the south pole and head north until they were well away from the rest of the Renegade forces. They would organize on the fly, units taking up stations as they moved. It was just as simple to shake out into battle formation on the move as it was while hovering around the headquarters, and significantly less confusing.

The Century swung away from the Renegade position. First Platoon took the left flank, Second took the right, and the command unit with the infantry platoon stayed in the center. The Century now formed a wedge, each platoon flying in a wide vee. Karstil took the point of his platoon formation. Ross was on his left, toward the center of the Century.

Ross had never commanded a Liberator, but she knew the drill from commanding the Viper. She was also blessed with an experienced crew. Blackstone was back as her driver, and Hamilton Hull served as her gunner. It seemed like coming home. Hull showed Ross around the innards of the tank while Blackstone took up their tank's assigned position in the formation. He was also getting used to a new tank. Driving the Liberator was different from driving a Viper. The larger tank offered far less thrust than the smaller vehicle, which meant the driver had to pay closer attention to what he was doing. Blackstone couldn't expect to jockey the Liberator's 273 tons around the same way he did the Viper, at one-third the mass. But he would have the hang of it before they made contact with the TOGs.

When the formation was sorted, Matruh ordered it to increase velocity, and it accelerated from 100 kph to 150, and finally to 200. As they approached the edge of the inner ice plain, the force rose to tree-top altitude. Its leaders did not want to repeat their previous experiences with the ice geysers. The Cohort leveled out and stormed north at 280 kph.

Eight hours later, the DDP in Karstil's Liberator flared with TOG units. "Unidentified vehicles. Range five-double-zero-double-zero. Bearing two-double-zero relative. Speed one-double-zero. Moving away. Range closing at three kilometers per minute. Targets will be in range in sixteen minutes." Karstil felt the familiar rush of adrenaline. The nagging pain in his arms vanished, his breathing and heartbeat became shallow and rapid. He knew that in fifteen minutes, a quarter of an hour, he would be leading his platoon into deadly combat.

"Unidentified vehicles. Range four-five-zero-double-zero. Bearing two-double-zero relative. Speed zero. Range closing at five kilometers per minute. Targets will be in range in eight minutes." The closest enemy units had stopped, probably to slow the pursuing Renegade forces. This would be a rear guard, bent on inflicting casualties at the longest possible range.

"Multiple Romulus vehicles. Range four-double-zero-double-zero. Bearing one-nine-zero relative. Speed zero. Range closing at five kilometers per minute. Targets will be in range in seven minutes." Romulus carriers meant heavy lasers capable of firing at four kilometers, supported by infantry. His own heavy laser could reach as far and inflict the same damage, but the Romulus had better armor and stronger shields.

"Multiple Romulus vehicles. Range three-five-zero-double-zero. Bearing one-nine-zero relative. Speed six-zero. Moving away. Range closing at four kilometers per minute. Targets will be in range in seven minutes." The Romulus carriers probably had dropped infantry on the ice and were falling back. The TOGs must be planning to use the dismounted infantry to paint from cover while the lasers fired at long range. This meant they were also facing TVLGs. But the infantry wasn't moving, which made them easier targets. He cued the DDP to continue tracking the first stationary position occupied by the carriers; that's where the infantry would be hiding. He posted the probable infantry to the plot.

"Contest Four-six. This is Contest Four-two-six. Probable infantry position at three-five-zero-double-zero. Carriers behind and moving away. Request permission to sweep right."

There was a pause as Matruh analyzed the downloaded data and the request. "Contest Four-two-six. This is Four-six. Permission granted. Break. Contest Four-one-six. Watch Four-two-six. Move behind TOG positions as you come up on him."

Karstil stared at the commlink in disbelief. His Century commander had approved his plan, and without comment. Centurion Alanton Freund never would have done it. Suddenly happy, he wanted to shout, "Let's go get 'em!" but instead he spoke calmly into the commlink.

"Contest Four-two. This is Four-two-six. Break right eight-double-zero. Speed two-four-zero. On the deck. Echelon left on me. Execute." The platoon swung to the right. The right-hand tank drifted across the back of the formation to take up a position to the left and behind Ross' Liberator. Karstil still led in the new formation, Ross was behind and to the left, and Tank Two was further back and to the left. When they made the ninety-degree left turn to attack the TOG carriers, they would be on line.

The DDP kept up with the change of formation and direction, murmuring, "Multiple Romulus vehicles. Range three-zero-zero-double-zero. Bearing five-eight-double-zero relative. Speed six-zero. Moving away. Range closing at three kilometers per minute. Targets will be in range in six minutes."

Karstil maintained direction and speed for four more minutes. The Romulus carrier stopped three kilometers behind the plotted infantry position. Karstil knew they would blow craters into the ice to take up hull defilade positions, but now the enemy faced a difficult choice. With the rest of the Renegade Century continuing in its original direction, the carriers were in danger of being turned from their right flank. Karstil's bearing off to their left threatened to turn the carriers' other flank. And both forces would converge behind the deployed infantry and out of range of their painting lasers. The TOG carriers had to choose between moving forward to retrieve their infantry and then running, staying where they were and fighting a superior force, or abandoning the infantry and trailing their retreating force. As Karstil expected, and in true TOG fashion, they fled.

"Contest Four-six. This is Two-two-six. Carriers breaking away. Watch for the infantry on the ice."

"Roger Four-two-six. I'll dispatch a carrier to pick them up. Rejoin."

Karstil turned the platoon to rejoin the Century. He kept well clear of the TOG infantry location, unwilling to take damage from an abandoned unit. He wanted to save his tank's strength for the real fight. His platoon had performed its first test well, changing formation quickly and accurately. The driver–commander combination in the other Liberator was a good one.

He listened to the commlink chatter as the Viper approached the TOG infantry. His estimate had been right; the force left behind was a single squad, heavily armed with TVLGs. The Viper sent by Matruh negotiated a surrender from out of range. Its task accomplished, the Viper dropped a warning beacon to keep the following Cohort, led by Martil, from stumbling unannounced on a squad of TOG infantry in the middle of the ice.

Karstil reassumed his position on the Century's right flank, his platoon re-formed into a vic. They were getting close to the edge of the ice cap now, and this time the TOGs wouldn't run.

59

1400, 16 Martius 6831—The lumbering TOG transports plowed through the towering waves, huge plumes of water breaking over the foredecks in a solid green wave that flowed all the way to the bridge towers. High above the bridge wings in the enclosed Glasser mounts, a single 200mm Gauss cannon, co-axed through three 7.5/6 lasers, swung back and forth as if looking for the landing coordinates on the south pole.

The water changed to ice as it met the frigid air pouring through the scuppers, bearding the ships with ragged silver. A sheen of ice sparkled on the upper decks and reflected the light cast by the round face of Rock Wall rising above the eastern horizon. Ahead, the ice cliffs marking the edge of Caralis' southern polar cap loomed white against the stygian sky. The transport captains nudged their huge craft into the narrow estuary, sheltered from the waves and the wind that howled over the exposed ice above.

The headquarters at Malthus had chosen the evacuation location for the retreating Penal Auxilia. Their coordinates preset, both forces had been guided to the rendezvous by electronic means. As the transports nosed up the estuary, a single, blinking recognition laser told them that the other force had also made their way successfully to the pickup point. The skippers scanned the sky, searching for signs of the air cover they had been promised. When it was obvious no such cover was there, they hunched themselves deeper into their duffel coats and tried not to think about the lack.

On the cliffs above, Legatus Maximus Rocipian Olioarchus looked down at the ships in the narrow harbor. His depleted forces would fit easily into the three vessels, each of which was big enough to hold a full-strength Cohort. It would be impossible to take the jouncing sleds down the steep grade without spilling their cargos into the frigid water below, so the infantry would have to dismount on the edge of the cliff and work their way down the steep slopes to their rescuers. The Ssora, in their Nisus-S carriers, would hover over and around the penals, herding them down to the transports' open clamshell doors. If they had enough time, the evacuation would be at least a limited success, but Olioarchus still wanted to avoid more than 80 percent casualties among the penals if he could; any higher number would look bad on his record.

The plan was to evacuate the equipment of Cohort Patrius first. The penals would establish a solid defensive line along the top of the cliff through which the regulars could fall back to the ships. Then the penals would execute a withdrawal under pressure by thinning their lines. Finally, the ships and the remaining Ssoran grav vehicles would cover the surviving penals as they moved down the cliffs. Once the infantry dropped below the crest of the cliff, the heavy weapons on the ships and the AP lasers of the Nisus-S light tanks would provide enough covering fire to get all personnel and vehicles loaded aboard the transports. The Ssoran vehicles could make the run to Malthus on their own if need be, as could the other vehicles of Cohort Patrius, but they would all be safer in the transports.

Matruh's Century continued across the ice plain at tree-top flight, geysers erupting below the flying tanks in spectacular gouts of freezing water and spray blasted to sheets of ice. The onboard navigational computers, the Terrain Sensing and Reaction circuits, measured each explosion, averaged it against the others it had recorded, then lifted the vehicle to a safe height. The tanks began to sink toward the surface as they neared the edge of the south pole.

The DDPs of the Renegade vehicles blossomed with targets at fifty kilometers, relaying the information to the combat helmets of the tank commanders. Karstil watched the "unidentified" amber indicators bleed to red as the computer acknowledged the distinct electronic emissions of the enemy vehicles. The TOGs were setting up in a series of fletches, three tanks or carriers in each vee-formation. The positions were spaced two kilometers apart, a wide setup, but well within range to take advantage of each other's TVLGs or SMLMs, even in the hands of dismounted infantry. The Renegade Century would have to break one of the strong points to make a breach in the line, but the commanders knew that the TOGs would willingly trade space for time, inflicting casualties as they fell back through another defensive line.

Sedden Matruh pulled the platoons closer together. He was going to use the Century as a hammer, overwhelming the defense with more targets than it had shots, closing to pointblank range, and blowing the enemy away. It was not a subtle plan, but given the nature of his current command and the type of defense the TOGs had established, it was a good one. Karstil fitted his platoon into a wing position; the other platoon would take the enemy point vehicle.

"Horatius tank. Range five-zero-double-zero. Bearing six-two-double-zero. Enemy vehicle stationary. Closing speed two-four-zero. Target locked. Target not painted." Karstil's DDP had chosen a Horatius tank and would disregard the other vehicles in the enemy formation until targeted by the enemy's sensors. They would be within range in seconds.

"Contest Four-two. This is Four-two-six. I'm going straight in. Two, follow as my wing. One, swing right for the flank attack. Execute." Ross brought her tank within two hundred meters of Karstil's left quarter. Tank One drifted away to the right to approach the enemy on an angle. Karstil switched his attention to the enemy.

"Horatius tank. Range four-five-double-zero. Bearing six-two-double-zero. Enemy vehicle stationary. Closing speed two-four-zero. Target locked. Target not painted." Karstil watched the enemy vehicle. The Horatius would be in defilade, the hull-mounted heavy cannon just above the lip. The tank would be difficult to hit, but the extra firepower of a full-platoon to single-tank attack should make up for the difficulty. "Horatius tank. Range four-zero-double-zero. Bearing six-two-double-zero. Enemy vehicle stationary. Closing speed two-four-zero. Target locked. Target not painted." He treadled the painting laser as the painting warning klaxon in his own tank sounded. The klaxon's low pitch told him that the enemy had not yet been successful, but had chosen to give Karstil his attention. The chances of hitting the target with a laser when the enemy tank was not painted and in defilade were almost nonexistent, but enough to make the shot worth a try. "Gunner. Horatius. Range four-zero-double-zero. Laser."

"Identified."

"Fire."

"Fired." Crowder paused. "Missed."

"Horatius tank. Range three-five-double-zero. Bearing six-two-double-zero. Enemy vehicle stationary. Closing speed of two-four-zero. Target locked. Target not painted." The pitch of the Liberator's warning klaxon went from a low howl to a high-pitched scream; the Horatius had painted its enemy. Karstil winced, pounding on the treadle of the painting laser system. An instant later the enemy's turret-mounted 3/6 laser scored on the Liberator's bow, drilling a neat hole through the titanium armor. A wisp of smoke appeared on the inner hull opposite the hit. Karstil smelled the caustic odor of incinerated paint and knew that the next shot hitting in that location would penetrate. The smell of burnt paint brought back unpleasant memories of other near-misses. He heard the high whine of his own 5/6 laser as Crowder fired again.

"Missed again," reported the gunner.

Karstil cursed silently. It was his three tanks against only one of theirs, and someone should be able to paint that Horatius. That is, if the rest of his platoon remembered to attempt it. He treadled the bar again. "Horatius tank. Range three-zero-double-zero. Bearing six-two-five-zero. Enemy vehicle stationary. Closing speed two-four-zero. Target locked. Target not paint—Target painted." Here we go! Karstil cheered inwardly.

"Gunner. Horatius. Range three-zero-double-zero. Laser and HEAP."

"Identified."

"Fire."

"On the way."

The screech of the heavy laser cut through the painting warning klaxon and the crash of the Gauss cannon, and the heavy tank trembled under the weapon's powerful recoil. A simultaneous hit by the Horatius tank doubled the recoil jolt and tore a slab of armor off the left-front glacis. Another laser hit scorched another dot of paint off the inside of the fighting compartment. Karstil's attempt to attract the enemy vehicle's attention was successful, and now the Horatius was almost within missile range.

Karstil glanced down at the display panel to check the firing systems of the hull-mounted TVLGs. When he looked back he saw the fiery trail of a SMLM describing an arc in his direction against the dark sky. The Vulcan swatted the missile away. The hull shook again as the 150mm cannon fired. "Horatius tank. Range one-five-double-zero. Enemy vehicle moving away," said the DDP. The next laser hit burned through the Liberator's hull, ballistic protection bubbling away under the heat of the aligned light. The front-shield control panel blinked red, then turned green again, and Karstil knew his front-shield generator system had suffered damage. The choking odor of burning electrical systems rose into the command hatch.

The Liberator slowed. "Left-front reaction system down," said Boutselis. "I need to move a little slower, boss."

"Okay. But not much. We don't want this guy to get away." Karstil caught sight of his left-hand tank sweeping past, its main gun throwing a huge ball of fire at the Horatius. The snub nose of the 5/6 laser glowed blue in the darkness, then was overshadowed by the flash from a 150mm cannon. Tank One was on the flank and pouring fire into the retreating Horatius.

The enemy tank had inflicted damage on the Renegade platoon, but it had waited too long to begin its retreat. The rest of its platoon had fired their lasers and main guns at long range and then had backed away. The Horatius opposing Karstil had been too successful with its opening shots, which had encouraged it to stay and keep shooting. Now it paid the price. Caught between the frontal attack of Ross' Liberator and the fire of the flanking tank, it was pounded into slag. The tank commander could not turn away from one attacker without allowing the other a clear shot. He fired at his attackers once more in desperation, then his tank dissolved. A flash of brilliant white shot across the ice, then it was completely dark again. There wasn't enough wreckage left to burn.

The trails of TVLGs lit the sky. A dozen missiles were screaming toward Karstil's platoon. The Vulcan systems on the leading tanks whirred into action, bursting most of the incoming fire against the sky. But some of the missiles broke through, pummeling the leading tanks' sides and fronts.

"Contest Four. This is Contest Four-six. Infantry in the area. Break away. Break away."

"Contest Four-two. This is Two-six. Break right. Break right." Karstil switched to intercom. "Boots. Hard left. Hard left." The three Liberators spun away from the infantry line, chased by more TVLGs. The enemy tanks escaped to below the edge of the cliff and drifted down to the waiting transports.

Liberator platoons down the line circled right and left away from the defending penals and re-formed behind their waiting infantry. "This is Four-six. At my command, smoke the infantry positions. Infantry will deploy short of the smoke line. After the infantry are down, we hit together." The platoon leaders acknowledged the orders.

"Boots, Spent. What's the damage?" Karstil listened to the reports while the Liberator hovered behind and to the flank of the Viper carriers.

The forward armor had been chopped away almost to the ceramic backing. The front shields were damaged, as was the TS&R computer. They both still worked, after a fashion, but any more damage to the bow would destroy both systems and much else besides. Ross' tank had taken several TVLG hits, but reported in as still combat-functional, as did the other tank. Karstil brought them on line as the Vipers began to move.

The DDPs had marked the approximate TVLG launch points, and so the platoons headed straight for those locations. Karstil checked to see that both the 150mm and 50mm were loaded with obscuring smoke, and then sent the Liberator drifting after the Vipers. On the signal, the Liberators would cover the enemy positions with smoke as the Vipers charged, releasing the bounce infantry as close as possible to the enemy. As the smoke cleared, the legionnaires, supported by the tanks, would close with the penals.

60

1500, 16 Martius 6831—"This is Four-six. Shoot!" The line of Liberators erupted in a long sheet of flame. An instant later the 150mm rounds spread smoke along the edge of the south polar ice cap. The Vipers raced forward over the last eight hundred meters, blowing the bounce infantry from their cocoons as close to the cliff edge as possible. As the smoke cleared, the Vipers wheeled away, covering the infantry with their snub-nosed 25mm cannon. The Liberators closed from behind to offer additional support. The peds dropped to the ice.

The sparkle of spike rifles, the flash of hand grenades, and the explosions of heavy weapons marked a line of fire across the TOG positions. A haze of powdered ice hung along the edge of the cliff, refracting the glow of the explosions that had lifted it. The penal infantry, following the established plan, slipped away from the fighting line as the Renegades pressed in. Those without immediate targets moved first, scrambling over the edge of the cliff and picking their way down the face to the waiting transports. A trickle of escaping men became a stream, and those waiting at the exit points had the opportunity to survey their situation.

The Ssoran-commanded Nisus-S grav vehicles assigned to add covering fire within six hundred meters of the cliff had drifted out over the estuary, no longer even pretending to support the penals trying to break contact. The penal infantry were on their own, but those in the fiercest combats were unaware that they had been deserted.

Three penal troopers dragged their Terere heavy assault rifle to the edge of the cliff. They knew they would have to abandon it when their turn came to run for the transport, but the training that required them to save the equipment, even at the risk of their own lives, was not easily shaken off. They had, however, come up with an unexpected plan for the weapon's use. They set the tripod down facing the hovering Nisus-S tanks, snapped the firing mechanism into place, and commenced firing. The *whack* of the Kess-Crusher echoed off the walls of the estuary. The team was well-trained in the weapon's use, and knew that the front armor of the light grav tanks could withstand the impact of several of the gun's heavy slugs. They aimed for the vulnerable flanks and sides. The Ssora backed away even further, returning fire as they moved.

On the deck of the transport closest to the foot of the cliff, Legatus Maximus Rocipian Olioarchus monitored the confusion on the cliff's edge from inside his grounded Pompey. He had hoped to reach the cliff with more than 20 percent of his penal infantry alive, but that number proved happily low as they counted the men who had escaped to the water. This gave him enough cushion to afford additional casualties, and so he leaned over the commlink and gave orders for the Ssora to pull away to safety. The rest of the infantry could escape on their own.

He turned to the commander of the three-transport escape detail. "Commodore, you may begin to withdraw. Please leave the barges behind to retrieve the maximum number of infantry, but do not endanger your ships."

The commodore raised his clenched right fist in the salute of New Rome. "Thank you, Legatus Maximus. I will give the orders at once." The commodore stepped back, turned on his heel, and exited the vehicle. Olioarchus turned back to the plot.

In an adjacent cubicle, Miles Stratton heard the command given, and once more adjusted his personal assessment of his commanding officer. The man had a unique concept of honor, and Stratton knew it would be in his best interests to keep that in mind. The operations officer returned his full attention to the confused mess of red and blue indicators covering his situation plot. Renegade vehicles were pressing toward the cliff, Ssoran Nisus-S tanks were hovering over the transports. Some penal infantry were fighting a desperate action on the ice shelf while others clambered down the face toward the waiting barges. Legatus Cariolanus Camus, under house arrest in the operations center since Rocipian Olioarchus had relieved him of command, had slipped from Stratton's mind.

Legatus Camus rose quietly from his chair and moved toward the seated centurion. He bent down to retrieve the officer's metal lunch tray, raised it over his head, and slammed it down with all his strength on the back of Stratton's head in one smooth motion. The dull crunch of the blow against the undefended skull filled the tiny space. The operations officer slumped over onto the plot display-screen, his breathing a soft, steady rhythm. Camus reached down, unsnapped the flap of Stratton's holster, and drew the Hantrus spike pistol. The polymer block of ammunition was loose in the stock as an extra safety precaution. Camus seated the ammunition block firmly and slipped the safety off the weapon.

Rocipian Olioarchus was engrossed in the situation plot and didn't hear the port slide open. Penal infantry were beginning to stream over the cliff edge. The sporadic attacks the penals had made on the Nisus-S vehicles had ceased because the alien guards had withdrawn to the decks of the evacuation transports. The barges were still against the shore, but the transports had begun to pull away. The Auxilia would take more casualties in the pullout, but he would return to planetary headquarters with a comfortable margin remaining. He was satisfied.

"Is everything going as planned?"

Olioarchus turned to face Cariolanus Camus. The legatus stood in the doorway of the command center, the Hantrus held loosely in his right hand, the muzzle pointed at the face of the legatus maximus. "You seem to have broken free," Olioarchus commented.

"No concern for your centurion?"

"He will either survive or not," said Olioarchus, shrugging. "It's of little interest to me." He leaned back in his chair. He was either supremely confident or trying to place greater distance between his face and the yawning muzzle of the Hantrus.

"And your command?"

"The same. Perhaps 20 percent will survive, and that is an acceptable number. Your former command has a slightly higher percentage of survivors, not that it will do you any good. I have already reported your negligence in command to headquarters. You will be dealt with presently." Olioarchus had recovered from his initial shock; in fact, he actually felt optimistic. The longer he could keep Camus talking, the better his chances of survival. Eventually, someone would come to the command vehicle, or he might talk Camus into surrendering, or some other solution would present itself.

"You have little future with the forces of New Rome, Camus. Your record is flagged for further action. In fact, you should not live to return to Malthus. A hero's death on the shores of this frozen continent would do much to soften your disgrace. I could ask that you be given a hero's reward, perhaps a triumph through the streets of New Rome." Olioarchus dropped his hand to the communications console, drumming his fingers on the surface. The call button that would summon help was only centimeters away.

Camus leaned against the door frame, considering what Olioarchus had said. Certainly his status within the TOG command structure had been blemished, and once marked, there was no way to erase the stain. But his time spent under house arrest had not been wasted. Having listened and observed, he was no longer sure that ambition was enough to carry him up the TOG command structure. Nor was he still sure that the careless attitude most TOG officers held toward their troops was the right one, or the only one. He could not remember the faces of the men in his command. Perhaps he was meant to do penance for this.

"It would be a nice thing for your family," continued Olioarchus, his fingers drumming ever closer to the call button. "Think what it would mean to your parents." His little finger reached for the button.

The crack of the Hantrus surprised Olioarchus even more than the sharp pain in his elbow. Looking down, he saw blood staining the rich fabric of his tunic. He tried to move his hand, but the rotator joint in his right elbow was completely smashed. A wisp of burnt polymer drifted through the cubicle.

"I'm sorry," said Camus. "When you checked my file, perhaps you didn't notice that I was the academy pistol champion for three years. I can hit a spot two millimeters in diameter at a range of twenty meters. I could put eight neatly spaced holes between your eyes. Please do not reach for the call button again. I need time to think."

Olioarchus hugged his shattered arm to his chest. "You fool!" he shouted. "Do you have any idea what you have done?" He gingerly felt the joint. It had been reduced to a soggy mush. "There'll be no triumph for you now!" he hissed. "Your name will be anathema to a generation of officers."

"I think not," Camus replied. "I will die facing the enemy. I fear, however, that you will desert. Or commit suicide over the destruction of your command. But no, suicide would be difficult with your present wound. Better that you leap over the side of this transport into the waters surrounding it."

"You wouldn't dare," sneered Olioarchus, not quite disguising a touch of panic in his voice. "But we can make a deal. I'll tell headquarters that I made a mistake, that you really did a fine job. That would be the end of it." Olioarchus looked into the other man's eyes. "Please. For the sake of the government, don't do this."

"Not for your own sake, Olioarchus?"

"Trust me. I can fix it."

"Yes," said Camus. Suddenly he was very tired. "You probably can." The muzzle of the spike pistol dropped slightly.

A brief look of triumph flitted across Olioarchus' face. "I knew you would see reason."

"But I haven't." The spike pistol cracked six times. Camus had been a little boastful about his shot pattern. The spikes struck a full two centimeters apart, the first in the forehead, the last in the throat. But Olioarchus didn't criticize. He was dead before the sixth spike penetrated his larynx.

Camus dropped the pistol and bent to lift the body. Bracing it with one arm, he opened the external portal and stepped into the frigid air. The walls of the estuary were randomly illuminated by the flashes of explosions high on the rim, the sides dark with the figures of the retreating penal infantry. No one on the transport deck noticed him, too intent on their own jobs, their own survival, to spare the attention. He moved to the rail. Ten meters below, the icy water of the bay swirled with turbulence as the transport backed away from the shore. He balanced the body on the rail. "New Rome salutes you," he muttered. A slight push, and the figure was gone.

He stepped back against the bulkhead. At his feet lay a dead legionnaire in a Penal Auxilia uniform. Camus bent down and removed the identity disk from the man's neck. He dropped the new cord around his own neck, lifting off his disk at the same time. In a few seconds he was transformed. Camus heaved the second body after the first, hurling the identity disk of Cariolanus Camus into the sea behind it. Then, as a veteran of a penal regiment, he descended the ladder into the hold.

The Nisus-S hovered over the stern of the retreating transport. The commander, a regular legionnaire, had two problems: landing the grav tank on the deck of a pitching ship, and explaining how three soldiers had acquired the vehicle in the first place. "Easy, driver. Take it easy," he said into the intercom. The superb electronics of the Nisus-S made the approach to the transport a simple matter. "Set her in a one-meter hover above the back end."

"The fantail," said the gunner, who hunched bear-like over the weapons system.

"It's the back end to me, gunner. I don't care if it's the moon. I just want us down."

"And then what?" asked the gunner.

"We'll worry about it then."

"No," said Stone. "Let's worry now. We've got to find a way to ditch this tank or there'll be too many questions."

"You got a plan?"

"Put it at a one-meter hover on autopilot. Then we get out. Last man out shifts to a one-meter-per-second climb. Then he jumps over the side. The thing shouldn't be more than eight or ten meters up by the time he jumps."

"Eight or ten meters? You could kill yourself from that height."

"Good point," said Stone. "What's your plan?"

The tank commander paused for a moment. "Driver," he said. "Put it in a one-meter hover on autopilot. We're going over the side." He looked back at Stone. "Your plan. You're last out."

"Sure, chief," Stone replied. "Just make sure you're clear before I jump. I don't want to land on anyone."

The Nisus-S hovered above the trembling fantail of the transport. Two figures dropped cleanly over the side to the deck. The tank continued to hold its position as the legionnaires scrambled away to the shelter of the bulkhead. They turned to watch.

Inside the Nisus-S, Stone bent over the firing system. He reached under the console and yanked out a cluster of wires. Breaking the bundle apart at the quick-release, he bent three of the prongs and recoupled the joint backwards. Almost immediately the AP lasers began to hum, the pitch rising as the gennium-arsenic crystals began to overheat.

Stone climbed onto the command seat, throwing his legs over the coaming. He reached back into the command station and adjusted the controls. The Nisus-S began to rise. Stone quickly rolled off the turret and onto the front glacis. As the tank climbed away from the deck of the transport, he slid down the armored bow to the front lip. The deck was five meters below, but there was no time to contemplate the distance. He leaped.

61

1545, 16 Martius 6831—"Contest Four. This is Four-six. They're breaking away. Follow them." The TOG penal infantry had abandoned their positions and were streaming toward the very edge of the polar ice cap, frantic to reach the evacuation barges at the foot of the cliff. Only the most disciplined made an effort to hold the line. Karstil's Liberators drove for the edge of the ice, pushing the Penal Auxilia ahead of them. Karstil hunkered low in the command hatch, aware that single spikes were snapping past the open command hatch over his head. The DDP showed three huge vessels in the narrow estuary just over the edge of the cliff, surface transports sent to evacuate the remnants of the battered TOG forces. They would be armed, but probably only with light weapons.

"Contest Four-two. This is Four-two-six. Let's be careful going over the edge. Those transports could be a nasty bunch."

"This is Four-two-one. Tally ho! I've got grav tanks in my sights." Karstil's DDP showed his right-hand tank scooting out over the edge of the cliff. The tank banked hard to the left, swinging its turret to engage a climbing Nisus tank. The main gun flashed, followed almost immediately by the secondary cannon and the heavy laser. "Burn, baby, burn! Break. Four-two-six. This is Four-two-one. The place is filled with barges. They're pulling out their troops."

"Acknowledged, One. This is Six. Let's go get 'em." Karstil switched to internal comm. "Boots. Take us to the edge. Those peds still have some sting, so be a little careful."

"You got it, sir." The command Liberator moved toward the cliff. The other two tanks of the platoon, eager to get in a final crack at the TOG infantry, raced ahead.

"Four-two. This is Six. Go slow. Go slow. They still shoot back."

"Four-two-one. Six! Look at the size of that cannon!"

The DDP flashed a weapons identification symbol. The statistics of the Glasser mount filled the screen of the DDP, and Karstil's mouth dropped open. He had never seen a weapons system that combined a heavy cannon with three lasers, but the hitting power it provided was immediately recognizable. The 200mm cannon would shear away vast chunks of a vehicle's armor, and the heavy lasers alone could penetrate the strongest armor in a single shot. The weapon configuration would direct the lasers to the hole blasted by the cannon. No vehicle Karstil knew of would survive a second hit, and the weapon was obviously designed to kill with the first. "This is Two-six. Get away! Run! Hide!" He broadcast on external and platoon push, and then his Liberator was braking to a stop, the forward thrusters firing in a continuous roar. His eyes stayed glued to the DDP as the other two tanks, well out over the estuary, broke for the shelter of the rim.

The warning klaxon sounded and immediately slid to a high-pitched shriek. Boutselis came down hard on the steering vanes as he continued to fire the thrusters. The Liberator turned sharply, the turret swinging to face the estuary to the rear. Karstil could see TOG infantry scattering away from the twisting tank as the driver brought it in low over the ice. The bow hit an outcropping of ice, grinding it into a soft powder that swept over the glacis. The design of the Liberator, two long arms extending forward from the main hull, funneled the spray directly over the turret. Karstil's face plate went white and Crowder yelped as a pile of snow landed on his sight console. Then they were in the clear again. Karstil wiped the grains of ice from his combat helmet.

A shattering explosion behind him threw vivid red light across the landscape. For an instant the peds, penals, and ice columns stood out in sharp relief, black shadow-fingers pointing away from the escarpment. The DDP went blank, then the landscape went dark and the data display returned. Karstil saw that he was one tank short. Nothing even showed where the tank had been. There wasn't enough left of the missing Liberator for the DDP sensing system to recognize.

"Contest Four. This is Contest Four-six. Heavy weapons on the transports. Cover with smoke before leaving the edge."

Thanks for the warning, Karstil snorted. A little too late for someone. He checked his platoon's other surviving tank. It was obviously damaged, cruising as if it had lost most of its thrusters. Karstil didn't dare call it. He couldn't bear to find out the truth.

"Contest Four-two-six. This is Contest Four-two-two. Our thrusters are almost gone." Ross had survived. Karstil was almost overwhelmed by relief, replaced instantly by anger.

"Contest Four-two-two. This is Four-two-six. What in the name of all that's holy were you doing that far out? I told you to take it slow! I said they still shoot back! Didn't you see the transports on your DDP? You could have gotten yourself killed!"

"Two-two. Sorry. I got a little excited." What Ross didn't say was that Blackstone, used to flying the more responsive Viper tank, had miscalculated the response time required to stop the heavier Liberator. Blaming her driver would not make her platoon leader any more understanding.

"This is Contest Four-two-six. Sorry? Got a little excited? That's not good enough." Even as he cut the comm, Karstil wondered what he would consider good enough. Too excited was probably the best explanation, but he was still angry. "Stupid woman," he muttered under his breath, regretting instantly that he had said it aloud.

"She's a good tank commander, boss." Crowder piped up on the intercom. "I've been watching her on the DDP. She's been sticking to you like glue. She knows her stuff. She was the one who blew the doors off that Horatius a while back."

Karstil flushed at the reprimand from his gunner. He had not paid much attention to Ross' position during the pursuit and the battle, and he knew he should have been. He also should have been aware of her tank's performance against the Horatius. Once again he was guilty of what Mullins had called being a high-priced tank commander rather than acting as a platoon leader. I don't need this, he thought, and was pleased with himself for not voicing it.

"Thanks, Spent," he said. "I should have remembered that." He didn't say what he meant, which was that he should have been aware of that. Admitting to the rest of his platoon that he hadn't been paying attention was something his troops didn't need to hear; they might worry about their leader's competence. He could worry about that well enough on his own.

"Two-two. Two-six. We're going over the edge again. Cover with smoke before you clear. Set the time fuse for one thousand meters."

"Two-two. Wilco. One thousand meters. Timed bursts."

The Liberators turned toward the precipice again. This time, Karstil paid attention, noticing that Ross brought her tank to his left quarter even though her tank's thrusters were obviously damaged. He would have to take into account the other Liberator's impaired acceleration and deceleration. He kept his speed down to allow plenty of lead time for maneuvering. As the tanks crossed the edge, Karstil gave the command to fire.

The air over the estuary was filled with obscuring smoke. The other vehicles in Matruh's command had been busy while Karstil rounded up his platoon. The transports were under such deep smoke-cover that the DDPs had difficulty even sensing the ships' positions. The smaller barges were still loading the evacuees, although some were already nosing away into the relative safety of the smoke. Two Liberators circled above one barge, their turrets pointed down at the ship below. The muzzle flash from their 150mm cannon illuminated the destruction raining down.

"Two-two. Two-six. Circle the one below me. Keep turning left. Shoot left." Karstil's Liberator began a tight, banking left turn, the turret rotating left to target another unfortunate barge.

"Unidentified vehicle. Range five-double-zero. Bearing four-eight-double-zero relative. Range steady. Vehicle is moving on a heading of four-double-zero true. Vehicle has no flicker shields." The DDP was completely confused by the target. It boasted a vast memory-bank full of vehicle outlines and other shapes it was programmed to recognize, but a naval barge was not one of those shapes. Sooner or later the computer would match it to something similar, but that would take time.

"Gunner. Barge. Pointblank. Load HEAP."

"Identified."

"Fire."

"On the way."

The Liberator rocked with the recoil of the heavy cannon, and Boutselis twisted the controls to bring the tank back to its original flight attitude.

"Hit," said Crowder, and then, "Up," indicating that the gun was ready to fire again.

Karstil examined the barge below. His first shot had hit the deck, blasting a crater into the surface. The laser had followed the HEAP round into the cargo hold below the upper deck. He could see crewmembers dragging firefighting equipment over the deck. Others huddled by the narrow bridge tower, their faces turned toward the Liberators that hovered like avenging angels some five hundred meters above. The light lasers on the bridge wings had been abandoned, and even the kicks of the officers responsible for the enlisted marines could not drive the crews to their stations. Farther out in the estuary, the transports turned toward Malthus. Ross' tank fired a heavy shell that struck just forward of the bridge tower, the laser boring in through the same hole. A knot of figures that had been sheltering by the bridge was not there when the smoke cleared.

"Up," said Crowder. "You want me to shoot?"

"Negative," said Karstil, and he flipped the master fire-control switch to safe. "Two-two. This is Two-six. Cease fire."

"Two-two. Wilco. Thank you." Even the impersonal commlink could not disguise the obvious relief in Ross' voice.

Karstil kept the Liberators circling above the damaged barge. The skipper, aware that he had escaped destruction for the moment, turned his vessel toward the transports and recognized his dilemma. The transports were ten kilometers away and accelerating. The first one had cleared the mouth of the estuary and was beginning to rise on its hydroplanes to assume WIGE flight. The biggest wave Rock Wall could attract between the ice cap and the coast of Malthus would not affect its progress. The wing-in-ground-effect flight mode created a solid cushion of air under the huge lower surface of the transport, and the vehicle's almost-vestigal wings added lift and steadied its flight. The air pushed down on the nearest surface, and so the transport followed smoothly whatever changes the surface of the water created. The other two ships, one of them spewing smoke from hits along the fantail, were about to hit the edge of the open sea. The evacuation barges had been left to their own fate. The skipper made the easy decision when a 150mm round exploded a hundred meters off his bow. He looked at the circling Liberators and turned the barge toward the icy shoreline.

Above the cliffs, the tanks of Cohort Harras gathered to watch the barges return. Fights broke out among the penal infantry on some of the barges, apparently between those who wished to escape and those who had given up all hope of rescue. Those who still believed escape was possible were either convinced otherwise, pummelled into acquiescence, or, in extreme situations, pitched over the side. The sea accepted the offerings of men and vehicles, and subsided into a watery gray-green graveyard.

Karstil reported his platoon's casualties to Matruh. One tank destroyed, no tanks combat-worthy. The two survivors could fly and fire, but neither could be trusted in any kind of engagement. The other tank platoon was in the same condition. Only the infantry command was whole, and its platoon leader wanted to pursue the departing transports while it was still possible, but his centurion decreed that this Century would not fight again until it had undergone an extensive refit.

Karstil grounded the Liberator and watched as Ross landed her tank beside his. The tank grounded in a swirl of snow, and Karstil had to turn away to shield his face. When he looked back, Ross was coming down the front glacis and dropping between the projecting arms of the forward hull. He walked to meet her.

"I'm sorry I yelled at you," he blurted out. "It was just that you scared the life out of me."

"Oh. I was all right."

Karstil gazed at the diminutive sergeant, whose blue eyes shone brilliantly from under her combat helmet. "When I thought that it was you who died, I didn't know what to do." He grasped her shoulders. "Honor, I've got to tell you how I feel. I..."

"Commlink, sir," yelled Crowder, sticking his head out of the command hatch. "Big boss says it's time to pull pitch. We are but a memory."

"You were saying?" prompted Honor Ross.

"It'll wait till we get back to Rolandrin," Karstil said softly. "Drive carefully."

62

1430, 18 Martius 6831—Both Renegade and Commonwealth troops lined the perimeter of the planetary headquarters landing-ground on Rolandrin. No one had ordered them to be on hand for the return of the 2567th Renegade Legion, but word of their coming had gotten around and the troops were gathered to see them come home. The air seemed to shake as the tight vee-formations of tanks, infantry carriers, and command vehicles swept in low over the trees, passing over the field and then swinging in tight turns to land amid clouds of swirling dust. The crews climbed out of the vehicles to stand at attention in deafening silence for their final inspection. Shouts of "All present or accounted for," rang across the parade ground.

It was the "or accounted for" numbers that showed the cost of Operation Gateway, for too many of the tanks and their crews would never answer the roll again. Shattered hulls and broken bodies were scattered from one edge of the southern polar cap to the other or else entombed beneath the ice in the Naram city.

Most of the spectators cheered themselves hoarse as the Legion arrived. The encampments around Alabaster rarely saw formations this size sweep in over the cantonment area. Kenderson had deliberately planned the display. Even the units of the 2567th that had not been called south for the operation itself had rendezvoused over the ocean with the survivors. Their presence filled out the depleted ranks of the Renegades that approached the field. It was an impressive display, which was what Kenderson had intended, as much for the benefit of those greeting the returning Legion as for those who had been there, fought, and died.

Kenderson also wanted the planetary headquarters at Alabaster to feel the thunder of the return. The 2567th was still classified as a "Provisional" Legion. Kenderson wanted the 2567th to become a permanent Legion. He wanted to reward its veterans for a job well done.

Those lining the landing ground who knew what to look for recognized the gaps in the Centuries and Cohorts. They saw the shattered hulls and dangling grav coils that spilled from the crippled vehicles, some so damaged that they were brought in on tow bars, dragged across the sky by those less-damaged. Some infantry carrier squads could barely form a complete section.

These cripples were not hidden behind the mass of replacement craft. Kenderson proudly displayed them in the front ranks, determined to present his command as it really was, warts and all. The 2567th Renegade Infantry Legion (Provisional) came home, not to the banners and trumpets and drums of the command, but to the wild cheers of the support troops and the common soldiers.

* * *

Half a world away, on Malthus, three transports descended from normal WIGE mode, landed on the water, and drifted up Frotik Bay toward the wharfs lining the water's edge. TOG command had cleared the stevedores and roughnecks from the dock area earlier in a massive sweep conducted by Ssoran military police. The survivors of Cohort Patrius and the 356th Penal Auxilia would be brought ashore in darkness and complete secrecy. There were too many questions that needed to be asked, too many conflicting reports to unravel, and Brigadier General Drusus Arcadius wanted no loose ends when he sent his final report to Grand General Oliodinus Severus Septimus at Sector Command.

Arcadius followed a strict policy of forwarding only complete information to Sector. He believed it was a waste of time to pass on incomplete information that almost always needed to be corrected or expanded at a later date. It was much better, he thought, to wait until all the ducks were in single file before presenting the flock to headquarters. Adhering to this policy in the present situation would be even more difficult because of the grand general's spies lurking in every corner of the headquarters, but if Arcadius and his personal staff moved fast enough, they just might accomplish the task.

This had been the reason for the dockside-area sweep. The disembarking troops were hustled into isolated warehouses secured by a phalanx of Ssoran police. All communications between the buildings and the rest of the city were carefully monitored. It was quite easy to slip into a building, but it was virtually impossible to slip out. The Ssoran guards were under orders to shoot to kill anyone trying to leave or enter the area from any point other than the single authorized one, and to pass that one point required a signed chit from Arcadius himself.

As the penal troops entered the holding area, the Ssoran police scanned their identity disks. Arcadius had decided that the combat on the ice cap would count as the one "campaign" the penal troops were required to serve in order to rejoin their regular units. Any members of the Auxilia whose original units were serving on Caralis would rejoin the regular troops immediately. Those whose units were on other planets would be confined to barracks until transportation could be arranged. Arcadius was delighted to be rid of the troublesome unit so easily.

He watched the line of troops stumble into the warehouse. The wounds and evidence of frostbite borne by nearly every soldier were mute testimony to the brutal fighting at the south pole. Half-asleep, they shuffled to present their identity disks at the tables, and when they tried to come to attention, most were too tired to do more than stiffen their weary poses while the interrogator studied their records. Arcadius thought that some of the penals looked vaguely familiar, and tried to remember if he had sent anyone to a penal unit during the past year. He thought he recognized one of them and moved to get a closer look, but just then an aide brought him a more urgent matter and he turned his attention away from the line of penals.

The most difficult problem Brigadier General Arcadius faced was dealing with the operation report from Legatus Maximus Rocipian Olioarchus, commander of the Penal Auxilia and the officer in charge of the final phases of the mission. His report was complete enough, but the operation had concluded with many loose ends untied. Olioarchus had disappeared from the transport on the way back to Malthus from the ice cap. Legatus Cariolanus Camus, the original commander of the Strike Cohort that had initiated the action, had also vanished on the return trip, even though he had been under house arrest in the command Pompey since being relieved of his command. Arcadius was forced to conclude that Camus had managed to slip away in the confusion of the evacuation.

Miles Stratton, the sole surviving officer of the Penal Auxilia staff, could offer few clues to either officer's whereabouts. He had been wounded in the evacuation, sustaining a nasty blow to the head that had left him unconscious for much of the journey, and he had not been able to satisfactorily explain the disappearance of the two senior officers. Unless Arcadius wanted to subject the officer to a potentially fatal deep-mind probe, there was probably little more he would get out of him. Stratton claimed dim memories of Olioarchus and Camus standing shoulder-to-shoulder on the deck of the transport, manning an antiaircraft laser mount. Then everything had gone dark. The transport Stratton came in on had lost such a mount, but it was positioned well forward, beyond the sight of anyone inside the command Pompey. The brigadier general found Centurion Stratton's report to be at best confusing, and at worst, improbable.

And then there was the matter of Prefect Claudius Sulla. The brigadier general had sent his chief of operations with the Cohort to the polar cap, hoping to get rid of him one way or another. Olioarchus' report painted the prefect's conduct as certainly less than brilliant and perhaps even obstructionist. But Olioarchus was unable to expand on his report, and Stratton had no conclusive evidence. Sector would have to act on their own evaluation. The brigadier general devoutly hoped they would find something else for the prefect to do.

Brigadier General Drusus Arcadius dictated his final report. Olioarchus and Camus had died heroes' deaths, honoring New Rome. The record of both officers would be so amended. The report would read that Camus had been relieved of his position as mission commander in order to place a more experienced officer in charge of the combined forces. Patrius would take command of the Cohort-Minus, as it would be designated until it was brought back to full strength. Sulla, Patrius, and Stratton would sign the document, attesting to its veracity, and it would be forwarded to Sector. The matter was closed.

Five officers settled into chairs around the desk of Brigadier Bernard Maxall, Chief of Commonwealth Operations on Caralis and host of the gathering. It was an informal get-together, as informal as a gathering of junior officers in the office of a brigadier could ever be, and Maxall wanted everyone to talk freely. Each guest had been served a Skuttarran Heartstopper by uniformed stewards, who had then departed to leave their superiors to their conversation. Maxall waited for the others to pick up their glasses, then raised his. "To Operation Gateway," he said. "A success, if not quite what we expected."

"To Gateway," chorused his guests. They settled deeper into their chairs.

"Well, Besta," began the brigadier, turning to the prefect of the 2567th Renegade Legion, "your luck seems to be holding."

NaBesta Kenderson stretched his legs, luxuriating in the kind of sore thigh muscles that a man could get only from doing battle. "It certainly has been an interesting few weeks."

"You have some very interesting people in that makeshift outfit," commented Colonel Holcomb Daubish, Chief of Intelligence for the planetary headquarters. "They seem to be able to pull things out of thin air or from portions of their anatomy."

Kenderson laughed. "They sure do. But some of the people on your staff seem to be able to do the same thing. You've got a centurion buried in your organization who put together that entire second relief effort. He pulled together units that didn't even exist. I hope he's getting some recognition."

"He is," replied Lieutenant Colonel Alban C. Tripp. "But I have to be careful about letting the rest of the system know about Pharker. If he gets too famous, someone at Sector is likely to grab him. He's quite a young man. Knows everyone, and uses the old-boy network to get things done."

"I was considering Pharker for a place on my personal staff, Tripp," offered Maxall. "He'd have a broader playing field for his talents." The brigadier saw his staff officer wince and quickly added, "But I can't be stealing talent from my working shops to stock my staff. You can keep young Centurion Pharker for now, but be warned; sooner or later, he'll be mine."

"Milt, here, did most of the fighting down south." Kenderson waved his hand in the general direction of his friend. "I thought you people would at least like to meet the man who took the mission."

"Milt and I go back a long way." Maxall grinned at Harras. "We were both Commonwealth before Milt opened his mouth to a field marshal when he should have kept it shut. Milt was right, of course, but it didn't do his chances for promotion much good. Nice to see you up and around."

Harras shifted his feet to a more comfortable position on the footstool and smiled. The Commonwealth officers in the room, with the exception of Tripp, were men he had known for a long time. "It's nice to be able to be up and around, sir."

"You can drop that in here, Milt. We're all equals with Heartstoppers in our fists. A couple more of these, and you'll be more equal than any of us. I remember how you used to put them away."

"That was a long time ago, Bernie, a long time ago." Harras could hardly remember the days when the two men were a centurion and a legatus, knocking back Heartstoppers and Tau Ceti brandy until the sun rose on their deep, philosophical discussions. Those had been interesting days.

"What about your Legion now?" asked Daubish. His interest was more than just casual. The TOG forces on Alsatia were due to make another push within the next thirty days, and he needed to know the availability of his troops.

"Sorry, guys," added Maxall. "But both Tripp and Daubish need to know when you'll be ready to go again."

Harras and Kenderson glanced at each other, then looked at the floor. Kenderson sighed and looked up first. "We should be ready for that push, but I want to give as many of my people as possible the leave they've earned, say, two weeks worth. Then we can pull them together for a quick organizational training period, which shouldn't be too bad if I can keep the people I've got."

"Some of your people are volunteers from Commonwealth units," said Daubish. "Do you want to keep them as well?"

"If I can."

"There'll be hell to pay with their commanders, but I'll arrange it," said the brigadier. "They've done without them for the past month. They can just get used to their absence."

"Two weeks leave, and then two weeks training," said Tripp. "I'll mark you on my calendar."

Epilogue

1230, 23 Martius 6831—The Commonwealth surface-based passenger liner *Queen Semiramide* hung suspended in the loading dock of the commercial hoverport nearest the Commonwealth's military headquarters on Rolandrin, waiting for its passengers to finish boarding. The main lounge of the ship hummed with muted conversation as the voyagers settled into the armchairs arranged in groups throughout the spacious accommodations. Stewards moved gracefully and silently between the groups, trays of drinks held high above their heads on the tips of their fingers. They bent solicitously over the seated passengers, serving drinks, fluffing pillows, adjusting backrests. They had performed these services so many times that they no longer noticed the people who occupied the chairs.

The external bulkheads were broken at regular intervals by large, rectangular viewing-ports. Small tables set with two easy chairs each were arranged in front of and between the windows. One such table was occupied by two sergeants in casual-dress uniform. One was a bulky man wearing the new stripes of a recently promoted noncommissioned officer. The other was a small woman with a mass of auburn hair that tumbled over her shoulders. They were talking in low, serious voices. So intent were they on their conversation that they did not notice when the *Queen Semiramide* left the embarkation station and began its transit to the Commonwealth Rest and Recreation Center. The passengers were headed for some well-deserved R&R. The spring night visible through the portholes sparkled with the lights of the receding city.

The couple also failed to notice the arrival of the Renegade optio who came up to stand beside the woman's chair. "Excuse me. May I sit down?" asked Optio Roglund Karstil.

The sergeants looked up in surprise. The man's face darkened with frustration. There were only two chairs at this spot, and he was fairly sure that he was the one who would be moving along. One look at his companion's radiant face confirmed his guess. "My pleasure, sir," he said, rising from his seat. "See you later, Honor."

Karstil sat down in the vacated chair. "I'm glad you're here."

"So am I."

"There were some things I wanted to say to you back on the ice that never got said."

"There were some things I wanted to have said to me," replied Honor Ross with a smile, "that never got heard."

The massive man pushed himself deeper into the scrub that covered the entrance to his hiding place. He raised the monocular scanner and searched the ground closest to his position, checking to make sure there were no enemy within that area. The immediate terrain clear, he scanned the rest of the area in overlapping sweeps until he reached the horizon. The only movement he found was normal TOG activity in the ruins of the city that lay ten kilometers away. Frotik had been reduced almost to rubble in the attack that claimed the city for the Terran Overlord Government two years previous, and the TOGs had been slow to rebuild. The dock area was filled with ugly temporary buildings, and the vehicle landing grounds had been restored, but the center of the city, the area occupied by the remnants of the civil population, was still a wasteland.

The spy had found his contact among the civilians. He had shed the TOG legionnaire uniform for civilian clothes, a guise that allowed him to slip unnoticed from the populated area. He did not want to endanger his contact by remaining, because he assumed the TOGs also had spies among the civilian populace. The cave had been a lucky find. His contact had also been able to provide the equipment necessary to continue the spy's work. The monocular was of TOG design, scavenged from a destroyed headquarters building. In a further stroke of luck, he had been able to scrape together the pieces of a Renegade militia kit, which meant that if he were captured by his enemy, military code would prevent his being shot out of hand as a spy. Of course, the Renegade agent didn't know if that were a blessing or a curse. It might be better to die a quick death rather than linger in one of the TOG interrogation chambers. He knew the terrible things mind probes did to a man's innards.

The man slipped back into the cave and downloaded the information acquired by the monocular onto a message disk. He rigged the thin wire that acted as an antenna across the roof of the cave, paying careful attention to the azimuth. The transmitter had limited power, and so he would need to hit the COMSAT directly on its receptor. He checked his perscomp, watching the seconds tick by as the satellite came on station. The computer's timer went to zero, and he depressed the send button. In less than half a second, the complete message leaped from the commlink to the ether. Seconds later the COMSAT reflected the screech transmission toward Rolandrin, and its addressee received the message later that same day.

A soft knock sounded on the open door, and Prefect NaBesta Kenderson looked up from the papers on his desk as Legatus Mantelli Lartur, operations officer for the 2567th Legion and general staff factotum, entered his office. Without a word, he handed Kenderson a sealed packet and left the room, closing and locking the door behind him. He was not surprised that the prefect had received a secret message; men in his position had their fingers in many pies.

But it was marked as double encoded, which meant that it was vitally important.

Kenderson broke the seal and began the long process of decrypting the notes, using a one-time tear sheet. It took him most of an hour to break the code. There wasn't much of particular interest in the message; only the signature block was important. It was signed "Stone."

Kenderson grinned at the blank wall of his office. He crumpled the message flimsy, the tear sheets, the scratch paper, and all his notes into tiny balls. One at a time he flipped them carefully into the burn basket, watching them flash as they crossed the rim. When the last traces of his task had been reduced to powder, he released the lock on his office door and went back to his paperwork.

Glossary

GROUND FORCE TECHNOLOGY

GRAV DRIVE

The most important advance in ground propulsion was the development of the grav drive in 2210. Named after its inventor, the Marshman Drive allows an object to fall parallel to the ground rather than toward it. Specialized anti-grav steering vanes allow the device to change direction. The military immediately saw the possibilities for the development of the modern-day grav tank.

The grav tank has significantly changed the nature of ground warfare. Depending on its altitude, a grav tank can travel from 100 kph up to 900 kph. At such speeds, a grav-mounted Legion can cover the distance between the old Terran cities of New York and Chicago in an hour and a half. With its terrain-following radar, a grav-mounted tank can maneuver in the densest terrain at unprecedented speeds. The firepower available to a grav Strike Legion could defeat a 20th-century army. Because of its great speed and ability to concentrate rapidly, a grav Legion can attack or defend an area hundreds of kilometers across. Grav armor has become the decisive arm of ground combat.

One of the disadvantages of the Marshman Drive is that it cannot operate farther than 15 kilometers above the mean surface of a Terra-like planet. Thus, most spacecraft use anti-grav generators for atmospheric flight. Even with its disadvantages, the grav tank has significantly changed the nature of ground warfare.

ARMOR AND PASSIVE PROTECTION

A grav tank's standard armor is a crystalline titanium alloy that is molecularly wedded to a ceramic matrix. It is proof against old-style shaped charges and low-kinetic energy weapons, very resistant to hyper-kinetic energy weapons, and offers good protection against most other energy weapons.

A grav tank's interior is also well-protected. All major components have redundant circuitry built into them, along with self-repair capabilities. A totally separate secondary system is provided for such critical components as shields and terrain sensors. Additionally, energy-absorbing foams and fire protection equipment are standard passive ballistic protection on all combat vehicles.

SHIELDING

Grav tanks are protected by flicker shields. The flicker shield is a thin wave of pressure-gravity that would normally be impervious to all forms of energy. Because power demands are so high, it was necessary to design a shield that flickered on and off instead of remaining permanently on. A flicker shield is effective against lasers, thermonuclear explosions, energy weapons, and low-mass projectiles. As the flicker rate increases, the power usage increases geometrically. No matter how fast the flicker rate, at least 10 percent of all shots get through.

PAINTING LASER

The painting laser marks a target with a laser, then the sensors in a missile or artillery munitions home in on the reflected laser light. As long as the laser is held on its target, the accuracy of the guided munition approaches 100 percent. When a painting laser hits a shield, the targeting vehicle can use the reflected laser light to analyze the defending shield's flicker rate. It can then target its combat lasers to slip in a shot during the flicker shield's off-cycle. The flicker rate can also be downloaded into other friendly fire-control systems and to the electronic circuitry of any guided missile.

As a countermeasure, the shield can be distanced from the hull of the vehicle so that painting laser light bounces off the hull and then strikes the reverse side of a shield in an "on" cycle. This reduces the amount of reflected laser energy and makes it difficult to lock onto shields with high flicker rates.

MASS DRIVER CANNON

The most modern form of projectile weapon, the MDC usually consists of a long tube made from superconductive material, to which twin rails of magnetic material are attached. A strong current passes through the tube, accelerating slivers of hardened steel down the barrel on the crest of a magnetic wave generated by the tube and the rails. Because of its weight and ineffectiveness against shields, MDCs are most often mounted on spacecraft or space-defense vehicles and installations.

GAUSS CANNON

A popular ground vehicle weapon, the Gauss cannon is a direct-fire ballistic weapon that functions similarly to a Mass Driver Cannon. The shells cannot be turned by shields and they use hyper-kinetic energy to penetrate a target's armor.

APDS Round

Armor-Piercing Discarding Sabot (APDS) rounds use kinetic energy to penetrate their target. The round consists of a long, thin, depleted uranium penetrator surrounded by a container, or sabot. Once the round has left the cannon, the sabot slips off to reduce drag caused by air resistance.

HEAP Round

The High-Explosive Armor-Piercing round is similar to an APDS round except that it has a directional explosive charge directly behind the penetrator that detonates when the penetrator enters the armor. This drives the penetrator deeper into the armor and causes some lateral damage.

Hammerhead Round

The Hammerhead round consists of a nose and a lateral-shaped charge. The nose has a self-destructive X-ray laser. When the round hits the side of a vehicle, the kinetic energy released is converted to X-ray energy. This energy is focused back toward the vehicle through a special crystal, causing it to laze. The laser bolt drills a hole through the armor, while the lateral-shaped part of the round passes down into the vehicle. When it strikes the bottom of the laser hold, the charge explodes perpendicularly to the sides.

MISSILES

Anti-vehicular missiles are fairly large, bulky, and have limited ranges. All missiles can be guided to their targets by active painting lasers, allowing for both direct and indirect firing. If the target is not painted, the gunner locks onto the target, fires, and the missile's internal guidance and control systems home in on the target.

SMLM

The Sub-Munitions Laser-Guided Missile (SMLM) is a standard, heavy anti-vehicular missile. When the missile approaches its target, it explodes and showers the target with high-velocity sub-munitions that can scour off large blocks of armor. If the missile is able to penetrate to the vehicle's interior, the explosion is directed laterally, causing extensive internal damage.

TVLG

The Tube or Vertically Launched Laser-Guided Missile (TVLG) is lighter and shorter-ranged than the SMLM, but has greater penetration. Its warhead is a modified 100mm Hammerhead round. Infantry squads normally use it as their primary anti-vehicular missile, with the indirect fire capabilities removed.

ARTILLERY

All field pieces are now mobile, armored, and capable of firing on the move. The guns utilize electromagnetic accelerators and rocket-assisted projectiles to respond with unheard-of speed and accuracy to fire missions from the forward combat elements. Artillery's ability to totally destroy any target that has stopped moving for more than one minute has ensured the grav tank's supremacy over cheaper and more easily constructed ground vehicles.

HAFE Round

The Hypervelocity Airburst Flechette Explosive (HAFE) round explodes into a cloud of thousands of flechettes, which are too large to be stopped by shields. Moderately effective against vehicles, HAFE rounds are most useful against infantry targets and to clear wooded areas for easier passage by grav vehicles.

ADM Round

Each Artillery-Dispensed Mine (ADM) round contains hundreds of mine sub-munitions. When the round arrives over its target, it scatters these mines over a diameter of 600 meters. Each mine is keyed to explode if a grav field passes over it or if it is touched. The mine is equipped with a transponder receiver that identifies friendly passing vehicles or infantrymen. Enemy units can clear ADM minefields by using engineering vehicles or Anti-Mine Artillery (AMA) rounds.

GLAD Round

The GLAD round is a laser-guided anti-vehicle round. When the round arrives over the general location of its target, a parachute is deployed. Sensors in the round then search the immediate area for a target being designated by a friendly laser. If there is no laser designation, the round chooses its own target and launches itself.

SMOKE Round

A Smoke round sets up a dense barrier of smoke that is opaque in the visual electromagnetic and infrared spectra. Smoke can be used defensively to cover the withdrawal or shifting of troops. Offensively, a barrage of smoke can be laid down in front of an enemy making a high-speed advance into a built-up area. The smoke blinds the enemy's terrain-following radar and will cause the vehicle to crash.

CRATER Round

The Crater round is an artillery version of the digging charges that all vehicles carry. They are used mainly to hastily create a defensive zone for a retreating force. They can also be used to quickly create dug-in positions for an attacking force.

HELL Round

When a HELL round detonates, it releases enough gravitic energy to cause a small, uncontrolled fusion reaction. This type of round is very clean, leaving little tactically significant radiation, but it does totally destroy any buildings, vegetation, or unshielded units in the blast radius. Shielding does reduce the blast effects of a HELL round, making it less effective against stationary vehicles than GLAD rounds.

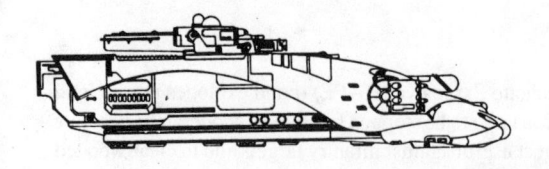

NAH TIKAL (VIPER)
LIGHT APC

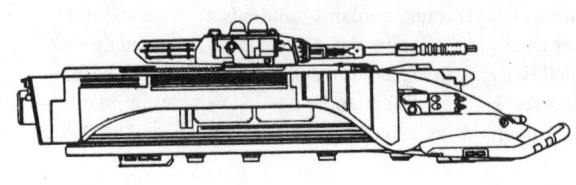

BATA REVO (WOLVERINE)
LIGHT GRAV TANK

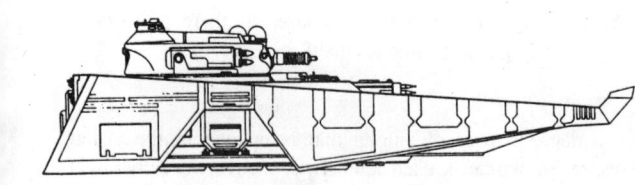

SPARTIUS
MEDIUM GRAV APC

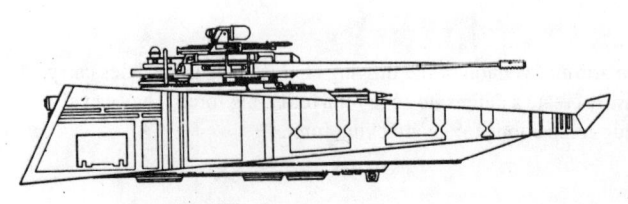

LIBERATOR
MEDIUM GRAV TANK

DELIVERER
HEAVY GRAV TANK

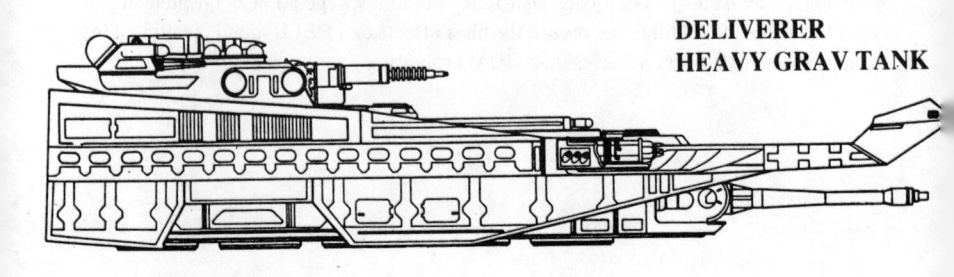

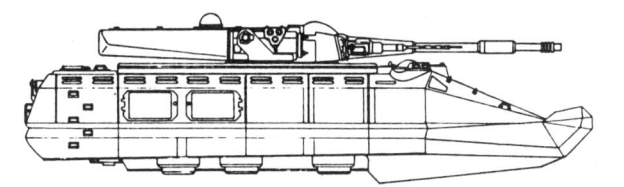

AENEAS
LIGHT GRAV TANK

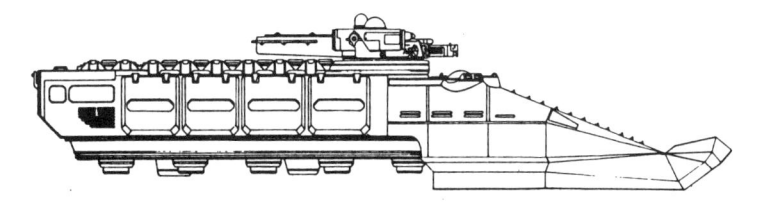

LUPIS
LIGHT GRAV APC

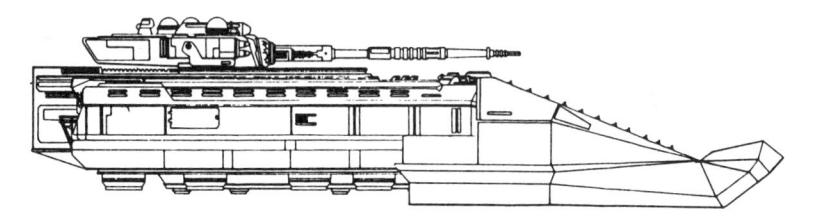

ROMULUS
MEDIUM GRAV APC

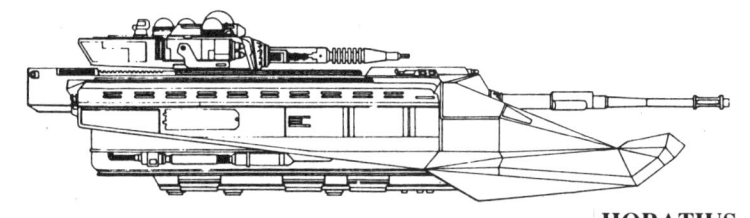

HORATIUS
MEDIUM GRAV TANK

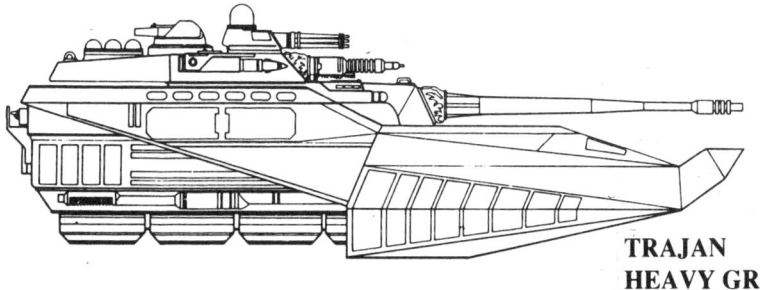

TRAJAN
HEAVY GRAV TANK

You've read the fiction, Now play the games...

RENEGADE LEGION®
CENTURION®
B L O O D & S T E E L

Centurion is a game of ground warfare set in the Renegade Legion universe of 6830. Grav tanks, bounce infantry, HELL rounds, Thor bombardment satellites, and orbital fire support are all part of this highly mobile, tactics-based air/land battle of the future. If you want to take a world in a condition worth having, you need flesh and blood men of iron conviction!

Centurion 2nd Edition contains 36 plastic grav tanks, two 24" x 36" double-sided, full-color maps, one rules book, one background book, a record sheet and scenario booklet, and more than 200 full-color information counters.

CENTURION® is a Registered Trademark of FASA Corporation. Copyright © 1991 FASA Corporation. All Rights Reserved.

RENEGADE LEGION®
PREFECT®
ASSUALT FROM THE STARS

Planetary invasions are complex & dangerous enterprises. The coordination of covering naval forces, orbital bombardment platforms, & troop transports must be precise & the timing of assault drops cannot deviate from the plan by more than a few seconds. Supplies & reinforcements must flow smoothly to the planetary bridgehead. Enemy grav forces must be located, fixed upon, & destroyed to gain a decisive advantage in the battle. Accomplish all this, and victory is assured. Fail, and face total defeat.

Prefect is a boxed game simulating a planetary invasion. Players plan and execute the space & group movements of the campaign.

Available in the Spring of 1992!

PREFECT® is a Registered Trademark of FASA Corporation. Copyright © 1991 FASA Corporation. All Rights Reserved.

RENEGADE LEGION®
LEGIONNAIRE®
THE ROLE PLAYING GAME

In 2056 humankind took to the stars. Five thousand years later, in the year 6831, humans dominate the Galaxy under the sway of the Terran Overlord Government (TOG). TOG holds that the Humans of Terra are superior to all other races, and enforces its absolute power through *any* means necessary. Faced with TOG's 8 million Legions and its 100,000 Battleships, who dares oppose the mightiest army the Galaxy has ever known? The answer lies 70,000 light years from Terra at the far end of the Orion Arm. Here lies a government known as the Human/Baufrin Commonwealth, the seat of armed resistance to TOG since the TOG first came to power in 6681.

In that year, a number of the Republic's legions fled the tyranny of the new TOG government, finding refuge among the peoples of the distant Commonwealth. They and their descendants are now known as the *Renegade Legions*, fighting side by side with their Commonwealth allies against TOG. The battlefield of the 69th century is a place of push button death and searing destruction where courage is as important as death-wielding technology.

Legionnaire is the role playing game for the **Renegade Legion** Universe. It provides all the information needed to create and play a character in this dangerous time. From star fighter pilot, a grav tank commander, or just a free-booting adventurer, this game will allow the players to fully explore the exciting Renegade Legion universe.

LEGIONNAIRE® is a Registered Trademark of FASA Corporation. Copyright © 1991 FASA Corporation. All Rights Reserved.

RENEGADE LEGION®
INTERCEPTOR®
THE FIRST LINE OF DEFENSE

SSI PRESENTS:

FASA's game of ship-to-ship space combat
ON A PERSONAL COMPUTER NEAR YOU!

24 fighter and ship types with options for new designs.

Powerful artificial intelligence can control both enemy and allied fighters.

Complete open-ended campaign system.

Over ten mission types including: fleet intercepts, space station strikes, intelligence gathering and wild melees.

Renegade Legion: Interceptor® is available for IBM & Amiga computers ($59.95).

To order, visit your local software store or call 1-800-245-4525 for Visa or Mastercard orders.

NOW AVAILABLE FOR THE AMIGA!

Renegade Legion® and Interceptor® are Registered Trademarks of FASA Corporation and are used under exclusive license.